BEHAVE

Also by the Author

Novels
The Spanish Bow
The Detour

Nonfiction
Searching for Steinbeck's Sea of Cortez

BEHAVE

ANDROMEDA ROMANO-LAX

Copyright © 2016 by Andromeda Romano-Lax

Published by
Soho Press, Inc.
853 Broadway
New York, NY 10003

Library of Congress Cataloging-in-Publication Data

Romano-Lax, Andromeda
Behave / Andromeda Romano-Lax.

ISBN 978-1-61695-653-0
eISBN 978-1-61695-654-7

I. Title.
PS3618.O59B44 2016
813'.6—dc23   2015028757

Interior design by Janine Agro, Soho Press, Inc.

Printed in the United States of America

10 9 8 7 6 5 4 3 2 1

To three strong women:
Juliet G., Karen F., and Kathleen T.

And to my mother, Cherilynn "Catherine" Cress Romano, PhD,
who has shared her love of psychology with many.

Give me a dozen healthy infants, well-formed, and my own specified world to bring them up in and I'll guarantee to take any one at random and train him to become any type of specialist I might select—doctor, lawyer, artist, merchant-chief and, yes, even beggar-man and thief, regardless of his talents, penchants, tendencies, abilities, vocations, and race of his ancestors.

—John Watson, *Behaviorism*, 1930

O brave new world, / That has such people in't!

—William Shakespeare, *The Tempest*, Act 5, Scene 1, quoted in the 1919 *Vassarion*, the Vassar College yearbook

I can almost hear you exclaiming: "Why, yes, it is worth while to study human behavior in this way, but the study of behavior is not the whole of psychology. It leaves out too much. Don't I have sensations, perceptions, conceptions? Do I not forget things and remember things, imagine things, have visual images and auditory images of things I once have seen and heard? Can I not see and hear things that I have never seen or heard in nature? Can I not be attentive or inattentive? Can I not will to do a thing or will not to do it, as the case may be? Do not certain things arouse pleasure in me, and others displeasure? Behaviorism is trying to rob us of everything we have believed in since earliest childhood."

Having been brought up on introspective psychology, as most of you have, these questions are perfectly natural and you will find it hard to formulate your psychological life in terms of behaviorism. Behaviorism is new wine and it will not go into old bottles; therefore I am going to try to make new bottles out of you.

—John Watson, *Behaviorism*, 1930

PART I

LITTLE ALBERT

1935

WHIP-POOR-WILL FARM, CONNECTICUT

"Why are you doing this?" John asks, coming home to the farm from Manhattan, finding me out of bed, at the corner desk, typing in my nightgown at 8 P.M., the boys already asleep and my dinner, a bowl of chicken soup, ignored at my elbow. Prescription for dysentery: hydrate relentlessly. And I'm trying. But it becomes tiresome, all these bowls of broth and cups of sugar water, and the inevitable visceral responses that become more painful, day and night. The stomach, regardless of what any other organ has to say, does not want nutrition. The stomach and the bowels and all those layers of unstriped, smooth muscle with their associated glands (how John loves to talk of those invisible places and their powerful relationships to our visible physical behaviors) want only to be left alone.

"Doing what?" I say, tugging out the paper, turning it over, neatening the edges of a growing pile.

"Working so hard when you're supposed to be recuperating."

I shield the paper with my forearm, like a teenage girl hiding her diary. We have been married close to fifteen years now, we have survived scandal, infidelities, and depressions (his, mine, the nation's), and mostly I feel we know each other as well as anyone can. And still, every human seems to remain to every other a mystery—despite John's strenuous disavowal of all things intangible.

It is the one thing any human can truly own: her private thoughts. But what do you do when you're married to a man who says "thought," as we generally refer to it, and the mind, and consciousness, and especially the soul, don't exist?

John runs a hand through his hair—now silver but as thick as when we first met. He remains as handsome to me now as when he was forty, and I was—well—half that age. I can smell the city on him. The stale cigarette funk of the train car, but also cologne, kept in his desk drawer, reapplied before leaving the Graybar Building. And the drink—bourbon, invariably—he stopped to have with a fellow ad man or behavior consultant. Even when he—*we*—worked in the lab with babies, he made it a point not to smell of sour milk. There are opportunities to be missed if you don't send out the right stimuli.

"Who's it for?" he asks finally, gesturing to the overturned pile.

He means which popular magazine. *Cosmopolitan? Parents?* John has written for most of them. I've had my own luck a couple of times. But this pile of fifty pages I've managed to accumulate in a week isn't meant for any magazine.

When I don't answer, he fidgets with his cuff links. A gift from Stanley, when John made VP. And still, he misses the days when he earned a fraction of what he earns now, but commanded the respect of real scientists and scholars, instead of salesmen and radio announcers.

"I heard you asked Ray to bring down some old Johns Hopkins boxes from the attic," he says. "I've always said I should get rid of all that stuff up there."

"Not the lab files, surely."

He starts to nod grudgingly, then shakes his head. "What's important is already published. I can't see the point in keeping every scrap of paper."

"I suppose that's true."

"And no one's ever going to have a need for my private papers, or yours. Burn it all."

"Burn it *all*," I repeat, making him smile. Haven't I heard him say that a hundred times? And he'll do it someday, I know he will, regardless of my own thoughts about posterity, or my own occasional desires to look back and see what we did, whether we're remembering things correctly, why our very own publications offer one version here and another slightly different one there, whether there are facts I overlooked in my youthful desire to be his indispensable assistant.

"When you're dead, you're all dead," he says.

"No proof to the contrary."

He's relieved by my pretense of agreeability, and yet he can see past it. Perhaps he knows me better than I know myself. John has always maintained that we are unable to observe our own behaviors, which is why others' behaviors are so much easier to predict and control. Which is always an "out" of sorts, if one chooses to take it. He certainly did.

"What *were* you looking for, Rar?"

I'm looking, I suppose, for how it all started: our love, his most important theories, our biggest contributions, our biggest mistakes. And at the same time, I find myself looking away, making excuses, as if I were too immature and impressionable to have known any better.

The most difficult part, you would think, is realizing that the person you idealized, whom you regarded as infallible, was imperfect all along. Instead, the hardest part is stopping to wonder what was so imperfect or unfinished within oneself as to impede comprehension of the obvious. There wouldn't be any experts telling us all what to do if we thought for ourselves, if we held our ground and asked the right questions. That's the most important thing a scientist can do, isn't it? Ask the right questions?

It's tricky for any woman to sort out her feelings, but most of all when her husband is a national expert on feelings, especially the unconditioned ones we are born with, which create the foundation for everything else. John always said there are only three: fear, rage, and love, the latter really only a reaction to erotic stimulation. The first and perhaps most powerful—fear—was the one that obsessed him, and the one we worked on together in the early years, by kindling small newspaper fires in front of babies, by letting our tender subjects touch candle flames, by sending rats scurrying across their laps, and rabbits, monkeys, and dogs jumping and lunging all over the place. (None of which frightened most infants, which was the point.) Only two things seem to stimulate an unconditioned fear response: sudden loud noises, or a sudden loss of stability. Having the rug pulled out from under you, in other words. Which is how I'm feeling now.

Don't blame him, I remind myself. He was more honest, even in his errors and duplicities, than any man I have ever known.

I'm not making sense of it yet.

There is one remembered image (John doesn't believe in mental images at all, but I can't find a better term) that refuses to leave me. It has always been playing on some forbidden film screen of my mind, but it has flashed with a particular insistency during the last two weeks of fevers and gastric distress.

The windowless psychological testing room is warm, as we wait for our camera man to return and to record the footage that will advance—so Dr. Watson hopes—the immature field of psychology. The first thousand feet of film alone costs $450, a considerable expenditure in 1919. Our nine-month-old subject—"Albert B."—is being remarkably stoic about all the fuss. His round head, bald except for a few flossy, sweat-dampened strands, swivels slowly in the direction of the closed door, though his eyes remain unfocused, lids heavy. A thin line of drool runs from his slick, ruby lips to the top of his velvet-smooth chest. As he tires, his chest settles closer to mine, so that I can feel his heat, and his heartbeat, through my blouse.

Dr. Watson's face turns toward mine. *What do you think?*

What I want at that moment is simply to avoid seeming incompetent, to avoid falling out of this swift-moving roadster in which I've managed, with great luck, to gain a seat. Drawing on everything I know as a budding scientist, I try to sound merely clinical.

"He seems . . . healthy."

"Yes," Dr. Watson says, inhaling deeply. He seems relieved. It is one of the few times I have witnessed him betraying any doubt. It is one of the first times he has seemed to need me. *Good.*

The little monkey, of the organ grinder's type, is penned up, outside the door. As is the dog. Somewhere there is a rabbit, too—it shows up on the film, later—but I can't recall where it's kept. (I don't trust myself, in other words. But that has always been part of the problem.)

In a corner basket, a rat scuffles, and next to it, in a large brown bag, a confined pigeon tries to lift its wings, making the bag shudder and jump. I pull Albert closer, muffling my racing pulse against his soft chest: pride, relief, adult desire, and an infant's vulnerability all mixed together in that moment which I can feel in my memory as damp heat in a small room thrumming, waiting. Later, he will be in tears, shuddering and terrified. Not from pain—we never hurt them physically, of course. (Does that make it all right? Would I be asking if it did?) For now, our uncomplaining subject releases a bubbling sigh and settles ever deeper, drowsy and trusting, in my arms.

Was Albert healthy? Was he normal? They are not the only questions—not by a long shot.

Perhaps none of the questions would even matter, except for what followed: years upon years of consequences for one silly, poorly executed experiment I'd much rather forget, no chance to temper or improve upon it and—no, I am understating things already, I am being a coward, it is bigger than all that—no chance to turn back a tide that washed a great many of us out to sea. If everything had stayed in the lab, it would be different. The lab was only where it started, I realize now.

One thunderclap of truth.

And now I am like one of those hundreds of babies we studied: grip loosening, falling with a pure and unconditioned panic, through the air.

CHAPTER 1

But I need to start before I ever knew John, and well before mother-hood, if only to prove to myself that I rose to challenges and coped with larger-than-life personalities before. I need to remember that I did have an earlier life, and my own ideas, too.

Vassar College, 1916.

The Vassar Brothers Labs.

Outside: that glorious musty smell of leaves starting to dry and color, shrivel and drop. Scarlet and amber brightening our world of brick and stone, skies fresh and blue overhead. September, that most hopeful month. Some people prefer May—lilies and hyacinths, white gloves and pearls—but I've always preferred autumn, the season of rededication, when one experiences that same thrill in the breast that one gets walking into a vast library with its smells of old pages and oiled banisters. All those books still to be read. All those centuries of knowledge. Feeling humbled within the context of all that intelli-gence—but at the same time, elevated. Made part of something larger.

Inside the labs: standing at attention in front of a microscope, paired with my dear friend Mary, waiting for our professor to enter the room—Margaret Floy Washburn, the first woman in the entire country to receive a PhD in psychology, from Cornell, four years before I was born. The author of a textbook, *The Animal Mind*, written just around the time I was first learning to read.

Mary was also a sophomore, but older than me, because I'd entered Vassar early. We'd missed crossing paths for most of freshman year—each lurkers in our ways, with noses in our books. But then we'd finally noticed each other—I recall the first time I saw her stiff corona of curls bouncing as she strode with an enviable sense of determination through Main—and I'd found someone with whom I could discuss Wilhelm Wundt and John Dewey all the way back to Rousseau and Locke, from whose work on education Mary paraphrased the very first day we met: "We are like chameleons; we take our hue and the color of our moral character, from those who are around us." Being always a chameleon of sorts and one who took pride in picking the right creature to emulate, I determined that she would be my study and lab partner, whenever possible.

On this particular morning in September, across the Atlantic, scores of French and German men (no one we knew) were probably off dying at the Battle of the Somme, while we girls rubbed tired eyes and rebraided loose hair, expecting class to begin. Mary, too restless to wait, was fixing an unlabeled slide under the microscope clip.

"What do you see?"

"It looks like a blob." She wrinkled her nose, turning the dials.

"An amoeba," I corrected her—though of course, she knew as much, and was only being flip. "I was just reading a paper about the periodic appearance and disappearance of the gastric vacuole . . ."

"Are you sure we're in the right class?" she interrupted without looking up from the eyepiece. "Because I didn't sign up for zoology. I thought we were here to study the complexities of the human mind."

The room, already hushed—girls in drab cardigans and ankle-length skirts, whispering in twos and threes—had become uniformly silent, but Mary was too engrossed in her slide to notice. Loudly, she said, "Our teacher may be one of Cattell's 'thousand most important men in science,' but perhaps she's mixed us up with some other class. How long are we going to have to wait, anyway?"

From the doorway across the room, through which she had entered on low-heeled, sensible black shoes, Miss Washburn answered. "You don't have to wait at all. You may be dismissed now, if you'd prefer."

A long pause, allowing us to behold her: firm helmet of wavy hair, just starting to silver, with a tiny, darker knot at the nape; deep lines around her mouth formed by years of rigorous concentration. "Name?"

"Cover. Mary Cover."

"And you're partnered with . . . ?"

I took a half step away from the microscope, chin up. "Rosalie Rayner."

"Rayner. Good." Miss Washburn took her time looking over the registration sheet in her hand. "Rayner, you don't have an objection to studying animals, do you?"

"No, Miss Washburn."

"Not even amoebas?"

"No, not at all."

"Do you think an amoeba has a mind?"

The back of my knees softened into jelly. "I'm sorry, Miss Washburn, but I don't know."

Miss Washburn pulled out a high stool and settled herself onto it, legs crossed at the ankle. A delicate chain of swinging black beads shifted against her broad chest and then settled, as we watched, listened, and faintly perspired.

"Don't be sorry, Miss Rayner. You don't know. *We* don't precisely know. Not knowing is a perfectly appropriate place to start. Sometimes it's even the right place to end."

Another pause, the tinkling of water in the plumbing, running in another lab over our heads. The distant, purring jet of a Bunsen burner. A faint sniff of some sulfurous chemical. I loved those sounds and smells. Even in my embarrassed concern for Mary, and for myself, I couldn't be anything but deliriously happy at that moment.

"Go ahead, everyone," Miss Washburn said. "Take your seats."

We did, and I could feel Mary holding her breath next to me, waiting to discover whether she had been merely warned or actually expelled from the class. But Miss Washburn was not interested in making things clear. Mary's cheeks held onto their red flush for most of that first hour. Turning the focus knob, her hand shook.

We would have to wait most of a week until Mary got back a graded lab report to know she hadn't been banished. But in a way that was slower to reveal itself, she had. For two more years we both progressed well in our studies, each of us optimistic if uncertain about our futures, each of us distinctly skewed toward the sciences. And yet at the beginning of senior year, when Miss Washburn invited a select group of senior students to enroll in her Special Projects in Psychology seminar, Mary wasn't invited. When Mary, intent on protesting, interrupted Miss Washburn on the way to one of her classes, Miss Washburn explained: "You weren't satisfied with the lab you took with me before. I don't imagine you'll be satisfied with this class either."

We were both shocked. Mary was one of the best psychology students at Vassar.

Mary thought that a private meeting in Washburn's office might offer a better climate for persuasion, and I offered to tag along, waiting on a plump, tapestry-covered bench in the hall outside faculty offices. From my seat on the bench, I worked at deciphering a German publication of new lectures by Freud—*Vorlesungen zur Einführung in die Psychoanalyse*—missing every third or fourth word, and swung my shoes against the floor, softly tapping out the rhythm of a popular tune while I absentmindedly played with the charm bracelet on my left wrist. My mother had given me the bracelet, and Mary had given me my favorite charm, the little magnifying glass, symbolizing my love for science (evidently, no beaker- or brain-shaped charms were commonly available).

As soon as I saw Mary emerge and walk right past me, I knew things had gone badly.

"Don't say it," she said, intent on moving as quickly as possible away from the source of her humiliation, her pointed chin with its faint cleft just starting to tremble.

"Oh, Mary," I said, struggling to catch up. "You'll be fine."

I took her arm so we could walk down the dark hall, past the sconce-lighted portraits and old windows. The wavy leaded glass of each window blurred the view of rust-colored trees outside. "You're our best and brightest. You'll be fine."

"How will I possibly be fine if I can't even rise to the top within our own little college? Three years of paying my dues and I'm being *excluded*."

"There will be a portrait of you hanging in the labs someday. 'Mary Cover,' our next famous psychologist."

"I don't want to be famous. That has nothing to do with it." Mary hurried our pace. Joined at the elbow, we bobbed out of sync, heels clicking and squeaking against the scuffed wooden floors. "I want to contribute. I want to understand. I'd just like to work with humans—if that's not so much to ask—instead of worms and rats and color-blind fish."

"It was just . . . rotten luck. You rubbed her the wrong way. Calling her one of Cattell's 'most important men,' and all."

Mary snickered. "Your fault, for telling me about that."

I was the one who read every journal announcement, every newsletter, every history of the newer "scientific psychology," from James and Hall to Titchener and Angell.

"Yes, my fault," I said, feeling the happiness well up inside me, glad that Mary wasn't feeling demolished at that moment.

"Self-righteous bat," Mary said.

How old was Washburn really? Early forties. She seemed ancient to us both.

"Cave-dwelling crone."

"Half-blind hermaphrodite."

"Don't worry," I said, buoyed by the snicker in Mary's voice. "We'll fix it."

"I admire your optimism, Rosalie," Mary said with faux formality, giving my elbow a grateful squeeze. Then she dropped into a huskier whisper, the sound of so many afternoon library conversations, so many sleepy picnics in the shade of ancient campus trees. "But don't hold your breath."

Mary was the type of woman Vassar was intended to produce, the type who wouldn't just run off and get married but would actually *do something*. She was needed. Goodness, we were all needed—and more than that, committed to making the world a better place.

In Europe, the Great War dragged on. Society, government, and even religion seemed to offer few solutions to problems of an incomprehensible scale. And yet, still, my fellow students and I retained our idealism, an unspoken sense that whatever was dismantled or destroyed, something else newer and better would rise up to take its place. Scientists urged us to believe that with the help of new education methods and a commitment to societal improvements, reforming man's worst habits was more than possible, it was *inevitable*. Look how much our own suffragette mothers had done to reform the world ahead of us, as they liked to remind us when we showed any sign of forgetting their labors and sacrifices.

Mary Cover's mother was more committed than my own. I was glad that my mother didn't distribute pins and handbills when she came to visit, but of course, we all wanted the same thing: equality of opportunity. And weren't we practically there already? A few more states to be persuaded, a few more legal details to be pinned down, but the battle had been won. Hadn't it?

We were meant to exceed our mothers' ambitions. We were meant to walk down that cleared path into a new American century of progress and enlightenment. Relying on experimental science, not phrenology or philosophy or voodoo, we would understand what made people tick. We would understand—in addition to how to mix a Manhattan and dance the fox-trot—how to make people healthier, happier, better in character and in conduct from the very start.

The day after Mary's snub by Miss Washburn, I walked past our teacher's house on Professors' Row. I had to circle back twice before mustering the courage to step up to the front door. I lifted and dropped the tarnished brass knocker: no reply.

To one side, a single struggling rosebush hunched, defeated, against the wall, next to a window I could just see into, pricking my hip on the branches as I angled in closer for a better view. The curtains, faded from years of sunlight to the point of near transparency, had been left parted. Inside, I could make out a small wooden desk of Quaker-like simplicity with stacks of papers, a typewriter, and a plain chair, with a white sweater folded neatly over the back. Also on the desk: one small and spidery green plant doing only a little better than the rosebush, pushed into a drinking glass full of tangled roots and brown water. No rugs or tapestries, no framed photographs or paintings, no side tables with crystal decanters, no other decoration in this monastic cottage. An answer to my question: How does a single, educated woman live?

When the curtain shifted, I startled and nearly fell into the rosebush again, but it was only a long-haired Persian cat that had leaped onto the sill, eyeing me skeptically through the glass, as if sensing with feline intuition my presumptions about Miss Washburn's choices and sacrifices. For why, at the age of nineteen, was I interested in practically any other person, except as an embodiment of who I should, or might, become?

I hadn't told Mary I planned to make any of these visits. Mary was pretending she'd forgotten about the matter. But I had my speech planned.

The next day, when Miss Washburn opened her faculty office door, I blurted, "I would like you to consider admitting Mary Cover into your class."

"Come in, come in. I *have* considered. You presume I haven't?"

"And?"

Miss Washburn invited me in and served us both Earl Grey tea on a small round table flanked by two peach-colored wing chairs. I took one sip of mine, but I made so much clatter setting the cup back on its saucer that I resolved not to sip again until the very end, and then to finish it off in one gulp. Miss Washburn took her time with her own cup, sipping and smiling, comfortable with the silence.

This room, at least, had more to occupy my gaze than her house would have had—proof of which place she considered her true home. There, across from me on the wall, were single and group portraits of men—the first-generation psychologists, clutching their cigars. There was G. Stanley Hall at Clark University, presiding over a group that included prestigious visitors from Europe: Freud and Carl Jung. There, in a separate portrait—and was his influence already fading?—was the father of American psychology, William James. Below a set of dark and piercing eyes, the bottom of his face was entirely hidden under a bushy mustache and square-cut beard. He looked grumpy and unapproachable, but from my own readings I knew that he'd actually helped one of the very first non-degreed women psychologists by allowing her to sit in on his class at Harvard, even when the other men boycotted in response.

That was the world from which Miss Washburn had herself emerged: victorious, fully degreed, recognized. Why was she making things so hard for another woman student?

"Rosalie," Miss Washburn said at last, setting down her cup.

"There's no shortage of competent seniors eager to fill those seats. Mary wasn't the only person who was told she'll have to choose another psychology class. And I'm not arrogant enough to think I'm the only professor with whom she'd benefit."

Damn the clatter. I drained my cup of tea. "But she's an excellent student. If Mary can't be in the class," I said, setting down my cup firmly, "then I withdraw."

Miss Washburn finally looked surprised, at least for a moment, until her startled expression softened into a rueful smile.

"You plan to withdraw," she said.

"Yes." I settled my hands atop the folds of my wool-skirted lap. "That's correct."

"No," she said.

"Pardon me?"

"No," she said again.

She stood and went to the window, looked out—there it all was, the world that had been her refuge for years. The world that had also been mine—*almost* enough. But no: not enough. Not at all. I felt the scratchy tingle of it, like some rash or fever just coming on. As a wide-eyed freshman, I'd been excited just to board the train to New York City, followed by the Empire line farther north, to Poughkeepsie. Away from my parents: Could there have been any greater excitement than that? Only in my fourth year was I starting to feel in want of something more than collegial, single-sex refuge. Only now was I pining for the invigoration of other places, other people, and perhaps moments like this: an opportunity to take sides, to sometimes go too far.

Miss Washburn returned to stand behind her chair. "Rosalie, you're a careful student. I don't mean timid. You're thoughtful and objective. You're deeply committed, with good habits and a solid work ethic, but you don't overreach. We need that."

Careful. Thoughtful. Solid. Was that the only impression I made?

She continued, "Psychology in our decade is like a three-year-old. It's at the runabout stage. It's growing by leaps and bounds, but it's also making messes—or it will be. It's separating itself from everything that came before, and it's still deciding who its friends will be, just as you're evidently deciding who *your* friends must be." She smiled. How amusing I was to her, with my narrow loyalties and small concerns. "Does that make sense?"

I nodded, but only to be polite. Never mind about friendship: evidently she knew nothing about that. Better to focus on academics. To her, the field of psychology might have seemed new and on shaky ground, but to me, it was old: thirty years, at least. James had called it not a science, "just a hope of a science," but enough with caution and modesty. Why this constant fear of everything new when the very point of science was to invite the new into our lives: the bubbling-over of beakers, the occasional shattering of glass?

"Do you get along with your parents?" Miss Washburn asked.

"As a matter of fact, I do."

"Any younger siblings?"

"No," I said, confused about what she was implying. I had an older sister, Evelyn. We were seven years apart and not close.

"I see."

But that *I see* bothered me. I was surprised to hear that kind of fainting-couch questioning coming from her, a scientist dedicated to objective laboratory techniques.

A secretary knocked and opened the door a crack. Miss Whitehall, a teacher of classics in her eighties, needed Miss Washburn to pop down the hall, just for a moment. She smiled apologetically. "Perhaps you could refill our tea."

I took our cups over and, alone in the room, found my eye wandering again, from the photos on the wall to the papers on the desk—was there something there about Mary, or anything that could help my cause?—and then to a piece of pale lavender stationery next to the typewriter, the letter half written. It was addressed to a female friend (fine, so she had *one*) in New York State. They were corresponding, evidently, about Emerson. Miss Washburn was saying that she could take a little Emerson—*as medicine, but not as regular food*—and about introspection in general, and about life. *The great thing is to look out for opportunities to help in little ways, and let the rest go.* And further down the page: *I am a very ordinary individual. There was a time when I feebly attempted to be other than ordinary, but I missed so much of wholesome fun and good fellowship that I was glad to give up the attempt.*

Resigned to being "ordinary." Well, that was another mark against her.

I refilled the cups hurriedly, hearing footsteps coming back down the hall.

"It was only about her cat," Miss Washburn said as she entered, smiling. "I'm watching Felix for her this weekend."

Turning serious, she continued. "Rosalie, you're worried about a friend. But I'm worrying about something larger: a set of ideas that will greatly influence society. The young women who graduate from Vassar and go on to advanced degrees will soon enough become my own colleagues. Someday, they'll be the women who challenge my own work. That's as it should be."

So she was open to change, but only change so slow we might not see it or feel it, or arrive at a new shore anytime soon. Change at the regal pace of an ocean liner. I'd made a trip, with my mother, in an ocean liner once. Three weeks of boredom and nausea, sitting on deck chairs, playing whist.

There was a knock at the door—another student, with an appointment.

"I'll see you in class," Miss Washburn said, reaching out to shake my hand, soft fingers—loose skin over bone—gently enclosing mine. I did not wish to be so gentle in return.

"Thank you for your time," I said. "Yes, I'll see you in Abnormal."

She cocked her head. "But you were signed up for Special Topics as well. You're doubling up this semester. I thought we'd understood each other."

"I'm off to see the registrar next," I said, pulling away. "It's so hard to fit everything in. I do the same thing at Thanksgiving dinners, loading up my plate with more than I can possibly digest. That's childish, don't you think? Better to make firm choices. But thank you for the tea."

CHAPTER 2

Of course, I rushed directly to the dorms, cheeks flushed with adventure, as if I'd just turned down a date with the most sought-after boy at a school dance. I couldn't wait to tell Mary. By dropping Special Topics, I'd be sacrificing the chance to be one of the seniors with whom Washburn co-wrote and published scientific papers—the real things, in actual journals. And if Washburn turned me away from Abnormal Psych because I'd withdrawn from Special Topics? She wouldn't, as it turned out. But at the time, I was willing to accept that additional consequence.

Yet when I arrived in the corner suite Mary shared with four girls, Mary was in the middle of entertaining some other friends: Cynthia and Strikey, the three of them sprawled out on the oriental carpet, with a phonograph warbling. In more than three years at Vassar, I'd heard a rude remark about my heritage only once, from Strikey's mouth. Regarding how to handle those sorts of comments, my father and my uncle, the senator, preferred optimistic stoicism. Only my mother seemed to think a biting response was appropriate. But then again, she would have been the first to call me home from Vassar if I'd been having any real trouble getting along, so I had to make sure never to let on that it was a challenge breaking into some social circles, even more so when you were darkly complected, quiet by default, a touch too book-smart, and young.

The phonograph was playing dance songs and the girls had pinned up their hair in back, to make it look bobbed from the front, and had rolled their skirts at the waist to pull the hems up to their knees.

"Mary," I shouted. "Something happened. Stop the music."

She wagged a finger at me and stood up to dance, and her two friends laughed all that much louder, jumping up to join her, grasping their knees and knocking them together in time with the song. Strikey had a charm bracelet much like my own, and as she danced, it jangled at her wrist.

Their giggles gave them away. I picked up Mary's teacup. Only a half inch of clear liquid remained, but it was potent.

"Tea time," Mary crooned. "Have some!" Her glasses slid crook-edly across her pert nose.

I always maintained that, despite her own protestations, Mary was pretty, but there were certain facts that couldn't be denied. Her eye-glasses were big and black-rimmed. Her hair tended to spread out into a brittle, electrified mass, creating a second, round frame for her oth-erwise small features. Late at night, in her humorously droning voice, she had praised my blue eyes, my silky (as she called it) dark hair, and my narrow ankles. I had always told her that none of it mattered. Neither of us wore makeup—not even powder. Neither of us cared, in fact, about whatever traits supposedly made a woman more attractive to the opposite sex.

But she had an indefinable charisma. She was revealing it now, dancing and slurring her speech, more glamorous and exotic in her honest, frizzy-haired dishevelment than some girls would be in perfect dresses, with fox stoles around their necks. She knew what she wanted and said what she thought, at the very least.

"What's in the cups?" I shouted over the phonograph. "British or American?"

British was our code name for gin. American was our name for rum. I didn't particularly enjoy drinking—yet—and the penalty for being discovered was steep, but we never let that worry us.

"See for yourself!" Strikey shrieked.

"But Mary, I need to talk to you!" I called out.

"Later," she said, and grabbed Strikey's hands, the two of them kicking and twisting. At the edge of the rug, they tripped and went down in a heap, with Strikey in Mary's lap. Strikey grabbed for her ankle, as if it had been sprained, but she was still grinning like an idiot.

When the song ended, I said too loudly, "I went to see Washburn."

"You didn't," Mary replied.

"I told her I'd withdraw if she didn't change her mind."

Mary turned to me, her eyes half crossed over the top of her glasses. Even though she'd unlinked hands with Strikey, she was still leaning over, shoulders slouched, waist widened by the padding of the rolled-up, hitched-up skirt, a skinny ape who has stumbled into a cache of fermented fruit.

"No need to talk to that witch on my behalf."

"I already said I did."

"I'd already talked to her twice. That was *my* battle to fight, Rosalie."

But what kind of person didn't want company in battle? If I wasn't getting any thanks for the attempt, I certainly wasn't going to get any credit for the result—which, it was occurring to me now, had not been in anyone's favor, just as Mary would have predicted.

"You're just convincing Washburn that I'm a moron," Mary said, holding out her cup for Cynthia to refill. "And if she decides to drop *you* from Special Topics, just for pestering her when you shouldn't, then *you're* the moron."

She wasn't getting the point. I hadn't risked being dropped from the class. I'd *chosen* to drop the class. For the sake of friendship. For *her*. Mary didn't even seem to need confirmation that my attempt had been futile. And now I realized this about her: she wasn't the best about holding her tongue, but she was always quick to accept the consequences and move on. She didn't need special favors or even recognition. Unlike many girls, she was impervious to pressure to sign up for the glee club, for theater productions, for the yearbook committee—and we'd had that in common, the lack of interest in being joiners.

I knew the several ways in which I didn't perfectly fit the Vassar mold. But Mary's set-apartness was different, not preordained by race, culture, or religion. You couldn't find her picture hardly at all in the yearbook, just as you couldn't find mine. She didn't need to be fawned upon by any one professor. She seemed to have an allergy to being a protégée. Whether or not she would ever need a devoted mentor or a fervent lover (I imagined she'd remain a bachelorette forever) Mary seemed to be proving at this moment that she didn't need *me*. Or rather, she didn't need any of her friends to pass a loyalty test. But I *did* want to pass that test. I didn't mind a spot of trouble if it was trouble that could be shared. I didn't need to be part of any Vassar daisy chain, but I still appreciated being attached to something or someone.

"Mary," I said. "I need to talk to you."

"And I," she said, holding her cup at an angle, "need to finish this, before Jo gets back."

Jo was the one roommate who disapproved of "dancing teas" altogether, and was likely to complain if she stumbled into the middle of a party.

"Couldn't we just be alone for a minute?" I beseeched Mary.

She responded, "Couldn't we *not* be alone for this once?"

My insides shrank, and with them, the last three years accordioned as well: a series of conversations and study sessions and lab-partner pairings that had meant too much to me, and nothing to anyone else.

"You're a pal, Rosalie. Just maybe stop trying so hard," Mary said in a softer voice, noting my crestfallen expression.

Oblivious, Cynthia slid a new record out of a burgundy-colored sleeve. "Everyone. You've gotta hear this." The record started up, with its lyrics about a soldier who'd been shot somewhere in France, and didn't want to get well, because he was so besotted with the woman caring for him. "Early ev'ry morning, night and noon, / The cutest little girlie comes and feeds me with a spoon . . ."

I wanted to grab Mary's arm and roll our eyes together at the stupidity of any college girls who could believe that being wounded in the trenches, probably shell-shocked and near death from some terrible infection, could be a giddy pleasure. But Mary refused to share my contempt. She sat on the floor, her lap occupied by Strikey's scarf-wrapped ankle, while Strikey reached out to paw at her own minor injury, drawing attention to her jangling little bracelet, from which hung a tiny magnifying glass.

I felt my stomach drop. The room was already warm, but now my face flamed with a heat so sudden and fierce it made my eyes water, while everyone else continued with their fun, singing and laughing. Mary had given her the charm, identical to mine. Strikey was *terrible* at science. How dare she wear it?

I was only another friend. Nothing special. And I'd judged Miss Washburn for her desire to be ordinary? I was ordinary, too. We were all sickeningly ordinary.

I could walk out, and no one would follow. Or I could stay—with a vengeance.

"Fill me a cup, Cynthia," I said, and proceeded to drink three cups of gin in all, choking back the astringent fumes, willing to prove I was as carefree as Cynthia, as silly as Strikey, as sensible and independent as Mary—if all those things could possibly go together. As if I could be someone more interesting by being everything to everyone. Lord knows I had many more years to keep trying.

I was the one who kept restarting the phonograph. I was the one who learned the lyrics of the chorus so that I could sing alongside the stupid soldier, "Early ev'ry morning, night and noon . . ." I was the one who remembered two dirty jokes that I had been told, in confidence, by my sister Evelyn, and I told them in turn to Strikey and Cynthia, who shrieked and groaned and laughed in pleased disbelief, which only proved they'd thought me incapable of being raunchy, a misunderstanding I was only too eager to disprove.

I was the one who, when Jo came home and opened the door, appalled at the noise and the suspicious vapors in the room, took the blame for the party, as if I'd started it rather than stumbled into it, and who talked Cynthia and Strikey into prancing outside, our skirts rolled scandalously high, while Mary—tired of me, or just tired—stayed behind. I was the one who vomited into the bushes outside the library building, and beamed, lying on my side, when Strikey patted my hair and pulled me up to a feeble stand: "I didn't know your kind drank."

"What kind is that?"

When she didn't answer, I filled in: "The dizzy kind. Strikey, help me. I can't stop everything from turning."

I was not the praying type, and perhaps I made my final spontaneous address to Adonai at that moment. *Stop spinning. Please stop. Oh, God, but look at those stars.* How those stars would keep spinning, all night long.

"You're skirt's a mess," Strikey said, after I crumpled on the lawn a second time. "But you're all right, Rar. You're all right."

Mary probably had no idea what had come between us. I had wanted a deep, passionate, risky, all-encompassing friendship. Sacrifice and loyalty—or nothing. So fine: nothing it was.

We occasionally still shared a table at the library, cramming for exams next to the soberly beautiful stained-glass windows. We even sat side-by-side once, during a winter sleigh ride when everyone else was talking about their upcoming New Year's plans—shopping for scarves and gloves, and going ice skating with a friendly batch of New England boys. Instead we compared notes on graduate schools for psychology, but in a formal, awkward way, as if we'd only just met and had not, seven months earlier, reclined together on the campus lawn, staring up at the starry sky, trying to picture our glowing futures, as if written between the constellations.

Never would I have guessed how similar our interests would remain, and how her life for years would always be the example of what *my* life might have been, professionally but also personally, if not for certain choices and—to be plain about it—if not for certain mistakes. I would begin to feel, only later, that we had been two saplings planted in the same field, and I had grown helter-skelter, too anxious for the sun maybe, or too sporadically watered, heavy with fruit at one moment and rotted the next, and then swarming with wasps, while she had grown slowly and more judiciously in a half-sunny, half-shady spot, taking her time, focusing on what mattered, neither overtended nor entirely ignored, maturing into something true and strong. A torturous metaphor, but poetry was not my subject of choice at Vassar.

But I must give Mary the credit for telling me about the John Watson lecture at the New School, in New York, at the start of 1919. It was just like Mary to seek out a psychology lecture outside Vassar's walls, for which she wouldn't even be awarded credit. It was also just like her not to seek a personal introduction to Watson that evening in January when we entered the lecture hall, crowded with Columbia and New School students familiar with Watson's 1913 Behaviorist Manifesto. Mary simply wasn't the flirting type and he—with his dark forelock and just-beginning-to-silver temples, his rakish smile, and his European-tailored clothes—was already encircled by students of both genders seeking his attention.

It was a Friday evening, and our own Miss Washburn was there, too, on one of her occasional forays outside of Poughkeepsie. When I stopped by her seat on the way to my own, she reached for my hand and said with a smile, "The youngest president of the Psychological Association, did you know that? He's made a name for himself. Listen well, Rosalie, but water it down by half."

I thought of the day I'd spied into her windows, and of the pale spider plant with the knotted roots, forced into the murky water in a dirty juice glass on her desk. I thought of the evening ahead, and what would follow: the gentle chatter, the crustless sandwiches and tables of punch. I wanted more than a half glass of cheap punch. I yearned for something purer—no, something downright stronger, and not just a drink. I wanted a torrential downpour, raining onto my head. I wanted to tip back my chin, close my eyes, and open up my mouth, drops pounding and splashing, soaking my throat, my dress, my skin.

As a speaker approached the stage to introduce the special guest, I hurried away to my own seat, several places away from Mary's. Then Dr. John B. Watson took the stage, patting his hair as he climbed the steps, smiling with faux modesty. He took off his wire-rimmed glasses to wipe them, which only drew our attention to his thick, dark eyebrows and soulful eyes, substantially deeper and larger without lenses in the way. Even from a distance, he struck me as both arrogant and vulnerable—a potent combination for a girl my age, whose romantic, inarticulate ideas were a mess of yearnings for both subordination and dutiful mothering.

I must have been distracted, my own thoughts spinning in circles or jumping from one loose association to the next, while he explained some of his main tenets—that we had no business wondering about abstract things like consciousness, that there was no such thing as a mind. If only *my* mind hadn't been so overstimulated at that moment, I might have heard and digested his opening words even better. As he talked, he kept the glasses hooked for several minutes between two fingers, until suddenly, he pushed them back onto his face and reached for something hidden beneath the lectern.

"Catch," he said, throwing a dingy softball toward the front row of seats. A girl—thick waisted, blonde head of curls—threw her hands up in alarm. The ball bounced and rolled between several rows, got kicked by someone trying in vain to retrieve it, and emerged in a row near the back, where a line of standing-room-only students had assembled.

"A negative early experience, I'm guessing," the visiting lecturer said good-naturedly. "Let's try that again."

Another toss, and another girl in the front lunged forward, elbows between her skirts, and still managed to butterfinger it. When the ball was returned to him, Dr. Watson took off his glasses and puzzled over the ball as if it had betrayed him.

"I've given this same demonstration at colleges up and down the coast, and it's never failed me before." He lifted one finger off the ball to scratch at his temple. "Then again, there were more men in those audiences. We seem to have an unusual number of women present." He pressed his lips together in a self-mocking smile. "Last time, then. Catch!"

Dr. Watson looked toward the far right corner of the room, the farthest front-row chair, where I was sitting, and in slow-moving pantomime, lobbed the gentlest possible underhand toss. I rose a few inches out of my seat, held my breath, and barely caught the ball between my wrists before scooping it inward, toward my heart. The room erupted in applause.

"What were you thinking?" he said to the first girl who had dropped the ball, and who even now couldn't organize her words into coherence.

"Never mind," he said, skipping the second girl and zeroing in on me. "What were *you* thinking?"

I was still tensed up, on the edge of my seat. "I was thinking I'd better not make a fool of myself."

"Really? All those subverbalized words, lodging in your larynx?"

My larynx? Well it's true, my throat felt tight. Is that where they had lodged? Wherever they'd gotten formed, and wherever they'd gotten stuck, yes—all those thoughts, and other things besides. He'd given us plenty of time to think and daydream since the moment he'd entered the room.

"I was thinking," I said, playing along, "*Don't drop it!*"

"Yes, well, we upset the demonstration, with those multiple attempts and significant delays. Usually, I do it just once, and the element of surprise is essential. I'm wagering that if the ball were coming toward you the first time, you might not have subverbalized at all, isn't that right?"

What did it cost me to agree? "Yes, that's probably right."

"No need for any introspective process. Just an action," he insisted. "Just protect yourself—if you're the first girl, and maybe had a ball smack you in the face as a child. A conditioned response, in other words." Everyone laughed at this, rubbernecking to see if the attention had made the girl turn red.

"And if you'd never had such a fearful incident," Dr. Watson continued, "you'd be responding in another conditioned and more complicated way, without even realizing you were moving. You'd be preparing to—why must we call it a thought?—preparing to simply . . . *catch.*"

The entire room was nodding, lips ready to repeat the word: *catch*. As he wanted it. But most of the young women gathered were just as ready to say, "Dinner at eight? Certainly." Or, "of course I'll dance with you." Or, "No, I don't have a ride, actually." Or any of a dozen other ready-made replies to this handsome and gregarious professor.

"No one asks a baseball player what he thinks every time a ball comes to him, as a way of understanding what follows in the game. No one posts his musings on a scoreboard, and no one should. Why should we care what you're thinking—*if* you're even thinking, whatever that means, and I propose that it means far less than you've been taught. I would suggest that our century's emphasis on thought and mind is as irrelevant as previous centuries' emphasis on the soul. We are interested in behavior. We are interested in what's observable, what's measurable, what's malleable. We are interested in what can be predicted, and what can be controlled. That's where our focus needs to be, if we intend to live in a saner world."

A saner world! So he was offering both the excitement of revolution and redemption from chaos, both change and security, upheaval and peace. Potent concepts, just a month after the armistice.

A college boy in a too-tight argyle sweater stood up from a seat in the back and called out a question. "But Dr. Watson, what are your positions on the structuralism of Wundt and Titchener versus the functionalism of James? And what about psychoanalysis?"

In one breathless expulsion, the student had managed to name three pioneers and three theories. The college boy glanced left and right, clearly proud of his performance, and sat down to receive his answer.

His seat was still squeaking when Dr. Watson replied, "Did you hear anything I've said so far? Are you a student of psychology, young man, or a student of philosophy? Every method you've just named is focused on one thing: introspection."

"But Wundt was an experimentalist," the student had the audacity to call back, although in a less certain voice.

Dr. Watson shook his head. His knowing smirk seemed to take in all the rest of us, granting us the benefit of the doubt. *We* weren't stupid enough to defend Wundt. (Until an hour ago, I'd considered Wundt brilliant, but I would never admit as much now.)

"You can't *perform* experiments involving introspection. You can only perform experiments involving behavior. Mental processes, whether the *what* and the *where* of structuralism or the *how* and the *why* of functionalism, do not concern us. What concerns us, and moreover, what we can study, is what the human animal actually does."

Dr. Watson gripped the podium more tightly, voice rising as he railed at us for our own benefit.

"The human animal retracts a finger from the fire. He lashes out in a rage. If he is a lazy medicine man intent on enslaving the rest of his tribe with superstition, he dances around the fire and tells tales about a frightening God. Whatever his views on religion, he eats and sleeps and copulates. He draws architectural plans and builds skyscrapers. From simple to complex, yet all structured of observable actions. Are these not interesting enough behaviors for you?"

No answer, now, from the college boy in the tight sweater.

"Let's forget about our game of catch, then, and forget with even less regret about the last thirty to forty years of introspective dead-ends," Dr. Watson continued to our roomful of fresh faces. "Let's talk about a range of unconditioned responses, and then we'll address the subject of conditioned ones." And Dr. Watson began to review for us the story of Pavlov, the bell, and the sal- ivating dog, and why, again, these things would make no sense at all unless we dismissed nearly all other approaches as outright hokum—*Listen well,* Washburn had said, *and water it down by half*—and we'd have to start all over and look only to what could be observed directly, and experimented upon, and thereby proven.

At the bottom of the stairs leading to the postlecture reception hall, Miss Washburn introduced us. Dr. Watson's forehead was gleaming; the act of overturning his predecessors' theories had been tiring. Working a finger under his high, tight collar, he explained that he was looking for a graduate student.

Mary was nearby, and she had already whispered a single comment in my ear: "Focus on what's observable. That's good sense." So quickly had she boiled down the parts that would be relevant to her, letting the rest blow away: his showmanship, his appearance, his claims to hold the future of humanity in his hands. And now she stood silently at my elbow: unassuming, staring at him through her thick, round lenses. I could feel the weight of her attention, the heavy outline of her personality. She would not pander, and if I'd been her closest friend that day, I might not have felt the need to pander either. But I wasn't her friend anymore. Colleagues, we'd be, and nothing more, after graduation. The mild loneliness I'd been feeling for months was, on this day, freedom: ejected from Mary's orbit, I could more easily respond to the magnetism of someone else's.

"There you are," Watson said, smiling as he turned, recognizing me as the girl who had managed to hold on to the tossed ball. "So why can't we come up with a roomful of women who can catch properly?"

"It's only because they didn't practice when they were younger," I said. "It's just something you learn, given half a chance."

"You must have had brothers."

"No."

"Then . . . ?"

"I guess I wanted to catch the ball badly enough. To help you with your demonstration, I mean."

"You like to help," he said.

"If the person is worth helping."

He stared at me openly, without guile. I had to hope against all hope that I looked more confident than I felt.

I said, "I should admit that I do have a father willing to play toss with his daughters."

"Good man. And what does he do for a living?"

"Real estate."

"Interested in planning and building the future."

"Yes, I suppose."

"And you? What do you think about the future?"

"That it will be much better than the past. It has to be."

He smiled again, and I felt as if I was passing successfully through a maze, choosing between turns, vaguely aware of some rewarding scent in the air, happy simply to avoid a dead end.

"And what do you imagine we do in a lab full of babies?"

With Miss Washburn, *I don't know* had often been the right, honest, admirable, and cautious answer, but with this man, I could tell that phrase would never, ever do.

My slight pause gave him an excuse to jump in. "Babies won't tell you their dreams, of course. Nor will they submit to hypnosis."

I plunged ahead, expanding on the ideas he'd just explained to us in the second half of the lecture. "I imagine you're looking at the senses: vision, hearing. You're seeing what develops, when and how. Issues of perception. Maybe left-hand or right-hand primacy."

When he frowned slightly, I backed up. "But in the lecture, you mentioned you haven't observed as much handedness as one might expect. It's one of those so-called innate qualities that perhaps isn't so innate after all. Perhaps almost nothing is innate."

Better, his tentative smile seemed to say.

"Maybe language?" I continued. "But I suppose that comes later, and anyway, self-reported thoughts or words of any kind actually lead us astray in a way that behaviors don't—which explains why Wundt and James aren't sufficient. So I imagine you're recording reactions to the simplest possible stimuli."

"What's a simple reaction?" he asked.

"Blinking."

"In response to?"

"Light, an approaching object, pain."

"And how about a more complex reaction—say, the turning of a man's head to follow a desirable woman as she passes?"

"It's merely a conditioned response, or I guess I should say, a complex and integrated set of responses."

I made no mention of where, as he had explained to us in the lecture, these responses led next: how mere visual stimuli, the simple sighting of a woman's bonnet, could initiate the building pressure of a liquid, male semen—the cause of most romantic entanglements, he'd said, easily reversed once the pressure has been released. All a bit much to spell out with Miss Washburn still looking on.

"It's the stuff of poetry," he teased.

"And the stuff of science."

"Which one tells us more?"

"I think we both know the answer to that, Dr. Watson. I don't blame the ancient poets, if that's what you mean."

"How about the modern ones?"

"I suppose they're wasting their time. But once a year, a little Valentine's poetry doesn't seem out of place. If they take one day and we scientists get the other 364, the human race still has a chance."

"You're assuming the scientist works more than five days a week."

"Is there a reason he shouldn't?"

He stopped me. "What's your name again?"

"Rosalie Rayner."

"And when do you graduate?"

CHAPTER 3

After receiving my degree that June, the summer stretched before me: a hot, dull limbo of Sunday Beef Wellington and mornings of tea and hard toast, and listening to the back stairs squeak as the servants carried laundry up and down, while I read about the adventures of career-minded bachelorette Una Golden in Sinclair Lewis's *The Job*. I held my breath near the end, afraid that Lewis would take away Una's desire for career once love and marriage were in the mix, but he didn't, thank goodness, or at least I thought he didn't: "'I will keep my job—if I've had this world of offices wished on me, at least I'll conquer it, and give my clerks a decent time,' the businesswoman meditated. 'But just the same—oh, I am a woman, and I do need love. I want Walter, and I want his child, my own baby and his.' THE END."

I read the last page while sprawled on my bed, avoiding the landing where our maid, Annie, was mopping the floor. "I will keep my job . . . But just the same—oh, I am a woman . . ." So did Una keep her job, and get the husband, and the baby? Was that even possible? I'd read Goldman and Sanger on the plight of prostitutes and factory workers, and Maria Montessori on the development of early education for the children of working women. But nowhere had I read about educated middle- or upper-class women with children and challenging professions. Did Lewis's last paragraph mean Una was giving equal weight to all her desires, and insisting upon them, or was it a second thought, a surrender of her determination? "Just the same— oh." Was that, "Oh, such a dilemma," or "Oh, I give up"?

Annie, bucket in her hand, called from the doorway, "Miss Rosalie, you're ready for luncheon now?"

"In a minute," I said. "Annie, do you think a woman can have a job and a baby and a husband?"

There was a long pause before she answered. "I think you do what you've got to do."

I called back, "I don't mean the kind of job you *have* to do. I mean the kind of job you'd like to do. To learn things and make the world a better place, for example."

She paused again before responding with a funny tone in her voice. "Why don't you carry this bucket down the stairs while I go get the lunch that's probably burning, and then I'll think on it awhile."

Good Annie, who probably had more lessons to teach me than Sinclair Lewis, who—reformer though he was—hadn't seemed able to make up his mind about Una Golden and her desires. "THE END" in those bossy capital letters came a little abruptly and breathlessly, as if he'd tired of trying to sort out fantasy and reality, or perhaps wanted to preserve the fantasy for his female readers: that everything was possible. Or not. My Vassar lit prof had tried to explain the value of ambiguity, but it seemed like a lazy, face-saving strategy for people who didn't know what the real answers were. No wonder I put more faith in science.

When I was young, we'd had two Irish women living with us: Ellen Shea and Mary Noon. Later, we had Pauline and Marye Duffy and Susan. Also Bertha, from Germany, and Agnus, a widow from Maryland, and Frank and Annie, from North Carolina. Annie was only a few years older than me, but she had the long, dry fingers, cracked palms, and weary-wise demeanor of someone much older. With so many servants attending the needs of three people, Mother was not overtaxed.

One stifling afternoon in July, a day in which no Atlantic breezes reached our Eutaw Place home, she joined me in the front parlor—a high-ceilinged room connected to our dining room via a massive pocket door—where the family bookshelves were kept. Mother asked Agnus to bring in the kitchen step stool and waited until she'd returned to scrubbing the front marble steps to reach down Hall's book on childhood and rebellious adolescence, which was kept on a high shelf, owing to its exciting and vivid passages about sexual urges, to which Hall had devoted much lyrical effort.

Mother and I took turns reading aloud paragraphs, determined to keep our expressions scholarly and dispassionate. Her profile was worthy of a sketch. She read with the book held out in front of her, searching for that magic distance at which her vision was still operating suitably—long nose tipped up, hair piled up in one of those Gibson Girl bouffants that was no longer fashionable but still common among ladies of a certain age, and Mother was not about to bob her hair anytime soon. At the point when the material would become too biologically specific, she'd wrinkle her nose as if trying to extinguish an oncoming sneeze.

"Go on," I'd urge her, just before we both dissolved into laughter.

But the more well-thumbed book—on a low shelf, no ladder required—was L. Emmett Holt's famous baby manual, *The Care and Feeding of Children*, the one that had been Mother's bible, at least in the beginning. Folded inside were my feeding schedules and weight charts, with spaces for measurements and elimination records and additional comments to be logged every two hours.

"Twelve days, that's all you managed?" I asked her.

"I meant to do better," she said, pausing to fan the back of her neck and coil and re-pin several damp, fallen strands from her upswept hair. "But then you cried, and wanted to be fed and be held. Other times, you were sleeping so soundly, and I hated to wake you up just to stay on schedule. And as for your weight, and stripping off your clothes all the time for all those required measurements, why bother? You seemed plump and cheerful to me."

"And then, what happened on day thirteen? You stopped feeding me altogether?"

She put her arm around my shoulder, stealing a squeeze. "Silly bird. I fed you all the time—more often than I was supposed to."

"Oh, Mother."

"I know, and look what happened!"

"What happened?"

"Absolutely nothing! As soon as you were old enough to run off into the gardens, run you did—and you grew up into a perfectly normal, slim, healthy girl."

She saw I wasn't satisfied. But what grown children ever are?

"I just wasn't as good with record keeping, Rosalie. And then the Irish girls, they had no interest whatsoever in writing anything down. How they laughed and laughed whenever I told them what to do!"

"That's not very nice," I said. But I had good memories of those profane Irish girls who chased me through the statue-dotted gardens that ran for several blocks down the middle of our newly constructed residential boulevard.

"It was positively fine," Mother said. "I might have felt a little bossed-about, but it was true, they knew a world more than I did. And as far as they were concerned, you were their baby, not mine. They thought it was ridiculous that anyone should learn about mothering from a book."

"But it would have been nice to have more records," I sulked, making my dear, patient mother smile her fretful smile.

"Yes, it would have. I failed you, and I failed Dr. Holt."

"And Dr. Hall."

"Yes, and Dr. Hall." She gave her own left hand a playful smack. "But he was wrong about the adolescent's need for drama and conflict. Look at how you've turned out: properly finished, and as level-headed as they come."

We knew of other students who had been accepted into universities out west—not as prestigious, or convenient. One girl's parents were actually moving two thousand miles away to live with her in a new city while she attended graduate school. It was touching to see how far parents would go to support their daughters' ambitions, while still doing everything possible to thwart any indecent behavior. This was the beginning of the Jazz Age, after all. And there was white slavery to consider as well. We were informed that thousands of otherwise innocent young women (well, a few dozen, anyway) were disappearing from city parks throughout the nation, drugged by decent-looking men in suits and overcoats. That's what happened when you let your daughters grow up, go to school, and get jobs.

My own good luck would save me from the slavers—as long as I didn't accept any drug-laced hard candy from strangers on the streetcar—and even from unnecessary long-distance transportation. Thanks to the proximity of Johns Hopkins, just a few mansion-covered hills away, I could live at home, while doing work with babies and children, and attend a school that my parents not only respected, but to which they and their own parents had also generously donated.

Everyone, for the moment—how difficult to imagine beyond any present moment!—was happy. So happy that my parents bought me, at summer's end, an automobile to celebrate: a gorgeous machine called a Stutz Bearcat, open topped and painted a bright canary yellow. My father, when he had time on weekends, taught me to drive it, and we made several excursions up and down the coast. These drives gave him an opportunity to show me his work, buying and selling land here, houses there. Such and such railroad had now extended farther down the coast and along some barrier island or through some drained marsh and this or that new seaside community had sprung up. He could say all this without seeming to boast more than was warranted, and he was just as happy to interrupt any tour and turn down a remote lane and give me the wheel, ready to delight in the bucking and swerving and my own look of horror at the engine's sputtering response to my uneven tapping of the gas pedal.

"I'm wrecking it, Father," I cried out one late-summer day when I still didn't have the full knack of driving my beautiful machine. "I'm wrecking it!"

"Well," he laughed, unbothered by the smell of grinding gears and burnt petroleum. "I bought you the first one. You'll have to save up and buy the second."

"So, you actually believe I'll earn an income someday."

"Or you'll meet someone who will."

But he caught my look of consternation and corrected himself. "Not that you'll need any help. You'll manage just fine on your own. Stranger things have happened."

"Thank you, Father."

"For the car?"

"No, for your confidence."

We drove home that night in comfortable silence, the setting sun glinting off the car's chrome, my left elbow pink with sunburn, from hanging out the open window during those spells when my Father neglected to remind me to "grip firmly, yes firmly" with both hands. Perhaps he only meant the steering wheel. Or perhaps he meant more. How often we underestimate our parents' abilities to see both into our hearts and toward the future, aware of their weakening influence, and children's ineradicable tendencies to blunder.

Then finally, that first softening in the air, the first cool mornings in late September and early October—waiting, still waiting for my supervisor to return from his summer vacation, for the semester to start—and then, at long last, the first official day, my golden future ahead of me.

"How many eggs, Miss Rosalie?" Annie asked me as I paced the front-parlor windows, fastening my charm bracelet and then thinking twice, and taking off my bracelet and the signet ring I'd worn since my sixteenth birthday.

"No eggs. Only toast, please. Dry. Forget that, Annie, I'm not hungry."

Annie lifted an eyebrow, hands pushed into the front pocket of her baggy blue apron. "I'll bring you buttered toast, Miss Rosalie."

"I don't think I could stomach anything at all, actually."

"Then I'll bring you a piece of fruit."

Was I dressed appropriately? A sort of Peter Pan–collared shirt, long front-buttoned sweater with wide sleeves, a calf-length skirt, and flat shoes. No jewelry now, and no makeup.

"You look beautiful," my mother said at the breakfast table, and then, seeing my eyes widen: "Not beautiful. You look professional. You look like you dressed without a thought. You look very admirably plain."

My father lifted his head just above his newspaper, eager to join in the teasing. "Won't they give you a lab coat, in any case? I suppose you could get away with pajamas."

I still wasn't a good driver in city traffic, and when my father offered to drop me off at Phipps Clinic, I insisted on taking two public streetcars instead. This wasn't primary school. I didn't want to be escorted by anyone.

Climbing to the third floor, clutching my purse and my gloves and a folder of papers (transcripts, some letters of recommendation—did I think he would review my credentials all over again?), I encountered John Watson just inside the clinic's main door. His manner in this sacred place was more reserved, at least on this particular day.

"Miss Rayner. I trust you had a restful summer?"

"Yes, and you?"

"A month at our lakeside place, in Canada."

"With your family?"

"My daughter was working on her lake swimming."

A perfect family man, with just the faintest echoes of the South in his voice—a lengthening of certain words, that "dawwww-ter" strung out long and soft. All summer, I'd thought about his New School lecture, reenacting it in my mind, and I'd remembered him as loud, almost brusque—but that was only the impression he made, with his outspoken opinions and his strong, masculine features. In fact, he spoke quietly, the loudest part of him the frequent laugh he used to punctuate conversations. His drawl and his laugh were both so pleasing to listen to, so worthy of trying to fix in my memory for recall at a later, more leisurely occasion, that I must have missed the final question he asked. He had to turn and say it a second time.

"I said, 'Are you ready for the rest of the tour?'"

"Oh yes. Please. It's all terribly impressive."

Dr. Watson was the ruler of a new empire here at Phipps Clinic, so recently remodeled it still smelled of paint and varnish and something else fresh—maybe it was only baby talc I was noticing—as Dr. Watson barely touched my elbow and gestured that we should turn a corner to peer into one of the labs. There it was again, stronger: a more complex scent than my father wore, more musky and liberally applied. With the sharp crease in his well-tailored trousers and the silver cuff links studding his immaculate pale-blue shirtsleeves, Dr. John Watson looked and smelled like a man heading out for cocktails rather than preparing for a long day doing science. Now there were two reasons to lean in closer when he talked: to catch each soft, drawn-out vowel and to note with appreciation his sophisticated fragrance, as effective to a woman as Pavlov's bell was for his trained dogs.

On our tour, Dr. Watson introduced me to Dr. Adolf Meyer, who had hired him before the war, and to everyone we passed, including several students, all male, who were also new to the program. One of them, Curt Richter, originally from somewhere out west—Colorado— was carrying a sort of leather-bound portfolio, looking officious.

"Here since last week," he said when we were introduced.

"Did you come early for a reason?"

"Just eager to start," he said, and offered me a loose and easy grin, but my own smile in response was nowhere near as relaxed. Should I have come earlier? What had he been doing all this time that I had already missed?

Curt tagged behind us for the next few minutes, hands in his pockets, looking so comfortable already, while I hadn't even found a place to stow my purse and gloves. Would we have white lab coats? Watson didn't have one. Curt didn't have one. I couldn't wait to stop looking and feeling like a special visitor instead of someone who truly belonged.

Everything in the clinic was clean and starchy or shiny: porcelain bowls and long rows of railed beds in the psychiatric side of the clinic, and at our end of the building, a half octagon of slanted windows with a stunning view out over a green lawn with more medical buildings beyond. Well, did I think we'd be working in Frankenstein's basement? The facilities had to be spectacular. I'd already heard that John Watson had gotten offers from every other major university, eager to steal him away.

In the newly remodeled lab side of the third floor, everything had been carefully selected and designed, down to each desk and chair.

"Special ordered," Watson said, tapping an armrest. "And the third floor's wiring, too—to my specifications. You can't let someone else design a lab who isn't fully aware of all the lab's potential functions. We plan to get a lot done here in the next few years."

In my college days, I'd heard endless praise for Vassar's architecture: its stained-glass library windows, which could make you believe you were in a medieval cathedral when you were simply studying for a chemistry exam. This was something else: everything modern, the vision of men still alive, still young. No ghosts here, and no hanging portraits of old men with square-cut beards.

This is where new things would begin—and also, of course, where some things would end. But we couldn't know that yet. There seemed nothing to stop us from rescuing a young field from irrelevance, from developing a new and better science, from creating a more rational and promising future.

CHAPTER 4

Right away, they started bringing us the babies from the pediatrics ward of the Harriet Lane Home next door, connected by a convenient corridor to the Johns Hopkins medical buildings. Watson—for that is what other graduate students called him and I would simply have to get used to it—had just shown me into one of the small testing rooms when two nurses entered, wheeling a nursery cart. Nestled inside was a red-faced newborn, small thatch of black hair plastered to its wrinkled, red scalp.

Watson's eyes lit up. He'd only started to explain to me about his theories of basic emotions: fear, rage, love—which wasn't love at all, he said, but only a response to erotic stimulation, a tickling of lips or genitals. But at the sight of the incoming nursery cart, Watson ceased his impromptu lecture.

"An angel from next door," he said to the first nurse, a fresh-faced blonde whose curls were pinned into a complex arrangement around the borders of her white cap. By angel, I thought he'd meant the baby. Later, I would realize he meant Essie, and any other pretty nurse who helped out at the lab.

Watson held out a stopwatch in my direction, then had second thoughts and handed the watch to the second nurse, a shorter, dark-haired woman. I was just looking around, taking it all in: a scale, a cabinet, a waist-high examination table in the middle of the room, and two open shelves with various items, including the flat white pillow that Watson handed me now.

"I want you as close to me as possible for this, Rosie."

"Rosalie."

"*Rosalie.* I recall that you were the only one in that lecture audience last winter who knew how to catch a ball."

"Oh, yes."

And still, I didn't understand why I was holding a pillow.

At that moment, the door opened a crack, and Curt poked his face into the room, eyebrows lifted, grinning. Another free and willing hand, conjured as if on cue, though I noticed he wasn't pressed into immediate duty. Watson nodded and Curt entered, slipping into the room, back against the wall, observing—the boy waiting for his turn to bat, squirming on the bench, which only made me focus more intently, privileged by this special duty with the pillow, whatever it was.

"Georgie, you're ready with the stopwatch?"

The dark-haired nurse stepped closer to the table, stopwatch held out in front of her face, thumb at the ready. Watson gestured for me to lay the pillow on the examining table, and on it he set the newborn, naked except for a diaper. The baby's eyes were still closed—he or she, *it* (for now), was just beginning to root around. Watson touched the baby's left cheek with a finger and the baby turned toward the touch, mouth opening, lips seeking. Watson chuckled with appreciation, never tired of seeing those basic reflexes at work. Then, from below the table he produced a short iron rod, about the diameter of a pencil, and worked it into the baby's left hand, the tiny fingers with their perfect little translucent fingernails clasping around it.

"Left side first, Georgie."

Watson began to lift the rod and the skinny arm went up, still fastened to the rod. A few inches higher, and the rosy bump of a shoulder lifted off the pillow, arm straightening, ribcage flexing as the body pulled upward. When I gasped, Watson smiled, but he kept his eyes fixed on the baby, whose splayed arms and bowed legs seemed even skinnier and smaller and redder, held apart from its solid little trunk of a body.

"You're not one of those people who thinks a newborn is weak, are you?" Watson asked me, with pleasure in his voice. "Hard to survive the jungle and the savannah all those millions of years without a few tricks up your sleeve."

Up the baby went, up and up, into the air. "*Ready, Rosalie?*" And now the baby was supported by nothing at all, I was holding an empty pillow, and the newborn, eyes still closed, red face screwed up with sheer effort or imminent protest, lungs filling with an angry cry, was hanging by one tiny, surprisingly determined fist and nothing else. I spread my hands across the space between the pillow and the hanging baby, all my attention focused on that vulnerable, exposed body.

Watson started to say, "But they lose this fierce grip . . ."

Just then, the baby plummeted, dropping into my cradling hands. Its skinny legs folded slightly upward as I stretched my fingers to catch the diapered rear end. At the same time, I angled my right hand, trying to make a suitable landing place for the soft, narrow shoulders. Breath held, arms trembling, I lowered the whole tender package down into the soft resistance of the pillow.

"Got the time on that one, Georgie?" Watson continued, absolutely calm. "They lose it, as I was saying, at about a hundred and twenty days."

The baby was fine. *Just fine*, I told myself, breath catching in my throat. Despite the solid presence of the pillow, the infant kept its arms up and held apart from its trunk, fingers splayed and grasping, bouncing back and forth a little, shuddering, still clutching for the branches or leaves that might have broken its fall, tumbling from that ancestral tree. Dark blue eyes open now, bulging, full of surprise: *Who did that? Where am I?*

"But you know," Watson continued, "we've even had an infant entirely missing a cerebellum who could still perform well at this test."

"But how did a baby live without a cerebellum?" I was thinking of the poor baby's parents. I couldn't help it.

"He didn't," Watson said. "But we made the most of his first few days, all the same. Sentiment is the enemy. Knowledge and progress, Rosalie. That's what we're concerned about here. Can you do it?"

"Catch the baby?"

"No, conquer unproductive sentiment. Most people can't."

I hoped it was a rhetorical question, but it wasn't. He really wanted to know, and it seemed to matter. *I* seemed to matter.

"I'll do my best."

The baby, breathless and outraged, was on the verge of squalling, and I wasn't sure if I should pick it up or rub its chest or find something to put in its mouth or offer some other kind of soothing. I was not yet indoctrinated enough to know that soothing any baby was counterproductive to its own healthy development. Before I could get in the way, Watson worked quickly, pushing the iron rod into the baby's right fist before the test could be interrupted. "Right side now, Georgie. Ready again, Rosalie?"

And up the baby went into the air a second time. This second trial was shorter than the first. Almost immediately, the infant dropped into my hands, which were more ready to break the fall in a graceful maneuver, guiding the baby back down to the safety of the pillow.

"A little off the predicted curve," Watson said, beaming, "All right, let's get a weight."

I glanced around, but the first nurse, Essie, was already taking charge, carrying the baby over to the scale. Georgie, holder of the stopwatch, passed a clipboard to me and I took it, pretending to know what I was doing, and recorded the weight, pressing hard to tame my shaking hand.

"There, and you didn't even drop your first subject," Watson said, enjoying the look of surprise still on my face. "Multiply that by a few hundred, and you've got only one of the dozens of experiments we're running here. We'll do some vision tests later this afternoon, and those you'll be able to handle with only one nurse assisting."

Georgie asked, "The next one right away, Dr. Watson?"

"Right away."

"We've got a little Negro girl, sixteen hours old."

He clapped his hands together. "Black, white, green or purple, makes no difference to me."

At dinner that night, I talked mainly about the vision tests, underplaying the grip test because as soon as I began to explain it, Mother brought her hands to her cheeks: "A baby can't possibly support its own weight!" But I was excited, they could see that. And Mother and Father were both excited for me.

I decided not to mention at all the demonstration in which Watson had handled a baby a little forcefully, to show how by confining the infant's limbs and placing pressure on either side of its head or pinching closed its airways until it turned blue he could provoke it into an explosive rage. Instead, I mentioned that we were studying babies of various races and backgrounds, all mixed together.

My father set down his fork and spoke slowly and deliberately. "So, your Dr. John Watson is not a believer in eugenics, then."

"He's more interested in early environment than inheritance," I said. "In terms of basic reflexes and inborn traits, his point is how few there are. And what he is most interested in tracking—like the development of vision—he tracks across racial boundaries. Across all boundaries. We don't know much about the backgrounds of the children we're given to study."

Annie came in with a creamer and sugar for the after-dinner coffee, and glanced around the table, looking for items to remove. Through the open door, from the distant kitchen, we could hear Bertha, muttering to herself in German, and then chastising Frank for something.

"A lot of well-meaning and important people take an interest in eugenics," Father said, still maintaining that curiously even tone. "Roosevelt does. Alexander Graham Bell does."

"And Margaret Sanger," Mother chipped in. "A number of progressives."

"It's a growing field," Father said, touching his napkin to his lips, pushing his plate away, though he hadn't finished his dessert. "A lot of government money in it, here and abroad. A lot of legislation in support of it. But popular support is rarely an indication of moral truth or even old-fashioned common sense."

From the stiff, careful way he was speaking and from the intensity of my mother's attention to his every gesture, I knew there was more he had to express, but didn't care to say without adequate knowledge or thought. I'd walked with my father around real estate developments, guided by surveyors and architects, and he was the type to nod, lean over a blueprint, rap on an unfinished doorframe. But he was the money man, and he knew it. He had always left politics to his brother—my uncle Isidor, the senator—who had passed away just before I left for college. Father was content to let the experts do their job, for the most part.

"I don't care for eugenics," he said finally with a sharp shake of his head. "People have suffered enough the foolishness of those who are obsessed with some notion of so-called purity, racial or otherwise."

He wasn't going to speak about our particular group of people— our family and our neighbors who had fled from Russia, Germany, and other parts of Europe where our family trees could become a legal liability or worse. Only "people."

He continued, "I've had enough with the conservatives and

progressives both, obsessed with trying to make generations of people genetically 'better.'"

"Well," my mother tried to say—she had no objection to expressing opinions, positive *or* negative—"they're concerned about the mentally deficient, usually, if you're talking about marriage laws and sterilization and such."

"No, Rebecca," Father said. It wasn't often he corrected her. "It's not just about the mentally deficient, or about illness, which in itself can be a red herring, make no mistake. It's about everything and everyone. And the deeper we can see into our cells and our chromosomes—you may correct me on my scientific terminology, Rosalie, but not until I'm finished—the more it should be clear that down in our marrow and going back through time we're all more alike than different. You wouldn't think that new science would only be used to confirm old prejudices."

Was he finished? He'd only started.

"You'd think science would make those problems go away, and instead scientists are misusing what they don't understand to divide humanity up all over again. I'm not trying to be alarmist. I'm just being plain." He nodded once—now he was done—and tried to smile. "But not your new mentor, thank goodness. He's not blinded by the so-called promises of eugenics. Aside from making babies cry, he sounds like a good man. Thank your Dr. Watson for taking a stand, at least."

"She didn't say he takes a stand," Mother said, gently.

"Oh, he does," I said with pride—a pride that had only grown, imagining my mentor at his very best, as seen through the eyes of my parents, whose advice I didn't always follow but whose opinions I most certainly did respect. "I think he takes a stand on just about everything."

"But I still think he shouldn't be requiring babies to hang from poles," Mother said, fitting in the last word, and reaching sideways across the table to give my hand a reassuring squeeze. "I can't imagine a person who would do that."

"Well, maybe you should invite him to dinner sometime," Father replied. "Then you'll be able to imagine him better."

My mother leaned back and shook her head, admonishing herself. "Well of course we will! I can't believe we haven't done it already."

CHAPTER 5

The next morning, I spent several hours busy with Watson in the testing room and an equal number of hours on my own performing infant tests involving grasping, blinking, and swimming (thrashing in shallow water, really). I did remember lunch this time, but ate it late and quickly at my desk, while perusing a scientific article. In the late afternoons, generally, Watson was pulled away from us, and there was nearly always a student, professor, or administrator coming round to ask for his help or opinion, to look at a piece of equipment, or to meet someone influential touring the clinic or adjacent hospital. Watson kept one small lab room furnished as a resting room—couch, drink cabinet, an extra filing cabinet, and small rolltop correspondence desk—so that he could read or write letters in seclusion, followed by a nap just as everyone else was leaving. Then he'd put in a second shift, long into the night and without distraction.

Even as I was finishing the article I was reading, trying to improve my own mind and efficiency, I was beginning to let my thoughts wander, thinking of Watson and how he worked so hard and so long, seemingly informed and connected to not only academic research, but government work, military work, and private business as well. We all aspired to his tirelessness and sense of mission.

"I'm not interrupting?" Curt asked as I was finishing up my sandwich. "John left a present in my office. I was hoping you'd come take a look and give me a little advice."

First *Watson* and now *John*—the younger men in the lab were quicker to adopt informalities. And what would I know that a Harvard graduate wouldn't?

I walked a half step behind, suspecting Curt's hangdog expression was part of some act or, worse, a joke at my expense. I hoped he didn't need me to tell him how to decorate a room or water a plant. But when we entered his small office, and Curt shut the door and gestured to the oak cabinet against the far wall, his somber expression remained.

"There they are. A perfect dozen."

From the back of the metal cage came the shuffling sounds of wood shavings being rearranged.

"I suppose I start by feeding them," Curt said, sounding glum. "Do they eat bread?"

"And just about everything else."

I stepped closer, pressing my fingers against the cage. The shuffling ceased. I unhooked the cage-door latch, pushed a hand inside, and drew out the nearest animal, holding it by the rough base of its naked pink tail.

When Curt flinched, I said, sounding a bit like Watson with our human subjects, "They're not that vulnerable, as long as you grab by the base, not the tip. This one's a juvenile. Someone has done a good job with regular handling, or it would be more aggressive. When you're not sure, wear gloves."

"I guess a big old male could deliver a serious bite."

"Actually, I've only been bit by a nursing mother with very young babies. They're protective that way."

When I held out the white rat, nose twitching and front paws pedaling in the air, Curt gestured back to the cage. "You can put it back. I've got all day to get to know them. Make that all year."

John had dropped off the cage with no instructions other than that this was something, at last, for Curt to do. Take care of them. Study them. Come up with a testable research question. Develop whatever apparatus would be necessary to gather solid data. And, by the way, John had told Curt, stop coming to the baby room except when summoned. Evidently, he had the only graduate assistant he needed to fulfill that role.

"You've really never worked with white rats?" I asked Curt, letting this one settle down into the crook of my arm for a minute before I put it back.

"Never worked with a white rat?" Curt said. "I've never even seen one."

It wasn't a fair question. Rat laboratories were far from ubiquitous in those days. It just happened that Miss Washburn had been an animal behavior specialist, so that nearly every small creature commonly used by scientists had passed through our Vassar labs. She'd once been offended when a friend's dog hadn't taken a liking to her; she expected all animals to respond to her as she responded to them, with genuine interest and affection. As for Watson, he had worked with rats extensively, even operating on them to isolate their sensory abilities (a newspaper reporter had caught wind of this and gotten a skeptical, anti-science column out of it), but he was a pioneer in that regard. It didn't seem to occur to Watson that any laboratory animals should like *him*.

I asked, "Does Watson know you're unfamiliar with rats?"

"Fortunately, he didn't ask."

But Curt was grateful to me for sharing everything I knew, about handling and feeding, life stages, reproductive cycles, and general behavior. And I was grateful to him for giving me the opportunity to demonstrate my expertise in one area at least, to prove to him and to myself that my own psych-lab preparation hadn't been too shabby, even if I'd still always wonder why Watson had chosen me instead of Curt as his right-hand helper. "They'll need hard foods, too, or their teeth will grow too long, up into their own skulls."

"They'll be old enough to mate when?"

"I'd say now or soon, even though they're only half grown. Don't wait until they're fully grown."

"The unstoppable drive to reproduce," he shook his head, grinning. "Powerful, isn't it?"

There it was, the decisive moment, an attempt at flirting, and I could see from Curt's embarrassed expression that he knew he'd bungled it. I flashed a quick smile—enough to show I could be joked with, but not so encouraging that he'd press the point further. "Yes, in simpler animals. Get them sorted and separated right away."

"And you say they're quick learners?"

"Exceptionally quick."

"Why are they scrambling about so much? Do they want out?"

"I have no idea. They just move around, that's all."

His glumness eased. Within minutes, he was pacing again, hands out of his pockets, talking animatedly about the free reign we were given, the excitement he'd felt on his first day when Watson had said, "You're on your own here. It's all up to you." Research, prolific and publishable research, was the thing with John Watson. Everything else was a distraction.

"Rosalie?" Curt asked when I was on my way out the door.

"Yes?"

"Never mind," he said.

I started to leave again.

"Actually . . ." he tried again, mustering his nerve.

But I cut him off. "If it's about rat care, ask any time. I've got to get back to my own work now." I needed to find my own thesis subject, in fact, if I ever got a break from helping Watson with the babies. I had at least a little sense in those early days, enough to know I must carve out my own area of distinction.

"All right," Curt said. And that was that.

In later months, I'd be too busy, but all the rest of that week, I checked in several more times with Curt and his rats, chatting with him as he built new cages, and letting one of the most docile young females curl into the pocket of my cardigan, where she would immediately fall asleep. But I knew not to get too fond of them, that depending on what Curt ultimately studied, they might end up in surgery or be made to do endurance swim tests or some other trial they might not survive. One couldn't be softhearted in this business, I told myself, again and again—and I was finally starting, by dint of sheer effort, to believe it. One had to have faith that the lessons learned were more than equal to any pain imposed. And even if the rats aged in relative peace, the effects of maturity alone—as well as having multiple litters of babies, or going without food and sleep, or suffering some normal hardship for any length of time—would change their personalities, making them irritable and untrustworthy.

I might have learned more about the travails of being a mother from watching those rats, if I'd been *less* narrowly scientific and willing to indulge some cross-species empathy. Easy for me to see the irony now: that "lesser" animals knew enough to protect their young and did not let a world of experts tell them how to live or raise their families.

It must have been on a day at the end of that same week when I found myself standing alone in my bedroom, taking off my sweater and lifting it toward my face, breathing in its various smells: sour milk, and Borax, from cleaning a lab table after a long series of tests. And also, at the edge of the cardigan's front pocket, the faint smell of wood shavings and that inescapable ratty smell—not dirty, just mammalian—even stronger deep inside the pocket, where I'd let the female take a nap.

I turned the cardigan over and held it even closer to my nose: a trace of Watson's cologne, perhaps from that moment he'd casually put his arm over my shoulder, guiding me toward the stairwell at the end of an extra-long day. (I'd missed dinner; he was hopping out to buy something but then planned to go back to the lab—perhaps for the rest of the weekend, for all I knew.) He'd leaned in close at that moment, and perhaps this is why I was thinking so much of scent, thinking of my own scent too, or the lack of it, because he'd said, "You don't wear makeup, from what I can tell. And you don't wear perfume, like some of the nurses do."

"Should I?"

He'd paused, weighing the question. "No. I think your freshness is your charm, Rosalie. You smell like a girl who has nothing to hide."

Later that day, alone in my room, I disrobed layer by layer: under the sweater, my white blouse with Navy-style lapels, neither dowdy nor fashionable, and under that, a camisole of the simplest type, only one ribbon of lace along the bottom edge. Seated at the edge of my bed, I rubbed my hands along my bare arms and held my hands to my face, breathing in deeply: nothing. Nothing to hide, or to show.

How could I explain? In one week, I felt like such a different person already, not just Rosalie of Girls' Latin School and Vassar and Eutaw Place anymore. But there was no evidence, nothing that would remain if in another week, another month, the work suddenly stopped. From the inside, I felt the claustrophobic tension, the sharp confinement of a carapace just at the point of bursting. From the outside, I looked no different. Only my thoughts marked me. But what were *thoughts*?

Who was I, seated there—bare feet long and narrow, bare arms, white slip, camisole, thin, plain, dark haired, blue eyed, a young woman of no clear heritage who could have come from any place or any time—who was I, beyond whatever latent reactions were poised for expression in my muscles and my larynx, beyond what could be easily and objectively observed? I was nothing. I was, still, unexceptional. I was unmarked and unspoiled—or so John Watson might have thought. At that age, I presumed that women attracted with some special, intoxicating trait they had. I did not understand that young women also attracted by what they did not have, for their very blankness and unthreatening malleability.

I was glad to have helped Curt get comfortable with his animal subjects and to feel that any envy had been resolved in favor of a new interest. Did I feel any attraction toward a man like Curt or any of the men close to my age working at the lab? Not particularly. I was too busy working and learning, most of the time, and I was determined not to let gender or any kind of sexual misunderstanding disrupt this job that was slowly beginning to feel rightly mine.

Curt's abilities only reinforced my own pride in being part of a larger body that was bound to be productive in multiple, innovative areas. Whenever I felt the temptation to question how I could have been so lucky to get the inside track, the choicest research, the most minutes of each day with Watson when there were always two or three other people wanting his time, I pushed it away in favor of working harder, learning more, proving myself worthy of the access I'd been given.

Taking care not to suggest that infant research was not my primary interest (for Watson, the simple availability of compliant subjects meant the world), I pressed him for ideas on how I might study learning in adults. In retrospect, I think I had a visceral reaction to the crying and distress of our infant subjects, but I can't claim that my concerns extended beyond that yet, in that middle period after my first anxious days and before my final ambivalent ones. After you've pinned down the arms and feet of your hundredth infant, pinched its nose to inspire rage, or plunged it into ice water to check whether it can swim, only to see the same infant contentedly cooing or snoozing a half hour later, you start to believe there is no harm. Maybe after you do something—anything—a hundred times you believe there is no harm in doing it. That's a form of conditioning, too, isn't it? Until a new stimulus comes along to change the experience for you: the cry of a baby who is your own, for example. Or even the cry of a baby you test more than once or twice, who demonstrates some evidence that one's unsentimental experimentation is producing an effect—a purposeful and convenient effect, but an effect all the same. But I'm getting well ahead of myself.

We did not have a large supply of animals, but that was just as well: people interested me more. As always, my inclination led me toward the abstract and the intangible, or the grandiose, while Watson was always more consistent and practical. If I wondered how society produced a Mozart, he wondered how a man or rat— made no difference—learned to turn right or left, and how various methods of "distributing" practice (more or fewer sessions per day) affected what was learned. These were the things one could possibly observe, Watson told me. Until the day when we could contain a full squad of subjects, completely controlling their environments—what they eat, how often they have sex—we would never understand the limits of learning. Ideal lab conditions always began to resemble some sort of prison or Utopia.

But Watson was right, and one had to concede that there was an art in turning a question into something focused and observable. If I'd had to muddle alone, I might have been back to those outmoded tools—written tests, mere observation—in no time. It was one thing to believe in Watson's behaviorism and another to emulate it consistently, objectively, affordably.

As a way to study learning, Watson finally recommended that I conduct dart tests. Darts, as in tavern darts—with targets. There could be nothing simpler. It might even be fun. Curt, with his rats, was finding interesting patterns in daily activity, disproving notions about randomness of rat movements, and I might investigate patterns of improvement or fatigue in people aiming for bull's-eyes. I drew up a plan, posted notices seeking in-house volunteers, and felt on my way to becoming a real and independent psychological researcher at last.

Infant studies and adult learning experiments aside, I tried to continue to better myself. If I had a free moment, I pulled out typed transcripts from Watson's speech files, or I read from the new scientific journals delivered to the third floor daily by our mailroom boy. Proceedings from a conference had just been dropped off one day during our third or fourth week, and I noticed it was something Watson had been looking for, because it was supposed to contain a rebuttal from another psychologist, questioning some of Watson's behaviorist tenets. He never let such a thing stand without firing off an immediate typed response. It was getting close to noon, I'd finished my morning tests, the nurses would be too busy with lunchtime infirmary duties to bring up any more infant subjects, and I hadn't seen Watson for the last hour but assumed he was still nearby, or if not, perhaps meeting some professors for lunch over on the Homewood Campus. I poked my head into one lab room and then another. I knocked—perhaps not loudly enough—on his resting-room door, merely out of habit. This wasn't even his late-afternoon resting time.

When I pushed the door open, I heard the answering sound of a drawer slamming, or a stuttering sort of rattle and slam, of something closed and then opened slightly and then closed again. And I spotted, first, nurse Essie's reddened face, turned over her shoulder, eyes wide, one blonde curl free of its pins and falling over one side of her cheek. I sensed more than saw what Watson was doing, standing behind her. Essie's arms were on either side of a tall oak filing cabinet, palms pressed against the sides and pushing, the way one pushes the handles of an accordion—a strange image, just one of many, as my eyes like a mindless camera recorded only one plate or picture at a time, refusing to put the images together, refusing to admit what I was actually witnessing—something I'd never seen in my life up to that point. Imagined, yes, with equal parts curiosity and anxiety, but never actually seen.

Then Essie was stepping back from the cabinet. Pretty, blonde Essie was dropping her arms to her side, and pulling down the back of her skirt, tugging at the fabric that had doubled up, exposing her legs well above the knees, garters and the thick ivory edge of a girdle showing, the skirt was so high. While at the same time, like a train-car decoupling, Watson was likewise stepping back and turning away, away from Essie and from me, toward the back wall, and fumbling, his hands busy in front of his trousers.

I hadn't seen his face—thank goodness I hadn't seen his face. I heard him say in a low, clotted sort of voice, "That drawer always gets stuck. Glad to help." And I saw, in the narrowing gap of the closing door, his hand go up to his hair and rake through it.

From behind the closed door came next a guttural laugh—his first, then hers—softer, followed by her gleeful, relieved whispering: words I couldn't make out, though I listened for another moment, as long as I dared. Then I heard him again: laughing, coming toward the door, clearing his throat. All of which got me quickly moving.

I couldn't go back to my own desk in the main room now, or anywhere I'd be found, not at this minute anyway. I couldn't go down the stairs, the same stairs Essie would use, en route to the pediatric ward in the adjacent building. So I walked toward the psychiatric clinic, the other side of the third floor, and then paused in the hallway, not wanting to arrive there, either, not wanting to see anyone, least of all Watson's own supervisor, Dr. Meyer, who I felt would see in my expression everything I'd just seen, just as clearly as if he were watching a nickelodeon flicker. Nor did I want to see any of the adult psychiatric clients, with their stony expressions and gaping mouths, mirroring back to me my own dim-witted expression.

I stopped in the hallway, breathing fast, confused not about the details of what I'd seen but how I felt about them, and why, and how it involved me or didn't, and how one could feel hurt and intrigued and somehow jilted but possibly violated all at the same time, if those were the right words, and most likely they were not. How could one possibly find the right words, or a friend in whom one could safely confide them? I struggled not to feel as young as I'd often felt at Vassar—young and excluded, always walking in on parties already started, wishing to be directly in the fray or well above it, but not this—hovering at the edges of adult secrets. I could not muster any feeling that Watson and Essie should be in trouble for doing what they'd been doing—where was my moral outrage?—only that I was somehow lacking something, for seeing and for not knowing how to respond to what I had seen, for being so easily mortified when I had done nothing wrong. *Silly, stupid child.*

It took more discipline than I had to stop replaying the image and the sounds, to stop not only revisiting the image, but feeling my own blood warm in response to it, with equal parts indignation and that other, inadmissable, thing—a quiver of excitement, which I tried to relabel as confusion and simple adrenaline fueled by my hurried flight away from what I had glimpsed. Essie and her red face, her exposed legs, and the edge of her girdle. Watson, turning away, fumbling with his trousers. The cabinet—could I ever file something in that cabinet again without thinking about it?—going rattle and bang.

For at least one moment, I considered racing out of the building, and never coming back, but then what would I say to my parents, what would I do with my life, and how would anything ever make sense again, given the steps I'd taken to come this far? In the time it took me to discard that preposterous idea, to castigate myself for even thinking it, I noticed I'd folded the conference proceedings, had crumpled them, the front cover dog-eared, and now it was even a little damp, from my perspiring, confused, inky hands.

Back at my desk, I pressed the booklet down and ironed it with the back of a dry hand, knowing that later this afternoon, he'd be touching these same creased pages, studying every word in the rebuttal inside, aware somehow of my confused feelings, when feelings were supposed to be irrelevant, or else exceedingly simple: rage, fear, love. What else was there, really?

CHAPTER 6

That weekend, I insisted on taking my Stutz Bearcat out for a late-afternoon drive, alone despite Mother's protestations. I drove with the top down, my father's raccoon coat draped over me, an old pack of cigarettes hidden in my purse, to be enjoyed only once I found some hidden spot in the countryside, taking in those sights and smells that had always reassured me: red and gold trees, country air, cheerful smoky leaf fires burning along the edges of the roads and fields. Another fall, and I was not at Vassar. I would never again be at Vassar. Welcome not only to Johns Hopkins, but to the school of life, and I was determined to be a better and quicker student: of men in general, of John Watson in particular. (An academic interest, purely. I was too smart to have a crush.) I was determined, more than ever, to be unflappable.

I started work the next Monday morning determined to be cool and collected, to betray nothing about what I'd seen and thought on Friday afternoon. But as soon as John Watson came into the main room with his hands full of mail intercepted from the mailboy, I started rambling.

"I just love this time of year," I said, standing up from my chair so that I'd be nearly as tall, and there'd be no chance of him hovering over me, should the conversation get tricky. "Burning leaves and haystacks, and apples and pumpkins. It's just wonderful outside the city. My head's all cleared . . ."

But he was distracted, sorting through the mail, brow furrowed, looking for something.

Had I remembered to put that conference publication into his hands? No. It was still sitting on my desk. Face warming, I reached for it and handed it to him, but he took one look and shuffled it back into the pile while his eyes stayed fixed on something smaller, a worn envelope with a handwritten address in the upper left corner.

"That didn't take long," he said, frowning.

My thoughts were still back with the burning leaves, desperate to launch a harmless conversation. The harder I tried to rein in my thoughts, the more they scattered.

"Do you go for country drives, Dr. Watson?"

As soon as I'd said it, I realized its implication—as if *I* wanted to go for a drive with him, as if I were suggesting something, as if what I'd seen had perversely inspired me to be suggestive. I added quickly, "I meant only with your wife and daughters."

For a moment I felt relief, but then a moment later, my face pulsed even hotter. I hadn't meant to mention his wife.

"Daughter, singular," he said. "I've got a daughter and a son."

He mentioned Polly often, but he hadn't mentioned the other one—whose name, I would find out later, was John. Little John.

He continued to stare at the envelope, frowning. "Pickens," he said.

"What's a pickens?"

"Not a what, a who. He can smell success from a thousand miles off, not that he can find it for himself, even if it were setting up a nest under his own front step." Watson's chin was still tucked into his chest as he stared down at the mail. "Some folks you just can't get rid of."

Watson pursed his lips and tucked the small envelope into his front jacket pocket. He glanced at me. "You were asking about drives? I ride, but I don't drive. Motor cars and I don't get along."

"Oh, I see." Another brilliant response.

"I need to take care of this," he gestured to his pocket "Would you ask Georgie to bring up two subjects?"

We'd agreed, the week before, that if we had the nurses fetch two babies at a time, we could process them even faster.

"Of course. Twenty minutes?"

"That would be fine."

Near the stairwell, I saw the young mailboy, Gerry, coming down the hall with his delivery bag over his shoulder. He always did the three floors of our building, Phipps Clinic, last, and then headed back down to the main mailroom before going to the neighboring buildings. "You're going to the baby ward next?"

"Yes ma'am."

"Would you save me the trip and tell Georgie we're ready for the day's subjects, starting with the little girl? They'll know the one."

"Happy to." He touched the short bill of his cap.

"Gerry—"

"Yes?"

"Oh, never mind. It was only that Dr. Watson seemed preoccupied because of a letter he opened. I shouldn't stop you from your rounds."

But Gerry enjoyed breaks from going up and down those stairs, too. He'd gab about anything if you prompted him. "I know exactly what it was, if that's what you're asking. Another letter from his father."

"From his father? How do you know?"

Gerry didn't blink. "Well, from the return address, with his name, and South Carolina. Interesting stamp, too."

He noticed the lift of my eyebrows. "Well," he said more carefully now, "and the doctor himself cussed the minute I put it in his hand—he's an expert cusser—so that's only why I took a look. Normally, I'd be too busy."

"Of course you would be. And I shouldn't be keeping you."

He started down the stairs, skipping a few. I called down: "Don't forget about the message for nurse Georgie!"

Knowing that Watson was inside, I paused outside the baby-testing room, waiting for Georgie to come walking down the hall so we'd be able to enter together. She had wide hips, a rolling gait, and a slow-developing smile that didn't entirely light up her eyes. But there was an evenness and reliability to Georgie that excused any lethargy. Even in an emergency, you wouldn't mind watching her deliberate walk down that hospital hallway because you knew, once she arrived, she'd be level-headed and proficient.

As soon as Georgie stepped through the doorway—I gestured for her to enter first and slipped in behind—he asked her, "You know about men's clothes, don't you?"

"I have a father and three brothers, if that's what you mean."

"You ever go clothes shopping with them?"

"Sure, sometimes."

"I don't mean the best places, not New York or anything expensive. I mean locally."

"Sure, sometimes."

Watson was sitting on a stool in the far corner of the room, heels hooked on the stool's lower rung, letter in his hands. "All right, we'll talk about it later." He nodded at me. "Where's the cart?"

I'd been too distracted to notice. No nursery cart. No babies.

"The little girl you asked for was taken home by her mother yesterday," Georgie explained. "They're moving."

That's exactly what annoyed him about research on human subjects, especially infant ones. Unlike rats in a cage, you couldn't be sure they wouldn't wander away, move, be collected by relatives or adopted by strangers. He was tremendously excited about the baby research now, but in the beginning, it hadn't been a first choice. He'd stumbled into it only because Johns Hopkins didn't have adequate facilities for a large animal population, and only later came to realize that babies represented the blank slates he'd always needed to prove his theories.

"And the other one? We asked for two."

Georgie paused. It was the first time I'd seen her with empty hands, unoccupied by any clipboard, tray, diaper, bottle, or cart. She seemed to notice the absence herself and clasped her hands just under her stout, uniformed chest. "The two-week-old boy passed away overnight, in his sleep."

Outside: the click of passing heels. The hateful sound of a man's tuneless, oblivious humming.

Finally, Watson responded. "Well."

Georgie took a deep breath and added, "We haven't told his mother yet. She's coming by for a visit this afternoon."

"I see." And a squeak of the casters as Watson rolled back several inches. "Well. *That's* a wasted morning, then."

"Would you want to speak to her, to say anything?"

"That's not my line. I wasn't even his physician."

Another sore spot. I'd heard from Curt that Watson had always wanted to get a medical doctor's degree, but couldn't afford the extra schooling. Though even if he'd had an MD, I was quite sure he'd leave a death notification to one of the nurses. No one liked delivering *that* news.

"But you might tell her," Georgie tried again, "that he was useful. To science, I mean."

Watson crossed him arms, stool squeaking under his weight. "But he wasn't, Georgie. That's the thing. You can't be very useful to anyone if they can't keep you alive for more than a few weeks."

I diverted my gaze to the white wall. Up high: a scattering of charts. The human eyeball: front, side, looking down. A chart of average weights and heights. Whatever I was looking for, it wasn't there, but at least it provided a distraction. I suppose I thought work might cease for the day, that we might gather and proceed to the hospital or take a lunch break and let the news sink in, the way my own family had once gathered silently in our parlor, when there'd been particularly grave news about troop mortalities or numbers dead of the flu. This was one infant, not a thousand dead, but it was one infant we'd held in our own arms. Just last week, he'd been strong enough to wrap his entire tiny, red fist around my finger. Surely any moment Watson would say something kinder or softer.

Instead he said, "I need a suit." He corrected himself, "Not for me. And not a good one. Just a suit. If I gave you the rough measurements and the money, Georgie, and a little extra, would you pick one out and mail it for me?"

"Sure, I could do that," Georgie answered slowly. "Who's it for, Doctor?"

"For my father."

"Is he visiting?"

"He sure as hell isn't. I'm sending him this gift and it's the last thing I'm giving him. And he can like it or he can lump it. With any luck, I'll never hear from him again."

I couldn't avoid looking at him now. His face wore an effortful smirk and he was cradling the side of his cheek with one hand, elbow on his knee, gaze focused out the doorway, watching Georgie leave. When she was gone, he turned to me.

"I always said we needed a bigger facility: more subjects, more controls. I've been talking with Meyer about a national baby farm."

I thought I'd misheard. "A baby *farm*?"

"We wouldn't call it a farm, of course. *Institute*. People always like that word better. A place where we raise hundreds of them. No bad habits introduced, no going home, a self-enclosed community. Every behavior tracked. Rotating adult supervision so there aren't any attachment issues. Better hygiene as well." The last part came out sharply, as an accusation—the closest he came to sorrow or regret.

Babies were born naturally strong, stronger than most people could imagine, and when they failed to thrive, there was inevitably someone or something to blame. As always, it was society that messed things up, not biology. He continued, "A carefully prepared environment with lower infant mortality and complete social-emotional stability. Parents entirely out of the way. That's the only way we'd get anywhere. There's government money for it, and a few of the right people are saying they'll support it. It's not out of the question."

For a moment, I thought he might be joking. He wasn't. But I also knew his idea was a big messy ball of rational notions and strange hubris and old-fashioned human hurt. I might have stated some objection to the "farm" idea if I'd thought it was the real subject, but I didn't believe it was. Not really.

I cleared my throat and said, "You're sure you want to cut off ties with your father, completely."

He seemed to see me for the first time that morning. "Yes, I'm sure." He breathed hard through his nose, shaking his head from side to side. He allowed himself a small chuckle.

He'd had no overtly sympathetic reaction whatsoever to the death of a baby, which shouldn't have surprised me. He always took the long, cold view. The historical view. Sentiment couldn't fix things. Only science and rational public policy could.

At my mother's insistence, two weeks earlier, I'd asked Watson and his family to dinner. He'd been slow in answering, and I'd hoped he wouldn't come, and then hoped that he would, and then that he wouldn't ("Get an answer, please, Rosalie," my mother demanded. "It's starting to get awkward."), and then that he would so we could just get it over with. Of course, I *was* curious to meet the woman who had married him.

"Your wife, does she get along with your father?"

He laughed. "My wife? She'd much prefer to pretend I was born of better stock, to use a despicable phrase."

"What about your mother—can she help sort things out?"

"She passed away when I was fifteen. Devout Baptist. Raised me to be a preacher. Named me after one: John Albert Broadus."

That was a surprise. I'd never met a less religious person in my life than John Watson. But I'd heard one or two people around the lab crack jokes about Watson's revivalist fervor for preaching science.

"He'd run off from her by the time she was shaping me up to preach," he said, "and clearly, the 'Good Word' had no good effect on *him*. Pickens Butler Watson was a bad-tempered, unrepentant rover. No number of dunkings in the Reedy River could wash it out of him. One full bottle of whiskey a day. Left my mother and all of us children to run the farm, which we didn't manage very well."

I opened my mouth to say I was sorry, but he fixed me with a look that discouraged any interruption. He was having more than enough trouble already.

"When he went to live in the hills with a couple Cherokee women, I was expected to make up for everything he wasn't, to be a perfect, morally upright son and a substitute husband, both. The absence of a man, even a lousy one, can encourage a kind of suffocating mother-love that's unhealthy to any child."

He'd gotten it out, but just saying it all had left him looking choked up, with a bad taste in his mouth. It wasn't just the memory of his father's intemperance or his mother's neediness, I didn't think—it was acknowledging it, letting the past show its mark on the present. I knew he'd betrayed his own beliefs in a way just by telling me all this, just by risking that I would find these childhood facts too important. He probably would have denied that his father's philandering and his mother's desperation and his family's backwoods poverty were essential to his present character. Allergic to Freudian notions about early traumas or sources of identity confusion, he was nonetheless offering up his own checkered past as an ante—a chip to buy his way into some larger game whose nature I didn't yet fully understand. What I knew for sure was that he had chosen to confide in me, as perhaps he couldn't confide in anyone else: not Curt or Georgie. Not Essie.

Neither of us had spoken for a long moment when he said, "I don't like this time of year, to answer your question. You were talking a while back about the leaves and the pumpkins and all that. It's all right for a few weeks more, but then there's the long downhill slide into the holidays: Thanksgiving, and that's bad enough. And then Christmas. That's murder."

"We'll get some time off, at least."

"Not if I can help it."

His tone had been irritable and he seemed to want to take it back, because he said next, with a deliberately casual air: "So, you enjoy getting out of Baltimore? You've got some college boy who takes you out for a drive, now and again?"

"College boy? Not hardly, Dr. Watson."

"You really can call me John, especially when there aren't bureaucrats around. Even the nurses do, behind my back."

"I've got my own motor car," I told him. "A beauty. I drive it myself."

"Well, well, Rosalie."

And with the change of subject, with the mention of my name, he returned to being the man I knew him to be, under the surface. His grin widened and his face relaxed. I could see the small gap between his two front teeth, the one where he occasionally stuck his thumbnail, when he was leaned over his desk, concentrating, worrying about something, unaware of being watched. That was all it took—that warming smile—to reassure me that his intentions were good and his future visions were sound, if occasionally extreme when taken too literally, of course, and that beneath it all was a lovable and sensitive person, someone worth not only helping, but defending. I wanted to be the one to defend him. And something simpler: I wanted to be the one to make him smile.

"You never fail to exceed my expectations, Rosalie," he said, as if the syllables of my name gave him pleasure. The way he pronounced it—slow and drawn out, twangy, with an impish flair—it was almost like a new name entirely.

The other infant tests were wrapping up, Curt and I had each embarked on our individual graduate projects, and Watson was eager for something more involving, something that would carry him through the holidays and into the next year, and even more important: something that would make a real scientific mark. He knew he needed the right subject. The pediatric ward had its share of children with significant medical problems (we only rarely used those) and babies born to mothers who couldn't afford care elsewhere, but those babies usually left the home quickly. Much harder was finding an infant who was normal and healthy but who would stay for months, who could be used for more than one trial.

Which brought us finally, in early December, after a few less-promising selections and another delay as we waited for the filming expenses to be approved, to "Albert B." John had come up with the pseudonym—part honor, part joke, a cross between my middle name, Alberta (one letter different from my father's name), and his own middle name, Broadus. We hadn't bothered with pseudonyms in most trials, but then again, we usually worked with infants we saw only once. If all went well, we'd work with this particular subject for as long as necessary to prove John's hypothesis, and we'd be writing about him in considerable detail, not just adding him to checklists and charts. Nine months old, the infant still lived at the home next door because his mother was an on-site wet nurse. It mattered greatly that Albert was suitable, if this work was to be started soon.

Which brings me to that day, when Albert was new to us, in a month when I was still new to the lab, uncertain of myself, of Watson, of everything.

"*What do you think?*"

"*He seems . . . healthy.*"

And then, the return of the camera technician, so we could get started, demonstrating on film that Albert had no fear.

That day in December, Albert stared, dully at first, at the leashed monkey being dragged in front of his line of vision, and at the rat crawling even closer, toward his legs. Drool glistening on his lower lip, attention focusing, he slowly and finally reached for the rat. As he did, later, for the dog. Even for the small fire kindled in the laboratory pan. I kept my hand just behind his hips, steadying him slightly as he leaned forward or side to side.

When Watson came close or jumped around, Albert became more still, scrutinizing the big male face that approached and then drew far away, the face that even returned once with a Santa mask. A stolid, imperturbable baby. No tears from our stoic Albert. And also no smiles.

"*What do you think?*"

"*He seems . . . healthy.*"

Albert showed only a little curiosity, a little puzzlement. And by the end: simple fatigue. Albert's head started to nod, chin falling to his chest. He was ready to go back to the ward next door. But not yet.

"Are you getting all this?" Dr. Watson asked Scottie, the filmographer. I could hear the excitement in his voice and the pleasure of evidence documented, of assumptions confirmed.

Now, the next step: stimulating a fear response. We tried pulling a blanket sharply out from under Albert, but even when he toppled forward or to the side, he barely responded. I was still more comfortable with animals than babies, but even so, I'd cradled and dangled my share of infants since October, and most of them had broken into tears easily and automatically. Admittedly, most of them were just days or weeks old.

We yanked and prodded and tried startling Albert, but this baby was stubbornly indifferent. Up until now, it had made our work easier. But I could see from Watson's concerned expression that a baby who refused to get upset would doom the entire experiment. Fortunately, he had something even more jarring up his sleeve.

It was my job to distract Albert's gaze. Behind the infant's head, unseen, Watson held a steel bar and a hammer. It was not subtle, but we didn't need subtlety. Watson struck the metal, making a clang so loud it made my molars hurt.

Albert inhaled sharply and flung his arms upward.

I distracted him again. Again, from the invisible place behind Albert's head, the earsplitting clang of steel.

This time, Albert turned down his lower lip. I stole a glance at Watson, whose eyebrows were furrowed.

A third time: *clang, clang, clang!*

Albert broke into sobs, leaned to one side, and toppled forward, his heavy head leading the rest of his slow-moving body as he tried to crawl away. I exchanged a smile with Watson, both of us momentarily distracted and terribly, unashamedly proud of ourselves. Then came the nearly spontaneous realization that our subject's terror had put him into full flight. "Come back, come back!" I grabbed Albert around one chubby leg and pulled him toward the center of the mattress, lightly speckled with his tears, while we laughed and congratulated ourselves, our elation too great to be diminished by anything or anyone.

CHAPTER 7

The Volstead Act had passed in October, extending the deprivations of the temporary Wartime Prohibition Act, and in mid-December it must have been—our family's holidays just starting, and Christmas still over a week away—two of Watson's old Chicago friends, Robert Tarr and Henry Follett, blew into town. They bounded into the lab, coats dripping, carrying the smell of tangy harbor-front air with them. Outside, streetlights gleamed on damp December pavement, where the barest snowfall had melted earlier that day, yielding again to early winter rain.

"It's just dinnertime, John," Robert said after the boisterous pleasantries had been exchanged. "You've got to eat, don't you? We came a long way, old boy."

While Watson made excuses, Robert conferred upon me an unearned wink. I'd been just about to offer to take their coats, but I decided against it and consciously turned back to my work.

"You got any coffee around here?" Robert said to the room at large.

John saved me the awkward moment of trying to decide whether I should play the expected hostessing role. "Aw, you don't want coffee. This time of day it'll give you the jitters."

They went into Watson's private resting office for just a few minutes. I heard the slide of his bottom desk drawer, which often meant a few inches of the specially permitted rye whiskey was being portioned out. They must have drained their tumblers quickly, because they were back in the main room just minutes later. I was writing up some results and planned to stay late. John's eye cast about desperately before landing on me.

"Please, Rosalie," he said. "That can wait until Monday. Come along."

When I started to protest, Henry asked, "You're not one of those girls who doesn't eat, are you? Because we know how much girls worry about their figures."

But I was already on my feet, heading across the room to grab my overcoat off the hook. "Not this girl, and not this figure." I made to push my hands into my sleeves quickly, before anyone insisted on helping. "I'm famished."

When John smiled at me, I knew I'd said the right thing, especially when he whispered in my ear as we crossed the Hopkins lawn: "Don't ever let them treat you like a secretary. You're a researcher, and my right-hand man, even if you're a woman. They'll catch on."

We walked half a mile to a steakhouse John knew about—a dark place with small sconces set into the papered walls, red leather benches and bulky chairs, dark wood tables, and steak knives already set out on top of each red napkin. After we'd ordered—all the same meal, no need to see a menu, just steak and potatoes, "and if there's any green vegetable on the plate, I won't eat it," Robert informed the waiter, who had already been jeered at for trying to talk them into soup—the volume continued, unabated.

The rain had started up again just before we'd ducked into the restaurant, and Watson's uncovered hair—he had a strange aversion to hats—was slick, his eyeglasses spotted with steam. He was bent over at the moment, wiping the round lenses with a handkerchief, while Robert and Henry erupted into laughter about some old shared memory of a college prank. When I sensed the presence of a large man behind my seat, leaning over my shoulder to get a better look at John, I thought it was a restaurant employee coming to tell the three men to modulate their voices.

Suddenly, an unfamiliar hand reached around and clapped John hard on the ear. John whirled and stood, knocking over his own chair. I gasped and struggled to push back my own heavy chair to get clear of the action. Henry was quick thinking and swept the steak knives clear of the stranger's grasp. We all had a chance to look at the ruffian: not tall, but broad, with a messy black forelock. Mashed nose. Brawny forearms with the cuffs rolled up.

Next thing, John was rearing back to deliver a punch that connected squarely with the stranger's cheek. Something cracked, either in the man's face or in John's hand.

The stranger bellowed in agony and then brayed with even greater rage at his sudden imprisonment as John's two friends—both sailor or longshoreman types, one bald and the other ginger haired—each took an arm and dragged him backward, out of the restaurant. We were left standing around our table, silent and incredulous, the dark restaurant claustrophobic now, the red walls closing in. John picked up the chair, shaking a little as he struggled to slow his breaths. Robert mopped up a puddle of spilled water and righted the salt and pepper shakers. A waiter hurried over, consulting in hushed tones with Henry, while a busboy replaced the silverware that had been swept onto the floor.

With his left hand covering his ringing ear, John apologized to all of us, "How ridiculous. I'm truly sorry."

Then he looked directly to me. "Darling, I can't bear to think of you going home hungry."

Maybe his head was ringing so hard he'd confused me for someone else, like his wife. Or maybe the fright of the experience had laid bare his feelings. *Darling.* He'd never talked to me that way.

"Stay and eat," he said. "Keep these two troublemakers company."

Troublemakers? He was the one who had just punched a man. I half-expected police to show up, but none did.

"I couldn't."

"You will," he said, dropping several bills on the table, then cautiously pushing his tender arm into his overcoat sleeve. "Or I'll give you the silent treatment Monday. Scout's honor. And I can always get a report from Henry later."

Robert followed John out the door and helped him get into a taxi, making sure the brute wasn't waiting out on the corner, before coming back inside. I didn't want to stay, but I was feeling nauseated and shocked. I'd never actually seen a real fistfight. The sped-up blurry images of that man appearing—just a shadow at first, a looming presence, and then the swinging hand, a wide clenched fist and ropy forearm covered with dark hair—were still playing behind my eyes. I hope I didn't feel excited, but maybe I did: pulse still pounding in my throat, hands shaking.

"A little something to settle your nerves?" Henry suggested, and pulled from beneath the table a flask of golden liquor, covertly pouring two inches into my empty water glass.

When the four steaks were delivered—one of them placed in front of John's now-empty seat, just next to my overloaded plate—Henry turned to me. "You said you were famished."

Now finally, with the relief surging through us and the steam rising out of our potatoes and the red juice pooling under our steaks, we all resumed talking. The two men's tongues had been loosened ever since their first tumblers of lab whiskey, a sneaky fresh round had loosened them further, and I gratefully joined them, needing to be indignant.

Of course, the irate stranger had been a cuckold. (A husband or boyfriend of some nurse? Not Essie—she wasn't even married. Then which one?)

"Men astonish me," I said, halfway through my steak.

"Only men? Women can get pretty crazy, too," Robert assured me. "John's love life is proof of that."

They looked at each other, then at me. Did I want to know? Of course I did.

"Mary Ickes," Henry started.

"No—Vida Sutton," Robert corrected him. "She was first. And last."

Vida was a University of Chicago student, it was explained to me in gleeful mock whispers, who had refused John's advances. Mary Ickes was another student, nineteen years old at the time and enrolled in one of his Introduction to Psychology classes, and as legend had it—it was John's version of the story, after all—she had spent an exam period mooning over him, resigning herself to failure by writing nothing but a love poem into the copy book. When he came to pick up the exams, she handed in her mostly empty pages, blushing.

I wanted to know: "Did he fail her?"

"That's not the point," Henry assured me. "He started dating her, of course."

Of course? So far, I was doing a better job of understanding Washburn's amoebas *and* Curt's rats than understanding John Watson or men in general.

Mary's family, including her lawyer brother, Harold, was involved in Chicago politics. The ambitious Ickes clan considered John an uncouth, social-climbing, backwoods Southerner. Perhaps it was the element of resistance that added a forbidden quality to their Romeo-and-Juliet relationship, because Mary and John wed secretly, in the year 1903, the day after Christmas—or maybe it was 1905, Robert suggested, unless that was only the public wedding. The dates were muddled, maybe intentionally so, since eight months after the 1905 wedding, Mary Junior, better known as Polly, was born.

The story from John, from Mary's brother, and even from Mary herself years later was that they never should have married in the first place. Vida Sutton thought so, too. She showed up again in Chicago some four years later to say she'd made a mistake by rejecting John and letting Mary have him. Mary's brother even hired a private detective to report on John's and Vida's clandestine meetings. Then Harold Ickes went to the president of the University of Chicago and asked him to fire John. There wasn't sufficient proof.

Harold tried to talk his sister into suing for divorce. John considered whether that outcome might be better than the marriage that had soured from nearly the beginning. But other voices, including some of John's academic mentors, intervened—recommending patience, fidelity, renewal, and commitment to their two young children.

I nodded silently, glad that Robert and Henry weren't asking my opinion.

When John was lured to the East Coast and Johns Hopkins about a year later, it seemed like more than a major career advance, Robert explained. It was also a chance to start over, to let the memories of a scandal fade away, to learn from one's mistakes. Even John's white rats at University of Chicago had managed to learn by trial and error, after all.

"More whiskey?" Henry asked.

I fumbled in my purse, the alcohol gone to my head, a wad of dollar bills in my hand, the room spinning as I stood.

"No, no," Robert protested. "John left plenty. We've got the rest covered. Put that away."

It was five or fifteen minutes later when Henry said, "Let's put you in a cab." His strong hand gripped my elbows, helping me down a small flight of carpeted stairs, out to the street and the cool, blissfully fresh air. "We'll take you home."

"Let's just stand here for a minute. Air is all I need."

I let them find me a cab, but refused to let them come along for the ride, and I could tell this parting of ways was their preference as well.

They still had the rest of the evening left, and more anti-Prohibition reveling to do.

Henry pecked me on the cheek just before opening my taxi door, and he relayed his best wishes to John.

"You're a nice girl," Robert called as the door was closing. "Nicer than most of the ones John finds. Be careful."

I woke the next day to a sour stomach and a splitting headache made worse by my mother's insistent shaking.

"Don't you remember, Rosalie? One o'clock?"

"No," I said, trying to pull free and bury my head in the pillow. "It's Saturday for heaven's sake."

She let go of my sleeve and went to my closet, where she started yanking dresses from hangers.

"You *did* forget. Well you're not getting out of this at such short notice."

"I can't."

"You mean you won't. A week ago, that would have meant something. But not when the poor boy is already more than halfway to Baltimore."

An hour later, fortified by a cup of black coffee and one hard-boiled egg, and wearing a sort of sailor-suit dress that made me look all of fourteen, I was seated in our front parlor, barely listening to the conversation between our guest and my parents, red spots playing across my eyelids when I let them mercifully close for stolen seconds.

The requisite questions—health and well-being of each sibling, update on his parents' vacation in France—were ticked off the list, and any moment now, Benjamin Fertig would rise from his seat and invite me out the door, where our chaperone-free date would begin. In the motor car, Benny, whom I'd known since childhood from synagogue and hadn't seen since my junior year at Vassar, would finally get a chance to turn and look me squarely in the eye, and tell me with a gee-whiz smile that I looked pretty, and now we could finally really get to know each other again, and he'd thought of me a lot since that summer sail two years ago.

It wasn't his fault I had a rusty lance embedded in my throbbing temple, a sandpaper tongue, and a tremor in my knees. It wasn't his fault I'd forgotten this date set up two weeks earlier, and that when I looked at his heavily oiled chestnut hair, parted cleanly down the middle with flakes of dandruff showing along that straight white part, and the little bow tie, cocked twenty degrees off center, I felt a dizzy unpleasantness only partly attributable to last night's whiskey.

Someone, someone would happily marry Benny Fertig and all those other boys my mother had mentioned as likely prospects—Sidney Cohn, Daniel Abrahamson. I was only wasting his time.

But at least we might have had a nice day of it, walking ever so slowly down a boardwalk, staring out at wintry coastal views, trading innocent childhood memories as I let last night's toxins percolate out of my system.

But no such walk was in the cards. Benjamin needed to show me an elevator, downtown.

Slipping a bill to the operator, a man who seemed to recognize him, and then a second one when the elevator operator seemed intent on balking—the poor man was risking his employment by leaving us alone in the elevator, with the vehicle in our hands—Benny purchased our solitude and made me spend ten minutes in that hot shuddering box, showing off his ability manipulating the motor control to joggle us to the right level at each floor, and lecturing me on the complications of modern elevator engineering and design, since that was to be his trade. He'd just gotten a new job designing them. My own father had put in a good word. My mother had also put in a good word, to *Benny's* mother, about what a delightful girl I was, and that I didn't date very much, and seemed lonesome on occasion.

"Is it true? You're feeling a little lonely?" Benny had asked.

"Well, not exactly . . ." but he didn't wait for the answer.

And how many children did I want? He wanted four: two girls, two boys. One shaggy dog.

And hadn't I had enough school, and would I be done with this rather pointless, unpaid interlude at Johns Hopkins very soon? Boy, he'd hated school. Women are lucky, Benny said. "School, work, all of it optional. And with labor-saving appliances, pretty soon a lady at home won't have anything to do but press a few buttons and then, what? Go shopping, I guess."

And did I have a favorite skyscraper in Boston or New York? His company's elevators were in all of them, and perhaps over ice cream—"*Yes, please!*" I said, anything to get out of the elevator and back down on the ground floor, where there was a soda shop with padded booths and water for my whiskey-parched tongue—he could tell me everything he knew about elevators and his dreams for the future.

It could have been worse.

He didn't try anything, either behind those closed elevator doors or in the car on the way home. And he talked so long and asked so few questions that my mind was free to wander back to the events of the night before, the stories about John, Mary, and Vida, my dazed distraction mistaken by Benny for confusion about the subject of weight maximums and hydraulics, safety mechanisms and vertical traffic patterns, about which he was willing to explain all over again.

"Ever heard of the elevator algorithm?" he asked. I had not.

Why does the voice and scent of one man make us cringe; the scent of another, swoon?

Those were the questions. Not what a lady at home would do once we all lived in a push-button world, or whether elevators would ever be fully automated, or how fast an elevator would have to travel once skyscrapers, many times higher than any built today, truly brushed the sky.

CHAPTER 8

On Monday morning I found a dozen red roses tied up with a spruce-green bow waiting for me in the lab, and raised eyebrows on the face of every nurse and technician I happened to pass.

Nothing happened, I wanted to stammer, my face warming in response to the insinuations. What could I do with the flowers anyway? I delivered them to a receptionist at the psychiatric intake desk.

Later that day, John Watson gestured for me to enter his private office, stepped carefully around me, and closed the door softly before returning to his desk.

"I'm sorry," he said. Only then did I notice the small bandage over a cut on his cheek and the way his right hand kept crawling into the front pocket of his jacket.

"It doesn't hurt too much," he said when he noticed me looking. "But it's true. My knuckles aren't as tough as they used to be. I guess you box all the time or not at all."

I'd been so caught up in the stories of his philandering that I'd forgotten to ask, until now, how he'd managed to throw such an effective punch.

"Oh that," he said, a hint of boyish pleasure in his voice, though he looked unsettled. "I'm afraid to say I was a shameless scrapper back in my South Carolina days."

He took off his glasses and rubbed the small red marks on either side of his nose. "I was arrested a couple times. For nigger fighting."

I waited for a moment, taken aback by the vulgar turn of phrase.

"I'm not going to defend that," he said. "You know where I stand now, on matters of race—and violence. I was looking for all kinds of trouble, and I found it. Are you going to take a seat or will I be giving my full confession while you stand there?"

I hurried to lower myself into the chair on the other side of the desk. He'd already told me a little about his upbringing on the farm, his parents and the riverside revivalist tent meetings he deplored. He told me now about coming to the University of Chicago with only fifty dollars in his pocket. When I got up my nerve to ask him about the Mary Ickes and Vida Sutton stories, he admitted that it was all true. It bothered him less that I knew about his early affairs than that I'd sat alone with two of his old college friends, not very good friends as it turned out, gossiping behind his back. Seeing his hurt look, I recognized he had a reason to feel betrayed. Yet how else could I have come to understand him, except by listening to their tales?

"And I suppose you might want to know about my present marriage," he continued.

"That's your own private business, Dr. Watson. All of it is."

"So we're back to 'Dr. Watson,' are we? Then what's the point of digging up my past if it doesn't even make us closer friends?"

His thumb went up to the gap between his teeth, until he noticed and pushed his hands down onto his lap.

"I've embarrassed you," he said. "First, with the fight and then with the flowers—I guess roses send the wrong message but I just can't stand those poinsettias—and now with all my pathetic boyhood stories. And that's without me even telling you that I'm stuck in a loveless, sexless marriage to a woman who can't stand me half of the time."

"I doubt that's true."

"What? That it's loveless? Sexless?"

I looked down at my lap. "That she can't stand you."

"Well," he said. "There I go. Embarrassing you again. Now you know the real John Broadus Watson, warts and all. But I'm getting carried away. I'm losing track of the point I wanted to make, about Friday's scuffle."

He stood up and came around the desk slowly, as if crossing an icy street, considering each step, finding his traction. I thought at first he was going for the door, but then he approached and stood behind me, hands on my shoulders, fumbling—the quiver of his own fingers perceptible until he rested the palms more firmly. That slight tremble, weighted with unclear intentions, accelerated my pulse.

"That silly fight at the restaurant," he said from behind my back, in a low and serious voice, "was about jealousy. A completely natural and utterly useless emotion. Do you understand what I'm telling you?"

I took a deep breath, tried to force myself back into a state of relaxation, to assume nothing, to take pains not to read too much into a gesture.

"No, I . . . I really don't."

"If you take away all the useless emotions, the errors in men's ways of responding irrationally to the world, do you know what you have?"

It was a test of some kind, but if it were merely a test, why was he speaking so huskily, his breath coming fast and shallow?

"You have no rage," he said. "You have no fear. Rosalie, you have *no war.*"

And I was back for the briefest moment at Vassar again, the morning we'd heard the war was over—millions dead, but it was over—and we'd all trooped out at 4 A.M. in our coat-covered nightgowns and skipped between the buildings, dancing and hugging. Someone had a German army helmet—a souvenir collected by an uncle in the army, who'd expected it to go on display in the library or in a history-club cabinet—and we climbed a hill and dug a hole and buried it, feeling like warriors ourselves. Several girls had broken down into tears. A girl named Lucy had thrown herself down on the ground, legs splayed, face melting—and I'd looked askance at those emotional prostrations. But listen now, here: even a grown man, a psychologist, Dr. John Watson of Greenville and Chicago and Baltimore, was trembling with the emotional residue of that Great War, that useless conflagration.

"It's so close, the changes we can make, but we're not there yet," he said. "I don't know sometimes if I can get there on my own."

A warmth spread from my throat down into my stomach and across my lap. "Rosalie," he said, the breath on his neck making my skin tingle, "You know I'm not a perfect man. And you know I'm an unapologetic flirt. Trouble finds me, on occasion."

I didn't dare to answer, or even turn my head. I only waited, the air electric, my mouth dry. I tilted my cheek toward him and lifted my chin just a fraction, admitting him into the curve of my neck, where I knew his lips would register the heat and rhythm of my own heart pounding. Anything to save me from having to speak: to say *yes* or *no* or *aren't there rules?* or *what about your wife?*

When he stood up a little straighter—backing away for only a moment, I thought, finding a better angle of attack—I took that moment to breathe and regain my composure. "I don't know what to think about this."

"So don't think," he said. Was there a hint of irritation in his voice? Of course. *Don't think.* I hadn't thought of that.

I closed my eyes, muscles tensed. I waited for his hands to move from my shoulders. I imagined them moving down my arms, onto my ribs, my waist, and up again, moving to the front, to my breasts, cupping them in his hands. When they got there, if he paused, I would whisper, *I don't mind.*

But it was too late. I opened my eyes again. He'd removed his hands.

I could still smell his cologne and feel the phantom pressure of his fingertips kneading my shoulders. I could still feel the ghostly longing coming from parts of my body he hadn't even touched, a taste of shame far in advance—because we hadn't done anything. Not yet.

I heard him step toward the door. Something had changed in his bearing.

"And the next time you want to hear stories about John Watson," he said, "just remember to come to me. I'm not a bad storyteller—better than that son-of-a-bitch Henry Follett." He cleared his throat. "Are you waiting for something, Rosalie?"

The words wouldn't come. I stammered, "You—you don't have a cigarette, do you?"

That stopped him short, hand on the doorknob. He went back around to his desk, watching my face, and opened up a little Camel cigarette tin. When he handed me the cigarette, my hand was shaking so much, I hurried it to my lip, where it still quivered as I took the lighter he passed me. He wouldn't do me the honors.

He said, "You're staring at me just now like you opened a hatbox and found a possum curled up inside."

"Yes, in a way I sort of feel like I did."

He cracked a smile, and then raised his eyebrows when I didn't laugh or smile back.

"Don't think," he'd said. The very word—*think*—wouldn't do. "I don't know what to make of you," I said.

"What to *make* of me? You thought I was going to kiss you. You thought I was going to seduce you, just a minute ago."

I was busy trying and failing to light the cigarette with useless fingers, which saved me the trouble of answering.

"Maybe I almost was," he said. "But first off, I sensed your considerable hesitation. Was I wrong about that?"

Was he wrong? What was I supposed to answer? That I was willing, possibly eager, a loose woman who barely needed persuasion? Oh, why couldn't I summon any excitement for the unmarried, appropriate Benny Fertigs of the world?

When it was clear I wasn't about to confess anything, he said, "Resistance might be appealing to some men. But it isn't appealing to me. Physical pleasure isn't something I try to trick another person into."

"I didn't think you were trying—"

"And second, I remembered. You're too old for me."

"Too *old*?"

"You've got to understand, when I was seduced by Mary, she was only nineteen. But you know that story now."

I couldn't believe what I'd just heard—the ridiculous, arrogant nerve of it. I was exactly half his age.

"And frankly," he said, "by the time we married, she already had plenty of negative traits that were too far gone to decondition."

"She was ruined, in other words," I said, finding my spine. "But not you. You have no bad habits."

"Oh, I've got plenty of them."

"Drinking? Being with women?"

Though it wasn't even lunchtime yet, he opened a file cabinet drawer and poured amber liquid into a small glass, the spilled drops betraying a mild tremor. "I never said either of those things were bad habits. Nothing bad about bourbon *or* about sex. I happen to like sex very much, especially."

I'd just managed to light the cigarette and take the first puff, which triggered an inexpert cough.

"That's right, sex," he said. "The most natural thing in the world. Doesn't even cause a hangover, which is more than I can say of my other favorite thing."

"So what's your bad habit, then?"

"Fear of the dark," he said, half-squinting. I couldn't tell if he was joking.

"How . . . how . . ." I said, irritated by his jocular tone, "how dare you call me too old?"

"That's better. Stand up for yourself. Don't just sit there like a scared rabbit. Where's that girl from the New School lecture, who kept out-talking me? She was smart, and mouthy, and driven. As I recall, she could even catch a ball." Try as he might to be incendiary, his tone was slipping. The act was falling apart. "I *liked* that girl."

I wanted to hear him say that. I would have given anything for him to repeat it. But I also clung to my righteous indignation.

"And what about Essie? What about all the nurses?"

"That's different," he said. "That's just play. And anyway, all men are attracted to nurses. It's just a fact."

"Which makes it all right, in your estimation."

"All right if the nurse doesn't mind. Did Essie look unhappy to you, the day you barged into my office?"

The proof that he had seen me come in that day added burn to my cheeks.

"You're saying it's perfectly acceptable for you to cheat on your wife."

"Is it cheating when she and I don't make love anymore? When we barely even talk? It's the law that's made things complicated, not me."

"Don't you love her even a little?"

"No, Rosalie. I don't."

When I didn't reply, he said, "What you're looking at, what you're studying with those big blue eyes of yours, is something rare in nature: one of the only honest men you'll ever meet."

I lifted my chin and tried to sound bravely offended, but my voice cracked. "My father's honest."

Whether it was the words or my sudden near-slip into inexplicable teariness, that ended the game for him. "All right, honey. I'm sure he is."

He got up and came around the desk again. "Only this once, because we're friends," he said, and then bent over to place a quick kiss on my cheek. "You may be surprised to know there are many women who want to be pursued—too many for a lifetime of pursuing."

I'd bought his line in that moment. I'd figured he went after the women he wanted most. I didn't realize that he wasn't used to being the one to cross the line.

All his life, women had hunted him. He had no trouble giving in to his urges, but it was exactly that: giving in. Reacting. Not initiating, except through design: surrounding himself with attractive women, making no secret of his appetites and inclinations. That strategy fit his model of human behavior perfectly: create opportunities for certain kinds of stimuli, and then—logically, naturally, faultlessly—simply react. Behaviorism was about control, certainly, but he wasn't the one who believed that sexuality or even adultery should be restricted. In his mind, sex was not one of civilization's problems. Things like rage and jealousy needed to be controlled, yes, but not sex itself.

And that line about me being too old? Preposterous, even for him.

Which meant, I suppose, that I had the upper hand. But I didn't feel that way. I only felt defenseless and confused. I had a brief sense of how our young, puzzled subjects must feel—fingers nearly poked in their eyes to assess their blink reaction times, bodies plunged into water without warning, furry animals sent scurrying across their legs.

Seemingly out of the blue, he said, "I was out hat shopping with Polly on Saturday." He added meaningfully, "*Downtown.*"

"That sounds pleasant," I said, too emotionally confused to fake interest.

"For the first thirty minutes, maybe. I left Polly to try on the fiftieth hat, and I walked across the street to get some fresh air, and I saw you in a booth near the window, with a young man. Not the most handsome, but sure of himself, I could tell from the way he kept tossing his head back, laughing at his own jokes. Rosalie, I couldn't help it. I kept watching. He kept talking, and at first, I tried to tell myself he must be an interesting fellow. And good for you. Good for the *both* of you. But then his mouth kept moving, and I looked at your face, and you weren't even looking back at him, and I felt a little surge of hope, because maybe you didn't have strong feelings for this young fellow after all, and then dread, because you're too nice for your own good."

"Is it so terrible, being nice?"

"You'd help a man like that find his way in the world, and one morning you'd wake up and realize how small a world you'd both decided to live in and that most people want so damn little that they're nearly dead at age twenty-two."

"Benny's already twenty-three," I said, pretending to miss the point.

"Don't be afraid of wanting the wrong things, Rosalie. It's better than wanting too little."

"And what do you want?"

I didn't say it with kindness. I expected him to answer with more talk about psychology and ending wars, and I was tired of all that for the moment: the abstract future, and pretending to be sure about big ideas or anything at all.

Instead he said, "I want what I can't have. I want to make love to you more expertly than any college boy, slowly and passionately. I think you might want that, too. But I don't think you're willing to pay for it."

CHAPTER 9

There was no one I could tell. Because here was the thing—I wasn't sure what exactly had happened, or whether I had myself to blame. What messages had I sent him with my actions? How seriously should I take his provocative words?

Later, when I told him I was leaving for the night, he looked up from his desk—unusually chaotic, with stacks of papers that represented his best attempt to avoid going home anytime soon—and said, "There are certain traits I have, that many men and some women have. Natural traits. Better suited to a world that doesn't yet exist."

Perhaps he heard himself stacking up the bricks of a would-be argument, and realized the rising wall was only obscuring the view of the very person he was trying to address. He looked down at the papers, the empty glass sitting in the shadow just outside the pool of light cast by his metal desk lamp. "I should be plainer, Rosalie. I made a mess of things today, and I said things I shouldn't have said. I'd hate to chase away my best assistant. Tell me I haven't done that."

"You haven't."

"All right," he said. "Then we'll never have to speak of it again."

I nodded.

"Good. Now find yourself a nice boyfriend this holiday break, won't you? Someone more interesting than the soda-shop boy."

"Benny," I said. "His name is Benny, and he's an engineer."

"My apologies. Go find yourself ten Bennies. It can't be hard for a girl as pretty and smart as you."

That evening, my mother met me in the hall, just as I opened the front door, seven o'clock, not yet late for dinner, which we often ate late on Fridays. The smell of roast chicken, potatoes, and rosemary in the air.

"Rosalie." My mother's hands were folded together, ligaments raised on the white knuckles of her clenched hands. "This can't continue."

My throat was so tight I couldn't swallow. I focused, wide-eyed, on her hands. If I so much as looked at her face, I might fall apart. How could she know? Did my own face give everything away?

"You simply must talk to him," she said. "It's become downright embarrassing."

I'd been distracted—at times moping, at times dreamy. And the sleeplessness had etched dark circles under my eyes. Of course she knew—not the details, but something. A mother's intuition.

I turned away, shrugging out of my overcoat, looking around for a place to set my purse in order to avoid seeing her eyes. "Mother, do we have to talk about this?"

"Yes, we certainly do." She blocked my way into the hall, insistent upon settling this here and now, without letting it enter the front parlor, spoil the dinner, or ruin the entire weekend.

"What do you expect me to say?"

"I expect you to get a straight answer."

From him, about us—to her, or to me? To our entire family?

Thank goodness for my exhaustion, which slowed my reaction time, because next she said, "Two months I've been issuing invitations. Nearly three. We can't just keep inviting them, Rosalie. We can't pretend, when we finally meet Dr. Watson and his wife, that we never did invite them to dinner."

It had been eating her up all day, this chess game beyond her control. I could breathe again. I could almost laugh at my own momentary terror.

"And now I realize—of course—that I should have been more formal," she continued. "I should have sent Mrs. Watson a note, not let you take care of it through him, word of mouth. It's like I've forgotten every last manner I ever learned. Who knows if he's relayed anything at all? And if he hasn't, whose fault is that? It's my fault. It would have been better if nothing had ever been said."

Four days before Christmas, my mother took me to New York, the city shimmering in white lights, bauble-decked trees in plazas and parks, the traffic at a near standstill, everyone in the world gathered into canyonlike, glittering streets—everyone except for the one person I couldn't stop thinking about.

"All you do lately is that lab work, all those experiments," Mother said. "What you need is amusement. Be merry, Rosalie."

The previous winter, the influenza epidemic had put a damper on most crowd-attracting activities, and my own mother had done most of her gift ordering by catalog, requesting a few items to be sent to orphanages directly from the department stores. We made up for that sober year now by stopping at a plaza in front of a children's choir, performing in front of a Christmas tree decked in gold and green globes. Mother clapped together her rabbit-fur-trimmed gloves: "Marvelous!" She did not sing any carols herself, nor did we have a Christmas tree in our Baltimore house—one had to draw a line somewhere—and even that word, *merry*, came to her lips a little awkwardly. But still she loved it all, and wanted me to love it alongside her. I dutifully stared at the red cheeks and taut, oval-shaped mouths, the words of cheer meaningless to me as I recalled John's description of Christmas: "murder."

For me, too. I wouldn't see him for two more weeks.

We pushed our way in and out of department stores, fought our way toward perfume, jewelry, and glove counters, stood in long lines to make purchases, carried overloaded shopping bags until our shoulders and wrists ached, and tried in vain to register for a table in the department-store restaurant, but the wait was too long.

At a toiletries counter, Mother asked a salesgirl about something for the shadows under my eyes. I'd always been inclined to shadows, but my overwork and sleepless nights all through December had made them more pronounced. I acquiesced to the gentle patting and smoothing of expert fingers.

"Better?" I asked my mother.

"Better."

"How about something for my lips?"

"Oh," my mother laughed. "I don't think we have to go that far."

I was still a girl to her, an appropriately natural and healthy girl. Noticeable makeup was reserved for actresses, eccentrics, or tarts. Rouges and tinted powders were becoming more commonplace, but to really get made up, you had to visit some special Helena Rubinstein or Elizabeth Arden salon—and prepare to pay a bundle and listen to long lectures about skin care and the new beauty culture, which was no longer for *those* kind of women but for everyone.

With Mother? Never.

"I'd give anything to sit down," my mother said, looking at the long lines queuing for the elevators. Bobbing heads and shoulders packed every doorway and aisle, swarming the display tables, puzzling over the store directory. It was the men I noticed most, in their black wool coats, scarves trailing from their lapels, enlisting the help of shopgirls in picking out appropriate gifts for their wives. A man with hair as thick and dark as John's bent low in front of a display case, directing a slim girl toward a display of bracelets, his smile faintly reflected in the glass as she pulled out a series of velvet-lined trays until he was satisfied with one particular item which she held up, glinting and twisting, like a jeweled snake.

He touched a finger to the shopgirl's wrist as she modeled the bracelet, demonstrating its clasp. The girl laughed a silvery laugh and brought her face closer to the man's, both of them intently focused on her narrow, blue-veined wrist and the beautiful object he was thinking—or perhaps not really thinking—of buying. She'd learned something I'd never mastered despite being on my way to a second university degree: How to read a man's intentions. How to flirt. How to go just far enough without going too far. Or how to go far and simply enjoy it—to be one of *those* people (men and a few women) endowed with certain "natural" if not yet socially acceptable traits— without falling apart.

My mother remembered suddenly. "Oh no—your salon appointment!"

It had been her idea to do this together, to get my hair bobbed, something I'd been asking to do since graduation.

"We could do it another time."

"No, no," she said, shifting her weight, no doubt suffering from swollen feet. "I insist."

At the third-floor salon, we made our excuses, and they hurried me off to the sinks in the back while my mother lingered, trading questions and suggestions with the barber. But at the first harsh rasp of the scissors, she turned away with an anxious giggle. When a single, dark lock fell to the floor, she leapt backward to avoid it, and turned back toward the waiting room. "I prefer to be surprised," she said, scurrying away.

Mother was lost in the pages of a *Saturday Evening Post* when I emerged. I stood waiting for her to notice me, feeling the strange lightness of my shorter hairstyle, swinging just above my faintly damp shoulders. Relieved of weight, the ends curled up naturally. My neck felt longer, more elegant. When I cleared my throat, my mother looked up. She was silent for a moment before breaking out into a single, plaintive sob.

I hurried to her. "Mother!"

She shook her head, struggling to stifle the downpour, laughing between choking little inhalations. "I guess you just look too grown-up to me now." She wiped an eye and then wrapped her arms around me. "How embarrassing."

Yes, for both of us.

There was still time, I thought for the briefest of moments, to be more honest with her than I'd been, to tell her about the mess I'd made falling in love with a married man, to create a new and more mature relationship to go with my new appearance. I reached inside of myself for the ounce of strength and character it would take—and came up empty.

Without any warning, I found myself crying in tandem, drenching her shoulder with hiccupping sobs.

"Oh darling," she said, patting me on the back. Then she pushed away, holding me by the shoulders so that she could look into my face, gaining control of herself while I lost the struggle, made all the worse by her concerned expression. Her hand reached up to touch my hair. "You don't like it?"

"No," I tried to say. "It's fine."

But she didn't believe me. And her complete willingness to imagine I was crying over nothing more than a haircut, to become the stoic consoler, provided the excuse for me to continue indulging my own confused melancholia. Each choking little gasp cleared some air inside my chest, purging the tight ache, but only temporarily. The next swell of breath seemed to dredge up an even deeper sob from someplace deep within.

"Let's make it better," she said, hurrying to pay the bill. "We'll invite someone to join us for dinner. We'll pay a visit to one of your school friends. What were their names—Eleanor? Hilda? The other one you liked so much. Mary?"

"Oh no." Not Mary. There could be nothing worse.

Because in fact, I had already sent a note to Mary, telling her I might visit the city over the holidays, and should we perhaps get together for lunch or tea? And she had written right back with exciting news: she—Mary, unsentimental, scholarly, unglamorous, nearsighted Mary—had fallen in love. *Appropriate*, uncomplicated love. To a good man named Harry, whom she'd met in a history course. He was also attending Columbia, also devoted to psychology. He was very smart (of course) and very kind (of course), and though Mary did not expect me to believe it until I met him (*You will have to meet him soon, please!*), he was completely enlightened and had no wish to disrupt Mary's graduate work and later career. In fact, it was possible that they might someday do research together.

I was still crying as we tried to exit the salon. A female voice called us back. We'd forgotten our packages, stored behind the counter. Loaded down a moment later, Mother pulled me closer to her as we wobbled together. "It really looks very charming! And it will grow back, of course it will grow."

"I know," I said, rubbing my face in my sleeve, and feeling bad not just about John now, but about the encompassing nature of my deceptions.

"Well, we certainly made a mistake," Mother said. "But at least it's one you'll outgrow."

"Yes," I said. And I really did hope so.

CHAPTER 10

I offered to feed Curt's rats so that I had an excuse to come back to the lab even before the holidays were over, even before the next series of experiments was to begin. But that did not make John return any sooner, of course, and when he did, he seemed to be in a strange, agitated state: anxious, volatile, rambunctious.

Maybe it was surviving Christmas, or some new truce that had been reached with his wife. Maybe it was the new year. The new decade.

He went to Adolf Meyer, demanded a raise, and got it. Every institution in America wanted Dr. John B. Watson, and if Johns Hopkins planned to keep him, well!—he said it still wasn't enough, and he planned to ask for another raise soon, he reassured me, as if I were a proxy for his wife, shopping list and threatening note from the landlord (yes, they rented), in hand. He deserved more money. "Don't I, Rosalie?"

Money wasn't a thing I'd been raised to worry about—and perhaps he found that extra attractive in me, the lack of nagging, the lack of that particular kind of knowledge or concern. What did a professional man need to earn? What did a professional woman deserve to earn? Even after reading Sinclair Lewis, I had no idea. But I knew what he wanted to hear.

"Of course you deserve more," I said.

He had several advanced classes to teach that semester, one held at the lab itself, others over at Homewood, but he did all he could to minimize the requirements, to oversee and delegate to other lecturers or cancel classes, to prioritize research and the development of new institutional partnerships. He assigned me some other simple infant tests I could do by myself, or with a single nurse's help, depriving me of his company unless I actively sought him out. I had come to recognize his footsteps, his particular gait, and my pulse would pick up whenever I heard him pass outside the testing-room door: the old Pavlovian response. First, the smell of him; then the sound of him. Eagerly anticipating something my body understood better than my brain.

But I didn't see much of him during that frantic January, because he was already hurrying off. To Homewood Campus. Over to the baby ward. Another lunch. Another meeting. Preparations for an upcoming conference.

And then, there was a diphtheria breakout in the baby ward. We canceled the baby tests and stayed secluded on our side of the clinic, out of contagion's reach. When the alarm passed, we got more bad news. Albert had contracted measles. He went through an outbreak, it worsened, we waited. Finally, on January 29, his temperature seemed normal again. We'd had our reference point for his behavior—unafraid of furry animals and so on, responsive to the clanging metal sound and therefore potentially fearful, but only of the sound, not of any of the other items we introduced. But he was maturing. We needed to get the experiment going while he was still essentially the same baby, and more important, while he was still on the ward, before his mother's wet-nurse contract ended.

On February 12, two weeks after his recovery from measles, we asked the nurses to bring Albert to us. He was eleven months old, with only a few more wisps of light hair, a shiny double chin, and a perennially spittle-dampened neck.

"Can't get much fatter," Essie said, carrying him on her hip into the room, now that he was too big for the infant carts.

"Picture of health," John replied.

Someone asked about the baby's mother, about whether she'd been at Hopkins long, and John made a crack about wet nurses: "One part cow, nine parts devil."

Essie smiled back, dimples flashing. "I do believe I've heard that one before. But I don't think you should be the one talking about devils, Dr. Watson."

There was a new nurse in the room, Rebecca—I'd never come to know her well, but I'd later remember that name because it was also my mother's—and I watched her bland face grow stony at the first comment, and even more at Essie's retort.

Now in the small, dark-walled lab room, Albert's head swiveled and his gaze seemed to locate me. But then it moved on, like a lighthouse beacon, a dutiful shaft of light passing over water and rock, without any innate intelligence. But of course, there was a lot of distraction in that room, and more than the typical number of people gathered: two nurses, Essie and Rebecca, and a stenographer, and Scottie, the filming technician. Now, the real work would begin. Now, too, I would get to see more of John.

Most of the observers and assistants gathered alongside the wall. In the middle of the room, several thin, striped mattresses were stacked. The camera, with its limited supply of film, was expensively rolling. Seated just inches above the ground with my legs tucked up under me, I presented Albert with a white rat. He'd gained better control of his hands over the last few months and was more eager than ever to reach out slowly, with a clumsy scooping motion. The rat scrambled toward him and Albert leaned forward, fingers grazing the stubby white fur, all his attention focused, a line of drool falling from his lower lip to the mattress as he concentrated and watched the rat scurry away.

John brought out the steel bar, positioning himself behind little

Albert's head. Though we could all see what he was doing, and knew the noise would come, we held our collective breaths, and when the bar was struck with an ear-splitting clang, all but John jumped. Albert whimpered.

I was the closest to Albert, offering a bit of comfort with my presence, but never too much. Albert's head swung toward me with bovine sluggishness, little hairless brow furrowed. I kept my own face neutral—the scientist's mask, which I was beginning to wear more comfortably—and risked a glance at John. His chest inflated with satisfaction, and a smile tugged at the sides of his mouth. His dark eyebrows lifted in anticipation. Oh, how he wanted to move on, to do more, to log more stimulations and responses. But he restrained himself. Pacing was necessary. To hurry was to ruin things. Experiments took time.

But of course they did.

It hit me then: Pacing. Testing. Time. And the long-term trial that love (or sex, if they were equivalent) is—that all human interaction is, really. What terribly simple creatures we all are. Yes, John and I were involved in an experiment of some kind, neither of us wholly in charge, both of us prey to the same impulses.

Stimulus and response. Uncomplicated. He wanted it; I wanted it. There was no question that anyone was forcing me to do something I didn't want to do. I was sure of that, now. He'd known I would have to be sure. Whether his waiting had been some kind of a trick, a function of his own insecurities, or just a habit formed in response to the women who had been happy to make the first moves, it had been the right thing to do. And more than right: tantalizing. A college boy would never have understood that. And now I understood, too: one did not need to suppress what should happen naturally. We were in the business of predicting and controlling behavior, but we were not in the business of controlling this.

"Are you taking notes, Rosalie?"

Not knowing how much I'd missed, I dashed off a couple words on a notepad tucked under my knee.

John had turned to Georgie, confirming some detail—Albert's feeding schedule, a communication about the measles issue and his temperament since then, the working schedule of his wet-nurse mother. The words were white noise, background chatter. Little Albert sat, with his large head balanced over his slightly bent legs, looking slightly troubled and unsure, but stable. Things were proceeding just as they needed to proceed.

A technician removed the white rat and a hand passed me a basket of blocks. I held out one small orange block toward Albert and he took it and brought it to his mouth, comforting himself with the familiar object.

"Should we return him to the ward?" Georgie asked.

John answered, "Let him play with the blocks a little while more. Rosalie will watch him. You'll bring Albert over to the nursery in ten minutes, won't you Rosalie?"

"Yes, of course."

Scottie, who had captured only frugal seconds of footage, left first, followed by Georgie. The rat was safely confined in a basket. The testing-room door was still open a crack, but I heard no voices outside. I absentmindedly handed Albert another two blocks.

I looked up at John, just as he was beginning to rise. "John, wait."

"Yes?" He smiled—a quick, pleasant, professional smile—but he paused, studying me, registering something in my voice and my expression, the use of his first name.

I repeated again, more quietly: "John."

His voice dropped a notch, softening into a playful, honeyed drawl. "Yes?"

I leaned to one side, behind oblivious Albert, and touched John's shoulder, and then retreated, setting my hand on the mattress again.

His grin widened. We balanced and braced ourselves, with hands therefore fully occupied, leaning into each other so incrementally, it reminded me of turning the focus knob of a microscope, careful not to make an adjustment too large—and then, closer yet, the slightest repositioning of chin, of neck. The most exquisite pause, well beyond the moment of feigned innocence, well beyond the moment of turning back.

And then: lips, mouth, taste of coffee and that hint of bourbon. My eyes were closed, not squeezed this time, in a paralyzed panic, but only closed so that I could shut out visual distractions and savor him. I could feel John's lips pulling back for a barely repressed chuckle, grinning in response to my clumsy eagerness, one quick bumping of teeth until we found lips again. He was making me come to him, making me convince him that I wanted his lips, his tongue. No one could possibly smell and taste as good as he did. It was delicious—a slow and decisive probing that was nothing at all like the handful of rushed, awkward slobbers I'd dutifully exchanged with college boys. For several minutes, our labored breathing accompanied the sounds of Albert's self-calming grunts and sighs.

My feet didn't touch the floor again.

My lips felt bruised all the rest of the day.

CHAPTER 11

The plan was to test Albert again in one week. Like a boy waiting for summer camp to commence, John was torn between eager impatience and reluctance, wanting to hold on to that moment when the experiment he had envisioned was on track, proving his theory, and disinclined to admit anything that might conflict with the elegant pattern taking shape—and yet, because he was curious and driven, also wanting to know more as soon as possible.

But he was thinking about more than just Albert. I could tell by the notes that began to arrive and would keep arriving all late winter and spring. Among my favorites: *Every cell I have is yours, individually and collectively.*

Now that my own love life and job were equally underway, it was finally possible to reply with authentic happiness to Mary Cover's last letter, as I had not been able to do over the Christmas holidays. *Harold sounds like a gem. Columbia sounds perfect. What wonderful news!*

As for my own news, I didn't feel secure enough to share any illicit details. *Dr. Watson keeps me extremely busy. I'm learning buckets and am convinced, as he is, that these experiments may be a solid foundation for the understanding and shaping of all human behavior.*

A week after the first post-baseline trial, we repeated the experiment with Albert. Even without the ear-splitting hammering on the steel bar, Albert seemed to remember his earlier fear response. When we presented the rat, Albert's hand withdrew. From the edge of the mattress, I wrote, "stimulus not without effect." Albert did not cry during that first stimulation, but when we handed him his blocks, he was even more eager to play with them, soothing himself with a familiar pastime. Familiar tactile explorations, in general, were his most frequent ways of self-comforting. He didn't seem to find much comfort from anything visual—least of all our faces, waiting to see him cry.

After a peaceful moment, we introduced the rat and the sound in combination again, twice, furry skitter and clang, furry skitter and clang. John with the hammer—Thor's hammer, Curt liked to tease—raised at shoulder height, all his attention focused, ready to rain down thunder again.

When we presented the rat alone, Albert puckered up his face, whimpering. But only whimpering. Trying to shut out the world, that room, and all the sources of his unnameable distress.

Again, the quick-moving rat, and the steel bar, and the hammer.

Albert leaned back, pulling his knees and elbows closer to his body, shrinking as best as he was able, defenseless against what would come next, on the verge of losing control of his emotions. I made a note, looked up at John, holding the bar, ready to strike. We both nodded, ready.

The combination again—*there*, the crack widening, the last defenses falling. Albert let out a series of choking gasps until he managed to tuck his bottom lip under his top, drying tears leaving white tracks down his pink cheeks.

We presented the rat alone. It had barely started to skitter when Albert exploded into fresh, bountiful sobs. He threw himself forward, determined to crawl away. I grabbed his chubby ankles just in time to catch him from tipping off the edge of the thin mattress. Smiles, all around the room, except from the newer nurse on duty, Rebecca, who watched us from a corner, baby blanket over one arm, stern. But we didn't need her approval, and there would always be the sentimental type of person who did not see that a few tears or a bit of subject discomfort were a small price to pay for unlocking the secrets of human behavior.

End of two sessions. Seven pairings of stimulus-response.

If you've ever felt that sad, hopeless moment when the past seems to splash over and inundate the present, when history—public or private—seems doomed to repeat and endlessly reinfect itself, then surely you can imagine the thrilling opposite of that moment, when the future, a new future of reason and control and radical reshaping of humanity's vestigial weaknesses, reaches back and extends a rescuing hand to the present. Never mind the apathetic finger of God reaching out, in that Michelangelo painting we'd all stared at in Art History class. This hand of reason had a firmer grip. It would pull us forward, if we grabbed back with enough determination, if we held on and didn't let go.

That's how it felt, then. That's how it truly felt.

John looked over my shoulder and smiled with approval as I wrote, "Proof of the conditioned origin of fear response."

The success of that second session surely merited a lunch out. I extended the invitation, to John's grinning surprise, and offered to take us both in my Bearcat, which in dark midwinter I had started driving to work, to avoid the gloomy and chilling streetcar rides home after late nights at the lab.

John suggested a cheap sandwich place in a rundown neighborhood near the hospital, but I needed a safe place to park, and besides, this was a red-letter day. There was a new hotel downtown, the Baltimore Regent, with an elegant dining room. When I proposed we head there, John's face tightened into an expression I couldn't read.

"It's a little pricey, isn't it?"

"Not for lunch, surely."

Still, he hesitated.

"But Dr. Watson," I said, with mock formality, "you deserve to celebrate your success in style, don't you?"

His face softened again, with what looked like pleasure and wonderment. "*Our* success, Rosalie. And you're right." He slapped the front of his trousers. "You're *absolutely* right. No one changes the world on a tuna-fish diet."

At the hotel, he made a big show of introducing himself and me to the maître d' and to the manager who stopped by our table. He explained to anyone who would listen that we were having a business lunch, celebrating some good news.

Waiting for our veal cutlets, we reviewed the progress of my dart-and-target study. I had completed two parts so far. In one, I instructed dart players to practice daily for two months, then had them throw darts once per hour from 8 A.M. to 8 P.M. Their abilities did not change significantly as the day wore on, suggesting no changes in diurnal efficiency. In another part of the study, I had taken less-trained players and had them throw a dart every two minutes for twenty-four hours, the last four with the added variable of various drugs. (John, a natural guinea pig, dosed himself with strychnine, cocaine, and whiskey—not all at the same time—and reported no ill effects.) For the first four hours, shooting steadily improved, then became less efficient. At the end of the study—and yes, our merry little group of volunteers had progressed from giddy to tired—the group was shooting no better than in the beginning. There was no point in practicing something beyond a certain point, in other words.

"The logical next step . . ."

I had trailed off, but John didn't notice. He was in his own world.

"He really did respond well, in that last session," he said.

"Which subject?" I was still thinking about darts.

"Albert. A textbook demonstration."

"Of something that hasn't yet appeared in any textbook, but which soon will."

He allowed himself a glimmer of unrestrained joy, but then his expression changed.

"If the next stages go as well. That's what takes us to the next step. No more needing to make up fairy tales or force people to recline on couches, musing about their own unpredictable emotional reactions."

"They won't be unpredictable anymore."

"Precisely."

"It's very exciting," I said, authentically eager, and willingly releasing my need to talk about the darts, adult learning, my dissertation in process. Because he was right. He was always right. This was something the public would be eager to know—even more than how a room of giddy graduate students did at dart-throwing after staying up all night and drinking hard liquor.

"I need this, Rosalie," he said. "*We* need this."

He looked at me, for something: assurance, permission, further encouragement.

"Your reputation is assured, John."

He managed a half smile.

"You just got a big raise. Surely, it's enough?"

It wasn't. Life was expensive. Life with a wife and mistress, even more so.

When I offered to pay for lunch, John responded with less surprise and offense than a good many men would, but still, he insisted upon sliding out the individual bills from his billfold with care. I wasn't particularly sensitive, in those days, either to what things cost or how it might make a man feel, when he couldn't afford to be a gentleman. There was some bit of negotiation with the waiter and manager at the end, settled just as I was returning from the powder room, but it was no trouble. He hadn't brought quite enough money, but they were setting up a special account for him, seeing how much we'd enjoyed the meal and might return on a regular basis, to continue celebrating the many laboratory successes sure to come.

Passing in the hallway the following Tuesday, John said, "So we're on, then, Saturday at Eutaw Place. Dinner for five. It's an odd number but I trust you'll make do."

I had an armload of files, a lock of hair free from my hair ribbon, falling over one eye. "Would it be better if I brought my own date, to make it six?"

He reached out a finger and pushed the hair back, tucking it behind my ear. "You wouldn't do that."

"Maybe I would," I said, egged on by his mischievous streak, wanting to equal him in self-assurance. But my attempt to be playful only made him put on a woebegone expression.

"You're getting back at me for that day in the office—for me saying that you were too old for me."

"What if I am?"

He moved closer, so that we were standing barely inches apart, so that he could speak softly, words rolling down the slope of his shoulder, into my ear. If someone passed, it would look like an almost normal conversation, our hands not touching, our bodies not quite facing each other.

"That was brutal for me, Rar," he whispered, using my college nickname, which I'd finally divulged to him.

"Was it?" I believed him, but I wanted to hear him say it, to make up for those many weeks I had pined, alone and confused.

"Stop teasing me, now. It hurt me to say those words. But I had to make sure that this was something you wanted."

"Of course I'm sure."

"I want to make love to you."

The way he could say it—so plainly, so nakedly and soberly, and not in the heat of passion or in some dark corner but standing here, in the most inappropriate public place, only made the words more stimulating.

"All right."

My mouth was dry. The files in my arms were heavy. I shifted to rebalance them.

"I want to see you. All of you."

I looked around—there was no one in the hall, but at any moment, someone could come around the corner, or open a door.

"I want to make love to you in the light," he insisted.

I lowered my voice. "We'll see about that. The light part."

"No, darling, it's important. Nudity is completely natural."

Later, he would tell me about a friend of his who was starting a summer camp. Boys and girls. All naked on an island. Like little monkeys running around, completely unembarrassed. He would ask me what I thought, testing my attitudes, trying to root out any latent Victorianisms. I envisioned pine needles stuck to narrow, sweaty rumps, and mosquito bites in awkward places, and girls falling painfully while rock-hopping and boys grabbing after each other's tiny penises. It sounded inconvenient, more than anything.

But what I told him now—the good student, the giving lover—was, "I'll learn to be more comfortable."

"That's a girl." He inhaled deeply and then said so softly I could barely make out the words, "You'll never know how much I hate the weekends. If I could see you seven days a week—if we could live at the lab—I'd be a happier and more productive man, ten times over."

He wanted to be with me at the North Pole, where the days were twenty-four hours long. If we could be together six days a week, he'd be twice as happy. But if we were together seven days, he'd be ten times as happy. I adored his ridiculous quantifications and schoolboy softheartedness.

"And you'd still make me fit in some lab work during all those sunlit hours," I said now.

"Well, why wouldn't I?"

"Tell me again," I said, "What you would do with me at the North Pole, to pass those long Arctic days."

In reply, he leaned down further, his lips ticklishly close to my ear, and said things I'd never heard him say—things I'd never heard *any* man say. He used long, Latin words I didn't know existed for various maneuvers I had imagined a man and a woman technically might be able to do, if they were limber and unselfconscious, but wasn't sure anyone really did do, outside of an ancient Indian text or modern red-light district. He broke down, step by step, a description of an erotic procedure I was sure wasn't common, or legal. My cheeks were burning.

"And at that moment, if you are very good, and if you say please . . ." he began to whisper, his eyes shining at the thought of bringing me to a place of gratifying discomfort, and then making me wait to discover an older man's secrets, his tricks for bringing the uninitiated to pleasure. But as his whispering had intensified, I had squeezed my knees together and at the same time tried to shift the files once more, to contain and rebalance them, and at that moment they all slid, slowly at first and then into a chaotic blizzard of papers, all over the floor.

As I struggled to pick them up, grimacing at the confused mess, he handed me one fallen file folder and glanced at his wristwatch.

"That's all right," I said. "Go ahead."

"It's just that Meyer is expecting me. Five-minute chat, before we gather back at the testing room."

"That's fine. Go." I took a few breaths, arms shaky. "I'll be there."

"We'll finish this little talk soon, I promise."

"You and your 'little talks,'" I said, but I was smiling.

I plopped down on my knees to better sweep all the muddled papers into a single pile, while the sound of his footsteps faded. Then I was alone, with a messy filing job to do, and my heart beating still too quickly, and a feeling of damp between my legs, and an exquisite and exasperating ache.

So this was what the big deal was about: the context for a third or more of all human behaviors.

Any day now, I fully expected him to seduce me in his office, but in truth, I didn't want it to be there. I could still picture Essie and her lifted skirt and ivory girdle, up against the filing cabinet, and maybe other nurses before her.

I wanted a fresh start for us. And just as John had his own ideas about how and in what conditions sexual intercourse should take place, so did I. Not that we didn't grab an intimate moment where we could. Yes, when we turned a corner in a stairwell, or closed the door in his office, the sound of a nurse advancing toward the door even as I stood with the doorknob digging into my hip, or the flickering shadow of a mailboy's passing feet, the sound of Curt calling out in the main room, or another Hopkins researcher or visiting academic friend—Kubie, Knight, Leslie—coming looking for John. Those moments were brief, and we cursed the limitations. But John must have known, even if I didn't. It's the limitations that arouse us most.

Meanwhile, we were drowning in data. We'd breezed through so many infant trials—not just our two satisfactory trials so far with Albert, but dozens of one-time tests with all the other babies, investigating a wide range of unconditioned responses. John wanted each finished sequence translated into a publishable paper, as soon as possible. I had my own learning experiments, to be continued after the completion of our Albert work. John wanted help polishing letters to editors and drafts of speeches, and help procuring and reviewing more papers for the psych journal he was helping to run, which had been interrupted by the war, trying to get it back on a regular publishing schedule again. It was because of our efficient partnership that John continued to take on more than he'd ever taken on before. It was because the experiments were going so well—and they needed to go well, he reminded me, they absolutely had to go well—that John could manage to be both sexually frustrated and yet still professionally energized, able to delay the full consummation of our union.

Of course, it hadn't been even two full weeks since our first consensual kiss, the one I'd initiated. But already it felt like a lifetime. I couldn't imagine that for four months we'd held back, when it was obvious that this was where things were leading—where things had always been leading, since the first day I'd watched him step up to the lecture podium, the man that every girl and woman in that room had been pining over. And I'd won him. John always said that the only things that mattered were those that could be measured, but this couldn't be measured: my luck, my longing, my infatuation.

As a woman, I'd never imagined such heights of happiness: of being both so wanted and so needed, my mind equally filled with our scientific tasks and, during the briefest of pauses or delays, immediately shifted onto a different daydreaming track, reenacting in my mind the latest moment of fondling and heavy breathing, teasing descriptions and tender endearments. When you are in love for the first time, when sex and all of its antecedents are fresh and new, your mind simply can't leave it alone. In the absence of the act itself, the lingering sensory impressions are dizzying.

And also, sex aside, if there's anything I was learning about the nature of human contentment, it was that we are happiest when we are occupied, completely occupied. The flirting and lovemaking—or even more distracting, the deferred lovemaking—were part of our shared bliss, no doubt. But it was the work, too, that made us fly through each day, always ready to take on more. It was being fully and busily absorbed, together.

I was still in the hallway, alone, picking up papers, and wondering what the hotel rooms at the Regent were like, and how one registered, if there was a way to do so discreetly. It would be reckless to stay overnight there—my Bearcat and both of our faces so recognizable by now, since we'd already had lunch in the Regent's dining room twice.

"Rosalie?"

I was so absorbed that Georgie, with her slow gait and heavy foot-step, had managed to sneak up on me. "I'm waiting for you."

I was supposed to be somewhere. What time was it?

"In the testing lab?" Georgie said, with a smirk in her voice. "With Albert?"

"I'm sorry, Georgie," I said, and tried to fix a stern expression on my face, as though I'd been crouched there intentionally, not only picking up scattered papers but mentally engrossed—multiplying sums, for example—when in fact, the only thing I was tallying was how many more days a man should be expected to stay with a wife he couldn't tolerate.

CHAPTER 12

Our session that day with Albert went well, even if I was distracted, thinking not only back to my hallway moment with John, but also ahead to the dinner that Sunday, when he'd be coming to my parents' house with Mary. The room was, as always, small, and the menagerie of animals made it feel more crowded yet. We verified first that Albert was still afraid of the rat. He also showed a strong fear response to a brown rabbit ("a most convincing test," we'd report in the final paper, later), to a short-haired dog, and to a sealskin coat. A package of white cotton elicited only a mild response. In a spirit of play, John lowered his head and let Albert run his fingers, still sticky from sucking, through his hair. Albert didn't mind. Nor did he mind when I moved my hair into his reach.

The generalization of the fear response, from furry rat to furry rabbit, dog, and coat was satisfying, but overall, the responses were mixed. Even so, that day, John didn't look antsy or disappointed, pushing too hard for certain desired results. I'd like to think he was as buoyed by thoughts of me as I by thoughts of him. It was hard to imagine our shared life as scientists would ever be anything but this: the successes shared, the unexceptional results made less disappointing, the truly significant discoveries celebrated. It was hard to believe there would come a day when I would not bring him joy, when he would not accept a modest outcome, when he would not retract an outrageous statement that might be hurtful. We were happy, that's all: productive and happy, and hurting no one.

The night the Watsons were expected at dinner, John arrived on foot, thirty minutes early, confounding my hostess mother, who was upstairs and trying to fix, with Bertha's help, a series of rhinestone hairpins into her upswept hair. Over our heads Mother could be heard calling out with effortful gaiety, fussing and apologizing at top volume, and in a hushed but still audible voice, issuing last-minute commands. "The hothouse flowers, they're still on the sink. Careful Bertha, you're piercing my scalp."

My father, who had been finishing his newspaper, ushered John into our parlor and provided a refreshment. I delayed my own entrance, lurking in the dining room on the opposite side of the hall, waiting for my overexcited heartbeat to settle. In the front parlor, John was saying, "No, of course we don't enjoy bothering babies. But you know, they're nowhere near as frail as the average person thinks. A hammered steel bar: how is that more damaging than a crash of thunder? Time away from a suffocating mother—well, that's a blessing at any age. If anything, infants are *made* to be frail by individuals without any interest in scientific parenting. Society's goal should be to make modern children *more* independent of their family situations."

"Speak of the devil. Here's my own independent child," said Father, noticing me standing at the threshold. He slapped his knees, as if he expected me to come and sit on his lap. Out of habit, I went to give him a kiss on the cheek and then stopped myself, several feet away, my hands behind my back, feeling like a schoolgirl in my plain blue dress and flat shoes.

"Good afternoon, Rosalie," John said, not bothering to rise.

"Good afternoon, Dr. Watson."

"I'm just a few minutes early. I hope you and your parents don't mind."

At first I thought John's arrival was a mischievous trick on his part, sneaking into our home early to catch everyone at their natural behaviors, all the better for a thorough investigation of me, his true love. But when I saw how quickly he sucked dry his glass and heard him explaining, in too much detail, how he loved a healthy walk and how Mrs. Watson preferred a drive—they didn't own a motor car, but she'd arranged to borrow a friend's vehicle, and a driver—and how difficult it could be to time their joint arrivals, I changed my mind. They must have been fighting. Something had come up at the last minute and he had stalked out, while she had gone on some errand without him, and he had simply had no patience for dawdling in the park in front of our house, when what he really wanted was a damn drink—preferably something stronger than the legal red punch my father had made available.

"And of course, Mrs. Watson had to stop by to pick something up. She isn't one to come empty-handed," John explained, halting his explanation when my mother entered the room. At the sight of her in the doorway, he bounded to his feet. She hurried forward and reached out to clasp his hands and hold him there, like a dancing partner, letting go only for the briefest moment to move her grip farther up, to his forearms, in that square-on near-embrace she reserved for people she was truly eager to meet.

"Oh no, no. Mrs. Watson can't bring anything, especially if it's an inconvenience. Absolutely not."

"Well, she already is, and Mary is unstoppable, I'm afraid."

"Dr. Watson," she said, looking at him again, unwilling to give up her grip on his sleeves. "It's been one half of a year that I've wanted to stand with you here in this very room."

My father, standing behind them both, started to lower himself back into his chair, looking to me for permission, which I granted with a quick nod.

"I'm ashamed at the delay," Mother continued. "But I feel like I know you already. And I'm so, so very pleased."

"Mutually," John said, his entire face ablaze with pleasure. "Mutually."

John liked to be liked. Certainly, he also liked competition and argument. But that came later. First was the pleasure of an openhearted dose of—no, not just affection, but *respect*, which both my parents were doling out lavishly, in greater supply than he'd ever received from Mary's family.

Later, when my mother took her own chair, she pressed John about my role in the lab. "You've done such a favor, allowing Rosalie to help."

"The favor's to me," John said, "She's the best assistant I've ever had."

My father winked at me, excess pride making his eyes glassy. He was more prone to emotion even than my mother, who was distracted anyway, with all of her attention turned toward John. She sat near the edge of her seat, feet crossed at the ankles, head and shoulders and well-bound bosom all pressed forward in the service of demonstrating concentration and interest. She'd stored up a dozen smart questions for John—about science, about funding, and about his behavioral recommendations to the military. I'd been worried about my part in the day's conversations, about what pose I should strike in order to give nothing away. But so far, I couldn't have added a word if I'd wanted to.

Then we heard Agnus at the door. Mrs. Mary Watson had arrived, with a driver standing behind her, holding a large white box that Agnus took and shepherded to the kitchen, allowing the driver to turn and leave with a touch of his cap. (Drivers usually came around back, separated from their passengers, but then again, I couldn't recall any guest who wasn't a close relative ever arriving with a culinary item.)

In the entryway, where we all hurried to gather, Mother radiated anxiety—where were the cut flowers? Had Annie still not put out the flowers?

Mary Watson stood in the hall, looking up and around: pert nose, fair heart-shaped face surrounded by a high bob of permanent-waved brown curls. She was pretty. Eyes tired, and with a downward slant at the outer corners that made her look like she was slightly sad, or shy. But undeniably pretty. Frank shuffled into the hallway and took Mary's fur-collared coat. She shrugged out of it without even looking at him, her eyes still diverted up and around, over all of our heads: the winding staircase, the large hall.

When I took her small hand quickly, introducing myself, she returned a quick, warm smile.

"My," she said, looking not at me, but past me. "Well, my. What would you call this?"

Father looked confused.

"The architectural style, I mean."

"Oh, it's just home sweet home," Mother said.

"Richardsonian Romanesque, actually," Father said. "If you're interested in buildings."

She took her time, fixed to that spot, clearly captivated. Since our Friday dinners and Sunday brunches were most often attended by family and extended family, which included a fair part of the neighborhood, it had been a long time since I'd seen our house through anyone else's eyes. Eutaw Place had many fine homes, but it was true, ours was at the top of the street, one of the largest and finest.

"Just around the corner," Mary said to my parents, "I saw the most impressive church."

"Yes? It's a lovely edifice," Mother said, more than willing to play along.

"It's a synagogue, actually," Father said.

Mary turned all her attention to him. "Is it?"

"This house was built four years after its completion," he said. "The entire neighborhood was farmland not so long ago."

"Well," she said, still having trouble communicating her admiration. "I've never been up here. It's sort of another Bolton Hill, isn't it?"

My father just smiled, not explaining that until just recently, our people would have been excluded from neighborhoods like Bolton Hill, which is why this separate neighborhood of millionaires' mansions had been built. We never called our house a mansion, of course. But I could see it confirmed in her eager, wanting eyes: it *was* a mansion. My father had worked to earn it. As had several other siblings and cousins, who had built houses next to ours, and farther down the street. Our family had come far in just a few generations. If she'd imagined my upbringing was hardscrabble, like John's, if she'd thought my own father was some sort of bourbon-swilling, hard-luck farmer, like Pickens Butler Watson, she was wrong.

Mary, gloves in one hand, thin-lipped smile unreadable, tipped her face and looked at me, ready to focus now, to understand who I was, to know how John's new graduate assistant fit into all this: whatever she'd heard, whatever she was now seeing.

"I'll go help with the flowers," I said, suddenly desperate to disappear.

"Oh yes," Mother said. "Bring a vase into the parlor, Rosalie, if you wouldn't mind. And tell Annie she can come in to serve."

I walked away from the sounds of contrition and mirth, as Mother teased my father for having allowed himself refreshments before the guests had all arrived, as Father shared the blame with John, as John in turn teased Mary for her separate arrival, and as all of them continued speaking in stage voices—a little louder, with clearer articulation— than any of them would use when they'd gotten to know each other better. It was clear even in those first moments, in the way they all hurried to laugh, compliment, and talk over each other that they were all on their best behavior, and all genuinely pleased to be together, in a strange confluence of mutual desires and anxieties I hadn't predicted.

My mother had tired of the social circles she'd relied upon in the years just after we'd settled on Eutaw Place: the philanthropy committees and neighborhood beautification clubs and women's self-improvement leagues. On top of it all, my older sister had moved away, and nearly all my college friends lived in distant cities, leaving our house less busy and cheerful than Mother would have liked. Mary Watson, too, seemed to have a less-than-full dance card, perhaps because her own tense marriage had resulted in a few too many canceled dinner parties, or because their strained budget limited attendance at various events, the places she wanted to attend in order to meet the right people. I'd wanted them to get along. I didn't think they'd get along this well, this soon, this desperately.

In the kitchen, Annie stared down into the open white box with her chin tucked into her neck, repulsion wrinkling her features.

"I can't serve this," she said.

"What did she bring?"

Annie leaned down into the box and sniffed. "I know where it came from: right down the block. But I don't know what she was thinking."

I hurried over and leaned down, too. A sweet smell I recognized from certain Baltimore street corners: seafood, corn bread, all mashed together in thick round disks.

"Are they good?" I asked her.

"They're tasty. But I'm not about to put them on your mother's china."

"No, of course not."

"Did that woman think we wouldn't be serving enough food to tide her over?"

"I don't know what she was thinking. I don't think she realized we were Jewish—or maybe she just doesn't know what that means."

My mother entered at the moment and came over to stand between us, hand soft against the small of my back.

"Mrs. Watson just told me. I made an excuse and said I was

hurrying up the punch refills. So here it is. Crab, in my kitchen. That's a first."

"You want me to dump it out back?" asked Annie.

"Heavens, no," my mother said, with a shrill laugh.

"It hasn't touched anything yet," I reminded her. "Maybe she didn't intend us to serve it with dinner. Maybe it's just a gift, because she was embarrassed about being late."

"She wasn't late," my mother said, already defending her new female friend. "Your Dr. Watson was half an hour *early*." She stood back, setting her shoulders in a posture of reconciliation. "Anyway, we don't keep a kosher kitchen. Not entirely. We've been bending the rules since you were born."

Maybe beef from the wrong butcher, on occasion. But not like this: not pork or shellfish. Not Baltimore crab. Not *trayf*.

Mother said firmly, "We're modern people and there's nothing to apologize about."

Annie turned and stared at Mother's face. She didn't need any theology, just directions. What to serve, and when, and on which dishes.

"Put them on the small dishes with the silver rims," Mother said.

Annie objected, "But they don't match the set I was planning to use for the roast."

"That's no matter," my mother said, trying to smile. "I've always been curious about crab cakes."

She left the room, and Annie looked around for Frank, who had been watching us from a corner, leaned up against the back counter with one big black work shoe lifted slightly and crossed over his better leg at the ankle, working a fragment of a walnut out of a half shell with a small pocketknife.

"Wash your hands first," Annie directed him. "Then reach me down those silver-rim plates."

He washed, went to find the small step stool, and laboriously set it up underneath the correct cabinet, with Annie watching him and me watching Annie, a knot of unhappiness lodged in my throat. All these years of keeping separate dishes, and now my own mother—yes, Reform and mostly secular of mind, but still—was going to let a Baltimore crab cake sit on her china?

Annie kept shaking her head back and forth. "Driver coming to the front door. White box full of nothing we need here."

Frank climbed each step slowly and balanced at the top of the stool. "You want the plates or you don't want the plates?"

"I didn't say I don't want the plates," Annie rebuked him. "Hurry up now before you fall off that stool."

"We could just leave them in the icebox," I tried. "There's no rule about eating whatever a guest brings. If it doesn't complement the dinner, it's downright odd."

Annie turned to look at me, chin jutting. Her sourness faded into a smug grin. "Look here who's the voice of tradition. Thought it would be your mama, but it's you."

"That's not it," I said. "It's just that—it's an insult to you. After all, you planned this meal with Mother. You cooked it. And you've made more than enough courses already."

"Oh, that's it," Annie smiled. "It's the insult to me you're all choked up about."

"Annie, one doesn't just change things on a whim."

"Sometimes," she said, "I think the only way things change is on a whim."

"Change," I countered in a firm voice, "should be a logical, measured, reasoned decision, at the very least. And, and—I don't appreciate how you're talking to me, like I'm a child."

"Miss Rosalie, you *are* a child."

"I'm twenty-one," I said.

"You can ride around in your canary-colored machine, wind in your hair, strange man in your passenger seat, but your Mama and your Daddy are supposed to live like their people. Old-fashioned."

Man in my passenger seat? We'd only gone to lunch twice. Or three times. How did Annie know about that? My face must have betrayed my panic.

"Honey, you think every time you're driving around in that loud, bright automobile, every person in town isn't noticing?" She chuckled to herself, narrow frame shaking with the pleasure. "Crab cakes ain't nothing compared to what you're up to."

I took my place out in the dining room, directly opposite Mary, throat tight, acid inching up from my gut, with Annie's words ringing in my ears. Mary knew. She had to. But no, I thought—not even tasting the consommé that Agnus and Annie brought out first. I ladled it quietly into my mouth, one shallow spoonful at a time, a reasonable excuse to avoid conversation. Mary couldn't possibly know. Look how happy she was!

When the crab cakes were brought in—looking down, I missed that first moment when my parents each took a taste—the conversation turned to differences between Atlantic coast life and the Middle West, Chicago in particular, where Mary and John had first met.

"And how did you come to Chicago, if you weren't born there?" Mother asked.

"I was sent there to live with relatives, when my mother died," Mary said brightly, earning my mother's cooing condolences in response. Orphans' tales never failed to excite Mother's sympathy.

Opposite her, my father made a sort of closed-mouth, gargling sound—a less skilled note of condolence, I thought at first. But then I realized it was the food he was reacting to. The possibility of what he was tasting had just hit him, and he lifted the napkin to his mouth, coughing.

"That's so tragic. You poor dear," my mother said to Mary, at high volume, eyes widening as Father turned in his chair, face hidden in his napkin.

"Tickle in the throat," my mother explained loudly on his behalf. "Don't eat so fast, dear."

His hand darted up in silent apology and he started to rise from his chair, napkin still over his mouth. Mother's eyes tracked to the doorway, urging him to get as far away from the dining room as possible. When he was safely around the corner, she nearly shrieked with relief, "What a wet winter we've had!"

"Lousy, hasn't it been?" Mary agreed, head cocked, cheeks rosy. She did look like a film star, like someone who might have been discovered on a street corner.

"Terrible!" mother agreed explosively. "Terrible for the lungs. But you were saying, Mary, about your poor mother. And your father, it was too much for him?"

"You don't have to worry about Mary," John said at his wife's elbow, food in his mouth, focused on shoveling. "Children are more independent than you'd think. Mary was no different. When I first met her, she was a spitfire."

"When John first showed up at the University of Chicago," Mary said, beaming as she turned toward him, fingers brushing the back of his hand, "he had to talk his way in. And he had to work for his tuition. As a janitor, isn't that right?"

I could see from the way his grip tightened around the fork that he didn't care for the janitor bit, not in front of people he'd just met, though it was true. "Nothing wrong with work."

"Absolutely not," my mother said. And then, celebrating the swift maneuver with which Annie slid my mother's barely touched plate of crab cake away from the table, banishing the last traces of that awkward second course, my mother said it again. "*Absolutely* not. You're an American success story, the two of you. What's his name? Rosalie, it's at the tip of my tongue."

Horatio Alger. But I didn't have time to say it.

"John was the youngest-ever PhD in Psychology from the University of Chicago," Mary enthused.

"Is *that* right?"

John—never averse to flattery, even from his own wife—smiled at this. The weight of their backstory, the ineradicable shared heritage of some fifteen years, nearly as long as my own life on this earth, bore down upon me. If I lifted my heels off the floor and pointed my toes, I might just slip under the table—*bump, bump*, until silently and mournfully prostrate on the oriental rug laid over the parquet flooring—and not be missed at all.

When my father returned at last, my mother turned toward him, inhaling deeply. He settled into his chair and took a long swallow of water, clearing his throat again.

"I have to say," he paused, "this is a little awkward . . ."

My mother lifted her chin, erect torso an inch from the edge of the tablecloth, shoulders pressed back. She glanced over at me with a tense smile.

"Father," I said, trying to help, "It looks like you lost your napkin. Do you need me to get a fresh one from Annie?"

He blinked once, shaking off my trivial interruption. "A little awkward," he started again, "not knowing your own inclinations or your feeling on the temperance issue, Mary. But I'll be honest. The next course would taste much better with a glass of wine."

Mary giggled. Actually giggled. "Or a few glasses, even."

"Lovely!" my mother called out, grasping the tinkly little bell at the table's corner—the bell that was mostly for show, since Agnus, Bertha, Annie, or Frank nearly always sensed our needs ahead of schedule and didn't often need to be roused. Annie came loping in, looking startled, with Frank at her heels.

I was the only one embarrassed: by the little bell, and even more, by the transparent desperation for liquor. "Four glasses, Frank," my father ordered, jumping up from his seat, "and I'll get the bottle myself. I've got something or other stored away."

Something or other. He had a perfectly good cellar, as did any other self-respecting Baltimorean who entertained.

Mary had caught the tally of the glasses. "I don't think I could take a sip if Rosalie didn't. You're not a teetotaler, are you, darling?"

"I tolerate a drop, now and again."

"Oh good," Mary said, clapping her small hands together. "If it's to be a party, we can't have anyone left out. And the first toast must go to Rosalie. I thought the lab was doing well before, but it was nothing compared to what it's been this winter. I haven't seen my husband this productive in years. And the second toast must go to John . . ."

She paused for effect, an effect that John and I noticed, and I counted my breaths, though my mother remained smiling, unaware.

"To John," Mary continued, though Father wasn't even back with the bottle. "Who recently got a raise, which we've never toasted properly."

John stabbed her with a look, which I took to mean, *Can you stop referring to money?*

But Mary only took it further. "And when you get the next raise, soon, when you're paid what you truly deserve, then we'll have a party. A wonderful party. Won't we, John? And our new friends can come."

After dinner and a postprandial drink in the opposite parlor, there was a final, customary tour of the house. Mary insisted she was fascinated by architecture, and she seemed determined to win over my father with increasingly detailed questions.

"You must know just everything about buildings," Mary purred.

Father looked down at his feet. "Maybe a thing or two."

John said that due to the prolonged renovation of the Phipps Clinic, he'd been on enough building inspections to last him a lifetime. "Go ahead, Mary. Fill me in later."

"Oh he's just tired," Mary winked. "Too many late nights at the lab. I guess that's just his constitution, but you better watch he doesn't overwork your daughter."

At the foot of the winding staircase, Mary pushed her hand into the crook of my father's arm, like a bride preparing to commence to the altar, while my flustered father—what on earth was that expression on his face?—jolted to attention.

Glancing up the staircase, Mother said, "I'll leave you with the expert, Mary."

But father turned stiffly, grinning over his shoulder. "No, no. It's all for one, and one for all."

"Yes, Mother, do go," I said, the only energy left in me heightened by sudden pangs of suspicious alarm, not only about what Mary seemed to know but by what she seemed willing to do, in the spirit of getting even. The dazzled look in my father's eyes whenever she addressed him was making me sick.

Up they went, Mary and Father in front, Mother trailing behind, to study the details on the upper hallway moldings.

"Now this," I could hear Mary say from the upper landing, with crisp articulation, as if she were in a speech class or play, "reminds me of the hotel downtown, the new one?"

"I haven't been," my mother said. "Do they have a good lunch service?"

"You should ask Rosalie," Mary said brightly.

The Regent. Where John and I had been going for lunch. The hotel where—and I balled one fist and felt the fingernails bite into my palm—we certainly wouldn't be going again.

Mary explained. "John takes all the lab staff out for lunch, on occasion. To keep the spirits up. It's the least he should do, considering the hours he imposes. I hear they serve a beautiful Sunday brunch. I keep asking John to take me, but he hasn't yet."

But no, she couldn't be rambling just for my benefit. Was it for his? John's face didn't tell me anything. He was only staring moodily at the empty fireplace, hands in his suit-pants pockets, no sign of reaction to her words.

They were still up there: How many light fixtures and mold-ings could there be at the top of stairs, anyway? But now they were talking about my father's other building projects. I heard his low, usu-ally humble voice becoming more formal as he responded to Mary's interest in beachside resort construction and hooks and spits and alongshore currents and sediment and storm damage and the new automobile bridge to Ocean City, on the Maryland coast.

"You haven't been?" I heard my father ask, incredulous. "Well, you should go."

"We should *all* go," Mary declared, then lowered her voice to ask something I couldn't quite make out.

In response, my mother sounded surprised at first—slightly off-put, but acquiescent, then warming to some idea. "They're just ordinary bedrooms, but I suppose it couldn't hurt. So you're planning a redeco-ration of your own home?"

My eyes dropped from the ceiling down to my feet when Annie trundled into the room with a large circular tray, loading it with emp-tied liqueur glasses. She glanced at me, then to the ceiling again.

"You've got gardens out back?" John asked in a flat voice.

"A few herbs. Nicer flower gardens in the front, where people can see them," I said. "Logically."

"Gardens all the way down the street," he said, with what I took to be sarcasm. "A little Versailles."

"That's right," I said, not appreciating his tone. "That's exactly right. It was a very nice place to grow up."

He looked a little taken aback by the sharpness of my retort, and he turned his head, looking thirstily around the room—but the last of the glasses had been removed. "I'm sure it was."

The chandelier's crystal teardrops danced as the tour proceeded heavily through my bedroom, overhead. I was tired. I wanted everyone gone so that I could crawl upstairs and burrow under the covers.

"So, what's in the back?"

"Not much. Used to be a coachhouse. Now it's a garage."

"We're thinking of adding a garage."

"I thought you didn't even own a car."

Annie walked out but she was still within earshot, in the dining room opposite, clearing the table. She'd be busy for a while yet, changing the tablecloth and putting salt and pepper cellars in the cabinet and pulling aside the candlesticks to polish—the tasks she did, drawers opening and closing, sighs audible, when guests were taking an unusually long time to leave.

"I could use a cigarette," he said.

"Suit yourself."

He lowered his voice. "Outside. Show me the garage, will you, Rosalie?"

Just go home already, I wanted to say, hearing the low rumble of my father's laughter upstairs, the little duet of ladies' laughter in response.

We were barely down the dark narrow hallway and out the back door when he grabbed me by the wrist and swung me around, pressing me up against the cold brick wall, knee cocked up and pinned against my leg, tongue plunged so insistently into my mouth that for a moment, I couldn't catch my breath.

I pushed him away. "I thought you were mad at me."

"Mad at you?"

"From the way you've barely talked to me all day. And you're in love with her. I can see it."

He recoiled. "*What* can you see? She's intent on tormenting me."

He threw his head back: one silent guffaw. When I leaned in, studying his expression, wanting desperately for more explanation, something to hold on to, he pushed his tongue into my mouth again, and this time I let him for a moment, and then tugged away, squirming under his arm, smoothing my dress into place. My teeth were chattering. We hadn't pulled on any coats. And there was a smell—a fishy smell. I looked around and saw, at the edge of the wall, the flick of an alley cat's tail, black triangular feline head down, gorging on something Annie had set out in a wide metal bowl. The cat looked up, legs tensed and ready to spring, with the remains of crab cakes flecking its whiskers. The cat was thin except for a dragging pouch at its midsection, a belly full of kittens, the weight of which pulled the back fur tighter over her knobby spine. When she went back to eating, the soft sound of the cat's overeager scavenging turned my own stomach, but there was something else aside from revulsion—that smell of sex and desperation in the air.

When John lunged for another kiss, I whispered, "Anyone could wander out here and see us."

"Show me the garage," he demanded again, his motivations pathetically clear.

I took another step back and craned my neck to try to see into the second-story windows over our heads.

"Why is she so interested in our bedrooms?"

"She's interested in everything about you and your family."

"Is she only pretending to like my parents?"

"I think she likes them very much," he said, voice growing huskier again. "And they like her. Nearly everyone likes her—at first."

He put his hand against the wall, blocking me again, body moving up against mine—a pocket of delicious heat as he pressed into me, stopping my teeth from chattering. "John, she knows, doesn't she?"

"She makes wild guesses."

"And . . . ?"

"And she likes to play games."

He stopped pawing finally, like a frantic animal that had just wanted one long drink and could now settle, wrapping his arms around me, both of us flat against the house, the rough wall at my back. He squeezed and I squeezed back, feeling simple relief. It didn't matter how adorable she was, or how long they'd been together. He did not love her even for a moment.

"So why did you let her come?" I asked finally.

"Because she truly wanted to. And so did I. To find any way to spend more time with you. Every second away from the lab, I'm miserable."

In the hallway, John and Mary made their formal goodbyes—Mary garrulous and repetitive, John reticent and unreadable. At the last minute, he said, "And I'll see you tomorrow, Rosalie. In the lab."

Mary and my mother said it almost simultaneously: "On a Sunday?"

I looked at them, and then at John, flustered. This was no ruse, although now that I'd actually met Mary, I was prepared to feel guilty even when we weren't doing anything wrong. Everything would be harder now that I could picture her charming face and imagine her silver-bell voice. The thing was: we really were scheduled to work on Sunday. We had our second-to-last session with Albert scheduled, and we had determined it should be five days from the last one, just as the last two had been spaced five days apart, and that simply happened to make this session fall on a Sunday. No one else working for the lab seemed to mind.

"See?" Mary said, only to Mother, who had spent plenty of her own Sundays deprived of a husband's company, when he was off motoring along the coast, inspecting a real estate investment.

Mother shook her head in shared exasperation. "These modern professionals. They lose sight of the important things sometimes, don't you think?"

Later that night at supper, hours after the Watsons had finally left, we all sat, quiet and listless, since any typical family meal, especially a small one, is bound to seem unspirited after a dinner party. I could have gone without eating yet again, but I didn't want to give any indication that things were out of the ordinary.

Father looked up, soupspoon halfway to his mouth, deep red broth just at the point of spilling over the spoon's edge and back into the bowl.

"Lillian Gish," he announced.

My mother asked, "The film star?"

"*That's* who she looks like."

I glanced to my mother, who did not ask who the *she* was, who did not pretend offense or even surprise at the sudden eruption, but only turned down her lips, considering. "The eyes and the rosebud mouth, a little. I can see that. Certainly."

And went back to spooning her own borscht into her mouth.

CHAPTER 13

The next day early, four of us occupied the warm, dark, crowded room, not counting all the animals, in boxes and baskets and on leashes—plus Albert, seated next to me on the thin mattresses.

I presented a rat. He whimpered and withdrew, his reaction less pronounced than the successful session before.

When the stimulus-response pairing was repeated, the sound of the clanging steel made Albert burst into tears. The subject was given the blocks again, followed by the rat. He played and gurgled a little. Even at eleven months, he was not a highly verbal infant, and when he did coo, it was often at an odd time, when he was distressed. We gave him the blocks again.

A brown rabbit was introduced. This produced a mild negative reaction.

We had managed to see a generalized response, the week prior, to the rabbit and the dog, but we had not yet tried to create a direct response, coordinated with the disturbing sound. We presented the rabbit, and when Albert was in contact with its fur, John clanged the steel rod. In my notes I wrote: *Violent fear reaction.*

The rabbit was presented again. *Leaning, whimpering, not as violent.*
Rabbit yet again: *Hands held up, whimpering.*

We presented the dog. Albert shook his head side to side, keeping his hands pulled as far away from the dog as he could manage.

Another joint stimulation: dog plus clanging steel. *Whimpering, violent reaction, up on all fours and trying to crawl away.*

John decided we should move to a larger, lighter-walled lecture room—I don't recall why. Certainly, it was warm and crowded in the original location, with the animals and the filming equipment and the dog now pacing back and forth in its corner. Typically, one would try not to introduce new changes haphazardly, as I understood experimental design, but John said we should change rooms, and we did, moving all of the needed supplies with us.

John, and Scottie with the camera equipment, and Curt with the dog in one hand and a caged rat in another, had already left the lab room and were moving down the hallway, voices fading. Georgie stayed back, arms loaded with a box containing the steel bar and hammer, Santa Claus mask, and some other effects. I went to help, reaching for a piece of cotton wool that was slipping off the piled items in the box, and when my face was close to hers, she made a quick quarter turn, shoring up the box in her strong arms, and said, "He's been happier the last few weeks. Have you noticed?"

There was no doubt about whom she was speaking, but as for the *why* of her comment, it gave me only a tight-chested feeling, as though she was on some fishing expedition, had just hooked me, and was slowly reeling me in. Her wide hip blocked me from squeezing past. There was no easy way to get around her or to leave the awkward conversation behind. "He's happy with the Albert study," I said, trying to sound both matter-of-fact and firm.

"Is he?"

"Certainly. The ease with which he has conditioned a fear response provides a challenge to Freud's primacy of love."

"Of sex, you mean."

"Yes, love and sex. Erogenous reactions. Still important, but not everything, and not the way Freud frames it, connecting it with suppressed fantasies."

"Hmmmph."

"Anyway," I said, trying to sound brisk, stepping closer to her with an intention to get through the doorway if she would only step aside, "I think he's more than satisfied with the project so far."

It was an odd time to say it, since John had started the day with a cloud hanging over his head. Just in the last five minutes, his mood had soured further, based on Albert's inconsistent responses: turning away, whimpering, not crying at the moments we thought he'd break down easily. We had only one subject, after all, and with that single subject, we had only limited time remaining.

Georgie said, "Mrs. Watson used to be his lab assistant here, you know. There's a paper somewhere around here, with her name on it, next to his. An actual published scientific paper." She took another step, into the doorway, and leaned against the frame with a deep sigh, face turned toward me, over her shoulder. "She did exactly what you do now: catching the babies, writing up the notes, head-to-head with Dr. Watson, the two of them chatting up a storm. But not anymore."

I'd always pictured Mary off elsewhere with society interests, her own hobbies and affiliations, pointedly uninterested in John's work, except for the money it brought in and the higher status it engendered. It didn't do any of us any good to imagine Mary as she was then, or even to understand her as she was now. It didn't help me, certainly.

"Maybe she got tired of helping," I said.

"No, I think she liked it quite a bit. She had a scientific mind, no surprise. Awfully smart. And pretty, too. Reminded me of the film star with the little heart-shaped face, what's her name?"

"Well, Mrs. Watson must have been less busy then."

"She was *more* busy. The children were younger."

"If they were so young, maybe she welcomed the break," I said. "Do you need me to take that box?"

"Just resting a moment."

"I think we'd better catch up with the others, don't you?"

Georgie gave a little heave, boosting up the box again. "Oh, it's a bit heavy for you, dear. Just come along behind."

Come along behind. It can never be a surprise for a younger woman to know she's following in someone else's footsteps: Vida Sutton's, Mary Watson's, nurse Essie's. And for some reason, other women want you to know it—want to prove you're not getting away with it, stepping on some other woman's shadow.

When I got to the larger, lighter-walled testing room, John looked cross.

We ran through the paces again: rat, rabbit, dog, rat again. Albert, looking placid if increasingly tired, watched them scurry, sniff, and hop past him in turn, avoidant but not highly bothered. We had less evidence than we'd had before today. The generalization hypothesis was key, but now he wouldn't even cry at the sight of the rat, the original animal in the stimulus-response pairing.

The rat and the rabbit were back in their baskets, but the dog was still free, snuffling at the bottom of the closed door, tail wagging, and then jumping up to scratch and be let out. Somehow the lead had gotten unclipped. John waved a hand toward Curt, and Curt stepped closer to the dog and squatted down, wrapping his arms around the animal like a harness, scratching behind one of its ears to get it to settle.

Scottie was still running the camera, but he backed his face away from the eyepiece, as if he expected John to say we were done for the day.

"Freshen the reaction," I said, feeling irritable. "Pair the rat and sound again."

John pulled the thumbnail he'd been nibbling out of his mouth. "Again, you think?"

"Yes."

John looked at me with gratitude, like a boy who'd let his balloon slip from his grasp only to have a bystander leap up and catch the very end of the string. Everyone else wanted to go home. "Georgie," John said, "the hammer. Quickly please." She'd been leaning against the wall and now she pushed off with her rump and bent over to retrieve the objects from the box and present them to John. I took the rat out of the basket, dropped it along the edge of the mattress, and gave it a further nudge, pushing it toward the open gap between Albert's legs, but he barely seemed to notice. He kept forgetting his fear. Then he needed a reminder.

I wanted the noise to be loud. I wanted the shrill clang to clean out the room—the sense of disappointment, last night's awkward dinner party, the lingering ghost of a certain previous assistant. I wanted most of all that little Albert would cry, as he was supposed to cry, so we could get on with things.

John, with the hammer in hand, cocked his right arm. At the moment Albert leaned forward, reaching out an exploratory finger, John struck the bar.

The clang sounded. Albert startled.

The rat was presented again. *Whimpering, pulling away, hands up.*

The blocks, again. *Played.*

The rat, again. *Whimpering.*

The rabbit alone, without the sound. *A stronger reaction.* But not strong enough. *Whimpering.*

Twenty-three presentations of animals and objects; whimpering and shuddering, hands up and hands back, tears and recovery, pulling away and reaching out, brief curiosity and violent aversion, acquiescence, recovery, and the *clang-clang-clang-clang* of the steel bar. My head throbbed.

"The dog, again," John said.

Albert put his hands up, without crying, as the dog was dragged by its leash, forcing subject and stimulus into close proximity. Then, just when the dog's face was near Albert's face, it strained against the leash, snout only inches away, and barked. Too loud; too close. Everyone in the room jumped. Georgie cried out. I pushed an arm out to protect myself—myself and little Albert—while the dog got in several more aggressive yaps.

"Get him," John yelled again. "Grab him. The dog. Grab him, damn it!"

Albert had fallen completely to one side with arms and legs splayed in a rictus of abject terror, like a marionette swiftly clipped from its strings. With the barking still echoing off the room's walls, I pulled him toward me. I felt his hot, shuddering body, face and chest slick with tears, dampening my own shirtfront. His fear was so acute, he couldn't get a breath. His sobs were airless, soundless contractions, silent trembling cascades of mucus and tears. Only after Curt had hooked a finger under the dog's collar and pulled it out of the room did Albert finally get a solid breath into him and manage to push it out in a series of shuddering gasps. His small fingers, the untrimmed nails surprisingly sharp, gripped me, and his hot face burrowed. When he finally backed away for one deeper breath, his neck softened. He tilted his face up, looking up at me through puffy, slitted eyes. Whatever he saw—no mother, I; no great supply of nurturing sympathy in this face—did not reassure him. More intelligence than I'd ever seen in his gaze so far, sizing me up accurately and making his decision—that I wasn't to be trusted, but that I was all he had.

Then he fell forward again, turned his head, and pressed it flat against my chest, surrendering to the meager comfort he could find. The breaths came, alternating between smooth and ragged, until they were all even and shallow. A few minutes later, he was asleep.

Meeting her had changed everything, and—I suppose—nothing. At the very least, it was more complicated now, as a clever woman like Mary, who had been through some of this before, would know and use to her advantage. At times I questioned all that John had said to me— that their marriage was essentially over, that he'd never really loved her. She'd said, according to him, that her feelings for him were "anesthetic." Occasionally I doubted what he was telling me, but far more often I believed what he said, recognized her manipulations, and felt more sympathy for him than for anyone. "One of the only honest men you'll ever meet," he'd said about himself. And I thought that was probably true. He was honest to a fault. And consider the person I'd admired before him, Mary Cover: honest as well, brusque to the point of insensitivity. I was consistent in my tastes. I was also reaping what I had sowed.

With the fifth Albert session completed, we had some variation in our lab schedulings. John had decided that our final test on Albert should be in thirty-one days, to ascertain whether the conditioning had continued having an effect, unextinguished by the passage of time. The baby's mother was finishing her wet-nurse contract and would be free to leave the hospital, where they both lived and she worked, a month from now. We might not see him again. In the meanwhile, we had to wait to conclude the experiment, as we seemed to always be waiting, biding our time.

"I can't wait any longer. We need a hotel," John said to me in a low, throaty whisper one day in March.

We avoided the Regent and went to another elegant Baltimore hotel instead, in the middle of the week—in the middle of the day, in fact, leaving minutes apart, claiming we were going to Homewood Campus—and I will refrain from delivering the blow-by-blow description except to say that we went the first time without consummating our union. When we pulled the blinds, the room went dark, and John put on a lamp, and though I tried to undress in a casual way, he noticed my slight shyness, my turning away as I lifted my camisole over my head, and instead of being charmed, instead of taking me in his arms and whispering encouragement and pulling me under the sheets and letting me take off the final layers with some modicum of privacy, he chose to make a point of it. A rather obnoxious, unyielding point.

He asked me to stand in front of him, to unclasp my brassiere, to continue standing as he looked at my breasts, and slowly, almost too teasingly fondled them, and each time there was something that displeased him—some flinch from a too-ticklish touch, some drop of the head. I was excited too, terribly excited, but I was a virgin, for goodness' sake, and he was controlling every move. And that damn light: he hadn't been kidding about being afraid of the dark. It was close to a phobia with him, because of some Southern mammy, a person who had helped his Mother from time to time—which I took to mean she had locked him in a closet or a cellar for being naughty, once too often. Conditioning, indeed.

The better I knew John, the more I knew about his many conflicted feelings about his childhood: not only his resentment of his father, but his confusion about his mother, who had loved him above all his other siblings, and expected the most of him, and—he refused to provide any more details—was more intimate with him, more smothering than any mother should ever be, in his opinion. He had an absolute terror of incest, especially mother-child incest, as well as homosexuality. He didn't particularly want to talk or even think about any of that, and I, standing shivering in my undergarments, struggling to please him sexually, didn't want to think about it either.

In the lamp-lit hotel room, I couldn't tell which he wanted more, to see me naked or simply to avoid the darkness. I'm not sure that even he knew. For a brief moment, I thought nostalgically about those college boys who would have gladly accepted a hand under the sweater, a strategic opening of the trousers and lifting of the skirts, which in those days were as thick as theater curtains, leaving both parties essentially clothed. I thought longingly of the quick grope that would get things quickly finished—sometimes, before the female of the pair even knew things had started. A streak of messy wetness here or there, but at least the groping was over, and no harm done.

But no, that was not enough for John. Not only did he want to see me standing, as naked as the day I was born, but he insisted that I not look uncomfortable. He plopped a large chocolate bon bon into my mouth, the juices running down my chin as he lifted up my camisole, and pushed down my slip, and cupped my buttocks in his hands, and drew up next to me—and no, conveniently, he was not undressed yet, he was not yet exposed, he was not being judged or measured, even if I could see the lump in the front of his trousers—and I don't quite recall what happened next, but I disappointed him. There was an argument. And at the end of it I sat in a huff, top layers still off, chin propped in my hand, breasts hanging down like some African bush dweller's in a *National Geographic* magazine, back hunched, unexcited nipples plump and unattended areolas pale, utterly bored with the entire situation. I lit up a cigarette and took a deep, soothing puff, and he looked around and said, "Now, that's better," and came closer. And I slapped him. Hard.

But I said I wouldn't dwell on those kinds of details.

We drove back toward the lab in silence, John in the passenger seat as I gripped the wheel of my beloved Bearcat.

"You like driving that machine," he said after a while.

"I adore driving it."

"You really know how to steer it."

"Of course I do," I said, gripping the wheel even more tightly. I may have pumped the accelerator, just to show off.

"I don't want to go back to the lab just yet," he said after a half mile. "I've been a little tense. I'm sorry, Rar."

When a sign came up for a northbound road, one that I knew led away from city streets and suddenly into farmlands, I took it without decelerating, and John, anxious, gripped my thigh, and with the other hand held the door handle as we took the curve.

I pulled alongside a farm—the green of spring plantings just begin-ning to thrust through the red-brown mounds, the smell of manure and clover in the air, the buzzing of insects audible as soon as I cut our speed—and then nestled the car along two ruts that ran behind a big, red barn.

"Take down your trousers," I said, as soon as I'd set the brake.

And there, behind a barn, in my beautiful yellow Bearcat, I strad-dled the lap of Dr. John Broadus Watson (yes, there would be private jokes between us about his middle name after that day), and we dem-onstrated together that it is in fact possible to perform coitus without fully reclining and without every last layer of clothing removed. It was not easy; it was not, that first time, completely pain free. But it was a memorable success, for both of us. John appreciated motor cars even more after that moment, even though he still refused to drive his own, and I'm sure we both thought we'd been the first to make use of a motor car's mobile seclusion in that way—that we'd discovered, like the equally deluded Columbus, a new and untouched continent. Like most explorers, we were more proud of our audacity than apprehensive about any con-sequences—including the biological ones. But we weren't the first lovers to be so selectively aware.

When it was over, John leaned his head back against the seat, sweat trickling down the subtly graying threads of his thick hair, down his strong jaw, and across my throat, where he nuzzled against my per-spiring skin and said, "For a beginner, you're terribly gifted. I should listen to you more often, Miss Rosalie Rayner."

And I threw back my head, panting, and said, "Yes. Yes, you should."

CHAPTER 14

But it wasn't all fun, and he didn't always let me steer.

The rest of the month was still stop-and-go, stop-and-go: hints that Mary was furious and knew something, hints that Mary knew nothing at all, or didn't care. During March, she saw my parents socially every other day, it seemed, as if we'd found a long-lost aunt or cousin, the telephone ringing at all hours, and every single weekend marked as something involving Mary: a luncheon or dinner, a shopping excursion with Mother, a drive with Father off to some place he was thinking of developing. ("And you must go along!" I kept reminding Mother, who didn't seem to have a jealous bone in her body. "She'll feel awkward, otherwise. You really all must go together.")

Mary was frantically befriending my parents, and John and I were feverishly having intercourse. I said I preferred to avoid the lab, but that wasn't entirely possible. Our moods were up and down, signals crossing, spirits high but just as often clashing. The search for affordable privacy consumed both of us, when we weren't actively fixated on a scientific problem. I haven't mentioned many Vassar friends, except for Mary. I wasn't particularly close to any one of them. But there were a few with whom I still kept in contact, and with whom I shared more in common as we all escaped the influence of our families and our alma mater, and as our circumstances sorted us into narrower niches—those who had not married, those who worked, and those who liked to go out dancing and date all kinds of men, not batting an eye at bawdy jokes or morally suspect situations.

Hilda had her heart set on an acting career, which put her in contact with all sorts of people and situations, some more bizarre than mine and John's. I'd let slip just once that we couldn't find a place to be alone, and she immediately volunteered her city apartment as a trysting spot, which we took advantage of several times, making the long drive into New York, sometimes for just a few hours before driving back, always inventing excuses for our absences from the lab and from each of our homes. Though we saw each other daily, John continued to write me letters, pining for the next love-nest rendezvous. "Everything will be lovely and we ought to play safe. Still, play we will."

Only occasionally did I crave an escape from the pulsing demands of our passion, the demands also of lying and remembering which lies had been told, and of learning to look into the faces of friends and family without blinking when they asked why my hours had been so long on Tuesday night, where I had been on Saturday morning when Annie or Mother came knocking at my door early, why I wasn't in the lab when my father stopped by unannounced one day to invite me to lunch. Sometimes, and only sometimes, I wanted a break from it all: from the lab and from the lying—just a chance to disappear into a play or a music concert or some other form of entertainment. John didn't care for the arts or many leisure activities.

One day at lunch, eating a sandwich at my desk, I was reading a new book that had just appeared fresh in the bookstore—the first novel I'd found time to open in over six months—and John came galloping in and whisked it, playfully, from my hands.

"Never heard of him" he said, reading the name, F. Scott Fitzgerald, on the cover. He was a new novelist, author of *This Side of Paradise*. John read aloud the first sentence: "Amory Blaine inherited from his mother every trait . . ."

John promptly walked across the room and ceremoniously dunked the book into the trash.

"*Inherited every trait*. On the first page. That's what we're up against," he said, grinning maniacally. "That's the sort of ignorance that will set this entire nation back a hundred years."

"But it's just a novel," I started to say . . . and gave up. Because he was right, I thought at the time. The ignorance was overwhelming. And there were so many new novels and new flickers showing at the cinema, new ways of spreading outdated ideas, that we were outnumbered in trying to combat it.

It's always good to have a cause, an enemy, somewhere to refocus your energies after you pull up your trousers and make use of a handkerchief or powder your face, trying to look merely sleep-deprived instead of sex-mad. Mary Ickes Watson would do, as would F. Scott Fitzgerald, as would quite a few psychologists who were publishing comments that didn't fully support John's behaviorism, as would any person at the hospital who seemed to raise his or her eyebrows as I passed.

Sometime late that month—Mary had already been over at the house three times—my mother approached me in the hallway and said, "I'm not sure about that red lipstick. When did you start wearing that?"

It's hard to imagine now, especially with the images we have in our minds of the 1920s, but up until the moment full makeup burst out into popularity and respectability, it teetered along a fine edge. In December, my mother had felt free to opine that I should wear no color at all on my face. Only three months later, and I may have gotten away with something subtle. Clearly, this wasn't subtle enough.

"Mary Watson wears nearly the exact same shade," I said, pulling away before Mother wiped my lips with her own bare hand.

"But you're so much younger, dear," she said.

"And it looks good on her."

"Well, practically everything looks good on her. She has that film-star face. I only meant to say . . ." Seeing my dismayed expression, she hesitated. "If it's because you want to look good for men, they don't even know *what* they want, half the time. And you must believe me, what they don't want is war paint."

"That may be what they say, Mother," I said, wanting to tell her everything, able to tell her nothing. "They say they like fresh-faced girls. But what they want is a girl who *looks* fresh and young, only because she has carefully applied makeup, and wears the right sort of undergarments, and the right sorts of shoes, that give her just the right sort of walk."

Mother frowned. "Well, that may be true. It's a brave new world, isn't it?"

I went away the last weekend in March. The previous weeks had been exciting, draining, and confusing. An old college friend, Bee, asked me to visit her in New York City, to enjoy an early taste of spring in the Big Apple. John expected that this would be another rendezvous—a convenient alternative to Hilda's, particularly important because Hilda was planning to go west soon, to try her luck in Hollywood. And perhaps it could have been. But for once, I didn't want him to come along. I sensed a rope being thrown, and I grabbed it. Bee was a fun girl—enviable figure, perfect strawberry-blonde hair, her face ruined only by a horsey set of teeth she tried to obscure with one hand—who had landed a dream job working at *Vogue* magazine. She would have lots of stories, a tiny but stylish apartment shared with two other girls who had their own interesting single-girl lives, and the inside scoop on where to shop and dine. I didn't want her pull-down Murphy bed for an hour while she went and had her nails done. I wanted *her*, a distant, easygoing, no-strings friend: another woman, and preferably one who did not want to discuss either married men or experimental psychology.

By chance, John's wife, Mary, had her own trip planned that weekend, which left John at home, deprived of all female company, except his fourteen-year-old daughter's. He thought I should stay behind and make use of the liberated weekend with him. I thought he should spend it by himself, to get a reminder that Mary and I weren't alternating courtesans, at his beck and call. Not one for being alone, John invited a good friend, Leslie, a fellow psych researcher from another university, to stay over at his house and keep him company. Leslie was unmarried, and an odd duck in his own way, which in certain, sometimes unpredictable cases, didn't seem to bother John despite his deep distaste for homosexuality—perhaps because it took another unconventional man to refrain from judging John. Whatever John had said or done, chances were that a man like Leslie might have done something just as frowned upon by the Victorian moral overlords.

What happened was reported to me only on Monday, back at work in the lab. I walked into John's office and saw him at his desk, head in his hands.

"Shut the door," he said, as soon as he saw me. "Polly had a sort of breakdown over the weekend."

"What?" I hurried to sit down across from him.

"Leslie slept over, and Little John was away with Mary, so we took his room with the twin beds. And we had a few drinks and then we stayed up all night—in the beds, you know, as if we were at sleep-away camp—just talking. I told him everything. I guess I was rather emphatic and descriptive. I probably enthused about some of our trysts, in detail. And the walls were thin."

"Oh, John."

"Like an imbecile, I talked about my plan to send Mary and the children to Switzerland for a couple of years, to get her out of my hair and enjoy the high life, if that's how she pictures it. And then sue *her* for abandonment."

"Oh, oh, John."

Polly didn't come out for breakfast, John told me. And when he checked on her, her eyes were so swollen and her face was so pink that it was as if someone had punched her over and over, through the night. "She'd just curled up in bed crying, listening to me talk about her mother and our busted-up sham of a marriage, and . . ."

He couldn't go on. He was sick about it. Mad at himself for being so indiscreet, mad at the situation most of all, since he'd never wanted to marry his wife in the first place, as he frequently reminded me.

"Is Polly going to tell?"

"She says she isn't. But then again, she's awfully protective of her mother."

With a sickening feeling, I thought of my own mother, and my own parents' marriage, and how I'd grown up securely never questioning that they would always remain together, that they'd never hurt each other.

John continued, "On the other hand, I think she's just old enough to know it would hurt her mother more than help her." He sighed. "So that's one good thing, anyway."

Maybe. But I wasn't so sure it was a good thing, imagining this young girl trying to hold in such a big secret.

"How did she seem today?"

"She wouldn't eat Sunday night supper. She didn't eat Monday breakfast. Didn't want to go to school. Says her stomach hurts."

Chances are, Mary already knew. But then again, if she knew, why had she gone hat shopping with Mother last Tuesday, and why had she knocked on the door Thursday with a Bundt cake, and why was she already set to come to Sunday dinner? You'd think the woman had no friends or family, the way she practically lived at our house. She'd hinted that she'd like to come to dinner Saturday, but there, Mother drew the line. Friday and Saturday nights were the Passover Seder. In fact, our entire house would be turned inside out this week in preparation, because Passover was the biggest cleaning any Jewish household—even a fairly secular one—does at any time of the year, with the search for *chametz*, any kind of breadcrumbs, the impetus to scrub every last drawer and closet, inside and out. I hoped my mother would use the ritual cleaning to throw away the set of dishes that now only reminded me of Mary's first inappropriate gift.

But there—my irritation at Mary had made me forget about Polly again. And the moment I thought of Polly—loyalties strained, eyes swollen—my own stomach hurt.

Tuesday was our final testing day with Albert, the epilogue to an experiment begun in December. We knew his mother's plans: she was definitely leaving Johns Hopkins. In fact, she'd just informed us she was leaving a few days earlier than previously announced.

We'd already started writing up the Albert paper to hurry into publication in the journal John helped run—the *Journal of Experimental Psychology*, the first issue of volume 3, already a month behind publication schedule, for lack of sufficient articles and staff. ("Do you see how hard this is, trying to improve the world?" John had said that morning, striding down the hallway several paces ahead of me, not even turning around as he spoke, mulling over a critical note he'd received from his boss, Meyer.)

I wasn't as observant as I should have been at the final test, still thinking of Polly, imagining John and Leslie gabbing away without any sense, and seeing, curled up on the other side of a thin bedroom wall, Polly alternately trying to block out the stories, the unweaving of her world, laced with erotic details equally puzzling. I could picture her putting a pillow over her head, not wanting to hear, and then taking it off again, pressing her ear to the wall, wanting to store up what she should tell her mother, and then hating herself for going against her father, whom she adored.

In the lab, there was more than the usual amount of pushing things at Albert, rather than just letting him look and reach. He was forced to touch the Santa Claus mask against his will (crying); he was forced into contact with the rat, which was placed on his arm and on his chest (crying); he was forced into close contact with the rabbit (hesitant curiosity, pushing away with feet, withdrawal and crying); and he was made to stay close to the very active dog. Several times throughout, Albert seemed to be fighting his fear— seemed curious, in fact, and wanting to touch. He would reach out for objects like the rabbit and the sealskin coat, in contradiction to everything we'd been trying to demonstrate. But with enough pushing of animals and objects into his face, he ended up in tears, hands over his eyes. The responses, John announced at the end with a sound of celebration in his voice, were likely to "persist indefinitely."

Would we decondition him, as I'd heard mentioned often back in December? Weren't we responsible for the consequences of what our experiment had done?

There wasn't time. The mother was ready to go, and that was that, John said. He would greatly appreciate the opportunity to study Albert for many more months, to see how the long the conditioning lasted.

"And to decondition him, you mean."

"Well of course. In time. But there just isn't time. Didn't I already explain this, Rosalie?"

John, who barely tolerated Freud's basic beliefs and despised the entire Freud mania that had infected the country for ten years (stylish young girls with ever rising skirts were eager to tell anyone their dreams), made a tasteless joke at the end of that session.

"Wouldn't it be funny," he said, "if little Albert here showed up in an analyst's office someday with a mysterious fear of sealskin coats? They'd turn it into something sexual about a hidden early memory. Maybe they'd think he'd gotten smacked for playing with his mother's pubic hair."

No, it wouldn't be funny, I should have said. But I didn't. Just as I hadn't said that John must do something, anything, to take the unfair burden of deception off Polly's shoulders. Just as I hadn't insisted that we couldn't let Albert leave without making some attempt to decondition him. Just as I hadn't said, about Mary and me: *choose, simply choose, never mind your theories about a more enlightened future. Before anyone else gets hurt.*

In response to John's vulgar quip, there was minimal uneasy laughter in the room. Albert—so big now, head tottering, face stained with tears—was being carried away on the hip of a nurse, sparing all of us any formal farewells, aside from the self-congratulatory banter. I didn't think John's final statement was appropriate. But I was even more surprised when he wrote that same jesting comment—pubic hair and all—into our final published scientific paper, released to the world just a few months later.

One of the only honest men in the world. If he had a thought, he seldom censored it. As I knew. As Mary knew. As poor Polly, the only innocent one among us, was forced to know as well.

CHAPTER 15

Mary arrived at our house on the first Sunday in April in a wound-up state, which persisted even after we'd sat down to a simple supper of leftover beef brisket, horseradish, and new potatoes.

"Oh, don't apologize," she said, stabbing a piece of beef without bringing it to her lips.

If anyone should've apologized, it was Mary. My parents hadn't wanted extra company during Passover, but she'd called several times that weekend, suggesting how much she wanted them all to see each other. Because of the holiday, they'd already sat through one enormous four-hour dinner and attended a repeat version at my Uncle's house the very next night, and by now, even my father, Mary-besotted as he was, would have preferred to sit in his favorite wing chair with Bromo-Seltzer and a copy of *Harper's*.

John ate without speaking. I matched him bite for bite, stealing looks, trying to judge whether he knew something he hadn't told us.

Finally, Mary pushed away her plate and said, "To tell you the truth, I have a rotten headache."

My mother leaned forward, reaching out to touch Mary's wrist while babbling consoling words. Mother was a well-meaning but not effortless hostess, and when someone seemed off or odd, she immediately took the blame, and became even more inelegant in her attempts to put every last thing right. Mary had seemed off from the moment she entered the house, and I could see the wheels in Mother's head turning: *Should we have invited her to the Friday Seder, even though she isn't Jewish? Is the cold brisket insufficient? Is it an insult we haven't brought out any wine?*

It did occur to me that Mary was an alcoholic, and that wine was actually the headache "cure" she was trying to acquire, by hinting, fretting, and ignoring her food. So perhaps it was a little heartless of me to suggest, "Why don't you go lie down for a little while, and see if it goes away?"

To my surprise, she practically leapt up and out of her chair, napkin dropping over her plate.

"That would be just the ticket. And then I'll be, I'll be"—she seemed to be stammering from happiness, or nerves, or both—"I'll be right as rain."

Mother summoned Annie and asked her to guide Mary to a resting couch in the opposite parlor, and to bring her a glass of fresh water, if that would help.

"It's quiet I need," Mary insisted. "You'll all be holding back your conversation if I'm napping right next door."

John, who hadn't spoken once since dinner was served, looked up and cocked an eyebrow. No one had been talking. What animated conversation would be interrupted?

"Don't trouble yourself. I know the way. Twenty minutes is all I need," Mary said, scooting to the hall and then up the stairs, quick as a scale on a xylophone, toward the bedrooms above.

She *should* know the way, I thought, since she had been here—was it possible?—nine or ten times in just four weeks.

After a few minutes, Mother addressed John. "I *do* hope she feels better."

He had just forked a parsley-covered new potato into his mouth. It stuck in one corner of his cheek, which went still for a moment, and then he resumed chewing, focused on the food, not at all concerned about his wife, who—it seemed, based on the silence over our heads— had made herself comfortable quickly.

In response to *his* utter lack of response, Mother gave John a look that told me she was beginning to wonder, at last, what kind of husband he was. She had asked him many times about Polly and Little John. He'd supplied some anecdotes about the golden "Stoney Lake days," especially those first years when he'd built a cottage up in Ontario, practically by himself. But no doubt she noticed how quickly the tales turned from children to his own interests in country life, building things, gardening, being self-sufficient, and his belief that the children—any children, in the abstract, for now the names of his actual children had vanished under the swift-moving waters of his perpetual self-congrat- ulation—really should do physical tasks, use their hands, do more and think less. I rationalized that he was simply nervous. Nerves generally sent him into a more grandstanding mode, just as they did for my father, who was otherwise the sweetest man on earth.

If Mother was beginning to question, it was a shame, because she had been so confident in the beginning, and that confidence had made her infinitely more happy. After that very first dinner with the Watsons, Mother had confided that she would no longer worry about me in a professional setting, now that she'd met the wife of the man I was working for. "You can judge a man by his wife," she'd said that day. "And I know that Mary Watson wouldn't settle for just anyone."

I didn't know whom or what Mary Watson would settle for. I knew only that she was in my bedroom, and I could just barely hear, above the sounds of halfhearted dinner conversation, some sort of scraping and scuttling that no one else seemed to notice.

"John," I said. "I mean, Dr. Watson . . ."

"No formalities required, Rosalie. Your parents have probably guessed that we go by first names around the lab."

"John," I said, "do you think that perhaps you might consider checking on your wife?" Drawers opened and closed in quick succession. I recognized the familiar squeak of my wardrobe door. Something, perhaps a hanger, clattered as it fell. "Maybe she's looking for an aspirin or a washcloth, or about to be sick . . ."

"Oh, I think she's probably fine."

Another few minutes passed, interminably, as I made a mental inventory of everything I owned and every reason Mary would have for going through my drawers and pockets.

"*John*," I said again.

At last he caught on to the urgency in my voice. His self-assurance melted. He stood and headed for the dining-room door, with me behind him, followed by Mother. Father barely turned in his chair, confused about the fuss, before turning back to his plate.

At that moment Mary came flying down the staircase, taking the steps so quickly, she missed one, grabbed the rail, lurched, and kept leaping downward in a half-galloping, half-cascading motion, skirt billowing. None of our reactions could keep pace with her. She was at the landing, eyes fixed straight ahead, and out the door with her spring wrap over one arm—but without her umbrella, still sitting in the stand. Mother called out just as Mary yanked on the door handle, but Mary didn't turn, didn't explain. There was a little grunt of satisfaction as the door opened, unless I imagined it and it was only the hinges groaning, and then only the open doorway, and a spring breeze blowing into our faces, with the smell of damp, fresh-tilled soil from the gardens at the center of the boulevard, and Mary gone, and all of us turning, Mother's mouth open, my hands over my face, John frowning, and Father still pushing up slowly, up and out of his chair, finally facing the right direction, toward the hallway, having missed Mary Watson's final theatrical performance.

CHAPTER 16

Two horrible weeks later, I was in New York City, in the apartment of Mary Cover, with two suitcases parked next to the arm of the sagging, floral-patterned sofa. Mary's fiancé, Harold, handed her a cup of tea and hitched up his trousers, revealing eight inches of black sock as he wedged himself into a comfortable position, fully attentive. In truth, I'd been hoping for a private female audience, at least for the first hours of my stay. But I could see from the moment that Mary opened the door with Harry standing behind her, his bushy-haired head floating above her smaller frizzy-haired one, that they were one of those couples joined at the hip—finishing each other's sentences, sensitive to each other's slightest cough or sniffle. It made me feel more depressed just sitting next to them.

"So let me get this straight," Harold said. "She's willing to divorce, is that right?"

"Most likely, yes."

Harold caressed his chin thoughtfully, as if he were a lawyer I was trying to hire—which he most certainly was not.

"But Rosalie," Mary said, leaning forward, "What do *you* want? Have you had any time to think about that?"

Mary made me a bowl of rice pudding and a cup of chamomile tea—"Do you have anything stronger?" No, she did not—and loaned me a pair of mint-striped pajamas, which I accepted, even though of course I'd brought everything I needed to live in the city for a month or two, or at least until things settled down in Baltimore. After saying goodnight, she disappeared into a back bedroom with Harold, and I tried to find a position between the springs, inhaling Mary's clean and comforting, astringent witch hazel smell—faint on the pajamas, stronger on the pillow. Breathing in, I could picture our dorm rooms at Vassar, that simpler time. I could picture sitting under a great oak tree, with her head in my lap, looking up at the sky, talking about a future we couldn't begin to imagine, which made it fairly boring, but also problem free.

Mary had accepted my desperate plea for help with few questions, had offered me a small stipend out of her own pocket for helping her teach a few weeks of a psych course at Columbia until the semester was finished, and given me a place to stay, on top of it all. Kind, practical, nonjudgmental Mary. Falling asleep that first night, I found myself on the cusp of dreams, puzzling: Where had that little charm bracelet gone? When had I last taken it off? I couldn't remember.

What had happened, two weeks earlier, was this.

John had waited for me to walk into the lab the morning after Mary's frenetic escape from our house that dreadful Sunday night, and then he'd immediately requested a ride in my car over to Homewood Campus, a subterfuge so that we could be alone, discussing what had happened, and what he would do, or rather—I had to remind him twice—what *we* would do.

"She knew what she was looking for," he said. "She found the letters in your wardrobe, and she gave them to her brother Harold, and he's already photographed them. He's trying to blackmail me."

I didn't know where to begin. *What do you mean, blackmail? How long did she know? Was she planning to search for the letters from the first moment she befriended my parents?*

But the question that came out first was: "Who has the letters now?"

"We had a loud quarrel. I got them back."

"And then?" I was having a hard time juggling talking, driving, and smoking—yes, I was smoking in earnest these days, the cigarette stamped red with the lipstick I was determined to wear, when I felt like it, with or without my mother's approval. And yes, in a sense, Mother had been right, as she'd discover in even more awful detail all too soon. Harlots wear lipstick, and I was a harlot, a trollop, a moll.

"And then what?" John repeated back to me. The more worried or excited I sounded, the more he responded by withdrawing, lips thinned and brow furrowed, eyes slitted as we drove.

"And then what happened to them? You wrote those love notes and letters to me. They belong *to me.*"

I took my eyes off the road to look at him. He was facing me squarely, a bland, annoyed expression on his face, questioning my priorities.

"He's tried to control me before," John said. "Now, he's got some powerful ammunition. The man is a professional scold. And he's very good at it, don't you forget."

Harold Ickes had wanted Mary and John to divorce years ago, back in Chicago, when John was having an affair with Vida Sutton. At the time, Harold had been having his own affair with a married woman, but no matter. Harold, a lawyer with political ambitions, still jumped to the moral high ground whenever he could. Sparring with Chicago politicians had given him hubris. It irked him that he could be a thorn in the side of mayors and business leaders but still have failed to get John Watson out of the family. Once and for all, he wanted his sister to get a divorce, under the best possible financial scenario. Basically, John should be forced to give Mary anything she asked for. Given that

John had always been plagued with financial problems, this would reduce him to abject poverty. I think Harold got the most pleasure from imagining John limping back to South Carolina, begging for occasional work as a farmhand, or living the life of a moonshiner perhaps.

"I'm surprised she's willing to divorce you," I said.

John hesitated. "She's mentioned it before."

"She has?"

John was honest, yes, but that didn't mean he volunteered every detail. I'd been under the impression Mary would never let go, no matter what she knew of John's affairs. But now I was getting the impression that she had always planned to let go, and only wanted the best timing and the best deal—and proof that would stand up in court, just to make sure he didn't pull any rabbits out of his hat.

"She's not just trying to scare you? She won't be trying to win you back?"

"I wouldn't put it past her," John said. "That could be her plan. She's not entirely stable."

The next morning, cloistered again in the apartment of friends I probably did not deserve, I moped about, allowing Harold Jones to serve me over-easy eggs, potatoes, and toast. Mary Cover refilled my coffee. Glancing at each other purposefully, like dancers in a Broadway show, they each pulled out a chair and sat down.

"We've been talking about this, Harold and I," Mary said.

Harold added, "We're only thinking of what's best for you."

"You know I respect John's work," Mary said. "In fact, we've been discussing conditioning and your infant trials and all sorts of things. It interests Harold and me, very much."

Harold nodded and tipped his head forward shyly, and I could see the hair thinning atop his head, a round patch that would soon meet the receding hairline a few inches to the front. "Do you realize that I very nearly almost came to work at Johns Hopkins last fall, just when you did?"

"No, I didn't."

"I was supposed to work with Knight Dunlap," he said. "You know Knight. And then something happened, I got rejected at the last minute, or they couldn't make room for me, or something." It still stung him a little. But he put an arm around Mary and squeezed. "Of course, look what I would have missed. These two ships would have passed in the night."

"I can't imagine," I said, marveling for the hundredth time that I'd gotten my position when someone like Harold hadn't. "Funny, how things work out."

"A shame missing the chance to work with John, though," Harold added kindly. "He's a pioneer. Good questions. Important work."

"The most important," Mary said, putting her hand over Harold's. "But about the personal matter. About the letters, and the divorce. I'm just not sure you're thinking through all the options and all the consequences."

I hadn't said a word, not that they'd given me a chance.

Mary glanced at my plate. "Aren't you going to eat?"

The two perfectly paired yellow yolks sat, dully shining, each covered by a rapidly cooling, opaque film. Harold had blackened the potatoes. I was sure that Mary adored his burned potatoes, but I could pass on them, especially this morning. Really, I wanted nothing more than the coffee, a cigarette, and a walk through Central Park.

"So what we're thinking," Harold said—and I noticed, only then, that he had an apron tied around his waist. It made me want to giggle, irresponsibly. To sober myself, I looked past him to the fire escape—backed window, and to the dirty windowsill, where a long line of small, ugly figurines sat in pairs: two little pigs, and two little lighthouses, two little haystacks, and two little railroad cars. They'd collected them together—slowly, methodically, agreeably, purchasing whatever pair was on offer at Cape Cod or colonial Williamsburg—on every weekend and holiday vacation away from Columbia. John would never collect salt and pepper shakers. Thank goodness.

Harold seemed to notice my inappropriate smile and tried to sally past it, toward the conclusion he'd worked up in the night, talking with Mary, the two of them part of a single hive brain, androgynous and fully fused. "What we're thinking," he tried again, in his crisp New Englander's accent—no honeyed drawl when he delivered the bad news—"is that perhaps you break things off. Stay in the city a year. Pursue some opportunities in the field. We have some promising suggestions."

"What he's trying to say," Mary said, running out of patience, "is that John Watson has a reputation. You're not the first, you won't be the last, and for all you know, they'll both simply drag your name through the mud, and your family's name, and they'll stay together, for the sake of the children, and he'll have more affairs, and get away with it, since men always do, and then what do you have? Nothing. There. I've said it."

"There," Harold Jones agreed. "She's said it."

Most troubling to recall is the look on my mother's face when John confirmed the reason behind Mary's bizarre dash, and her plan for the letters. After two days, I summoned the courage to sit down with Mother and finally answer the questions that had been batting against her worried brain like june bugs against a screen door. It was as if she'd lost two daughters, or a daughter and a very dear new friend, in one fell swoop. It took her a while to absorb it all and to travel mentally backward, dinner by shopping trip by Sunday drive, and realize that Mary had never meant to be friends. Even more shocking—I could see her eyes slam down like shutters against a storm when the subject came up, when she even tried to think about it—that I'd been having some sort of intimate relations, and worse yet, with someone she knew, with the man who had sat in their house on multiple occasions with his very own wife, breaking bread with all of us, or—at the end of Passover, since we'd had no bread in the house, breaking matzo. Unthinkable.

"Well, there's simply no question," she'd said during that midweek evening tête-à-tête, in her own boudoir off her bedroom, all doors closed, even our servants no longer trusted—*no one* trusted now, for the moment. She sat on a padded ottoman pulled up next to her dressing table, facing me, while I stood. She patted the seat, but I just couldn't. I didn't want the feel of her soft warm hip and arm next to mine, as if we were both sitting on a train together, facing the same direction, looking off into some shared future.

"You'll get far away from him, as far as possible," she said. "And they'll simply have to sort it out. And shame on him—on them—for bringing us into it."

She chose her words carefully. "And Rosalie, you know there are other fish in the sea. You don't think we're expecting you to date and marry someone from our own circles, do you? Other parents try to push that sort of thing. We don't."

In her mind, because she and Father were so open-minded and didn't expect me to marry within the Jewish faith or select a person of any particular occupation, the choices were dizzying. In what other era did a young woman truly have choices at all?

"You're pretty. You're smart. You can't begin to imagine the number of men who will come knocking."

"John's different," I said.

She turned around, facing the dressing table, and occupied herself with clearing its surface. She opened a drawer in order to put away a bottle of lotion, then pulled out two tangled necklace chains and started trying to unknot them, clumsily. "It's useless, isn't it? Trying to talk to someone who's in love?" She was making the knot worse with her tugging, but she didn't want to stop or look up, couldn't bear to look at me. Her voice walked a taut line, with unruly emotions seething below. "It'll wear off, you'll see. It'll wear off."

"Here, Mother. You're just making it worse," I said, trying to untangle the chains before giving up and dropping them back into the drawer.

She looked up. "And what about children?"

I took a breath, I considered the best course, and I lied. I told her that we simply couldn't think about children yet, that it wasn't even appropriate to think about that, which wasn't true. *I* wasn't ready to think about it—that part was true. Spending every day with babies didn't make them more appealing; for me, they were simply test subjects, things that arrived on gurneys and entered bright eyed or yawning and exited crying and red faced and wet.

John, on the other hand, had already thought about it. As usual, he had a better sense of the future than I did. He'd said that his two current children were more than enough.

Mother took a deep breath and tried one last time. "I know you won't listen. I fear you won't, and that you'll only resent me for saying it. But I just have to ask: Can't you see what he's done to you? Don't you even want to see?" Her neck was red, where she'd been raking at it absentmindedly with her nails. Hairs had come loose from her upswept bun. "How could two smart people be so horribly stupid?"

"Is that what you think, Mother? That I'm stupid? That I'm horrible?"

"No, no." She was looking at me, in the mirror. I could see us both, and how we were hurting each other. "You were perfect before he came along."

"But now I'm ruined." I blamed her for saying it, but it's what I thought, too. It's what I saw in my own reflection.

I waited for her to correct me, but she didn't. And that only drove me back into the arms of the one man who knew how to make things better, the one person who still loved me, the one person who believed that people and futures could be fixed, that fortunes—like behaviors—could always be changed, even if it took a while to figure out how, even if it took aligning oneself against nearly everything and everyone.

"Getting away" was a common, repeating theme. Distance meant more in those days. Split the lovers apart. Separate the warring parties. But who would go and who would stay?

When I met John later that spring in Baltimore, on a campus park bench (his lunching-out budget being more strained than ever), he handed me the published journal with our Albert paper, to reassure me that he had indeed shared billing—John B. Watson & Rosalie Rayner—for this historically significant report that was bound to stir up great interest, generate further infant studies, and strike a blow against those who used terms like "instinct" carelessly. (Yes, yes, I thought, as he gabbled, but what about us and our families and everyone we'd hurt and everything we desperately wanted, right now?)

Then he explained his latest plan. Before the day of the purloined letters, he'd been trying to send his wife away. Now, he'd decided it was my duty—no, my opportunity—to go. I would be the one sent to Europe for an unspecified time period, to stop the gossips' tongues from wagging and to redirect the Hopkins administrators' attentions back toward John's plans for fall research. (Had they even noticed my sudden departure, or simply assumed that women were fickle and easily uprooted in springtime, when semesters could naturally be cut short?)

My absence would allow Mary time to come to her senses, to plot a slower course toward divorce, one based on objective logic instead of rash emotions, and one that wouldn't leave him as impoverished and publicly shamed. He'd even had the nerve to contact my own father and meet with him privately, to review the plan—and the costs for the plan, which of course, my father would be expected to bear. My father had also noted, John now informed me, that there were excellent educational opportunities in Germany for an American—even for an American woman. I could read some psychology there, among top names in the field, improve my command of the continental languages, and look up a few old relatives.

No, I told John.

"But, you'd have a good time in Europe."

"No. John, I said *no*."

And no, I told my father later that night, reinstalled in my childhood bedroom again for a weekend—as I would also be for some unknown number of months that summer and fall, until I charted my own post-Hopkins future.

No, I told Mary Cover and Harold Jones when I returned to the city the next Monday, where I would continue to sleep on their couch, commuting to Columbia together on those days I helped her teach, sometimes for a change of pace sleeping at Bee's and sometimes at Hilda's—our love refuge. My legs were marked with bruises along the outside of each calf, where my suitcase banged as I hauled it from one tiny apartment to another, up staircases in buildings with broken elevators and across subway platforms, building up my courage to ask my father for money so that I might rent my own apartment, but not ready to beg quite yet, for I knew he had other plans for me.

I would not wear the scarlet letter. I would not be sent away, even temporarily. I would not let John and Mary return to their marriage of convenience, and get comfortable together again—disloyally, hypocritically comfortable. I was angry at John and yet trying to save him from himself, even then. I wanted him to be a better person, living by his stated principles, and in pursuit of that end, I was willing to make us all desperately unhappy. To be right and to win, one simply had to be the most unbending: either I'd learned that from John, or we'd been drawn together by that shared trait, which could make a person the most virtuous in the world, or the most self-deluded.

At Mary Cover's, I felt most like the interloper, because unlike my other city friends, she was not a dedicated bachelorette. Both she and Harold were finishing their master's degrees, both to be awarded that late spring, and they had set the date of their wedding as September 1, which also happened to be Mary's birthday. In the fall, they'd both begin their doctorates, which surprised me, because a married couple would almost certainly not be hired at the same university and probably couldn't thrive even in the same field. If a professional woman wanted to help her husband, she might be allowed to shadow him, unpaid, a two-for-one. But Mary and Harold still seemed under the impression they would have equally serious careers, investigating the very same issues and subjects that most fascinated John: behaviorism, conditioning and deconditioning, fear responses, infants and children. If anyone could manage working together, I figured John and I would, because I did not have the ambition of equaling him in status or accomplishments, and if that seems a reversal from how I'd imagined myself on college graduation day, perhaps it was only because John was so ambitious and so influential that I couldn't imagine any student of his expecting equal billing.

I listened from the bedroom one night as Mary and Harold made dinner together, banging pots and pans and cupboard doors as they discussed first their wedding, a casual affair that would take place on a Wednesday, and what kind of cake they should order—lemon yellow or white—and adding up the expenses, down to the last cent, because they were frugal and practical people. And next, without a pause, Harold was asking her what she thought about galvanometers—electricity-measuring devices—that might record subtle fear responses of babies, completely objectively, without disturbing the baby in any way. Models had been tested in Paris on children from three months to four years, with good results. Mary asked how they worked, and Harold described, in numbing detail but with an admirable lack of pedantry, how they measured minute amounts of perspiration gathering in pores, via two tiny silver plates placed on the ankle and on the sole of the shoe.

I reclined on the bed, rubbing the sore spot on my calf mindlessly, listening to her excitement rising as they both developed ideas for experiments—not only Harold's ideas, for he had access to test subjects thanks to his new position at the city children's hospital, but Mary's as well, including experiments that she was more than capable of doing independently. She asked about measuring blood pressure, as another nonintrusive means. And I thought of John, recording the most obvious of signs in Albert—shuddering, tears—and also John wielding the hammer, and pushing the rat with its small sharp claws toward Albert's legs.

"No," Harold said on the other side of the door, talking with his mouth full of something Mary and he were cooking together, the smell of oregano and tomatoes—slightly burnt again—wafting into the bedroom. "Even a blood pressure cuff would be too disruptive. The child should continue playing, completely unaware."

I sat up, wanting to join the discussion, and equally not wanting to, feeling defensive and contrary. Response measurement aside, the item stimulating fear or being introduced as a substitute, whether noise or rat or rabbit, would still be disruptive, I told myself, the mute member of this three-person conversation. There was simply no way *not* to distress children in such experiments, whether significantly or mildly. I had to believe so. After all, my name was on that "Conditioned Emotional Reactions" paper. Uneducated people might have questioned our experimental design, but no one at Hopkins had objections, that I could recall. I had sat in that room, eager for a strong reaction, urging John to freshen it, and watching Albert nod his head in a strange, repetitive shuddering rhythm we hadn't seen before, legs kicking out against the rabbit and the dog.

"Of course, we'd study only the fears the child came with. And the moment we detected any fears, we would attempt their removal," Mary said to Harold, and I could practically see her pushing her glasses back up her nose, and pursing her lips, looking serious and noble. "That's really the point of it all, isn't it? Anyone can make a child afraid. How to make a child *unafraid* is the important and more interesting question."

And off they went, brainstorming the possibilities, from distraction and verbal appeal to direct reconditioning—all those things we hadn't done with Albert, all those things we hadn't made time for, and that, frankly, seemed to interest John a good deal less.

I packed my suitcases and left again the next morning, thanking them sincerely, not burning my bridges because I might very well need to stay with them again. And after they'd both said their good-byes and then stood there, smiling at me, this guest who said she was leaving but still hadn't quite left, when they were both busy in a corner, oohing and aahing over some tender seedlings that had just burst from a little planting tray Harold had set up two weeks earlier, I walked past the window sill, nabbed one of the paired lighthouse shakers, and dropped it into my cardigan pocket. I don't know why I did. I wasn't thinking, and how could I be, when thoughts may not even exist? I just did, and that's all that matters.

John discovered, if he hadn't known before, that I had a stubborn streak. I discovered that John, though he enjoyed argumentative epistolary relationships with fellow researchers and seemed to invite controversy at every turn, had a surprisingly low tolerance for social friction. He'd leave the room if pressed into a difficult conversation. He'd go for a walk. Or he'd give in—as Mary knew. Which is why my own future with him felt beyond my control.

By July, I had tired of New York City sofas, bread-and-butter sandwiches, and life on the cheap in general. I returned to my parents' house, which had become, in the heat of summer and in the wake of all that had happened, an even more unnaturally quiet place. The parquet flooring squeaked under my step, as I avoided rooms in which my mother sat reading or embroidering, as I tiptoed out whenever Agnus or Annie or Bertha or Frank stepped in, dusting or fixing something. Reading even light novels felt too hard; I stopped in the middle of a page, realizing my eyes had been tracking without taking in any of the words. Walks were short: I did not want activity, and I imagined the eyes of every stranger on me. When my mother brought me some new plants for the back garden, I was too rough with the roots and too negligent with the watering, and ended up with dead brown sticks.

For a while that summer, despite all my previous feelings, I still had moments when my frustration with John, and my own sense of futility became so great that I considered going to Europe. Never mind Germany—I would go to Paris, or Rome. I would go, alone, to nightclubs, and I would go to art museums and cathedrals, and I would eat at sidewalk cafés where no one recognized me, or knew my parents' name, or John's. I would begin my own life over again, and no one would tell me what to do or think. I might even turn my back on centuries of progress and decide I had a soul! (Well, I probably wouldn't go that far.)

Except that I still needed him. I still loved him. I wanted to have him whispering in my ear again, forcing my knees to buckle. I wanted his hand on my leg as I drove toward the city, his fingers pressing and walking, one inch at a time, higher up my thigh, as he pretended to look off at an angle toward the passenger-side ditch, identifying nonexistent birds using invented names, "brown bunkeroo, variegated titty-tit finch," as I tried to breathe deep from my diaphragm, my vision fuzzing, his hand buried in my skirts, skillfully manipulating my reactions, and his own voice growing husky with his own arousal, with his own sense of pride and gratitude for all we'd manage to seize for ourselves by ignoring everyone else's outmoded rules and inhibitions.

CHAPTER 17

When I received the news that John and Mary had finally and legally separated, I packed a bag and picked him up from the lab in my Bearcat, and we drove, not to New York City this time, for a new frugality had set in, but just outside town heading north, to a hotel, or rather, boarding house, if it would have merited even that nice a name. We parked and I approached slowly, a step behind John, one of my hands clasped in one of his, and my arm lifting as I trailed behind. He dragged me a little, wanting to be inside, where the fun would begin. It wasn't the sex I was hesitant about, of course, it was the look of the place: wood so weathered it glinted silver, a flash of some tailed critter slipping under the porch ahead of us, and on the front porch itself, gaping planks that grabbed on to the heel of my shoe, so that it twisted off entirely, and I was caught balanced precariously there, one shoe in my hand, when the sullen landlady opened the door.

John knew a man who lived in the house and had told him everything about it—the weekly rates, the daily rates, and even the hourly rates in the upstairs rooms: in each, one bed and not a lick of any other kind of furniture, not even a dresser. The shared bathroom was down the hall. Downstairs, there was a kitchen with a round table in the middle, where bachelors fried up plates of salami and eggs for dinner, and drank bourbon and played cards. We joined them on occasion, after our two or four or at the very most eight hours in the upstairs room had expired, and we shared whatever food and drink we'd brought, if John's own bourbon bottle hadn't already been emptied on the drive up and during our first minutes of undressing, up in the room. More and more, we sipped from others' flasks and bottles and didn't provide much in return, though I tried to bring extra cigarettes at least, a little embarrassed by how we took more than we gave, from such sad, down-on-their-luck men, no less.

"Don't worry," John said once. "You give them a free peep show every now and again. That's worth a nickel."

He meant only that I often had to stand outside the bathroom door, waiting for my turn, in John's robe, which he left there at the boarding house. I suppose I was less careful as the weeks went by, roaming the upper hallway, unkempt, with tangled hair, and smelling of salt and bourbon and sex, not even minding when another man exited his room, and stopped in his own bathrobe and socks, hungrily staring—all of us a little charged up by what we knew was happening behind all those doors, by the sounds of knocking against the thin walls and the opening and shutting of car doors late in the night, and the trip of a woman's footsteps in the gravel and next on the stairs, and then the five-minute wait, and the grunting and mewling, authentic or exaggerated.

"What do you think they're doing in there?" John said one night, and shook me more awake to make me listen with him. He'd left a lamp burning low. I could make out the bulk of his shaggy head, hanging over me. "Go ahead, Rar. Paint me a picture."

When I summarized the action to him, succinctly and objectively, he pouted. "You have a much more extensive vocabulary than that.

And you're a much more precise observer. Be serious for a minute. Try again."

And so I did. No doubt they weren't doing anything all that special, just whatever was simplest and most efficient, and the woman was on bottom and perhaps mostly motionless and—for all we knew—on the clock. But I painted a more interesting picture for him, one step at a time, one new position at a time, with endless erotic fussing and fretting and tormented rearranging and alternately vexing and arousing attempts at novelty elaborating the coupling. At that moment in the next room, we heard the sound of a quick final series of flesh-slapping sounds in triple meter, and then another simpering, climaxing mewl, and John's lips parted slightly and I could see his wide eyes flashing in the half dark.

"Imagine," John said, turning on his side, hard from listening to the final echo of our neighbors' bedsprings—or more likely he'd been hard since the very moment he'd first jostled me awake. "If we could set up a lab here. Imagine the tools we'd need. Imagine the behaviors we'd discover."

"Don't you wish," I said, and if only to change the subject, I let him push into me, finding his release—a maneuver that didn't take long on that particular night of auditory stimulation.

I'd be dishonest if I claimed our boarding-house visits didn't stimulate my own scientific curiosity, in my own way. I was less interested in positions, performances, and tumescence in general than in practical matters, like how the women avoided getting pregnant. Quietly broaching the subject on the front porch, when I happened to share a cigarette with one of the more experienced lady visitors, didn't entirely enlighten me. Some of the women did in fact have multiple children as well as unfounded confidence in all manner of over-the-counter "women's friends," "monthly aids," and "pearls of health." (Dangerous abortifacients sold under misleading names, in other words.)

Then there was Lysol, that product in which we'd put our trust while the Spanish flu had raged. It wasn't yet advertised euphemistically as a feminine hygiene product, but even at Vassar, the girls had whispered about it.

A few women who visited the boarding house simply claimed they rarely got pregnant. I suspected they'd been injured by abortions or infected by men enough to compromise their fertility. Many a Great War soldier was discharged critically ailing from syphilis or gonorrhea, and the army didn't make things any better by pretending that patriotic "self-control" was the best solution. (No more than a third of soldiers agreed, I'd learned from John.)

One of John's better-funded projects, just the year before, had been a detailed study of the extremely limited efficacy of a wartime anti-VD motion picture on military men *and* civilians. The lengthy paper and the exhaustive postwar surveying—nearly five thousand people from all walks of life were shown the motion picture—was one of the best conducted and least remembered of John's works. Looking back, two things strike me: that despite John's lifelong fascination with emotional manipulation, he had no trouble admitting that arousing fear about sexual disease was not the best way to control behavior; and that he had been much more methodical when studying sexual activity than when studying babies. Without any sarcasm, I can say that it was a calling overlooked.

Despite John's clinical interests and my own willingness to pry into other women's lives, we weren't as candid about our own concerns or as well informed as we should have been. No one was, in those years. Suffrage leaders had frowned on the use of rubbers, which only encouraged promiscuity. Margaret Sanger had more good sense— enough to land in her jail—but our opposition to her stances on eugenics kept John and me from ordering many of her publications. Privately, I took an interest in her introduction of "birth control," as she'd started to call it, but John was not as interested in forgiving someone such backward views on race, immigration exclusions, and other matters.

What did that leave? I'd heard of coitus interruptus, and John knew even more terms—coitus reservatus, coitus obstructus—and questioned the usefulness of many of them, whenever we broached the subject together, which was less often than you might think. Various pessaries and caps were illegal and hard to obtain. Then there was the calendar method. It certainly fit John's fondness for charts. The problem was knowing when, exactly, a woman was fertile. Was it during menstruation, or just before? A dog's fertility coincided with bloody discharge, and I was the last to tell John, still fond of quoting Pavlov and recalling his own days studying birds and rats, that humans and animals aren't always the same. But why am I chiding John? I had no better idea, myself.

My parents caught on pretty quickly where I was going, with whom, and probably why. "Men are disgusting," Mother said to me once, on the verge of tears, as I was hurrying out the door on a Friday afternoon, just hours before Shabbat. My father was away, as he'd been away increasingly since the infamous day of the stolen letters. He claimed his absences were due to work. It would have been a terrible irony if we'd awakened in him any longings previously suppressed, or provided some justification for being less cautious about behaviors he'd previously concealed. It was John's goal to free every American from unnecessary and outdated moralities, but did I really want my parents' generation to be part of that change? Maybe we could start with our own generation, or the one to follow.

Things were becoming so awkward, with spells of two and three days when we didn't even talk or share meals, that my mother convinced us all to go on a family motoring vacation to the Great American West. I consented, knowing that I'd be alone and silent in the backseat, not getting a clean break as my mother saw it, but only brooding on Baltimore, my head turning with the memories of every conversation, every negotiation, every debauched tryst, trying to sort through it all.

At the first fill-up stop we hit, heading out of state, a man who was looking under the hood of his car glanced up at me standing near the pump, rubbing the sand out of my eyes, and said, "Well hello, Sugar, aren't you sweet."

And I smiled back, as innocently as I could muster, thinking, *You have no idea.*

Most of the time was en route, with a week or ten forgettable days in between spent at Colorado and Yosemite—and that's all I have to say about that, not enjoying backseats or endlessly dusty roads or terrible food or nature camping. But it did give me a cover story for part of the summer, and when I filled out my alumnae news card to Vassar, I mentioned that I'd just returned from an out-West trip, extending the time it had taken us, and fudging the time I got back, for the very same reason I pocketed one of those salt and pepper lighthouses, which is to say, for no reason, or none I'd care to admit.

Early fall continued as late summer had been spent, a dozen or more visits with John to the flophouse, where I was getting to know everyone by name, and where no one ever told me my lipstick was too red, or my new haircut too short, or my arched eyebrows plucked too thin, or my eyelids painted too dark silver. We put on records and danced, John shuffling side to side, or more often sitting, fingers gripped around a glass, watching me dancing with other women, who left all too quickly after they'd finished their visits and eaten their tuna sandwiches or salami and eggs. Or, just as often, with other men. The men all said they were charmed by my laugh, and so I laughed even more to please them.

But I'm confusing the order of things slightly, and failing to remember that just after the Yosemite trip, the very first thing I did was go to the city for two days and apply for jobs in advertising. I'm muddling that for good reason, as one does when logical lines begin to split and go in different directions: the researcher and decadent paramour I had been, and the confident lover and future professional woman I wished to be, for whom doors were no longer opening so easily. Make no mistake: my own Johns Hopkins days were over, and Albert had gone away, but there is no such thing as a clean break. Our most famous experiment would inform every professional and philosophical position John ever took, and everything we'd ever done together during those Hopkins days, every pain we'd ever caused, like every self-deception we'd ever practiced, would have shadows and echoes.

I did not realize it at the time, of course. I embraced optimism. What other choice did I have?

Staying with Hilda and her friends, with all their talk of fashion magazines and new opportunities for women, had given me the courage to think about a new direction for myself. My writing skills were more than adequate, and of course I felt I knew something about what women would like to buy, and how to speak to them. Ad agencies were thriving and I would love being in the city in my own apartment. John could visit me often, of course. It would put us on a more balanced footing, for him to have his world, and I to have mine, at least until he brought his marriage to its conclusion. Maybe if we came to the next stage of our relationship with equal independence, we could create something different and more lasting, exceeding the expectations of anyone who had an opinion about modern marriage.

My most exciting moment was a call to interview at an ad agency on Lexington Avenue. I actually included in my alumnae note to Vassar that I was fairly sure I'd gotten the job. I shouldn't have been so eager to spread that news prematurely, but I suppose I wanted everyone to know I had plans, I was charting my own course, just in case word got out that I wasn't continuing at Johns Hopkins.

All summer, John had exhibited no concern whatsoever about his own professional standing. A dozen universities had tried luring him for the last decade, he'd spent more time turning down jobs than seeking them, and he was utterly convinced of the merit of his own theories and experiments, especially the most recent work. He felt he was indispensable. Each step toward divorce, including the most recent July separation agreement, had added to the rumors circulating around campus, about the cause of the divorce and the various dramatic steps leading up to it. John did nothing to counter the gossip or to prove that he felt any remorse. The problem wasn't just that he was divorcing, of course; it was that he was having an affair, and not with anyone, but with a student.

Adolf Meyer, in John's corner more than not, had written John a letter in September, when we were visiting the flophouse often and were at our most incautious, expressing that he hoped John would continue at the university, but that he must sever his relationship with me and acknowledge, without reservation, the impropriety of what he had done. John ignored that warning letter. Then in October, John was called into President Goodnow's office. Even if Goodnow had failed to notice my small role in the lab, he recognized my last name. My own grandfather, William Solomon Rayner, had made a sizable donation to Johns Hopkins in the year after my birth. That hurt our case, rather than helping it. The university seemed to feel even more of a custodial responsibility toward me. If John were a different man—if he'd simply apologized, or acted contrite, instead of wagging a progressive finger at anyone who restricted his social and sexual imperatives—things might have turned out differently.

John may have known more than most of his peers about psychology and biology. What he didn't care much about was history. We'd both heard the story, from the time just before John had come to Baltimore, of the prof who'd been let go after being caught in a bordello. The administration had made one stand against such shenanigans, more than adequate rehearsal for standing firm against another. But John didn't see how that former case applied to him.

That day in October, John walked into Goodnow's office. When he walked out, he'd left a letter of resignation behind, scrawled at that moment, spontaneously and irritably, on a blank piece of university stationery sitting on Goodnow's desk. John packed his bags and went to New York, to temporarily live with a sympathetic friend, a sociologist named William Thomas, who had been dismissed from the University of Chicago, for similar reasons.

Meyer had wanted John to admit his errors. John didn't want to, especially at first, and he maintained it was their loss for getting rid of him. But he did have one moment of doubt after all his bravado. He asked me, the next time I saw him, "You don't think I should go back and try to explain, do you?"

"Apologize, you mean?"

"Not that." But he was considering something close, I could tell. He was deciding what it would take to eat some crow.

"You don't need to go begging. You can do better," I said with my heart in my throat, hoping. "We both can."

Maybe I thought that the least reward I could get from this debacle was John all to myself, in a faraway city preferably. We could run away, self-righteous and unrepentant. At the time, it seemed an easy enough thing to do.

There were some inconvenient details, however. I left Hopkins with a blank transcript—no degree, no courses listed, certainly no published dissertation. At the time, I judged it—I *had* to judge it—as a mere setback. I might try another type of job here or there, to add some spice to my life, but I didn't expect never to study or work in a university again. That simply wasn't imaginable. Those had been the happiest and most productive days of my life.

If the city visits and flophouse stopovers had been debauched fun appropriate to the steamy days of late summer, the headlines that appeared in later 1920 were a cold autumn shower.

I came down at breakfast time to the rattling sound of my father hurrying to hide a newspaper on the table, and then changing his mind and pushing it in my direction, wrists balanced at the edge of the table, fingers still flexing in aggravation.

"What am I doing? You're going to see it. You *have* to see it. I can't protect you anymore."

"Protect her?" Mother asked rhetorically, in a dead voice.

Father was near tears. Mother was already temporarily drained of hers. She sat at a right angle to him, eyes pink, handkerchief in her fist, next to an untouched bowl of oatmeal.

I took the newspaper without making eye contact. There it was, in black and white. The newspaper article discussed John's dismissal and the fact that his wife was suing for divorce following an affair. It hadn't named me yet, though anyone at Johns Hopkins would know my identity. It could be worse. It *might* be worse, in terms of my equilibrium as well as my future prospects, very soon.

I was trying my hardest not to blow things up out of proportion. But there were other people and situations to think of: people involved in my father's business, my mother's social circles, our extended family, our synagogue. My family had come to Baltimore and labored hard to create a life here. And thanks to thin newsprint suitable for fish wrapping, that life might never be the same.

I could guess how many people had seen my name in print a few months earlier, when my first scientific paper had been published. Enough to count on the fingers of one hand. No one would have actually read it, first page to last, but my father would have carried a copy to his synagogue board meeting and waved it in front of a few faces, just to show what his daughter was doing with her education. I held my breath now, naively hoping that if my name did finally appear, no one would notice it under this particular circumstance.

In the days that followed, Frank was instructed to visit the nearest newsstand every two to three hours, checking the headlines of every large and small East Coast paper for the Rayner family name. When he came home with a dozen printed copies, nearly sending my father into apoplexy, we realized that his reading skills were even more modest than previously estimated, and we sent Agnus with him on all subsequent times, to monitor the news together. Her first language was German, and she had a little trouble with reading herself, but she could certainly skim the pages quickly for our surname. I think my father was sure it would be buried somewhere, easy to overlook, damning but obscure, in a column of tiny print. If only.

My father stayed home from work, and each time Frank and Agnus left, we gathered in the parlor. Each of us pretended to read a magazine or novel (not a newspaper; now they all seemed contaminated) and awaited the sound of the kitchen door opening, at the back of the house. Each time Frank would step in, with Agnus behind him, and tiptoe quietly through the hallway, as if our house had been transformed into a funeral parlor, and come to stand in the doorway to the room where we three sat, mostly ignored books and magazines or knitting across our knees. Frank would clear his throat and say, "Nothing yet, Mr. Rayner," and then wait to be excused. Each time, as if it had been the very first time, my father would say, "Of course. Thank you, Frank. And check again in about two hours, will you?" Frank would look across at the grandfather clock and look up at the ceiling, doing a mental calculation and say, "Sure, I can do that. Thank you, sir."

That first evening, at a dinner that was scarcely touched, my mother invented her own theories about journalistic protocol, including her firm belief that no newspaperman worth his salt would publish the name of a girl alleged to be involved in an affair, without proof, or even—she stammered here—with proof. The married man's name yes, but not the girl's. The divorce proceedings were scheduled for November—which is why the newspapers were chasing every lead—but the court had been discreet. They had not released my name. One could hope, my mother surmised, they never would.

The phone rang several times that first day, and the second, but I was never called to the phone and hadn't the heart to ask if any of the calls had been from John.

It began to seem like sitting shivah, that seven-day Jewish period of mourning, with its rituals of remaining in the house with bodies and hair unwashed, clothing torn as a sign of grief, mirrors covered. The difference is that, during shivah, loved ones all gather with food and condolence. In this case, the few who gathered, my mother couldn't bear to see, and many others turned away, pretending not to know, their sensitivities offended.

The second night, in the parlor once again—my mother commented, "I'm just glad Isidor already passed." My uncle, the senator, who had died in 1912, would have been dragged through the mud on account of this, an occasion of frivolous joy for his enemies.

"He was only the fourth Jewish senator, you know," my father said—which of course, I did know. And he was Maryland attorney general, and chairman of the *Titanic* hearings, and a great many other things. "He was asked to run for vice president. Twice. But he didn't. The only time he mentioned his Jewish heritage . . ."

I knew the rest of the story as well as I knew about Washington's cherry tree and Lincoln's log cabin. The only time my uncle had mentioned his Jewish heritage in a political setting was when he was fighting an amendment that would have disenfranchised colored voters in Maryland. He said that if such legal wording had been adopted earlier, his very own father from Bavaria would have been denied the vote.

I still remembered the first thing I'd ever told my father about John that had earned his respect. He had admired John for not believing in eugenics, for not damning a person or assuming inherent weaknesses because of supposed "innate" differences due to ethnicity, religion, or race. That was all still true. They were not the most common popular positions in those days or for many years to come, and to eject from professional scholarship a man who was willing to stand up for them, vocally and tirelessly—even obnoxiously—was to risk changing a fine balance in the world of science, which because it was the field that spoke for progress, overlapped the world of politics. John's views in this regard very much matched my father's. But my father wouldn't be able to stand hearing the name John Watson for a very long time.

Father finished telling the story of Isidor's famous political stand. Recalling this moment of political honesty, his voice trembling, my own eyes began to fill, and the harder my father labored to finish the story, the more my own lips began to quiver, my own nose to redden and run. I was so sorry for what I'd done—but only to my parents and the good memory of Uncle Isidor, that rabble-rouser. Only to them.

After what had seemed an endless wait but was, in truth, only a matter of days, Frank came back with the final edition of the *Washington Times*. He stood in the doorway, hands behind his back, and we waited for him to say the routine line, "Nothing yet, Mr. Rayner." But he didn't. He just rocked back and forth slightly until my father lost his patience and said, "Delay won't make things any better. Bring it here, then."

Above the newspaper's banner title, the large headline ran: BLUE-EYED MYSTERY CO-RESPONDENT IS ROSALIE RAYNER. And further down: DC BEAUTY IS NAMED IN SUIT.

My father got the first look. After all, it was his name: Rayner, son of William Solomon Rayner, son of William from Oberelsbach, a simple schoolteacher, who had come to America and worked as a dry-goods merchant in Fells Point until he could afford to send for his children and sweetheart, Amalie.

"So there it is," Father said. "One name, one reputation. That's what we get in life."

How old-fashioned he seemed at that moment, but what he said felt true. I never wanted to leave my house again.

Still, somehow in my ignorance, with that first journalistic exposure, I thought the worst was over, not realizing that press only begets more press, and that now every newspaper wanted to run the same story, with or without its own supplementary details and color. The attention lasted a full month, fueled by Mary Ickes, who had invited a reporter into her living room in her new home in New York City. She pretended that it had been her intention to keep my identity secret all along. But now that the word was out, she felt compelled to explain, adding the color and drama she knew newshounds fall over themselves to get: that I refused to hide away in Europe, that John's attitude toward a mistress like me was "out of sight, out of mind," in her gentle opinion. She came off sounding like the tired wife who had put up with much and was still willing to put up with more, if only her husband would mend his ways. I was the one painted in the bleakest colors by her one-sided portrait. I came off not as a glamorous hussy, but only as a young, dim-witted, marriage-wrecking fool.

Reporters came to our door, confusing the servants, and baffling Father, who had never had to turn anyone away. On one of the first occasions, a reporter came while we were eating dinner, and he was allowed in and invited to sit on a bench in the hallway while we finished. After choking down a last few spoiled bites, Father called his lawyer, then went back out to the hallway and told the reporter to leave. After the door closed, he muttered to Mother, "I'm not a criminal. I don't know what's expected or required in these circumstances."

"Well of course you don't, Albert," she said, and looked at me.

CHAPTER 18

Which left only the divorce itself, just weeks away. One year from the time John first kissed me on the cheek, one year from the beginning of our research with Albert, the court proceedings began. John had made it clear he would contest nothing, and he'd already agreed to the settlement, which granted full custody to Mary and would reduce his income to a third. I was not called to testify, and the only witnesses who were called in were not our close friends—not Leslie or William on John's side, not Mary Cover on mine, and no one at all from the lab, thank goodness.

It was bad enough that, outside of a court, John had started to hear that lab colleagues and friends were speaking about him in disloyal, demeaning ways. They'd said to his face that he was the most brilliant psychologist of his day, second in influence only to Freud, and now they were saying that his experimental design was faulty and his research record not very deep. Most of them would be ready to take it all back whenever John managed to reclaim his professional glory, but still. I'd never felt closer to him than when I saw his vast circle grow smaller and smaller, his enemies emboldened by the rising swell of snide comments, his so-called friends weakening in their resolve to defend him.

John reenacted the trial details for me only later, in William's Thirty-Fourth Street apartment, after the proceedings had concluded. William, who had heard it all once already, got up and left the room, leaving a bottle of bourbon and two glasses on the table.

The judge—John explained to me now, voice caustic and slurred—asked Mary how she knew. We'd been seen, "at various lunch rooms, and in her machine at all hours of the day."

William MacGruder was brought to the stand. He was the boarder with whom we'd shared laughs and drinks at the flophouse. The judge asked: "Do you know the cause of the separation?"

"Yes I do."

"Can you state what it was?"

"A brown-hair girl with blue eyes, was the cause of the separation."

Why on earth had he been so coy? It was like he was quoting from the headlines.

The judge asked, "Do you know her first name?"

"Rosalie."

"Do you know what the relations were between the Defendant in this case and the girl named Rosalie?"

"I know that they were intimate from all appearances."

He'd seen us in the flophouse, MacGruder told the judge, "many times. A great many times. I hate like thunder to say it."

Then there was Feeny, who had been a tenant in Dr. Thomas's house, this very same house. He, like MacGruder, had seen me coming and going from a bedroom, wearing a man's bathrobe.

The pièce de résistance, the part that all the newspapers had been waiting for, was more details about the love letters, thirteen or fourteen of them, which had already been leaked in part. These were John's words, immortalized in the public record now, not in my own possession anymore as keepsakes: "Could you kiss me for two hours right now without getting weary?"

And: "My total reactions are positive and toward you. So likewise each and every heart reaction. I can't be any more yours than I am even if a surgical operation made us one."

All those wonderful, silly notes, about the North Pole and our cells and his reactions and our love. Only evidence now, thanks to the newspapers, which had reproduced them in bits and pieces, converted into jokes for dinner parties happening in DC, Baltimore, and New York.

The fact that it was all over didn't make it any less aversive. What had John written about the lasting effects of Albert's fear conditioning? That the effects were likely to "persist indefinitely."

"I don't know what you're willing to pay," John had said to me last December, that first teasing encounter. Now I could answer: *This*. We had lost the good faith of our families and some of our friends, and we had lost our professions and our reputations and our right to privacy, together.

I reminded myself that people have fled a great many things worse than what we had suffered. I had to remember and be gay. It was up to us, now, to create our own life of luck and fun. John has always maintained—and I hoped now it was so simple—that it was Mary's sourness, in addition to her lack of interest in sex, that had pushed the final wedge between them. We would have the last laugh *only* by laughing. And—John would remind me—by succeeding.

John had been writing letters, making phone calls, and squeezing every last faithful friend and colleague for letters of reference to find a new job. Some were willing to vouch for him. One academic colleague wrote a letter emphasizing John's integrity, though even he conceded that John could be immature and impulsive. But then again, we were in the Jazz Age now. Some kinds of self-control were old-fashioned, and there was nothing more dangerous, if you were trying to make a name for yourself in 1920, than being called old-fashioned.

In December, after the trial but before the divorce was completely finalized, John finally found something. His friend, William Thomas, had made the connection and secured him the all-important interview. It was not the path I'd envisioned for him, but John was determined and strangely eager. He was going to work in a skyscraper on Lexington Avenue. If he lasted the rigorous training period, they promised to pay him many times what he'd earned as an academic, which was essential, since the divorce meant he kept so little of it, and Manhattan living wasn't cheap. He was going to have power and money, and most important, influence. He was going to be an ad man.

It wasn't enough, of course, that he'd get a desk job in the city, writing up copy, as so many people begin—as I, frankly, would have been happy to begin. I hadn't heard back from many of my applications or interviews. Sometimes I wondered if John even remembered that I'd interviewed for an advertising job before he did—if he even remembered his early admiration for my professional ambitions. This wasn't the time to remind him. Despite his bold intentions, his ego was more fragile than I'd ever seen it, and he countered that fragility by being more vocal and more audacious in his claims for his own as-yet-unproven corporate abilities.

J. Walter Thompson was a prestigious agency that had been bought a few years earlier by a man named Stanley Resor, who had already conceived of the idea of a research division, and specifically, of finding scientists interested in investigating the "psychology of appeal." John's friend William, though he had personally helped John get a foot in the door, was intrigued but skeptical, wary of this use of behaviorist principles. There was no such skepticism on John's part. He was going to transform the entire business, using everything he'd learned about behavior in the service of selling products. John had been trying to change the world one way. Now he was on the rebound, completely convinced he would change it just as much, only from a different angle.

After failing to hear back from the advertising agency that I had been sure was interested in hiring *me*, I attended a final interview that month as well. This second agency was smaller, at a less impressive address. I walked up a dusty stairwell to a third-floor personnel office, and with no secretary showing me the way, rapped on the pebbled glass door of a room at the end of the hall. Inside, an old fan was blowing with such vigor, failing to stir the overheated air, that I had to strain to listen to the tired words, "It's open."

From behind his desk, a man ushered me in, pointed to the less damaged of two ancient leather club chairs, and squinted at my résumé. "Rayner. That sounds familiar."

"My grandfather helped found Har Sinai Congregation, in Baltimore."

"No, that isn't it. Rayner. *Rayner.*"

"My father is in real estate."

"No. So let's see. You were last working at . . ."

I'd already pulled out a pocket steno pad and an envelope containing several transcripts and letters of recommendation.

"Johns Hopkins. *Rosalie* Rayner? Of DC?"

"I don't know why they claimed I was from DC," I said. I might as well have said, *I don't know why the newspapers claimed I was a beauty.* Even he looked disappointed, ogling me for one long, lousy minute until I stood up. I held out my envelope of papers, but he didn't reach out to take them. I slid my papers back into my purse and leaned far over his desk, reaching out a hand to shake—to insist on shaking, as if this were just one stop in a very busy schedule, and I had to be going.

"Thank you, anyway, for your time," I said, though a mischievous and distinctly unfriendly smile had formed on his face. "I'll show myself out."

The divorce came through on Christmas Eve, timed so that John's wife and children would never forget it. Christmas was murder, John had always said. Well, now all of the Ickes-Watsons, including little Polly, who had refused to go back to school that fall, would think so, too.

We waited a week and married on December 31. Finally, 1920 and all its bad memories would be behind us. The New Year, 1921, would be ours. Just as we raised our glasses to toast the uncounted hours we'd soon be spending together—in our very own home, together at last in New York City, a domestic honeymoon but all that I needed—I was informed of a slight hitch.

"There's a traveling requirement, a sort of probationary period, at least for the first two or three months," John told me, turning away to refill his glass.

"Together?" I asked hopefully, just as willing to swap domestic bliss for a working honeymoon. I always liked to be around John when he was working. Frankly, I couldn't imagine him spending much time *not* working.

"Not together," he said. "Regrettably."

He hid his expression behind a lifted glass, but once he put it down, I could still see, from his squint, that he was worried how I'd take it. I determined to take it in stride.

"The more challenges they throw at you, the faster you'll rise," I said.

"But how about you?"

He might as well have been throwing me a ball again, as he'd done that day back at the New School lecture, seeing whether I'd wince or fumble or show any fear. John was always willing to reach. That's what excused his tendency for overstatement and excess. That's what I loved best about him. I had to reach just as far, and sometimes blindly.

"I'll be busy making us a home," I said, trying to sound unbothered. "I'll be busy proving what people seem so inclined to doubt. That we're in it for the long run. That we're not just man and wife, but true partners."

The love and pride in his eyes at that moment was undeniable—a force to see us through gossip or scandal, and any kind of public or private opposition, months apart if necessary. I might have convinced myself I was glad for this additional challenge, if only to prove my faith in him and in us.

He came close and took me in his arms. "And if people don't believe?"

"They'll just have to believe. You'll be the first to tell them."

PART II

DR. WATSON SAYS

Under sex excitement the male may go to any length to capture a willing female. Once sex activity has been completed the restless seeking movements disappear. The female no longer stimulates the male to sex activity.

—John Watson, *Behaviorism*, 1930

The young married woman today brought up on the poetry of motherhood written for another era has a rude awakening when she becomes pregnant.

—Rosalie Rayner Watson,
"What Future Has Motherhood?" 1932

CHAPTER 19

"It's rich and tasty, you have my word. Would you consider . . ." John said, just as the door slammed in his face. "Son of a bitch. I'm not here to violate your daughters. I'm just here to give you a complimentary sample."

He was "Yubanning it," as he liked to say, through towns of Tennessee so small they didn't appear on most maps. Reading his postcards, my imagination would take flight and I'd envision long, footsore days of muddy backroads, twitching curtains, barking coonhounds, and old women with stumps for teeth pausing their rockers only long enough to say, "Listen, feller, I don't know what Yuban is but I don't want any."

"It's coffee," I imagined him telling them. "Only coffee." And then, remembering his training. Not *only* coffee: "The Private Coffee of the Greatest Coffee Merchants."

Given his Valentino looks, I felt sure that there were also days he was invited into kitchens that smelled of roasted chicory and apple pie and maybe a spot of rotgut whiskey. It was wintertime, after all, so I gathered there were more folks huddling around their stoves than rocking on their porches—more toasty scenes of hospitality, like the mother fixing up a plate while the slim-legged daughter in a tight white cardigan inquired as to John's place of permanent residence and plans for the future.

At J. Walter Thompson, every male employee, no matter his background or ambitions, had to train in each department, including traveling sales and retail, so that he would understand what it was like to try to sell a product—not just write up copy for a magazine, but actually look a customer in the face and get them to say not only yes, but "yes, please."

Later, he would reassure me that it hadn't been private residences so much, but rather small-town grocery stores he'd been visiting—the retailers themselves—and maybe it was my own worried fantasizing about the temptations of a traveling salesman's life that planted all those domestic pictures in my mind. But whether it was a pretty clerk in a store or a daughter in a shack at the end of the lane, I'm sure he charmed plenty of girls during his salesman days.

Then he was back, neither deeply humbled nor unduly triumphant, just his regular self, a Boy Scout with one badge, ready to go for the next, which required another training stint—this time at Macy's. At least that was in the city, where we could be together.

My job was to set up housekeeping.

"Go ahead. Shop, decorate. Do what women do," John said, leaving for his department-store shift. And then he'd remember to smile, that closed-lip smile that still evoked mischief, even though we were no longer hiding or sneaking around.

It was hard to shop when the money went so quickly and the future supply was not yet secure. There was no point in endlessly comparing sofas and china sets when we couldn't afford them. Our windows needed coverings, and it occurred to me after an afternoon spent looking through expensive catalogs that there must be a cheaper way. The next day, at the fabric store, it occurred to me that I didn't know how to sew. Or how to clean. Or how to cook, for that matter.

Mother had felt no need to teach me the domestic arts, since I wouldn't need them; there were always other people willing and able to scrub a stoop or roast a chicken, she'd assured me. John wasn't suggesting I should become a domestic expert, either. He didn't necessarily want a wife who cooked. When we had lots of money, other people would do it. Anyway, hadn't some of our best dinners been nothing more than salami, eggs, and bourbon? No need to get fancy now. What he wanted most, he told me, wasn't chicken Kiev or steak tartare, but a lively person to come home to.

John had burned most of his bridges, but he was happy with this new side of the river. Rather than feeling put-upon working as a sales clerk at Macy's, he saw it as a fascinating challenge. What made people buy certain things? Where did the desires come from? How did they choose? He came home each day bursting with new questions and hypotheses. He started experimenting, by reorganizing the display cases. He moved inexpensive items onto the countertops so people could touch them more easily and spend time gazing at them while they waited for larger purchases to be rung up and boxed. He imagined how impulse-nurturing could change the look and layout of every department, from grocery to footwear. John had been criticized, even in the otherwise positive reference letters that had gotten him this job, for being impulsive. He was determined to prove that *everyone* was impulsive. Customers could be steered into buying much more than what they'd planned to buy on any given day.

"And what did you do today?" he asked one evening over drinks, when he had no more stories of his own to tell.

I hesitated. "This and that. It was just so busy, I've forgotten."

"Good. Oh—I almost forgot." His face broke out in a schoolboy grin. "Office day tomorrow. We have a speaker coming."

J. Walter Thompson prided itself on being the "university of advertising," with not only the biggest billings of any agency, and some two hundred employees, but also a philosophy about ongoing education, research, and self-improvement. Every two weeks, a prominent figure was brought in to talk to the staff.

"Darrow," John said, loosening his tie.

"Clarence Darrow, the famous lawyer?"

I tried to look lively. Not envious, just attentive.

"That's right."

"Aren't there plenty of people who hate him for defending murderers?"

"Anyone who's great at what he does—anyone with a new idea, period—excites the common man's wrath."

As a sometimes beloved, sometimes reviled man, John was in good company, in other words. But I didn't want to hear Darrow speak because he was controversial. I just wanted to hear about ideas that mattered, one way or another. Maybe I just wanted out of a boring apartment.

I'd been scrimping for several weeks, limiting our food budget, skipping my own lunch at home altogether, pretending at dinner that my half-size portion was all that I really wanted, trying to set aside money to buy the curtains I didn't have the talent to sew, and several other items, besides. Though I was feeling under the weather the day after John mentioned the guest speaker, I knew better than to waste money on a subway token when my own two feet would suffice. I arrived at the JWT building lightheaded but happy. I'd made it in time to casually stop by just in advance of Darrow's late-morning visit.

Up I went to the JWT offices, gloves in hand, trying to catch my reflection in the shining gold-trim surface of the elevator doors as the elevator boy stopped at one floor after another. Since John had gotten the job, I hadn't yet visited him at work, delaying purposefully until he'd finished his training period. But I couldn't wait any longer. The flutter in my stomach as the elevator cage whirred and shuddered, pulling us up and into those higher reaches of Manhattan, that world high above the noise and street smells, reminded me of my nerves on my first day at Johns Hopkins. John had been excited then to show me every room, every outlet and cabinet and custom-ordered chair, because he'd been instrumental in the lab's design. This would have to be an even grander tour, given the size of the company and its near monopoly of the top advertising accounts up and down the East Coast. When the elevator boy announced my arrival: "J. Walter Thompson. Have a good day, Ma'am," I stepped out, not knowing if this were the only floor or just one of many.

The agency entryway was guarded by two receptionists seated side-by-side. "John Watson, please," I said.

Twenty minutes later, John came into the reception area, still laughing over his shoulder at some joke he'd just heard in the hallway. He stopped.

"Rosalie. Everything all right?"

"Of course I'm all right. I just thought . . ."

He took a chair next to me, while I craned my neck to see past the framed soap advertisements on the wall.

"I can't go to lunch, you understand."

"Oh, I understand completely. It's just . . ."

Four men entered the agency, strolled past the receptionists and continued down another hall, into some inner sanctum. One of them might have been Darrow, though I'd seen only the back of him, and surely the man in front was Stanley Resor, whom I'd met once, very briefly and just by chance, when I happened to be standing on a platform with John at Grand Central Station. But then they were gone, off with their kind.

"Rar, why are you here?"

It made no sense to me either, now. John wouldn't have his own office until he finished his training. The biweekly lectures weren't open to just anyone. I didn't even care about law or Darrow, especially. I just wanted to hear what one idea man said to dozens of other idea men. It had to be more interesting than trying to make curtains. But I realized now it had been a wasted trip, and I was only tired and a little headachy from walking all those blocks with the horns beeping and the people late for their jobs, pushing to get around me, all of us dwarfed by the city itself, and made acutely aware of our roles or lack of significant roles in the towering buildings.

John lowered his voice. "This looks a little peculiar—like my mother noticed I forgot my lunch and came to school with it."

"I did bring you something," I said. That morning, he'd been running late, complaining that one of the socks he'd just pulled on had a hole (one of us really did have to learn to sew, and quickly). I'd thought to pack a different clean pair, folded inside my purse, just in case of this moment, when a better excuse was needed. "Something you were wishing for with great enthusiasm this morning."

A mischievous smile formed on his face. We'd had a discussion—I wouldn't quite call it a tiff—about the manner in which we each woke up, and what our first priorities were, aside from coffee.

"Not that, of course," I said.

"Clean socks?" He put a hand up to his neck, rubbing it, and made an exaggerated head-roll motion that was equal parts fatigue and disbelief. "I hope you're joking."

I was an inch from unsnapping my purse. I pulled back my hand. "Of course I'm joking. I was just in the neighborhood. Before I leave, is there a place where I can freshen up?"

"Fran will show you. I've got to get back." He gave his own neck one more rub for good measure, reached out to pat me on the side of the arm, and walked away.

Fran, who looked about my age, turned to the woman at her side, older by ten or fifteen years. "Mel, are you going to the cafeteria soon? I might want a sandwich. When I come back, don't let me forget. I'll give you some money."

Fran walked me down another hallway, opposite the direction John had gone, and waited as I used the facilities and composed myself. She seemed satisfied with getting a chance to be away from her desk, and when, on the way back, I slowed to look at more pictures on the wall, she loitered alongside me. I noticed another short hallway, with a large interior window onto a conference room filled almost entirely with women.

"Secretarial training?"

Fran was still putting her lipstick back in her purse. "Them? No, they're not secretaries."

"What are they, then?"

She squinted. "Copywriters, mostly. Gladys there is an illustrator—one of the best. Melba is in Research. I think Evelyn just got promoted."

The woman standing at the head of table looked up and noticed us.

"That's Helen, of course," Fran said.

"Who's Helen?"

". . . Lansdowne Resor. Stanley's wife."

So wives did make impromptu visits—dropping lunch, socks, or a clean shirt. Or maybe she was socializing with the female employees she'd come to know through Stanley. But it took only another moment for me to look again at her posture, bent over, one hand braced on the table, the other still holding a pencil with which she'd been marking up a large illustration, until she looked up and noticed us staring. One of her legs was extended slightly back in a general's stance, directing the attention of the whole room. She looked to be in her middle thirties: hair medium long and loosely pulled away from her face and knotted at the nape of her neck, not exactly the latest style. She was handsome more than pretty, with slightly dark skin, as though she enjoyed being out in the sun and didn't care for heavy, pale powder. Over her long skirt she wore a double-breasted jacket, mannish at the shoulders, but with a softer collar, and her lace-up walking boots, though freshly shined, were at least ten years out of date, more suited to a former suffragette than a currently fashionable Manhattanite.

A pane of glass stood between us, but still, I kept my voice to a whisper. "And what does she do?"

"Why, she runs JWT."

"I thought Stanley did."

"He runs client services: you know, shake hands, have a drink, and here's the bill. She designs the ads and comes up with new ways to run campaigns."

"Isn't designing ads and running campaigns the *main* thing an agency does?"

"I suppose so. I guess you could say she runs the meetings that the public doesn't see and Stanley runs the meetings the public does see, if that makes any sense."

Helen Lansdowne Resor was still looking back at us, eyes narrowed, as if she was trying to place me. Whenever someone *did* recognize my face or name lately, it didn't go well. I instinctively hunched down a bit.

"She must know my husband," I said.

"He's hard to miss," Fran agreed, stifling a smile, which raised a tickle of bilious worry in my gut. I wanted John to do well here. I didn't want him—or our marriage—to be the butt of jokes. We had to prove somehow that we didn't care, even if I did care. The only way to come up with snappy retorts was to know what everyone was saying behind our backs in the first place.

"I didn't mean that in a negative way," Fran said, hurrying to correct the misunderstanding that was etching new worry lines into my face. "It's just a story we've all heard, that's all. Mrs. Resor interviewed your husband. He had to say what new ideas he'd bring to the company, of course."

"Only natural," I said, to encourage her.

"So he said he would use . . . well, *sex* . . . to sell products."

I exhaled. Yes, that certainly sounded like him.

"And Helen—Mrs. Resor—said, 'My dear Dr. Watson, I was using sex to sell products while you were still running rats through mazes.'"

Fran turned, gesturing with her chin toward a triptych of framed advertisements that lined one side of the hall. The nearest read: "Woodbury's Facial Soap: The Skin You Love to Touch."

"That was hers—one of the most successful ad campaigns of all time."

I followed Fran out to the reception area and asked if I could take a seat—just a spot of dizziness again, and I wanted to store up enough energy to last me the long walk back. Fran's deskmate had come back already with the sandwiches.

"Oh, I thought you'd wait," Fran lamented. "I was going to watch the desk for you."

"Jane went down," the other woman explained. "She picked them up for all of us."

I took a deep breath, trying to look relaxed and not out of place, as Fran lifted a corner of bread. "Egg salad drowning in mayo. Just what I was afraid of. Do you want it?"

Her deskmate shook her head. "I'm borrowing my cousin's dress for Saturday and it's a tight fit already."

Fran sniffed again. Her eyes lifted and happened to meet mine.

"You don't want a sandwich, do you, Mrs. Watson?"

I didn't register what she was asking at first—though I practiced using the name, I wasn't fully used to hearing myself called Mrs. Watson. I'd been staring with absentminded hunger at that sandwich in her hand, white bread with tan crusts and white-yellow creamy cubes of egg salad spilling onto the wax paper. Her kind offer caught me off guard and brought me, inexplicably, to the edge of teariness. At home, I liked egg salad. But suddenly now, the queasiness hit, as if I'd hated eggs my entire life. I had to drop my head toward my knees.

It took me a moment to say, "No, thank you." I studied the herringbone pattern on my skirt, vision darkening for a moment, and then brightening again, the lines of my skirt amazingly sharp, every stitch visible.

"Are you all right?" Fran asked.

I looked up, every ounce of effort poured into clearing my expression and looking serene, even while the pinpricks of sweat moistened my forehead. In a flash, I was hot and just as quickly cold, armpits and legs under my skirt and scalp all damp in that quick flash of heat.

Just then, Helen Resor entered the reception area. She put on a bright, just-in-case smile and sang out, "Are you a client?"

"No," I said, hurrying to my feet. *Steady; steady.*

"I saw you in the hall. You looked like you were searching for someone." Her voice rang in my ears, unnaturally loud, softening into normal tones as my stomach settled and my vision cleared. "We have a special guest here today so I just thought perhaps you were looking for him . . ."

When I explained that I was only John Watson's wife, she responded with what seemed like genuine warmth. For the next minute or so, I tried to sound moderately intelligent and interested in advertising but not desperately so, hoping my face wasn't shining with too much sweat, hoping that my words were coming out in more or less sensible fashion.

At the end, she looked over her shoulder, in the direction Darrow and my own husband had gone. She had to get going. "Call me Helen. I so look forward to getting to know you better. I can tell we'd get along. I do hope you'll be joining us."

My breath caught. Joining her, joining them? Joining J. Walter Thompson? John must have put in a good word, explaining I'd been on a job hunt of my own. Perhaps he'd made it clear how well we worked together, or even better—perhaps she simply recognized a modern woman with vitality. I would do anything, in any capacity. At that point, it didn't even matter whether they paid me. I'd continue skipping lunches if only my brain could be fed. My days in the apartment had become more empty than I'd been willing to admit, even to myself.

"Joining us two weeks from now," she added, studying my face.

So much to do between now and then. So much to learn. "Two weeks," I repeated back.

I was glowing—sweating—smiling. Helen looked at me quizzically.

"Joining us for the celebration dinner?" she clarified. "I take it you know the address. After your husband officially completes his training period?"

Good thing my face was already moist and red from the queasy spell. It couldn't flush any darker, and I couldn't look any more sickly or strange.

"Oh, yes," I said. "The dinner in two weeks. Of course."

I should have been mortified by my misunderstanding, but I was less embarrassed than determined. Those nickels and quarters I'd been saving by skipping lunch and walking block after sooty block? I spent them downstairs at the newsstand, buying five magazines to study as soon as I got home: every ad, every picture, every slogan. The next time I met Helen, I'd have more to say. I'd press John for more details about JWT's campaigns, what they'd pioneered and what they were still trying to figure out. I'd fill my change purse again and keep saving what I could, in the hopes that I might buy the right kind of dress for the upcoming celebration dinner: something fashionable but not too feminine, striking just the right balance for Helen's taste.

That night in bed, John put an arm over me and pulled me close, forearm against my ribcage, palm against my spine. "You are getting a little bonier these days, aren't you?"

"Am I?" I said, pulling away.

He tugged me closer again, so that my breasts crushed up against his own soft, warm chest.

"Don't worry. You've still got plenty where it counts. I don't care for those new flat-chested fashions."

"Careful," I said, feeling tender in his strong arms. "That's a little tight."

He loosened up an inch and smiled, looking down at me. "I just can't get enough, is all."

"Even with all those beautiful women surrounding you at your office?"

"Oh, Rar," he said, chastising and forgiving me in the same moment, mistaking my comment for the first pangs of marital jealousy. But I was not—or not yet—the jealous sort. What I really wanted to know was why he hadn't told me that one of his bosses was a woman. That this was a more egalitarian field than I'd realized. That there might be opportunities for me to work at JWT as well.

He started to nibble my earlobe.

"Tell me about Helen Resor," I said.

"Later," he mumbled, face buried in my neck.

"You're hiding her from me, and that means you think I'll dislike her, or the opposite, and you don't want me fawning."

"That's right, darling. And fawning is prohibited at JWT. We're too sophisticated for that."

"You think I'll have a girl crush." His tongue darted into my ear. "That tickles. In the wrong way."

"I know they encouraged that sort of thing at Vassar," he said breathily.

"Tickling?"

"Girl crushes."

"Oh, wouldn't you like to think so." His discomfort with homosexuality extended to both genders, but at the same time, he was intrigued by the idea of women "being" with other women.

"I'll tell you about her later," he said, pushing off the covers that were getting in our way. "I'll tell you about *all* the gray-haired JWT spinsters later."

"She's not a spinster. She's married, and she must be no more than thirty . . ."

"There, you know all about her already. For now, news trailer finished. Feature entertainment to follow."

As a man in his forties, he was at his prime, and at times, it seemed, insatiable. I didn't mind his pushing. And when it came to work news, I didn't worry terribly that he was withholding. It was a dance, both ways. We all had things we wanted, precious treasures we needlessly hid, appetites that rose and fell and sometimes needed a little doing-without to stimulate. I still remembered John warning me away from the Benny Fertigs of the world, who did not want enough. Marriage, physical satisfaction, professional ambition: there was room enough, and time, for both of us to have everything we desired.

"Promise," I said, letting him unfasten me, refusing to help as he fumbled with the ribbon lacings that cinched the top of my negligee. Dear man, with his thick fingers and thumping heart.

"I promise."

"All right. But I won't let you forget."

CHAPTER 20

For the next two weeks, I pressed John for more details about Helen, which he parceled out in teasingly small bites. She was a legend already in the company, which controlled three quarters of all the advertising accounts in New York and Boston. She had increased the sale of Woodbury soap 1,000 percent. The common man outside the company didn't know much about her, and didn't need to. People inside the company seemed to take her genius and authority for granted.

But how had she found her way into such a position? That was the question I put to John. Was she the daughter of a famous businessman? I teasingly hinted that perhaps it simply ran in her family's blood. If you wanted to bait John Watson, you had only to emphasize ancestral predilections.

Refusing to give inherited traits any unearned credit, John told me what he knew about her up-by-the-bootstraps career, explaining that Helen had started working various ad-company jobs—bill auditing, writing retail ads—directly out of high school. When Stanley and his brother opened a small branch of JWT in Cincinnati, he brought her on to work for him as the sole copywriter, and she followed them when they transferred to the New York headquarters three years later.

Five years ago, Stanley had bought out the company for a half-million dollars, and a year after that, they married and continued to run the company as a team. In her position at JWT now, Helen had been known for hiring women, including suffragettes and women with science backgrounds.

"Surely, that's all you need to know," he said the night he coughed up most of her background. He'd come home after 9 P.M., skipping dinner in favor of a long evening of liquid nutrition. "I admire your interest, Rar. But you know, I go with the men for a drink after work, and the shop talk never ends. By the time I come home, I'm about done."

"Then let me come for a drink. Especially if you're not going to make it home in time for dinner."

I'd let him think I'd eaten alone, when in fact I'd made only a half portion, nibbled a few bites, and then set aside the rest for him, in the icebox. He'd told me he was going out that night with the other Research Department fellows to a "teahouse"—one of the many speakeasies doing a lively business now—and I'd known that meant I wouldn't be seeing him for hours.

Half of the time lately, I felt ravenously hungry, and the other half of the time I felt nauseated. I didn't tell John. He'd only tease me for finally living like normal people—no longer pampered by maids and cooks, forced occasionally to deal with an empty icebox or my own inferior cooking abilities. But it wasn't my bad cooking that was making me queasy. I chalked it up to anxiety and my own feelings of rootlessness. I refused to believe it could be anything else. I had the records to prove that John and I scheduled our intimacy with some care.

Loosening his tie, John said, "Never mind about Helen—you'd like these boys in Research. You really would."

I didn't need to be convinced. Working in the Hopkins lab, I'd occasionally socialized with other scientists who, at lunchtime or day's end, didn't want to talk about science anymore. But these ad men were more like John: equally obsessed, wanting to tinker and test. John was convinced they were the practical scientists of our day. People throughout America were their subjects and the experimental design was elegant. Will a certain photograph interest women in a new kind of lotion? Run the ad, offer free samples of the new product, and count how many requests are made. In the lab, it had been hard work to get hundreds of babies for testing and sometimes, to make sense of the results. It wasn't hard at all to get twenty thousand women to respond to an advertisement in a ladies' magazine, requesting free samples of a new beauty product, proving that the stimulus had worked.

"If an ad man is right," John liked to say, "the consumer behaviors prove it." I would always nod when he made those statements, showing my interest, while my brain lingered a step behind, noticing he'd said "ad man," never "ad woman." I knew it was just a turn of phrase, but as advertisers know, a turn of phrase changes everything.

John had always enjoyed the argumentative side of our science work, but not me—I'd enjoyed the sense of urgency and collaboration, the way the hours and the days flew, the stalking down of some new idea, the nailing down of an answer to some question. "Let me come out with you, John," I said.

"Listen," he tried to reassure me. "It's just a little different than the lab. I was at Hopkins years before you came along. I could make a case for any assistant. But now it's different. I have to make a name for myself first. I can't sneak a wife into my briefcase."

He was right. But I'd never imagined that word, *wife*, would sound quite so unappealing.

"Rar, you know me. I don't like to wait for anything. It won't take me very long. I could be running the place in a few years' time."

"Not if Helen and Stanley Resor have anything to say about it."

"Running it with them, I mean. One of the VPs at the very least."

He never erred on the side of modesty. It was possible. Anything was possible.

But I didn't like to wait, either.

❖   ❖   ❖

We didn't have a telephone line in the apartment, which made it easier not to talk with my mother and to ignore the fact that she might not wish to talk with me. Letters were easier: one-sided, brief.

When my mother sent a note asking about our plans for Passover—Passover again already, the last one still a bad taste in all of our mouths—I made excuses. *John's too busy. He can't miss a day of work.*

John wanted me to patch things up. He'd even hinted that it wouldn't be terrible if my parents provided us with a belated wedding gift—cash would do—that might ease us through this period until John was past probation and more generously compensated at JWT. But I couldn't ask. I wasn't even sure I'd accept if help were offered. I wanted proof that the world recognized that John and I had been a good match from the beginning, that we were right, and that I, as John's new wife, could make a household run just fine, even with scant resources.

Mother wrote again, suggesting it was just as well that John was busy. It was better, in fact, that I come alone. But that's where I had to draw the line. If he wasn't truly welcome, I couldn't go. I didn't want to become one of those daughters who ran home whenever things were difficult, to be comforted by a family whose objection to a marriage was clear. That was not a strong foundation for our future. They had been ready and eager for me to exile myself in Europe. A briefer exile in New York would have to be just as acceptable, at least until John had proven himself and they were ready to admit that our lives were not an unmitigated disaster.

The restaurant chosen for John's postprobation dinner was below street level: windowless, dark paneled, and clubby. The smell of frying fat hit us as we came down the steps. With one hand, I gripped the banister as we descended into the warm, loud, overly fragrant dark. With the other, I rested a hand over my unsettled stomach. The maître d', who immediately recognized Stanley, put us in a special room at the back.

Stanley liked to deny that he was recognizable or any kind of Manhattan bigwig, and Helen reinforced their shared modesty. She quipped, "If we were a better looking group, they'd keep us in full view."

"You'll hurt Mildred's feelings, saying that," Stanley joked back. Mildred was in Personnel. "She tries to get us handsome people. She signed off on Dr. Watson, didn't she?"

I liked hearing my husband's good looks praised. I liked even better knowing that at least two women had needed to approve his hiring. How could one wish to be living in any other place, at any other time in history? I had every reason to be optimistic. Lab science, even with its Margaret Washburns and Mary Covers, had been a closed, masculine world compared to this.

I felt his hand at the small of my back now, escorting me toward the table and guiding me away from unproductive contemplation. Why on earth should I be thinking about the past? It was only my fatigue and anxiety talking. This was a time for celebration.

At the table, John's co-workers jockeyed for their positions. Helen was at one end of the long table, and Stanley at the other, and John, the man of honor, stood between them, waiting to be tugged in either direction, while the other men—researchers and copywriters—made quick dashes for middle-of-the-table seats, like children playing duck, duck, goose.

"Here, Rosalie, you'll be next to me," Helen said, indicating a seat at her right. "John, you sit next to your lovely wife." I felt honored, and grateful to collapse into the chair, scooting into place, all our legs tucked in tight to avoid kicking one another. The food here was good, not great, John had told me beforehand. But there were cocktails, and supposedly a back wall connected to chutes where the liquor bottles would drop at the flip of a switch, if the police came in. The police who weren't already here drinking, that is.

Seated, my dress felt even tighter around the middle. It was the first major purchase I'd ever had to save for carefully, a quarter here and a dollar there, sacrificing along the way, and it was nearly perfect: panels of dark navy and white, sleeveless, slim-cut. I kept the matching blue jacket on, even thought it was too warm at the table, because the ensemble looked more elegant than the dress alone, and plus, I could feel sweat rings already darkening the cloth under my arms. In a moment of daring, using kitchen shears, I'd cut my hair even shorter, and now I wore a close-fitting hairband, with a cloth rosette on one side, over the right ear. Hearing about Helen's love of art, I'd trekked all the way to Brooklyn for a free museum showing of Art Nouveau works, and I hoped the subject would come up, that I'd be able to find a subtle way to mention it to her.

She turned to me, "Now that's a smart suit. Rosalie, you could give me some good advice on my own fashion regimen. I'm afraid I don't take the time to keep up."

"Oh, but you do. Your clothes are gorgeous."

"No, no," she laughed, looking away—and I made a note, no unnecessary flattery, no bending the truth, not with Helen. I thought I'd lost her attention already, but she was only flagging down a waiter. She turned back to me and said, "I'm frugal. It's neglect, on my part. Really it is. How can you understand consumers if you don't understand women? And how can you understand women if you don't understand what they like to wear?"

"Oh. I agree."

"That reminds me," she continued, tapping her water glass with a butter knife until everyone stopped fussing with their chairs and their napkins and looked up. "Some of you may have heard, and some of you may only have hoped, but the research is in . . ."

"Tell us already, Helen," some male voice had the gall to interrupt. I looked around. It hadn't been John, thank goodness. But everyone was smiling; Helen, too. I had to get used to this: everyone interrupted, everyone bantered, everyone joked. No wonder John fit in so well here.

"I *am* telling you. It's official. Ladies are discarding their corsets."

A male copywriter at the end of the table wisecracked, "Goodbye, lingerie departments."

"Not at all," Helen corrected him. "The undergarments are shrinking, but their place in women's hearts is only growing. What portion do you think women are spending now on flimsy pieces of silk and satin that do nothing to define a woman's waist?"

When no one volunteered, she answered. "Half. Fully half of women's clothing budgets are now spent on undergarments."

"It proves women are irrational," Stanley suggested, smiling.

Mildred spoke more loudly, "It suggests women are perfectly rational."

A man whose name I hadn't caught interrupted her. "What's rational about spending so much on garments that aren't seen once the lights go off?"

"Don't blame us," Mildred interrupted back. "Who says women want the lights off? I've got nothing to hide, with or without lingerie."

A young busboy had just approached the table with a pitcher of water. He paused, face reddening, and turned on his heel. Stanley waved him back to finish the job, and raised his cocktail glass. "A toast to Thomas Edison."

A flurry of competing toasts filled the room with a roar.

"To light."

"To lovely, unashamed women."

The man opposite me said good-naturedly, "To—what's your name again? To Rosie."

I took a sip and wished I hadn't. It was water I needed. Plain water. The busboy had barely finished filling my glass when I lifted it to drink, desperately.

More toasts: "To John—isn't he the reason we're here drinking this terrible stuff?"

"To Stanley for hiring John."

"To Helen—the brains of the operation—for marrying Stanley."

"Enough of that," Helen said, laughing. "I only meant to toast the end of corsets."

I was wishing for a corset now, something to hold my own tummy in place. I was bloated, my cycle delayed. Maybe I was coming down with something, or maybe it was the way we were all crowded around this table, with our elbows pinned in close to our sides and our ankles crossed and our feet tucked underneath our chairs. And the heat, especially in this windowless back room. And that smell again: thick steaks frying, breaded fish sizzling in pans. When the menus were passed around, the dense curling script danced in front of my eyes, and I had no desire for anything and no idea what to order.

"John, choose for me," I said. "Whatever you get, I'll have the same."

At the table, a more earnest debate started on the topic of how consumers made decisions, on whether they used logic. Either way, no one present believed that advertisers should lie to consumers. That was one of the Resors' strongest positions. Outright deception had gone the way of old patent medicine ads. The new game was about mass education and finding a fit between products and people—a people who wouldn't stay put, who no longer lived in the same towns and shopped in the same few stores as their parents had. The new game, someone at the table said, was storytelling: the skillful use of story and imagery and the perfect phrase and testimonials that made clear that a product had real value and appeal.

I made mental notes: Find out whether Mildred is married, and how she got hired, and whom she prefers to hire. Read more magazines. Watch women in department stores. Eavesdrop. What did people want? What did *I* want? This: to be in the middle of it all, a lively and opinionated crowd, a step ahead of things, excited by the future, rather than scandalized by it. To be wanted and needed for what I could offer. To rub away the tarnish of the last year and be interested—and interesting—again.

John entered the fray. "But the point isn't to accept the customers' opinions and their tendencies. The point isn't to tell them a nice bedtime story. It's to *shape* their wishes and desires. Let's take baby powder. What is it for?"

I'd been too quiet. I wasn't keeping up. "To keep babies dry," I volunteered.

"No, no, no," he said loudly, so that two other conversations at the table—one about the latest census news proving the US population balance had tipped from rural to urban, another about the new law in a Pennsylvania town, requiring skirts to be at least four inches below the knee—came to a halt.

"And you're talking about behavior, there," John said loudly, pointing to the census talkers, "and you're talking about behavior, there," he said, pointing to the two men and Mildred, who were disagreeing about whether skirt laws would only make new skirts even shorter, just as Prohibition had made everyone thirstier. "And that's our business and that's all well and good. But if I can direct your attention to this particular behavioral question: What's talcum powder for?"

I was still swallowing back my surprise at how quickly he'd cut me off. *No, no, no.* Aggressive, even for this crowd of assertive banterers. And he hadn't meant anything by it—he loved to argue and to jeer— but this was my informal job interview, even if he didn't know it. I had to say something correct. I had to say something informed and clever.

Well, what on earth *was* baby powder for?

"Perhaps," I tried to say, leaning in closer to John and speaking as loudly as I could manage, "it's more healthful for the child, in some other way. It treats rashes or prevents them. It's antiseptic."

"Ah," John said. "Health. Good feelings." And he turned to me and winked. I was a student again, a very new student. I might even pass this particular test.

"We've tried for years to sell things by stating their positive qualities," he lectured all of us. "This product is good for digestion. That product suppresses your cough."

A waiter had come by and taken orders for cocktail refills, which couldn't come quickly enough for this group. John frowned and raised his voice above the murmur.

"But my lovely wife is wrong. We've all been wrong. We won't sell best by pointing out what works. We'll sell best by telling the customer what dire circumstances she faces—and yes, I'm aware that four times out of five it is a *she* who holds the purse strings—if she fails to buy our product. We sell by stirring the most basic emotion there is."

"Fear," I said, but too quietly.

John said it louder, rising an inch off his seat, speaking over the waiter, even over the voice of Stanley Resor, who had just started a new conversation at the end of the table about baseball. "Fear!" John shouted.

"It's not enough to say that powder actively prevents something mildly negative. What if," he continued, "there are serious diseases Baby might get if Mother does not use baby powder—our preferred brand of baby powder, the only kind Mother can be certain is completely pure. What risks if she chooses the wrong brand, or none? What regrets does she face? We focus on the cost, the guilt: if she does *not* buy this, the door is open. Not to one specific thing, but to an abstract quantity of things. Not to a single factual problem, but to fear itself, which is more powerful when it is generalized across many possible causes."

One of the junior copywriters at the end of the table asked, "But how do we convince a consumer that diseases, in the abstract, pose a threat?"

"That's easy," John said. "You get the expert to say it."

"A mother, you mean," the copywriter said.

"The mother? Heavens no," John said. At this, everyone laughed, and I sat back, out of my league. "I meant an expert, of course. I meant a doctor."

A waiter placed a fresh drink in front of me. From the other side, over my shoulder, a second waiter set down a small dish: at the center a crenulated, pearlescent shell, and at its center, a shining mucilaginous orb, gray around the edges. A cataracted eye. Seeing and unseeing. Like me. Oblivious to my dwindling chances, the nature of my own constricted future. Half aware at best. Dumb as an oyster. And queasy.

It was hard, extracting my chair from the tangled seating arrangement. Standing, I leaned hard on one of John's shoulders to catch my balance, and then, feeling my knees go soft, spun and hurried forward, in what I hoped was the right direction.

I was just leaning over the bowl in the ladies room when I heard the door open again, and Helen's voice asking the woman attendant, "Is she all right?"

When I came out into the powder-room area, Helen had a damp handkerchief ready.

"I'm sorry," I said, nose sniffly, arms still trembling. "Let's join the others. It's John's big night."

"No, let's just sit here." Helen directed me to a padded chair. "That rowdy bunch can occupy itself just fine without us."

She held the damp cloth to my brow, and after it had lost its coolness, I handed it back, and she wetted it again, the freshness welcome if short-lived. I'd neglected to bring my purse, but Helen brought out her own powder compact, which she urged me to use, since my entire face was shining with perspiration. I thought of making some joke about powder and diseases, and selling to anxious women, but the words wouldn't come. The required cleverness wouldn't come.

"He definitely holds his own, your husband," Helen said.

"Yes, he does."

I waited, still catching my breath, and Helen sat on a chair next to me, quiet and kind, as if she had no desire to be anywhere else.

"How do you do it?" I finally asked her.

"Work with Stanley?"

I'd meant more than that. I meant, how had she done it all: come so far, accomplishing so much without being pushed to the side, even as the company had grown, even after she'd moved from one city to another, even after they'd married.

"I let him take the credit," she said. She clicked her purse shut—an exclamation mark to a statement that sadly, I'd never forget.

The dizziness had ebbed, but the nausea remained. Every smell was more acute. The scented powder masked the restaurant's strong odors just enough to keep me from retching again, but I couldn't eat. I didn't even want to be near food.

"You're looking better now," she said. "Feeling better?"

"A little."

"But not entirely?"

"No."

"Well, it can take a while. I was the same way. First three months at least." She added, smiling, "John made it through the training period—gold stars all around. He'll be making a good salary now, and that will help."

That will help.

"With your new addition, I mean," she said, and waited for the possibility of a correction that wouldn't come, that couldn't come.

How could a modern woman have missed the obvious? But I had. There are some things you know but don't want to know—that you're not going to get that job, or that your monthly visitor is late for good reason—until you suddenly, in a brief flash, know them undeniably and want only to disappear, shamed by your own willful ignorance.

"That is it, isn't it?" Helen asked. "But darling, it's wonderful news. We'll all get to celebrate again together before the year is out."

CHAPTER 21

Seven and a half months later, they handed him to me: Albert William Rayner Watson. *Billy*. But not Billy yet. Only, for now, a red-faced, puffy-eyed worm, with little threads of dark hair plastered against a wrinkly scalp. I was still fighting my way out of the ether clouds when they put him in my arms, wrapped up tight in a striped hospital blanket. I remember looking around and thinking, "Is this grip strength or vision we're testing today? Where's the nurse who's supposed to be setting things up?"

I was lost. I would be lost for weeks and for years. Because I had not intended to be a mother, certainly not so soon. Possibly not ever.

When I'd informed John about the pregnancy, he'd been magnanimous. These things happened. Make the best of it. While I suffered through a hot New York summer, waddling to our apartment and the corner store and the laundry and back—John gone, most of the time, working his way up the ad-man ladder—he grew increasingly comfortable with the idea. Excited, even. There was nothing better than a blank slate. Polly had never gone back to school after last year's upset; in fact, she'd never go to school again, and before long she'd be married young, with troubles of her own. Little John was struggling, though intent on college. But it made sense that they'd turned out badly, given the strain of the marriage and Mary's histrionics and her inconsistent parenting style. Without even trying, I'd surely do better, John reassured me.

I needed that reassurance, since my own family had taken the pregnancy news badly. My parents, I now believe, had thought the marriage would discreetly dissolve if we had no children in the first two or three years, and now that such an easy exit wasn't possible, my father went into a prolonged funk, attended by my mother, who had said, the only time she came to New York, "You'll have to give him time. He doesn't know what to make of all this now."

At the moment, in the hospital bed, I didn't know what to make of it all either. Not the distance of my family, and not the high expectations upheld by John, who seemed certain I'd be a better mother than Mary had been, though he disregarded mothering in general. It was like saying my temporary maternal condition was a disease that could be contained. I'd be the *better* kind of disease: the manageable, treatable kind. Not a chronic condition.

The baby was out of me, and that was a start. My distended abdomen was a pillowy mess of floating organs, rearranged by the trauma of expulsion. My backside ached, and I was glad I hadn't the strength to pull down the covers and peel away the absorbent cloths wadded up between my legs, to see what damage had been wrought. I was still bleeding, though the nurses said it was normal. But here was something new: my breasts had ballooned and were hot to the touch, so full they seemed ready to split the thin, mottled skin barely encasing them. The left in particular was rock hard and pulsing uncomfortably, a delta of thin, blue veins visible on the stretched skin.

A nurse entered the room with the two-day-old infant in her arms and lowered him, for the moment, into a bassinet in the corner. Good. Keep him there. Silent, sleeping, attended by a nurse who knew what she was doing.

Where was John? He'd been in the room the last time I'd opened my eyes.

"I'm afraid there might be infection," I said to the nurse, who was standing at the far side of the room, studying a clipboard.

She didn't look up. "Vaginal?"

"No. My breasts. One more than the other. But maybe both."

"Why do you think they're infected?"

"They feel . . . different."

"Well, they should."

She came closer, and I could read her name badge: REBECCA. Familiar. My mother's name. Was that the only reason?

"It's only your milk coming in," she said.

It's strange to say, but there was some confusion about this. There'd been so much to sort out during the last few weeks, and John and I had danced around the issue of breast-feeding, both of us preferring to avoid the topic. It was much easier to use our limited time together to debate baby names. It was easier to study classifieds for the various houses John was considering renting for us; I wanted to be as close to an urban center as possible, while he wanted trees and a good yard. It was easier to flip-flop on whether we should hire some kind of home nurse or helper, and how, and when. We wouldn't accept just anyone, of course. John's firm ideas made for some high and particular standards not easy to spell out in twenty words or less.

"I hadn't decided whether I would breast-feed," I told the nurse, who finally looked up from her chart.

"Well, your body isn't interested in waiting for a decision. It's gone ahead and started making the milk."

She came closer and stood alongside my bed. "One part cow, nine parts devil—is that how you're feeling now?"

Rebecca.

John had been the one to make that disparaging comment about wet nurses, during one of our Albert sessions more than a year earlier.

Rebecca had been a new nurse standing in the corner: face grim, especially once Albert started sobbing. Yes, I did feel like one part cow, now. Never mind about the devil.

I said, "You worked at Hopkins?"

"That's right. And now you have your very own baby to experiment with. How interesting."

She didn't sound interested. She sounded darkly amused, glad to see me uncomfortable, unable to escape my own biology, and paying for something I'd done.

"Isn't there something I can take, to make the milk go away?"

"Here's a curious thing," she said. "The baby himself can make some of the milk go away, if it's being over full with milk that's giving you pain now."

"But then what?"

"Then your body will make more milk. But things will even out."

I shrank away from her, my arms tight against my sides, chest throbbing.

She crossed her arms loosely over her own chest. "We'll try some compresses later. Crushed cabbage leaves are helpful."

Cabbage? I wanted my mother, and at the same time didn't want her to see me like this, unknowing and uncertain, and using old folk remedies suitable to the nineteenth century.

Rebecca crossed the room and picked up the baby. "Here's the big boy. William, you've decided to call him?"

"Billy," I said, surrendering only after she pressed the blanketed bundle within an inch of me. My arms reacting in delayed fashion, closing around his blanket-bound body only at the last moment.

"Look, he recognized his own name. He turned toward you as soon as you said it."

"That isn't recognition," I insisted.

"Well, he heard a familiar voice. And he smelled you. He's hungry."

"Here . . . I can't . . ." I stammered, but she was already at work, pushing back my pillow, rearranging the sheet, unbuttoning the top of my nightgown. I turned him—"That's right," said Rebecca—and pulled him toward my aching breast, feeling his surprising strength as he rooted around, pushing his face into me, deciding for us both.

But he didn't know anything a baby was supposed to know. His mouth failed to grasp the nipple immediately. His tongue worked at it, and seemed to reject it, as if he'd tasted something bitter. He pulled away and redoubled his strength and charged against my breast again. I was sure he couldn't breathe, the way his mouth and tiny nostrils were buried in my skin. He seemed both powerfully determined and horribly fragile, likely to suffocate or shatter, likely to die in my incompetent care. In a flash I had a vision of him rolling out of my arms, off the side of the bed, an image so terrible I squeezed him closer to my chest, despite the ache.

"Billy," I said again, more surely this time. And to the nurse, Rebecca: "He's not getting it. There's something wrong with him."

"There's nothing wrong with him," she said. "He'll get it."

I felt the heat of frustration as the baby raised one clenched red fist, which had broken free of the blanket, and beat it against the taut white drum of my breast. Then, for a moment, he managed to latch on and suck. A moment of relief spread in radiant waves, only to be pierced, in that briefly rosy bull's-eye, by a sharp thin arrow of pain that ran from nipple to spine. All my muscles tensed, and down in my uterus there was a deep postpartum contraction, a ripple that rolled up and over me like an enormous wake created by some distant passing ship, or something bigger, a tidal wave. I reared back into the pillow, squirming away from him, and the baby lost his suction. His head waggled back and forth in a fit of frustration.

"Stop fighting," Rebecca said, and I couldn't tell if she was talking to me or the baby or both of us. "Calm down, Mrs. Watson. Take a deep breath."

I tried, puffing in and out, flooded by sensations and memories of sensations: of holding slippery baby bodies; of watching the strain of a newborn as it clung to an iron rod, about to fall; of feeling the hot tears of little Albert, desperately pressing into my chest; and of other babies, too, rooting and twisting and flailing and seeking, but none with as much determination as this one. This one, who was intent on mastering this situation, mastering me, and yet feeble and easily snuffed out.

"He's going to starve," I said, unable to contain the shrill melodrama in my own voice. "Bring something for him. Get some . . . get some help."

"He isn't starving," she said. "You don't need help."

"Tell me what to do. Get a doctor."

"You certainly don't need a doctor."

"Find someone who knows."

"*You* know—a good deal more than you think."

"I don't," I said, near tears.

"You only need some time and a little dose of common sense. He's a beautiful, healthy baby boy, Mrs. Watson. You'll be careful. You'll do fine. And he's strong."

She paused a moment, her voice shifting, in a way I didn't care for at all, from a tone of comfort to one of command. "Listen to me and get ahold of yourself. You won't hurt him."

CHAPTER 22

We came home from the hospital to our new cottage, snow on the walk and boxes still unpacked, on a Friday. On Monday morning, John came in to give me a kiss on the forehead before he left for work.

"You'll get around all right?"

John was sensitive to my physical ailments: residual bleeding, normal postpartum complaints with a simple timeline for healing. Anything else was filed away under simple fatigue. It was my job to beat my way out of that fog, and to do much more than that—to seek, once the air cleared, a new world.

Conqueror's glory be damned. I hadn't even managed to wash my hair in a week.

"I left the breakfast dishes on the table," he said. "Hope that's all right. Coffee's still on."

"Coffee," I tried to smile. "Sounds marvelous."

"You eat a big breakfast now, hear me? Get your strength back up."

The goatlike bleating of Billy, waking up, issued from the bassinet in the small, undecorated nursery.

"I'll miss you both today. You're in charge."

"Instead of who—you?"

"Instead of him." John laughed. "Don't forget to take some notes. These first weeks are priceless. You won't get them back if you sleep-walk through them."

John was at the door, making a swift exit before the soft bleating became a breathless, choking cry.

"Notes," I repeated. "Schedule."

In that moment before the door closed, I listened for the sound of a car idling out on the drive, a colleague of John's who was sharing the commute to the train station, over the grand cantilevered span of Queensboro Bridge, and then into the city. Then: only quiet. A whisper of traffic on the narrow road outside our rented Long Island home, which John had finally chosen.

John had said no American should be allowed to bring a new child into the world unless he could afford to give that child its own bed-room, preferably one protected from the nerve-straining clamor of the modern world—though not overprotected from the more salu-tary challenges of nature, with some yard space for a child to get daily, scheduled fresh air. I would have preferred the tighter confines of a Manhattan apartment, a less isolating place in the middle of the hubbub, closer to friends, frivolity, distraction, the occasional extra helping hand. But he was right. Billy would need his room. And we would need our privacy.

I strained to hear the traffic passing, to imagine the cars and where they were going today, to imagine the world out there, which hadn't stopped buying, selling, and speeding along while I had swelled and gone into seclusion and finally burst and been emptied and returned to the world, a little softer inside, a little broken.

I said, to myself and to Billy: "Sheets." They smelled fusty, but washing them would require a trip to the village laundry, two miles down the road. "We're not very clean, are we?" A drive along snowy streets, or a walk followed by a trolley ride. Not anytime this week. "Bath—for me, this time."

When would he nap again: two hours, or three? How long would he cry if I ignored him? Would he stop? Quiet enough in the hospital, and moderately quiet for those first two days when John was paying closest attention, he seemed to be gaining strength and volume now that he was home alone with me.

The properly raised baby doesn't cry except when it's been stuck with a diaper pin. I'd found that typed on an otherwise empty page at the top of a box I'd opened on the weekend, searching for my old address book in the vain hope of sending out birth announcements in the next few weeks. Well, all right then. We'd put an end to crying, soon enough. Underneath the single sheet of paper was a folder, still empty, labeled "Psychological Parenting Guide." It was just like John to start organizing notes on how to raise babies the very week we came home with our first. Nothing like one project to spawn another, and nothing like the voice of expertise to quell any first-time jitters. We were alike in at least one way, John and I: made uneasy by uncertainty or by lack of structure. Better a fantasy blueprint than no blueprint at all.

But first, Billy was hungry. I had to feed him, of course. But first, before that other competing first, I had to get off the wet diaper that would soil the bed, which was already far from fresh. I had to change him, feed him, and then I would have to change him again. One weekend, and we were already out of tiny clean shirts and fussy little rompers with tight cuffs and too many buttons. They were all squashed into a basket, damp or mustard stained.

I went to Billy and lifted him out of his bassinet. He'd been crying so hard for the last few minutes, he'd slipped into short silent spells of rage, unable to catch his breath, red body a single taut muscle of unsatisfied needs.

"Come now, Billy. Stop that."

My nipples were cracked. I'd never discovered whether cabbage leaves worked or whether that was just an old wives' tale. I dared not ask John to buy or bring home anything that suggested I was toying with old-fashioned remedies. They would just have to heal. My body could manage that much on its own, I hoped.

When I sat up in bed and put Billy to my left breast, a cramp seized my calf. Without realizing, I'd been pointing my toes, clenching all my muscles in pain as the suck broke the scabby skin and allowed a thin gray cloudy stream to flow through. Then the answering wave, getting softer each day, of my uterus contracting. Breast and uterus talking to each other, while I hovered absentmindedly above, trying to remove myself via my breathing, wondering why women let themselves be turned inside out this way, wondering if other women wondered, wondering why I felt so glum at this moment. Smell of burnt toast still in the air. The dishes. The sheets.

On top of that, the cupboards we'd meant to clean out before the baby came: sticky paper-lined shelves, littered with mouse droppings. Country living of the type John idealized, remembering with rosy nostalgia the Stoney Lake summer cottage he'd enjoyed with Mary, Polly, John, and visitors, plus a half-dozen assorted child cousins. But a cottage in summer with lots of people helping was one thing. A suburban cottage in winter—with neighbors on each side, but no one we'd actually met and no one whom John seemed interested in meeting yet—was another.

Billy kept working away at one breast and then the other while I wondered: which dress would fit me, when I finally found time to get dressed today? Half of them were too small, the others, far too large, enormous ugly circus tents I couldn't wait to give away. Even my feet had gone up a half size, which meant my only pair of winter boots wouldn't fit, and outside, the walk to the car was along a narrow unshoveled path, under two old evergreen trees whose boughs hung heavy and threatening with their loads of damp snow. John's trees. ("A boy needs a tree to climb." "Yes dear, aren't you sweet—but not for the first three years of his life." "Well maybe our son will be advanced.") I would have taken a closer laundry and corner grocery over those sunlight-blocking, snow-gathering trees.

The doctor had said I should stay off my feet for another week at least. A great sense of humor, those doctors have. I could try kneeling down and washing the baby clothes in the bathtub. And I could walk out into the snowy yard like a farmer's wife, with clothespins in my mouth. I could hang the clothes and the sheets out to dry—to attempt drying—in the damp winter coastal air. Would it warm up just enough to rain? Was there a line out there, between the trees? Were there clothespins in the mousy drawers?

A thin line of pain from my left nipple. *Breathe through it. Breathe through.* I'd thought one left pain behind following childbirth. Clearly not.

"How long?" John had asked, the night before.

"How long, what?"

He'd smiled at me. Then I understood. "Oh, I don't know. Six weeks, maybe."

"Long time," he'd said, leaning toward me until his cheek rested, briefly, against my own. Yes, from the neck up: that part he could touch. Even I was reluctant to touch anything much farther down, except when absolutely necessary.

Billy was making good progress, nodding off, satiated, gums still clamped to the nipple, until his head began to drop back and he startled himself awake, suck-suck-sucking again. The fingers of my free hand went idly to his back, smoothing down the fabric of the sleeper, and then up to the folds of his neck, the soft and nearly hairless back of his head, which fit so neatly into the curve of my palm. I had started humming, absentmindedly. For a moment, I felt peaceful, made drowsy from the nursing, enchanted with the weight of his head against my outstretched fingers and the curve of Billy's cheek and the velvet of his perfect skin.

But then I pulled my hand back, remembering what John had said, about the biggest danger, the biggest temptation. Too much touching. Too much needy mother love—the mother's own attempt to satisfy her own sensual and emotional needs. I felt suddenly ashamed. This was how it happened. This was where it went wrong from the start. I let the pillow do the work of holding up his head. I let my hand fall, and felt a morose weight drop onto my entire body in turn, pressing down upon me, anchoring me to the bed.

I was struck with a greater thirst than I'd ever felt, but the kitchen tap seemed too far. Before he'd left, I should have thought to ask John to bring in a cup of coffee or a glass of water. Getting up was necessary but getting up too often started the blood between my legs flowing again, the pads dampening, and I only had so many. The last thing I needed was more things to wash and wring and hang out to dry. Out in the small kitchen beyond my view, there'd be a plate with toast crusts waiting, tempting the cockroaches. There'd be a sink full of dishes from last night, sitting in the tepid, crumb-filled water.

I looked down at Billy's face and he looked back up at me with large, gray eyes. Then he squinted and clamped down hard, screwing up his face as he pushed.

"No, Billy."

But even the "no" was unnecessary. Less touching, less directing, less empty chatter, just instruction, delivered in the most neutral voice possible: that was the goal.

"That's for the toilet, Billy. Let's get you there."

Get you there, or I'll be out of nappies. Get you there, or your father will know we're not keeping to the schedule we agreed upon yesterday. And I'll go mad if I can't do at least one thing right. No place for me at Hopkins and no room for me on Lexington or Madison Avenue and now this. Third strike if I can't do this right.

Shuffling into the bathroom, I held him over the toilet, little legs bunched up and peddling until he registered the pressure of the large cool seat against his little thighs. No outcome, no product, but at least we were started. First trial, at age eleven days (Infant Billy), and age twenty-three years (Mother—that would be me). Something to record. A thought and a goal that gave me enough strength to dig a fresh robe out of the closet, fasten it over my nightgown, and return to the bathroom, baby in the crook of one arm, one hand free to splash water on my face. There was a new baby scale on the long sink counter, taking up the space where my cosmetics and hair things had been. Where had John put all of my private things? No matter. Focus on the daily measurements.

Seven pounds, one ounce. (And now he was fussing again, unhappy with having been set on the cold metal scale.)

Somewhere in a box, there was a big pile of notebooks, a carton of typing paper. But I'd only located that one page of notes started by John. I went looking in that same box and under the page found instead of blank paper, rubber-banded piles of mail. The topmost had fancy, looping handwriting, an exotic return address from Madrid, Spain—perhaps one of the members of royalty that JWT was trying to talk into offering a hand-cream testimonial. I didn't actually open that envelope or any of the fancy, perfumed letters beneath it to read the personal messages that John had felt valuable enough to move into our small new home with its shortage of drawers and cabinets. My own survival instinct told me to use my limited reserves to create some sense of order for my days. Maybe when I knew who I was again, and had a job of sorts I knew how to perform, I could be more suspicious of my husband's letters from various women in Madrid and Paris and New York and Washington, DC. But of course, his job did involve so many women—as consumers, as colleagues, as celebrity endorsement providers. I noted the postmarks, yes, but that was the limit of my curiosity and energy.

Finally, I located an ivory card—on the front, an invitation to a Vassar classmate's wedding we hadn't attended, a much more sumptuous affair than our own quick dash to city hall. I flipped it over to write on the back in light pencil script, "7, 1," with Billy still over one shoulder, and through the diaper and through my robe, a feeling of warmth spreading onto my shoulder, the front of my chest.

A diaper change. A walk around the kitchen, dropping the breakfast dish into the sink, grabbing an old spotted apple from the ice box and because it was next to the apple and easy, a leftover pork chop, cold, tearing at the bone with my teeth. A quick hair-brushing, but no time for styling or anything else. There was spit up on my nightgown, beneath the urine-spotted robe. Who would wash the nightgown? Who would wash the robe? Who would wash the sheets? Then somehow, it was two hours later, and he was hungry again. How could he be so hungry when he wasn't doing much more than bicycle-kicking on his back? *Billy. His name is Billy.*

"Like William James," John had cracked, a few months ago.

"Only psychologists and philosophers will get that joke."

"The first one we'll call William. The second one we'll call James. Every child needs a sibling."

But John had always liked making sly references with names—the same way he'd made a joke at Hopkins of naming little Albert after my own middle name. To think that I'd felt honored, at the time.

There he was again: that heavy-headed, drooling, and stoic subject of our shared past. Floating up to remind me of that earlier road I'd been on, not so very long ago, and also to make me wonder: how had Albert been so stolid, those first weeks we'd known him?

Once I had my own first child, I realized: babies cried. They had needs. They didn't like to wait. They whipped themselves into frenzies. Evolution had favored them with this: determination to get the food, the attention, the nurturing they required. Babies shrieked, and at least in those first weeks, a mother's heart pounded in response. (And shouldn't John have known the same things? He'd had two of his own children by then. Had he really spent no time with them as infants, or had he pushed those observations to the back of his mind?)

This was natural. This was the stimulus and response that nature intended—that a mother should listen and answer. Not silence. Not stolidity on the baby's part. Why had Albert been so imperturbable, until we'd finally made him more reactive and fearful? As a twenty-year-old I couldn't have known, but now I did, at least in part: Albert had not been a typical child. And then I pushed that thought away, not to resurface again for several years. What point, in those difficult early-motherhood days, entertaining it?

As a graduate student at Johns Hopkins, I couldn't have imagined myself like this, a disheveled mess, with my own crying baby set on a blanket on the nubby couch, rolling toward the back cushion in his little tantrum, red face against the cushion. (Where did one set a baby safely when there wasn't a nurse standing by with waiting arms or those handy rolling carts we'd had in such abundance?) I couldn't wait until he was old enough to sit up at least, to play with blocks. At this age, he could only nurse and cry and sleep. And babies weren't supposed to cry—so said John, regardless of Mother Nature's intentions.

I made Billy wait. He fussed and cried and went red and nodded off and immediately woke, fussing and crying again. More waves washed over me: not physical pain anymore, only bone-deep fatigue. I carried Billy into his dark bedroom and lowered him into his crib, his small red arms flying up reflexively as I lowered him, breath catching between airless sobs. Shut the door.

Eleven. Eleven twenty. Eleven thirty-five. In the living room, near the front hall closet, stood the rocking chair that my mother had sent as a gift, which the department-store deliverymen would be picking up tomorrow, to take back for a refund.

John had laughed when we'd first seen it, Friday afternoon. "What century do they think we're living in?" Even the most outdated, prewar baby books said rocking chairs weren't good for babies because they discouraged independence. "Quickest way to raise a baby who can't put himself to sleep," John had said. "I'll telephone the store from the office on Monday."

"What we might need," I said carefully, tentatively, knowing that cost was always an issue, "is our own telephone, in the house. For emergencies."

"But it's darn expensive," John had said. "Did you read the paper? Price of sirloin and milk both doubled in just a few years. Stanley owes me another raise, and I won't let him forget it." And then, for some reason I couldn't follow, he'd starting talking about a boat show two weekends from now, on Long Island. Two weekends: I couldn't imagine that far into the future. Babies weren't the only ones obsessed with toys. Something about having a baby brought out the baby in the man.

In the dim light of the hallway, the rocker's varnished wood shone. It may have been old-fashioned, but it was more beautiful and new-looking than the furniture that had come with the cottage: the sagging checked couch, covered with a scratchy red flannel blanket, and the single overstuffed armchair, and the wooden kitchen chairs with their uneven legs, many times badly repainted, patches of pale green showing beneath the dark brown overcoats of paint.

Through the thin nursery door, I could hear the stuttering lamb's cry. Moments of silence that seemed like a reprieve, but weren't true and lasting silence, only breathlessness.

I lowered myself into the rocking chair for just a moment, looking around cautiously as if someone might be peeping through the window. Just out of curiosity, I pushed back and forth, and then lifted my feet from the floor, until the rocker slowly came to a stop again, and then pushed again, savoring the glide. The motion relaxed my cramped legs, lessening the ache in that torn hollow between my tailbone and my abdomen. But I could see the problem and the temptation. I could grow prematurely old in that chair, rocking away my own overattended miseries, rocking babies into feeble and dependent sleep. It had to be removed from the premises, the sooner the better. I would do this right or not at all—as if "not at all" were an option. I tried to laugh. It came out in one soft wheeze—as though someone had slapped me on the back. As if a mother had any choice, once the deed was done.

The brief lull was followed by a renewed squall.

Eleven fifty-seven. Eleven fifty-nine. Noon.

"Fine. There. Are you happy?"

The baby was in such a state when I finally pulled him, red and spasming, up from his bassinet, that I had to walk him around in circles just to quiet him into spacing out his cries, from breathless shriek into a more rhythmic and negotiable complaint. Then I sat down in the ugly armchair, put him to my breast, felt the milk let down, a little stab of needles followed by a softer warm pulse, drowsy-making for us both.

One gray eye opened and looked up at me, with only a little interest. *One part cow.*

To restore my sense of dignity and purpose, I remembered something else John had said. "No well-trained man or woman has ever watched the complete and daily development of a single child from its birth to its third year. Plants and animals we know about because we have studied them, but the child is a mystery."

I whispered to Billy now: "You are a mystery."

I wished I could put a name to the heaviness in my heart. Deep sadness feels that heavy, but so does deep, tormenting love.

I was supposed to be better at this. I was supposed to be good at something. If I were meant to be a mother, I'd have more patience and more confidence. If I were meant to be a party girl, a real flapper, I'd have handed this child off to a nurse from day one, let my breasts dry up, bound them up tight, and gone out to dance, even while my knees were still wobbly. If I were meant to be a scientist, I'd have more curiosity and drive, and would have filled one notebook already with hour by hour observations: every sensation, every change in Billy's reactions to external stimuli.

John had always talked about three powerful drives: fear, love, rage. Rage was something I'd never yet felt in its fullest expression (time enough for that, in later years). Because all love was essentially erotic in origin, my new love for Billy was both suspect and complicated: a thread that got snipped and reknotted daily, a push and pull of acceptable and unacceptable urges and responses. But fear, steady as an undertow, with or without a name—I'd known that forever. Maybe my own malaise now was the same fear I'd always had. A fear of disappearing. From the world. From myself. And now, from John's affections.

I had to swim harder. I had to keep my head up. I had to be useful.

As Billy nursed again—it might have been during that same late-morning session, or it might have been the next time, a few hours later—I made light noises at his ear. I spotted an old receipt pushed into the armchair cushion and pulled it out and tore it, seeing if it would make Billy startle or take notice in any way. I tapped with a closed fist on a bureau within reach. He was neither fearful nor particularly curious. Uncorrupted. The very best thing. A blank slate, so far—as John would have suggested.

It would be a woman who would ruin him—a mother, a grandmother, a nurse or nanny. The trick was to ruin him as little as possible. Scientific parenting couldn't advance quickly enough to save me, save my son, save a million other little boys like him. Consider my own thoughts that day: I'd already made excuses for Billy's crying, even mustering scientific justification for the belief that newborns must indeed shriek for our attention. John never would have done that. He looked to the future. He knew we all had the power to change within us.

Billy's small fist had gotten tangled in my hair. He tugged at it, and the gentle, rhythmic tug on my scalp was soothing. The flow of milk through my breasts, the milk itself pooling over the nipples and drying there and softening the scabs, was soothing, too, like having a knot worked out of a cramped muscle. I wanted to sleep in that chair. I must have slept.

What felt like mere moments later, I heard the slam of the door and John's innocent words—"Dinner ready?"—before his recoil of surprise at the slothful sight of the baby and me, pressed together and drooling. Making mistakes already.

CHAPTER 23

It's hard to believe we found much time at all together that year. I was learning to take care of Billy—in a professional rather than maternal way, whenever possible. And John, meanwhile, was doing three or four times as much: making contributions at the ad agency, lecturing occasionally at the New School on evenings to earn his way back into academic respectability, and talking with some Rockefeller people with deep pockets, about some new baby research to be conducted under his supervision at Columbia—with our old friend Mary Cover Jones, in fact—even if he could assist only tangentially, by advising and signing off on protocol forms and grant paperwork, since his days were well spoken-for now. He would remain an ad man, first and foremost, but for many years, he still pined to be let back into the academic club.

My own days had gotten, if not easy, a little more manageable. I remember walking in the coastal park near our house: a bright winter Sunday, and Billy asleep in the buggy, his head covered in a crocheted cap, his tiny button nose red with the cold, eyes closed and long lashes fluttering when the buggy jounced up and over paving stones or got briefly stuck in an icy rut where the park path was not entirely clear.

John was navigating the buggy, and my mittened hands were completely, wonderfully free—one hand snugged into my coat pocket, and the other pushed into the crook of John's elbow. Like someone recovering from illness, I was grateful for simple fresh air and easy movement and tender companionship, my senses tuned up to better appreciate the diamond sparkle of sunlight on water and to note how the piercing blue of the winter sky lifted an anvil-like weight off my head.

"Look at that," John said, and I thought he must also be appreciating the glinting water or the delicate arch of a snow-covered tree bough alongside the park's curving paths. Instead he was studying two women who had parked their own baby buggy in front of a bench, ahead of us. The older of the two, a stout woman with iron-colored curls under a black cloche hat, was lifting the child out. The baby, swaddled in a checkered blanket, looked about two or three months older than Billy. John slowed our walk, to stay within sight of them.

"There she goes," he whispered into my cheek. "Four, five, six."

That's how many times the grandmother had kissed the baby, one cheek and then the next, twisting him back and forth to get full access to his rosy skin. Settling onto the bench, she dandled the baby on her knee, facing her—"seven, eight"—so she could push her face into the crook of his neck and plant her lips on his cheeks again.

We were almost immobile now, creeping along, just far enough away to be out of earshot. I tugged on John's arm a little, but it was no good. It was a Sunday, and even so, John couldn't stop working, making a behavioral observation—a criticism—that might later prove useful in a speech or article.

"Why do women do that?" he asked. "You're not the perfect mother, Rar, but you're better and more sensible than that."

"Thanks for the small compliment," I said, jerking his arm playfully.

"The only honest kind."

John wouldn't have noticed that I had weighed Billy just that morning, gone to enter it into the chart, and then—noticing I had missed the last three days—back-filled the spaces with some credible, invented figures. It was just as easy to record, post hoc, an entire week's worth of bowel movements and nap durations, if I'd let those recordings slide; sort of like telling someone you had your first highball at 5:00 when it was really at 3:15. Did it really matter so much? Even *I* could manage to forget my lapses as both scientist and mother if I didn't have blank lines staring me back in the face.

"You should be the one writing articles for parenting magazines," John said, and I felt a little surge of warmth at the vote of confidence, quickly offset by what he said next. "Of course, it's a shame we didn't manage to get you a PhD. Then you could really fire from two barrels, like Mary Cover Jones."

"She'll only have the PhD," I objected, not getting his point. "One barrel, to use your metaphor."

"I didn't mention? She's expecting this fall. Just told me at the last Spellman grant meeting."

"Expecting? Well I'd like to see her finish a dissertation with a baby underfoot."

He shrugged. "I think she'll manage. She always seems to."

I expected him to say something funny, or sharp—that Harold wasn't much of a man's man, that Mary worked hard but didn't have much charm. When he didn't add anything, I put on my best smile. "We'll have to have a baby shower for her."

"Oh, I don't know. She and Harold have plenty of friends and family to do that sort of thing."

"*Plenty* of friends. More than we have, you mean."

John screwed up his face. "What are you talking about? I don't keep track of Mary and Harold's social life."

I hadn't meant to irritate him or let the morning's good feelings slip away. "We'll have our own social life again, once we have some help. Won't we?"

The wind had whipped up, turning the channel from sparkling to gray. I tried to turn John's attention to something we'd discussed at breakfast. We'd had a local girl around to help—Louisa, seventeen years old, from midmorning to 4 P.M.—but we'd let her go after two weeks. She'd come from a large family, but we'd neglected to ask about birth order, and it turned out she was the baby herself. She'd had no experience raising younger siblings and was more comfortable cleaning the dishes and making beds. When she tried to lift Billy out of my arms, or tend him while I was in any part of the house, he fussed—and more problematically, she gave in to his fussing, and handed him back over. I'd wanted to keep her services until we found a replacement. Clean dishes were something, after all. But John was easily bothered about wasted expense and let her go.

On Friday, I'd interviewed two replacement baby nurses. Neither had reassured me.

I tried to hold his attention. "As I was saying this morning—about the Hoboken woman, Mae. At least she has a sister to live with nearby. The others expect accommodations."

"Oh no."

"Exactly right. We don't have the room, unless you count the den."

"No good in having a nurse for the baby if you can't close a door and get something done," he said, and I moved closer to him with gratitude. How many husbands would have understood in an instant that a wife at home still planned to study, or write, or do something? It almost made up for him reminding me about Mary and her impossible list of successes.

"And," he added, squeezing my arm affectionately under his, "I don't plan on dressing for any nurse. Whether it's an old hag or an innocent waif, if she wants to come early, she may catch a look at more than she bargained for."

It needn't have been said. There was a reason I'd told young and impressionable Louisa never to show up before 9:30. A robe would have solved the problem, but this was John's house, a very small house, and if he wanted to saunter to the bathtub nude and shave with the door open, he'd do it.

How different things were from my own childhood, in a large house with rooms and privacy for all, with hired help who were much more than that, really a part of the family, and given a kind of autonomy that wouldn't be permissible now. Besides that, my own father never would have walked around in his underclothes, never mind nude. I couldn't even remember the last time I hadn't seen him with collar and tie. And my mother was content not to get much of anything done, and could be interrupted by servants at any time. It made her feel needed as house manager.

John would howl at an Irish immigrant nanny intent on raising a baby any way she saw fit, given that he insisted upon scientific parenting but wasn't around to actually do it. And Billy was all too quickly getting used to being held by only one familiar set of arms—mine—when that was the very opposite of John's ideal situation. Back when no dream was too big, he'd wanted to create a baby farm, after all—a place where children were raised away from their parents altogether.

In trying to invent a new type of family in a modern new age, we'd not managed to create anything new at all yet. We'd only given ourselves cramps trying. Perhaps it had been the same just after the Civil War, when the slaves had been set free: a bunch of confused ladies who didn't know how to care for their children and their china. Perhaps this was how our modern weddings and funerals would seem to old-time true believers: a graceless kind of fraudulent bungling, trying to keep rituals alive after religion was dead. It must be the same during any kind of major social change. Messy and illogical at first. Easy to lampoon. Hardest on an uncelebrated or foolhardy few.

But I couldn't say that to John. He thought we were doing admirably, which is how it must have seemed when you left the house every day early, came home late, knocked back a few drinks, and drifted into sleep, dreaming about the next day's campaigns, meetings, and three-cocktail lunches.

I was still mulling as John walked more and more slowly, gait stiff, lips thinned in concentration, still watching the two women. Instead of enjoying her moment of freedom from baby tending, the younger woman was leaning over the infant, bringing her face close to his, and making raspberry sounds, which made the baby squirm and giggle.

"Ten kisses so far," he said. "But look: it's only made them hungrier. They don't even care that they're making him fuss. He'd rather be sleeping in the buggy. Grandma's turn now. Eleven, twelve, and why not one more? Thirteen."

I knew why the grandmother was getting under his skin, even more so on this particular outing. My parents were coming to visit for the first time that afternoon, and John was not looking forward to the delayed inspection. At home, the roast was in the oven, surrounded by parsnips, carrots, and potatoes, the entire house aromatic with rosemary and thyme. The house was more or less clean, if a bit chilly from the airing we'd done all morning, every window thrown open to bring the winter freshness into every dark corner. The only thing we could have done better was to have arranged for help already, so that we might show off our household in its fully operational form. I wasn't sure how I'd handle last-minute sauce and side-dish preparation, never my strong suit, and serving and baby tending, even with a husband's help, all under the eyes of two parents who had reason to find fault with us both.

But I was nervous enough without talking about it. The stakes had been climbing since we'd come home from the hospital, in November. Already, my father had canceled twice on successive

Sundays—supposedly because he had a cold and didn't want to pass it to the grandchild he'd never met.

As if thinking about my father at the same moment, John said, "And people bother to wonder why babies get sick, with so many adults spitting on their faces all the time. A cold wouldn't have mattered anyway, if your father would promise to keep his hands to himself."

"Anyway, Alboo says he doesn't have a cold, now."

"He really wants us to call him Alboo?"

My father had informed me of the nickname by letter just after Billy was born. He didn't want to go by Grandfather or Grandpa or Papaw or anything else. Mr. Albert Rayner felt he was too young to have grandchildren. Which meant, of course, that I had chosen to have my own progeny far too young. He saw himself as a still-virile man. If only he and John got along better; they both prized their virility so much!

"Yes," I said, trying to sound both firm and charmed. "He's decided on Alboo. I think it'll catch on."

Shifting back to more neutral territory, I said, "Mae has good references—not as a nurse, exactly. But at least she's already been around children, and won't be as timid as Louisa was. The other one, Lizette, has much more experience, but the letter from her last employer was lukewarm."

"Lukewarm," he said, still frowning at the women on the bench. "Well, lukewarm can be better, in some cases. We should run an ad: 'Neglectful Nurse Wanted.' Subhead: 'Must be averse to spoiling, the bane of our age.' Then maybe we'd find some competent help."

He shook off his surliness, turning at last away from the bench scene that had offended him, and pushed the buggy forward with a jolt. When I leaned my cheek against his shoulder, he leaned back, and turned to kiss me—just a peck at first, but one that slowed and softened, extending nearly to indecency. Just as we had been watching the mother and granny, I'm sure now they were watching us: a man and his wife still affectionate with each other, our sensual needs fulfilled as they should be: by each other. Still lucky and in love and trying desperately hard to do everything right.

John and I had discussed the ideal schedule to which we had nearly managed to train Billy already. The same schedule we'd explain to my mother and Alboo, if they pressed for details.

Just as he had for most of the last two months, and as he would for the rest of his childhood, Billy was expected to wake at 6:30 to have a sip of milk (at a later age, orange juice), and be set on the pot, for urinating only. Back to bed to play quietly, without supervision. Quiet breakfast an hour later.

(We couldn't know it that day in the park, but Mae would be fired, as it turned out, for being a chatterbox. Her insistence on playing games as she spooned cereal into Billy's mouth couldn't be tolerated.)

After breakfast, he would be set on the toilet for a bowel movement. Suppositories could be used, if necessary, and sometimes were. It was only a matter of conditioning to make these movements routine. Billy—and later his brother as well—were to be strapped, safely and contentedly, in place. No toys, no company or distractions.

(Eleanor would be fired for joining Billy in the bathroom, no matter how many warnings we gave her. She hated to see a child left alone for long. She hated to see me left alone as well, in my bedroom at midday, for example, revising part of a chapter for John's forthcoming book on behaviorism into a stand-alone article for a national magazine. Her endlessly social company was terminated after six unproductive weeks.)

Outdoors by 10:00. Buggy rides for baby, but by age two, the child should be free to exercise his own legs. In the best scenario, an outdoor area would be safely penned. Should the child be left alone? Certainly, within reason. Our yard wasn't haunted by overflying birds of prey, after all. A sunny room was a less ideal option, but the important thing was for baby or child to play or "work" (as John liked to call solo activity) alone. Endless minding and interacting would only create dependence.

(A string of other nurses were let go for being either negligent and unsafe, or conversely and more commonly, safety paranoid and determined to respond too quickly to a child's every movement and burble.)

Lunch with nurse, or alone. Good dining habits emphasized, regardless of age.

Bath at 5:30 P.M. Shallow water, no celluloid toys, a simple but not gloomy affair. We were never shy about nudity—theirs or ours—but John still insisted, once we had two boys, that they should always be bathed separately.

(Nicole, who would be enviably firm in most matters but also highly efficient in the matters of dressing and bathing, seemed not to understand the depth of John's feelings on this matter. She was one of our very best nurses to yield to a swift termination. I'm afraid I cried the day she left, and off and on for a week, though never at a time when John was home to see. He would have thought I was going soft in the head, and maybe I was. My fault again, for all these problems, for not choosing the right help or delivering our instructions clearly enough to make things stick.)

A light meal—child or children alone, manners enforced at a distance but no adult company necessary—and then bed by 7 P.M.

Did this mean, as Billy grew old enough to notice, and was later joined by his brother, Jimmy, that they almost never ate with their parents, especially their father, who often enough returned home after they were asleep? Well, yes. But it was just food, after all. They ate alone, and often enough, after they were sleeping and the house was quiet, so did I, with a stack of newspapers and magazines at my side, relishing the quiet moment to read *New Yorker* columns about the latest speakeasies and dance parlors, the nightlife just across the bridge, the life of ease and entertainment—and yes, relaxed morals—that still called to us, even though our hired help kept coming and going and John worked so very hard.

John was helping to create the mood of the 1920s, but we weren't getting to take part in it. Maybe no one was playing all that much, but the columns and the ads—ads my own husband was helping to create—certainly made it seem that there was an endless party going on. Had men ever looked so charming? Had women ever looked so lovely? Had nightclubbing and drinking, now that it was illegal, ever seemed so much fun? Other people would characterize the 1920s as a time of frivolous excess, but for most of us, I realize only now, it was a time of vicarious, incomplete pleasures. John was in the envy trade himself, making people want more in order to sell them things they didn't usually need, because that's what scientists-turned-ad-men—regardless of their previous inclinations and callings—did.

But much of that came later. For the moment, in the early winter of 1922, I *was* inexperienced, and Billy was only Billy, or an infant with the potential to become a child named Billy—not even able to "work," or to read a book, or even to hold a little wooden block in his chubby hands. Infants are the hardest. The blankest of all, and so—you would think—the easiest, but also the most manipulative, the most able to shape a parent's behavior with their tracking gazes, and their cries and coos, their silky hair and soft cheeks and appearances of endearing vulnerability.

On that day of my parents' first visit, I already wanted Billy to be older. I already wanted to be in that near future, in which our routines would be firmly established, our help hired at least for the moment, even if personnel changes would be frequent over the years. I wanted to be irreproachable, with our standards very much time-tested and in place. But that sort of true expertise was hard-won.

"It's time we write a book—together," John mentioned that very morning, on the way back home from the park, with Billy asleep in his buggy. Maybe he noticed my baffled response to Mary's combined maternity and dissertation ambitions; maybe it was our talk of where to lodge a nurse and the need to maintain the den as a professional sanctum. "It should open new doors for us," he continued. "Something for the popular market."

I hadn't said anything yet about stumbling across John's notes for what appeared to be a parenting guide. I didn't mention that I had wondered how a person who had raised only one baby at home—and not even raised him fully yet—could imagine himself capable of writing a how-to guide for the next generation. So I said simply, "How about a general overview of behaviorism instead? A textbook for the layman?"

"Maybe that to start," he said. "Establish the science a little better, and then write down to an even simpler, everyman level after that." And off he went, not only about the parenting book that might follow, but all kinds of books: about marriage, about personal investing, even about boats, his latest nonpsychological interest—even though he knew very little about boats, beyond what he'd been learning by visiting various Long Island weekend boat shows, his way to relax when he wasn't at the office. Did I mind? Not very much. When John was home, Billy had to behave perfectly, which only made more work for me. When Daddy was away, I could choose to ignore unfinished lunches and failed bowel movements.

John's hubris seemed the key to both his happiness and his tremendous success. I didn't resent it; I admired and envied it. My relative insecurity and anxiety wasn't a sign of healthful modesty or cautious wisdom, but only proof of lesser energy. He dreamed, more than ever, of changing the world. On an exceptional day, I dreamed of going out for a night on the town, drinking champagne, and splashing through fountains. (Perhaps I had been reading the gossip columns too much.)

On an average day, I dreamed only of taking a long, hot, silent bath.

CHAPTER 24

"It smells delightful," Mother said, leading the way into our cottage, trying to push past me even before I was able to slide her second arm out and pass the coat to John, who was standing by, looking handsome in one of the new gray suits he'd bought with his latest JWT raise.

Mother barely looked at John—me, either, except for the quickest of ribcage squeezes. "How did you lose the baby weight so quickly? Aren't you a little too thin? And oh my." She paused long enough to stare me in the face. "Those eyebrows are a little severe, aren't they?"

"The style is to pluck them," I said. "I might have been rushed."

But she was already in the center of our small living room. "Well, where is he?"

My father entered more slowly, patting down his overcoat before handing it wordlessly to John. "Hello darling," he said to me, sounding tired. "Evelyn intends to come later, if she can manage it."

My sister had changed her plans several times, and I was under the assumption that she wouldn't be eating with us, and most likely wouldn't show at all. Still, my parents seemed to need to pretend, and I pretended with them. "You gave her our new telephone number, didn't you, Mother?"

"I think your father did. Yes, I'm certain. But I'm so glad you have a telephone, finally." That word—finally—wouldn't sit well with John, I knew. But never mind: he'd promised to be on his best behavior. I'd made sure he was given plenty of quiet since our walk, leaving him to read in his armchair, with a bowl of nuts and a ham sandwich, even if it spoiled his appetite, and a drink at his side. Anything to take the edge off.

Mother added, "I'd hate to think of an emergency without any way to get help, all the way out here."

One neighbor's house was visible from the kitchen window, the other was directly across the road, close enough that John had promised that, come spring, we'd smell their lilacs blooming through our very own windows.

"We're not exactly alone out here."

Mother asked, "And do your neighbors have telephones?"

"I'm not sure. I think we're the second on the street."

"*We* were the first at the top of Eutaw Place," Mother said. She seemed to have become, even in her letters lately, a little more brittle, a little more vain. "There's pluses and minuses. You may have all kinds of people bothering you to use it. You'll have to set limits."

I had to laugh: First, it seemed the problem was that we lived in the wilderness. Now, we were on the verge of being ambushed by our neighbors. But I'd been just as uncertain about Long Island that first week—thinking of it as somber and rural, when I now saw it as a little whirlpool of activity, with new houses springing up near us, and tony neighbors moving into the older, larger mansions to the east. I suppose I was accepting this new life and trying to make the best of it, if only I could get others to see it the same way.

Father joined Mother in front of our small fireplace, from which we had a view of—well, almost everything. Living room, small dining area, doorway into the kitchen.

"It's rustic," Father said.

Mother added apologetically, eyes lifted to the low ceiling, "It must be affordable to heat."

John was busy in the closet, hanging coats, but he'd heard everything so far. When he came out and faced us, hand already patting at his pocket for a calming cigarette, I saw his eyes narrow, in that Valentino stare that women found handsome. With a big intake of breath meant to last the next three hours, his shoulders broadened, preparing to bear the brunt of being judged.

"It has a nice yard," I hurried to say. "That's important for a boy."

Mother hurried toward me, taking both my hands in hers. "See, Albert. I told you we drove too slowly. A boy, already! We missed his babyhood."

"Actually," John said, crossing to his easy chair and lowering himself into the seat, "You *are* late. Billy is down for his nap."

"But it's only a few minutes past three," my mother smiled, purse still over her forearm, pinching my hands even more eagerly.

"Half past," John corrected, rotating his wrist to confirm. My father had a pocket watch he carried only on workdays or when he was in formal attire, not for a simple Sunday drive, in other words. My mother didn't wear one at all. At home, there was a grandfather clock in the second parlor, and if Mother needed to know the time, she'd call out to one of the servants and ask them to go check it for her and come back with the news.

"You said we should come for supper at three," Mother said. "I wouldn't call that late."

I gave John a warning glance. "It isn't late. But all the same, we do put him down for his nap at three o'clock."

"On Sundays, too?"

"Do you think an infant can tell a Sunday from a Wednesday?" John asked.

"Yes, every day, the same routine," I said, trying to sound cheerful and matter-of-fact. "That way we can have pleasant adult conversation before he wakes up and gets hungry or tired again."

"You couldn't have waited a few more minutes, just so we could help put him to bed?"

John tapped a cigarette on the back of his hand. "Oh, it doesn't take any help. He's a good baby."

Mother, surrendering, fell back into the sofa. "Well, of course he's a good baby! He's our grandchild!"

I gave John a steadying glance, hoping he would restrain himself from saying what he was surely thinking: that their genetic contribution had nothing to do with it. It was all environment: an environment in which they'd had zero influence.

"Have a cigarette, John," I said. "And I'll get us all drinks. Father, have a seat."

"Just any seat?" he asked, standing next to the only available armchair. When no one laughed, Father coughed into his hand. "Doctor says a little smoking will be good for this irritated throat. Darn cold lasted about three weeks."

"We were so sorry to cancel last weekend," Mother hurried to add, the first of what would be many apologies about prior absences. "Both weekends. We know you're both so careful."

"We're not unusually careful," John said. "In many ways, we're less anxious and convention-bound than most parents."

"Just with germs, I meant."

"That was your concern, not ours."

Father interrupted. "That isn't a pack of Luckies you have there, is it, John?"

He'd finally acknowledged John by name. We were moving ahead. The ice was melting. I actually felt a little tingle lighten my step and hurried to get the glasses tray.

"No," John said. "They're not Luckies."

There was an awkward moment, as John lit his own cigarette and didn't offer Father one.

"I do wish Evelyn would come," my mother said. And then, giving me a meaningful look, "I'm afraid she isn't very happy. Not like you—you and John." She was saying this to be encouraging and complimentary. But to John, I knew it would all sound like meddling. Evelyn was nearing middle age, already divorced once, with a daughter from her first marriage, and now a new husband with whom she already seemed at odds. If she wasn't happy by now, it was her own job to fix things and square up her life, John would have suggested, if he hadn't been holding his tongue as a favor to me.

When the telephone jangled from the guest bedroom we'd converted into a den, we all turned toward the sound. Mother smiled, as if her expressed wish for Evelyn's arrival had magically triggered the call. John jumped up to get it and closed the den door behind him, as he did whenever the telephone rang. A workplace habit, I supposed. He wasn't sheltering Billy, asleep in his nursery one door down, from the noise; John believed in exposing babies to a steady thrum of normal noise, or else they'd become too sensitive and wake at every murmur. Even when we made love, John made no attempt to quiet our sounds. Let the baby get used to it. Let the baby—and later, the child—understand that love between a man and his wife came first.

"It wasn't Evelyn," he said when he came out from the den. "Wrong connection."

We'd only had the telephone for a week, and we'd had more wrong numbers than right ones. Perhaps they'd assigned us an existing number. It was still a novelty for us, that telephone, and one of the best gifts John had ever given me, knowing I yearned for a way to reach him at work, or to telephone our small handful of city friends and acquaintances who had their own telephones, to make all the festive plans we'd be making once Billy was a little older, once we had more hired help, and once we became real adults with real lives again—not a moment too soon.

Later, John was serving the roast and I was carrying more dishes to the table when we heard Billy's halfhearted, soft, and stuttering cry. It was the cranky sound of a baby waking too soon, musing over his options, perhaps on the verge of going right back to sleep. (I'd watched him do it, in the half dark: roll over, fingers of one hand stuffed into his mouth, and find sleep again. I needn't have been watching, but once in a while, I did.)

Mother clapped her hands over her plate and then, noticing John's glare, set both hands flat on the table, reaction contained.

"Carrots, Mother?" I asked.

"You don't really think we came for the roast and carrots, darling. It will be so much more fun when we get to have our new grandchild at the table with us!"

John flashed her a cool smile. "That reminds me of a story."

"Oh, do tell it," I said. Anything to spark conversation.

"Well all right. I was speaking to a New York audience. After the event, I was signing some programs. A matronly lady—I'm sure you know the type—came up to me, arms crossed over her very large bosom, and declared, 'Dr. Watson . . .'"

The little crying lamb sound came from behind the door again. Mother interrupted John's story. "Rosalie, let me."

I didn't answer or look up. I could see everything without looking: Mother's plaintive face, body perched at the edge of her chair, frantic to rise; John's irritated expression, dark eyebrows scowling at his story being derailed.

I swallowed. "Go on, John."

He didn't.

"Please, John, tell the rest of your story."

"You're sure?"

Mother noted the tension only belatedly. "Yes, John. I'm sorry. Go on."

I dared to look up. I smiled at Mother. *Thank you. Thank you for at least trying.*

"All right," John said. "So the woman says, 'Dr. Watson, I'm so glad I didn't hear your talk until *after* my own children were grown, so that I had a chance to enjoy them.'"

Mother looked at him blankly. "Yes?"

I explained, "She thought it was a cutting remark."

"And wasn't it?"

"No," John said. "It was only a revealing one."

Mother said impatiently, "And what did it reveal, *John?*"

Only two years ago, her use of his first name was a compliment, an expression of acceptance. Now it was a rebuke: He might wish to tell stories about himself in the third person—"Dr. Watson"—but she'd stick with a more common address.

"It revealed," John replied, "that what most parents and grandparents really care about is enjoying themselves, not about doing what's best for their babies."

We were halfway through the meal when the stuttering cry came again and John looked to me, honestly confused. Hadn't I said that Billy napped two solid hours, like clockwork? Why this awkward break from a well-established routine, only now?

Perhaps I'd exaggerated. An hour and a half, two and a half hours, and on exceptional days maybe a solid three hours of blissful rest— there was some variation and sometimes I lost track of the time. If he was sleeping deeply and I was busy, typing or folding laundry, I certainly didn't wake him, unless I knew John was coming home on time that night—a rarity—in which case, I might even wake Billy a little early, to make sure he got enough wide-awake afternoon time that bedtime would pose no problems.

This nap had undoubtedly been on the short side, and as I watched my father chewing his last tough forkful of roast, oblivious, and as I noticed my mother hurrying to spear just enough of her vegetables to qualify as being done eating, should her grandchild appear, and as I heard the sound of a cranky distant cry gathering steam, I knew why. John and I had gone on that long, fresh-air walk together, before their arrival, never talking to Billy or lifting him from the buggy, and even when we'd come back, I'd been so busy doing last-minute cooking and cleaning that I'd chosen to leave him sleeping, still in the buggy parked in the entry hall, overly warm in his cocoon of blankets, cheeks scarlet red, head muddled with toasty dreams. John, eager to read a newspaper before guests arrived, hadn't objected to the quiet one bit. Now Billy had slept far too much for so early in the day.

John didn't realize that when I went to the park on my own, I wasn't so different from those two women we'd seen. I didn't smooch and nuzzle endlessly, but I did play with Billy. I dandled him on my knee, facing this bird or that squirrel, talking to myself, and even occasionally—yes, I'm aware we teased and scolded nannies for doing the very same thing, and so I had to be extra careful not to do it when others were in earshot—talking to *him*. It was how I tired him out *before* his nap. There was some strategy involved in training a baby, and even more strategy in helping a baby *appear* well trained, in protecting a mother—or a father—from seeing that a baby was less than perfect in his habits.

"How about that smoke now," John said to my father, the first thing he'd said since shoveling a large serving of meat onto my father's plate.

"I wouldn't mind it," Father said.

I was only midway through my own dinner, having been the last to start.

"I can go take care of Billy while you're eating, dear," Mother said.

I focused on my plate, cutting up the tough meat—I still wasn't much of a cook—and turned toward my father, who was accepting a light from John. I fully understood my mother's frustrations and her visceral longings. But it didn't make me feel any better to be reminded of our similarities, especially since I was trying to be a more modern kind of mother. I was trying to do and be good: by John's standards, by everyone's. If only they could stop wanting such different things.

"Tell him about the brand testing you've been doing, John," I said. "Father, I bet you think you can identify your favorite cigarette brand, isn't that right? You said you prefer Luckies?"

"I do."

"Or you *think* you do, rather," I said with a quick grin and a wink toward John, so he would take up the thread.

Trials conducted at JWT had shown that smokers were responding not to a specific chemical signature in their preferred tobacco—as even John had expected—but to a yearning for less tangible satisfactions.

I said, "It's opened up all kinds of doors for advertisers, because people can't identify their brands. They're not looking for a specific taste or chemical so much as an association, an emotional satisfaction—and that can be manipulated. Do I have that right, John?"

"That sounds a little funny," Father said with a morose look on his face.

John grudgingly joined the conversation. "The test subjects didn't like the findings any more than you did, Albert. Quite a few were forlorn. They didn't enjoy discovering that a known, loved product couldn't actually be identified reliably. We build our identities from these things. When we realize the foundations aren't solid, it disturbs us."

Even after John laid out the specifics of the trials, Father looked unconvinced. He said, "So you're saying we can't even identify something we experience every week or every day. We can't even identify what we like. Careful, Rebecca. I'd thought I was fond of you, but maybe I was only mistaken."

Mother turned at the sound of her name. "Oh, you're talking nonsense." She hadn't been paying any attention to John's science-of-advertising anecdotes. She had a talent for selective hearing; ears turned up high to catch the next peep from Billy, she could nonetheless manage to screen out some voices and subjects altogether. When Billy's wail picked up again in earnest, she turned her body away from her plate, eyes fixed on the nursery-room door.

I'd prompted John to talk about smoking in part because I wanted my parents to understand he was doing real work—*scientific* work—at JWT; and also because I knew that once I got him rolling, he would warm to the topic and keep going with minimal encouragement, helping the afternoon pass. I needed to focus on finishing my dinner, barely able to attend to the conversation because Billy's distant cry was unnaturally loud in my ears. I felt a warm needlelike tingle in my chest as my milk let down, leaking into the thick pads stuffed into my brassiere.

This leaking of milk was one of those facts of life I'd never heard women discuss. From my early college years, when I first started menstruating, my prematernal "monthly" had always reminded me, more than I cared to be reminded, that gender was inescapable, that I was a woman, even when I was doing the work of men. But leaking breast milk made me feel like an animal. So why hadn't I weaned Billy, who was already nearing three months old? Maybe because it was the only time I could touch and hold him with unquestionable justification. In the guise of nutrition, it provided a blind of sorts, more than I wished to admit. I had on more than one occasion offered Billy the breast even when I knew he could stretch between nursing sessions. At other times, I'd denied him, even when he was crying. It was just as John would have predicted—all my fault for being needy and most of all, unpredictable. A stranger would have done at least as good a job, I thought on my darker days. A machine, even better.

"Rosalie," Mother said. "You don't have to get up. I'll take care of it. I don't mind."

I shook my head and kept eating, though the roast had all the flavor and moisture of sawdust.

"Well, I don't believe it," Father was saying to John about the cigarette brand trials.

A loud clatter made us all jump, as John dropped his fork and scooted back his chair, scraping the wooden floor.

"With all due respect, Mr. Rayner," he said, voice hard, "I'm starting to think that you won't believe anything I tell you."

John dropped his napkin and stalked off toward Billy's nursery door. I started to push back my chair. "John?"

"Finish your dinner. Visit."

"I'm finished enough."

"No. I insist. I'll take Billy to the backyard for some air."

My mother called after him, "Oh, John, this is ridiculous. I finished my dinner ages ago."

Without looking up from his plate, Father said, "I don't suppose he can change a diaper as well? A modern father, indeed."

"It's not like I changed all that many diapers myself," Mother apologized—on Father's behalf, on John's, on her own. "I had more help. Rosalie, dear, can't you simply hire some help?"

"Of course, we want to." The telephone rang in the den, interrupting my thought. "I mean, we *are*. We have already, and we are again. It's hard to find the right person." Despite my efforts to stay calm, my voice, which had been gaining volume with every word, cracked from the strain. "It's just hard, Mother, don't you know that?"

She looked wounded. "Of course I know that, Rosalie. I hired plenty of help, in my day."

"It just isn't that easy to find help now," I objected.

"Well maybe," she said delicately, "we were less demanding."

John stalked through the house again with Billy, wrapped in a blanket, red cheeked and wide-eyed, startled from his sudden exposure to the cold, crying successfully paused. He passed Billy off to me—bottom damp; John hadn't taken care of the diaper after all, which didn't surprise me—and dashed back to the den, catching the call by its fourth ring, too hurried to close the door. We could all hear his words. "This isn't the best time, but all right. I understand."

The rest was drowned out by Mother's thrilled exclamations. "There he is! Our dear one! Rosalie, his little fists are like ice!"

Across the table, Father—a shock to me—was silently weeping. He did not speak, did not move, just sat with his eyes glassy, one big tear spilling onto his cheek, staring at our first child. My heart cracked, looking at him. Love, without theories. Pure, unbridled sentiment. But there was pain in Father's face, too. Perhaps when it comes to love, there always is.

Mother was too enraptured to notice Father. She was too happy to see the baby at last to spend any more time worrying or criticizing. And she showed not a single sign of disappointment when John came back to the table, explaining that he had an emergency appointment to keep. Yes, on a Sunday, at dinner time. But it was about a boat, you see. A boat being kept down at the Long Island Shore Club, on which he'd made a casual offer. He planned to look it over and most likely pass, but he had made the offer, after all. He had to follow through or risk looking like a cad, which wasn't good form, considering we hoped to join the Shore Club as members.

Oh, did we? It was news to me.

I didn't reveal to my parents that I hadn't been consulted about John's supposed offer. Given his recent boat madness and his recent raise, it didn't seem impossible. I believed him about the strange Sunday evening call, just as I'd believed him about all the wrong connections of evenings prior. John had a way of making unquestionable declarations.

Aside from the boat, and the telephone call itself, I was simply grateful for the relief of tension, the eased denouement of a nearly concluded family dinner. Now I could let Father sit in silence, staring at Billy, without trying to foster peace talks between him and John. Now I could let Mother hold her new grandson without limits. I might even run off and take a bath, in case she wanted to smother him with kisses without anyone watching.

After a diaper change and a quick nursing session (hard to tear Billy out of Mother's hands and leave the room to fulfill these functions in private, but I managed), and delivery of grandson back to her arms, I went into the bathroom and locked the door. Tap running, I spent a minute in front of the mirror, trying to tweeze my eyebrows more carefully than I'd done a week earlier, during a rushed moment when Billy was fussing. Yes, they were a little severe, just as Mother had said. Nothing an eyebrow pencil wouldn't fix, but who had time each morning for an eyebrow pencil?

When the bath was full, I dipped one toe into it and heard the telephone ring. I pulled my foot out, drips pooling on the floor.

A moment later, Mother's voice was just outside the door, with Billy—I could hear him grunting slightly—in her arms. "Darling, it's your sister. She really is eager to talk with you."

"One minute. Just have her wait."

The sound of my voice alone was enough to make Billy start fussing again, with vigor.

A moment later I was wrapped in my robe, leaving wet footprints as I hurried to the telephone. The call was brief. Evelyn sounded anxious and apologetic, not necessarily eager to talk, as Mother had claimed, but dispatching the duty to make excuses. "I do want to come," she kept saying. "It's just not convenient, and there are things that I can't really explain briefly. Things aren't so good."

It was her marriage, I knew. She imagined we had nothing in common, and I couldn't bear to tell her any differently. To put my own confusion into words would make it real. The less we said, the more we might gratefully forget later.

"It's a busy time," she said again. "I can't talk about it now."

"That's fine, Evelyn. Of course I want to see you, but I more than understand."

"I'm not sure you do," she said, sounding harried.

The back room was drafty. Billy was fussing in the living room. I may have sounded a little harried myself, which only made her more defensive.

"Oh, Evelyn, I just miss you, that's all. I want you to see the baby. Of course it's fine. We'll reschedule."

Sneaking back down the hall, back in the bathroom, I could feel the invisible pressure of their curiosity about the conversation with Evelyn, but I ignored it. The water had cooled. I turned on the tap, hot as it would go, steam pouring forth, and stepped as close to the fresh water as I could manage without getting scalded.

I sank lower and lower. Eyes under. Then lips. Finally, nose. Comfort. Forgiveness. Erasure.

Only once I was fully immersed under the water, holding my breath, trying to think about nothing at all, did the thought forcefully intrude: That boat for sale was, supposedly, at a club ten miles down the shore.

There'd been no call for a taxi, no knock at the door.

He'd left in an instant.

Yet John—still and always—didn't drive.

CHAPTER 25

"Daddy go wook," Billy said, rhyming the word with *look*. He was two years old now, still forming his words.

John was sipping his coffee, finishing the newspaper, a trace of jam on his cheek. Billy was seated in the kitchen, head peeking out from the space under the sink, running a truck along the floor.

"Daddy go wook."

"Yes, in just a few minutes, Daddy will be going to *work*," I said, pronouncing the word carefully for him.

Billy said it again, louder. He wasn't making a prediction, he was making a demand. Time for Daddy to leave, so we could get on with our day without him, especially the best part, our hour alone, before Cora the baby nurse came. I tried to suppress a smile, not sure how John would take this display of toddler impudence, but less anxious than I might have been a year earlier. Maybe it was the natural sedation of mothering hormones in my blood, preparing for the change to come. Maybe it was my bovine girth: eight and a half months and nearly ready to pop all over again, and too aware of the chores ahead to get anxious over minor family tension, though I expected John would be mildly offended.

John folded the paper and looked down at our son with a serious expression. "What's that, Billy? You want your mother all to yourself, do you?"

Billy didn't know what John was getting at, but he was suspicious of the tone. He pulled his heels in closer to his body, knees up in a froglike posture, short-legged overalls riding up to bare his sweet, chubby calves. He leaned over his truck, as if John had been talking about taking it away.

"Oh, he's just used to the routine," I said. "You're running a little late, and he can tell."

John asked, "Is that it, Billy?"

Billy, neck bent and face angled downward, rubbed his palm against the textured surface of the tiny truck tire, rolling it back and forth.

"That's very interesting," John said, looking past me even as I leaned toward him to wipe the jam off his cheek.

"*Very* interesting," he said again, not offended at all, but rather oddly pleased. I patted the knot of his tie for good measure and gave him a quick kiss that he seemed not to register.

The maternity clothes had been boxed up for only a few months when I'd told John to bring them down from the high closet shelf again. John and I thought it best to get the set finished in short order. (Two was plenty, we both agreed.) And maybe I was more eager the second time around, thinking a playmate in the house would be good for Billy, and another voice and bubbly spirit good for us all.

Maybe, also, I was competing, via my own reproductive competency, against some opponent I couldn't see or name. How many more times since Billy's infancy had the telephone been a wrong caller, or some secretary contacting John about a work matter, as late as 8 or 9 P.M.? How many more times had he spent Sunday afternoon out of the house, frustratingly unclear about his plans?

When he started to spend one or two evenings a week sleeping over at work, on the couch in his office, I questioned him. He reminded me of how many evenings he'd slept at Johns Hopkins, getting in his best hours—writing the bulk of his published papers and designing his most promising experiments—when everyone else had gone home. He had quite typically worked two separate shifts, napping on his office couch between them.

"Isn't that true?"

Of course it was.

Then why was I pestering him with these questions?

"I'm not sure."

The arguments increased over my final trimester. Did I want to be married to a less ambitious, less productive man?

"Goodness, no."

Had I fallen in love with him because he was temperate, cautious, conventional?

"Not at all."

Did I feel threatened, anticipating some loss, whether of him, of my own youth and beauty, financial stability, or the prospect of a future reproductive mate?

Now he wasn't really talking with me; he was studying me, and ticking boxes off some theoretical checklist. I was displaying something of interest to him. I was depicting the emotional trajectory of a typical wife and mother, operating not out of instinct—this was no instinct—but in reaction to some change in my environment.

The primary environmental change *I* recognized was John's own aloofness and increasingly frequent absences. First, all that time he had spent shopping for boats—and yes, he had finally bought one, christened *Eutopia*. In August, we'd taken the motorboat out for a spin together, but I'd been about three months pregnant with Jimmy, and the slamming over the waves had made me so nauseated, I begged John to turn around and deposit me back at the shore club, where I stood in the window, sipping a tonic water with lemon, letting my stomach settle as I watched him depart again, thrilled with his new purchase. A woman had come up to me—she introduced herself as a fellow "yacht club widow"—and pointed out her own husband in the small harbor below us, busily shouting introductions to the fuel jockey before backing out his own motorboat.

"Rodney hates traffic, straight lines, and speed limits, any kind of obstacle," she'd said, lifting her chin toward the shrinking figure of her husband, speeding into the distance. "At sea, he thinks he doesn't have to follow any rules. Your husband the same?"

"Yes, actually," I said, grateful she'd explained this latest male mystery to me.

But the boat was only a weekend distraction. The rest of the week, always in addition to his day job, of course, John busied himself with an ever-increasing amount of work at the New School and Columbia, overseeing Mary Cover Jones's research and teaching the occasional night class, as well as recruiting interesting speakers to come lecture. The tide was turning back toward scientific positions John had tried to stamp out while at Hopkins: increasing emphasis on instincts and innate qualities, and from there to measuring and selecting for intelligence. A Princeton prof we knew was working on a book about Nordic superiority. John, playing the fair-if-never-wholly-impartial referee, tried to get the scientists, including the ones he disagreed with, talking openly about their claims. The ad man part of his personality was being continually reinforced, most tangibly by his ever improving salary, but it hadn't laid claim to all of his allegiances. His belief in logic—and in his fellow Americans' ability to see through others' dangerous, sometimes racist illogic—remained strong, regardless of his primary profession, in which he took advantage of people's illogical emotionalism. Even though academia didn't count John as a serious member anymore, he hated to see ignorance flower there.

Lately, John had been exchanging barbs with a British-born Harvard professor named William McDougall, who was strongly invested in the notions of instinct, inherited traits, and eugenics. Negroes, McDougall believed, were inherently inclined to violent emotions but also had, conversely, "happy-go-lucky dispositions."

John was reading a review copy of McDougall's newest book one Sunday evening in his armchair while I knelt on the floor not far away, sorting through a bag I was packing in advance for my maternity trip to the hospital. As I counted undergarments and tucked in a few comforting items—thick slippers, a favorite rose-scented hand lotion—he quipped, "So he thinks the colored are irascible idiots. Well, I think the same of him. Listen to this: about the 'tall, elegant, white race,' McDougall writes that we have 'great independence of character, individual initiative, and tenacity of will.' Well, obviously, we should rule the world, then, and breed only the finest of our own Nordic specimens to create an even purer race."

"Obviously." I picked up the two new novels I'd thought to bring in case I was stuck recuperating longer than expected. Janine, our neighbor from the corner, had told me that her second childbirth created more complications than the first. Her first, born when she and her husband were newlyweds restricted to a tight budget, had come into the world with the help of a simple midwife. Her second child, born three more-affluent years later, was delivered with the help of a doctor of considerable repute, known for his belief that all childbirth was inherently problematic. His prediction had come true. He'd tried a few experimental procedures, from which she spent six weeks recovering.

Just in case my doctor was equally innovative, Janine loaned me *Men Like Gods*, the new "scientific romance" by H. G. Wells. Flipping open the dark green leather cover now, eyes landing on "utopia" and "liberty" and "perfected anarchy" and "the promises of advanced science," I felt I was proofreading a more flamboyant version of my husband's next lecture or ad-man-club speech. Janine might have thought it a playful fantasy, given its setting on a distant planet, but it bore no trace of the exotic for me. I rejected *Men Like Gods* and put my faith in a British collection of comic stories called *Jeeves*, instead.

John interrupted his McDougall reading long enough to squint at the cover of *Men Like Gods*, sitting in the discarded "don't pack" pile.

"You get that from Elaine?"

"No, from Janine."

He nodded, satisfied. Janine was acceptable. She didn't drop by uninvited early in the morning or late at night; she didn't seem to endlessly smooch or baby talk to her son Tommy, with whom Billy was allowed to play on occasion; and she didn't press her religious or political views on us.

Elaine, by contrast, had relocated from Indiana soon after we'd moved in, and she'd brought some less-than-cosmopolitan views with her. I hadn't planned to tell John, who was already so dismissive of our neighborhood women. But then I'd started to notice how frequently he was chatting with her after work, on his way into the house. Somehow, his arrival home—whether at six, seven, or eight o'clock—seemed to coincide, more often than random chance would suggest, with Elaine being outside, planting bulbs at twilight or picking up a forgotten child's toy from the sidewalk. It was almost as if she listened for the sound of the cab that John took home evenings from the train station, and raced out in time to banter. I finally thought it prudent to mention: yes, she was nice enough, and pretty, too, with those dimpled cheeks and cute figure. But she was also a little too insistent about those meetings, always wondering when we'd like to give one a try.

"What meetings?"

"Oh, you know. The Ku Klux Klan."

Who knows? Maybe it wasn't even a fib.

John had blown his top. Did he look like a Klansman? Did she really think he'd walk around in a white bedsheet and pointy dunce cap, like those *Birth of a Nation* imbeciles? That was the end of his friendly banter with cute Elaine; the end, also, of getting sprigs of spring lilac and summer tomatoes from our across-the-street neighbor.

The 1920s rise of the Klan and the growing conservative backlash—both paradoxical and probably predictable, given the explosive liberality of popular culture—made views like William McDougall's more concerning, even if he claimed not to be a racist. The Harvard professor agreed to debate John publicly at the Psychology Club in Washington, DC, on February 5. The vast majority of those attending were not psychologists or even up-to-date on psychological terms, which only showed how many people knew of my husband through his more popular writings and speeches.

John won the Battle of Behaviorism debate, as it was called, but only narrowly. That was fine with John. He didn't truly want to vanquish his enemies. He needed them. Without open debate, ideas—including the superstitious or jingoistic ones—just became common currency, unquestioned.

A thousand people attended that historic debate. I was not one of them, having given birth on February 3rd to little Jimmy (yes, after William James—John had gotten his way with both part one and part two of that little inside joke). My mother had taken Billy for a few days—something John might have objected to, except that he had his debate plans and was won over by convenience. I was kept in the hospital for fewer days than the doctors wanted, but more than I personally desired.

I arrived home before John, who had extended his public performance with some business and research meetings. He apologized later, but I reassured him: I was happy to have been released early. When your name was on everyone's lips, you didn't squander the week-long whispers, the collegial nods days later from someone who had heard about the big event. Surely, John must have spent several nights in a row, dining out on the notoriety. But where, and with whom? I just wanted to know, that was all, especially because I'd missed the big event.

I hadn't resented John's absence at the birth—I'd missed it myself, of course, being heavily sedated. I hadn't resented his absence when I first walked into the door of our home, leaning on the elbow of the temporary nurse I'd hired. Irene drove me home from the hospital and helped me bathe and dress on the first few tender days, scheduled to depart when John and Billy came home. After then, I'd also have Cora to help with both the children during the midday hours. I wasn't going to put myself in the same position I'd been in last time, too tired to make a sandwich or clear out a bathtub's clogged drain.

My mother still wondered why we didn't have a live-in baby nurse, or at least someone who worked full days, but Cora's limited schedule suited Billy and me both. It gave our son those quiet mornings after John left to play alone, constructing block towers or rolling his trucks near my feet as I folded towels or picked out socks for us to put on our hands for impromptu sock-puppet theater before the serious part of the day began—but only when no one was watching. Billy had started noticing: fun was something easier to have when witnesses weren't around. Cora's early departure also gave me a few hours while Billy napped and before John came home, to do whatever *I* wanted: bath, cocktail, looking at old photos, and wondering—I was doing more wondering, even then—how our lives had become as they were, the very opposite of what I'd expected as a younger woman.

John planned to leave Washington, DC, travel by train up through Baltimore to pick up Billy, and from there to New York. I mentioned that my own mother had offered to drive Billy to us, but John was adamant. He wanted to arrive at the same time with Billy. Meeting a new brother for the first time was a milestone.

Cora had departed for the day, leaving me a chicken casserole in the oven, when I heard stamping feet and voices at the door: Billy's happy recounting of his Baltimore winter adventures, missing some consonants, so that "snow" came out as "no." John, who spent less time with Billy, sometimes had a hard time translating, but today, he seemed unusually patient and willing to try.

"Alboo played outside with you, did he?" I heard John say.

Billy answered in high falsetto, "Alboo like da no!"

A few more lost syllables, Billy's excitement about the rare big snowfall and a new sled pushing his voice higher and higher, and tipping over into a tinkling cascade of little-boy giggles, remembering his first snowball fight with my own dear father, who'd clearly taken him to our boulevard-long park, where I'd had my own very first snowball fight.

"That's just fine," John replied, most likely understanding only one word out of three. "Let's focus on the boots. Keep pulling."

Billy's giggles had turned to grunts. The final one—I heard the *thunk* of it landing—suggested a sudden dramatic victory over the tight boot.

"Where did the sock go?" John asked in a serious voice.

A puzzled pause. Then Billy erupted in laughter all over again: "It's still in da boot!"

I smiled, on the verge of giggling myself, listening to that youthful insistence on humor and joy, knowing that even if John was scowling, Billy couldn't help but find it hilarious that his boot had swallowed his sock.

"That isn't funny, Billy," John said calmly. "It won't be funny tomorrow when you can't find the sock."

Billy didn't care what anyone else thought. And he didn't care about tomorrow. Why should he? "Dat silly boot!"

Listening to his continuing giggles, I had to press one hand over my mouth to keep from laughing with him, even from the next room. Having adapted to motherhood less than gracefully, it surprised me now when I had these bursts of visceral joy, triggered by something as simple as a little boy's high-pitched laugh. It was a feeling of bubbly pleasure that bypassed my intellect and went right to my stomach and toes, making everything feel lighter.

Then Billy remembered where he was and what was coming next. Snow, sled, boots, socks: done. "Where Mama?"

John issued a quick, but still gentle, rebuke: "Mittens off. Coat on the peg. No, you can reach it if you stretch. I'm not hanging it up there for you. There you go."

At that moment, as I listened to the two familiar voices negotiating a routine I'd shared with Billy many times, little Jimmy was nursing at my breast. The milk had come in as it had before, with a pulsing, prickly heat. But there was less engorgement the second time around, less pain even in the first days. Was my body more practiced and better able to manage the flow, or was I just more relaxed and less of a silly baby myself, better able to handle minor, passing discomforts?

I looked down to watch the little movements of Jimmy's round cheek and tiny pointed chin, the rhythmic sucking, his eyes closed, eyelashes and brows so light they were almost transparent. He twitched once, sighing hard through his tiny nostrils as he swallowed. So happy. And I was happy, too. The most contented I had ever been—thinking of Billy and his lost sock and the good Baltimore visit he'd had and my own father playing in the snow, and John warming to all of it, getting more used to his own son's playful nature, perhaps. We all made accommodations and were better off for it, every one of us. *Finally.*

They were just outside the door now.

"Where Mama?" Billy asked again.

John's voice remained steady, betraying nothing out of the ordinary. "In the nursery."

Around the corner they came. Billy's eyes lit up. "Mama!"

He trundled ahead and bumped into my knees, patting them, folding his hands for a moment behind my calves, so that I could feel the winter-cool freshness of his sweater against my shins. Then he let go and came alongside, reaching up to pat at my nearest shoulder with his flat hand, cheek pushed up against the back of my arm. I freed the hand I'd been using to cradle Jimmy's head and reached back, shaking Billy's hand, and held it a long moment. What I wanted, of course, was a big breathless hug. What I wanted was to bury my face in the top of his head, to fill my senses with the touch and smell of him. Oh, why didn't I? Because we were handshakers in this family, especially when John was around, and that's what Billy was used to.

All the jostling had wakened Jimmy. His eyelids flickered, but then he closed them again, resuming his diligent emptying of one breast.

Billy looked at Jimmy, reached out a hand and patted one sleeper-covered baby leg as if he were clapping the shoulder of an old working buddy in a bar. Then, after what appeared to be a tranquil and even half-bored moment, he looked across the room at the toy shelf he hadn't seen in nearly two weeks. His eyes lit up again. "'Dere you are!"

Hurrying across the room, he retrieved his favorite red truck, which we hadn't allowed him to bring to Alboo's house, and set it down on the ground at my feet, immersed in play. It wouldn't be the first time a boy had decided a truck was more interesting than a baby.

From the doorway, John said in a commanding voice, "Billy, you know who that is?"

My sweet boy answered without a pause and without looking up, "Dat's our baby. Dat's Jimmy."

"That's your brother. Do you understand? Mother is home from the hospital with your new brother."

I'd talked to Billy for several weeks about what would happen, and what we were planning to call the new baby if it was a boy or a girl, and what he would probably look like, and about how little he would be able to do at first, and how we'd have to take care of him until he could talk and walk and eat regular foods and play. After the birth, I'd even telephoned my parents to confirm the gender and ask them to use Jimmy's name in conversation. Billy, who didn't seem to need any more explanation from John or from anyone else, continued playing.

"What's Mother doing now, Billy?" John asked.

Billy shrugged, but he didn't look unhappy, just excited to see a toy that had disappeared from his little-boy universe for too many days.

I asked more gently, "What's *Jimmy* doing now, Billy? Do you think he's sleeping?"

Billy looked up and smiled. "He's eating."

Well, well. My advance explanations had hit the mark. Billy even looked a little proud, as if to say: *You're all grown-ups, and you can't tell what the baby is doing?*

I looked from Billy's bright uncomplicated face to John's. I knew that look: eyebrow cocked, mouth a tight line, a shadow of a smile, but not a convincing one.

"Hmmm," he said.

"The baby's eating, John," I repeated, smiling. "That's all. And thank goodness he's almost done, since I'm hungry myself and that casserole Cora left in the oven smells divine."

"Hmmm," John said again, looking back down at Billy, utterly absorbed, on the watch for any sign of anxiety or duplicity.

In all the excitement over Billy's first response—over whether he would show signs of jealousy, preparation for a life of more complicated and damaging jealousies—even I had forgotten something basic. This was *John's* first exposure to little Jimmy as well.

"John," I said to get his attention. "Would *you* like to get a closer look at your new son?"

CHAPTER 26

Billy's equanimity had puzzled John enough that he was still mulling it over, days later. I tended to drift into exhausted sleep even while John was having a last nightcap in the living room, reading journals or catching up on correspondence. Among his newer pen pals was the British philosopher Bertrand Russell, who had been attracted to John's behaviorist theories as a reconciliation of the mind-body dualism that had bedeviled philosophers for centuries.

But on this night, I struggled to stay awake long enough for the soft footsteps and the feel of the sinking mattress as he climbed into bed next to me.

"If it's about Billy," I said, feeling the tug of blankets, "I know his first reactions to Jimmy weren't what you expected."

John rolled toward me and put a hand on my cheek. Even now, with my body stretched and sore, I still appreciated his touch, and found him enormously attractive. I hoped that he felt the same toward me, or would, once I shed this latest baby weight and smartened myself up again.

When he didn't reply, I continued, "Isn't it a good thing that he isn't jealous this early? It demonstrates what you're always saying: that so few behaviors are inborn."

"True," he said, kissing the tip of my nose. "But the introduction of a new sibling is how we would expect jealousy to begin."

"Maybe he simply isn't the jealous type."

Another pause in the half dark, John busy thinking as he rubbed a hand lightly up and down my arm. The first touch had been sweet, the kiss gentle, and even this rubbing felt good—an immediate answer to my question, a sign that he did in fact still find me appealing. But I hoped it wasn't a sign that he was expecting anything more. I had a lot of healing to do. John loved speed, but some things had to proceed at their own pace.

"Oh, John," I said, feeling the caul of exhaustion slipping over my head, knowing we'd made our way through one tiring infancy and we'd do the same again. "I love you."

"To understand a behavior," he mused, his own thought stream unbroken by my declaration, "we need to see how it's initially conditioned, how it becomes generalized to other situations."

He didn't have to explain. I'd been there during the Albert trials, stimulating a fear response in a baby who'd been initially unafraid. I couldn't tell whether John was reviewing obvious facts, or really puzzling, or only treading carefully, preparing to counter objections.

"Did you hear me? I said, 'I love you.'"

"Of course, Rar. I love you, too." With effort, he paused. "But don't you see? Catching things at the beginning has always been a challenge for psychologists. The worst of them count on what adults recall on their own, as if memory is the same as third-party observation. Of course it isn't. Look at your own memories. Anyone's memories. Worthless."

Well, not *worthless*, I thought to myself, feeling the urge to guard the chambers of my own heart. Maybe it was having children that did that: showed you how fast things changed, how quickly the past receded. I wanted to save and store and treasure. I was married to a man concerned only about the future, and as a young, tired mother, I was very much wedded to the present, but I could see a day soon when I'd want to look back and find comfort and even pleasure in the past.

He continued, "It may need a little push to get started."

"What do you mean, push?"

"The first stimulated behavior. How else to show clearly the before and the after?"

"I'm not sure we want to trigger a negative behavior in our son. If it starts to show itself naturally, that's one thing, and then we can try to decondition it, but . . ."

"You're sounding like Mary now."

They were on such familiar terms with each other, my husband and the old college friend I almost never saw. But he didn't always praise her. Publicly, yes, but privately, he occasionally questioned her methods.

John's caressing had stopped. I tugged the blankets higher, trying to draw a little extra padding around me, feeling protective.

"Whether you're endorsing or disapproving, you do talk about her work an awful lot," I said. "Mary this, and Harold that. Columbia this, and Rockefeller that. On balance, she seems to be advancing the field. What's wrong with emphasizing deconditioning? What's wrong with using a little caution?"

"And going slowly," he said. "And publishing a tenth of what someone in our field needs to publish in order to put a finger in the dike."

"What dike?"

"The ignorance and mumbo jumbo, the antiscientific rhetoric and political opportunism that's threatening to turn the clock back to the 1800s. She does good work, but she'd rather study one child for three years, or even thirty, than three hundred children for . . . oh never mind. It was Billy we were talking about."

"Exactly. It was Billy. *Our* child. Not some random subject. Not little Albert."

He rolled away from me, and I heard the sound of the nightstand drawer. Rummaging for a cigarette. And if he didn't find one, he'd go into the living room, light up, pour another bourbon, and probably be up half the night, writing another letter to Russell or Mencken, another exchange in their gleeful tirade about the stupidity of Freud—Freud, who had identified the Oedipal complex to begin with, and wasn't that what John had been expecting our dear firstborn to demonstrate?

I wanted John to stay next to me, to comfort me with his strong, warm body. I wanted him to leave work at work, to leave our own family out of it.

But I wasn't being fair or honest, was I? Because at the same time, I wanted him to bring work home, so I wouldn't be bored to tears, so that I could stay caught up with his latest thinking and feel I was making a contribution as well. I hated when he slept at his office. I hated not understanding the latest Rockefeller funding and whether Mary had deconditioned a girl to be less afraid of a dog, a boy to be less afraid of a rabbit. I didn't even like it when John's JWT secretary helped type a clean draft of some psychology article he'd written on the side. The JWT girls were supposed to help him with his advertising projects. I was supposed to help him with his after-hours psychology work. But John had always managed—the nurses at Johns Hopkins being just one example—to persuade people to take on extra duties.

John's new book, *Behaviorism*—the first for a truly lay audience—would be published in just a few months, and I'd spent much of my pregnancy with Jimmy in our bedroom, typewriter on a nightstand, cleaning up his drafts, sorting through editorial notes from the publisher, condensing and expanding, all while preserving John's authoritative, acerbic voice in the text. I could do a good job parroting him after five years together.

And so I knew, even as he left the bedroom and went to sit in his armchair alone, what he would have said to me next on the subject of jealousy, if I'd pushed. He would have said, "The future will be no

better than the past until we understand these behaviors in the present."
He would have said, "No one can master scientific parenting, because
no one asks the hard questions. No one takes the risks." He would
have said, "All I'm suggesting is that we create a controlled situation in
which to observe and record more carefully. Billy's bound to get jealous
soon, whether we try to make him that way or not. Everyone becomes
jealous, at some point. After all, aren't you?"

Perhaps it was that late night conversation that convinced me to stifle
any behaviors of my own that I may have been exhibiting in moments
of weakness: asking too many questions, protesting John's absences,
noting strange postmarks on letters delivered to the house. When
I'd first met him, he'd been fascinated by fear, and he'd staked his
career on investigating that emotion. Now, as he developed an equal
or greater interest in jealousy, I didn't want to feed it, even if I did
wonder: Why this, why now?

Was it really just because we now had two children, and one might
logically become jealous of the other? Was it because John was in
fact jealous of *my* relationship with the children, even though I tried
to keep our marriage top priority, and tried my best to follow his
principles of nonattachment? Was it because John had noticed, ever
since our marriage, that I was in fact a little more jealous, a little
more suspicious? Or was it because he was actively doing something,
out of my view, that should cause me to be very jealous indeed? That
would have been an irony of Watsonian proportions—and unfortunately, entirely credible—if John's own infidelities were shaping his
scientific hypotheses, regardless of any behavior that Billy, Jimmy, or
I exhibited.

But John was too busy to actively pursue his scientific interest in
jealousy that spring. He had been made a vice president at JWT. It
was what he had predicted back in 1921, when no one else had been
willing to hire him, and he'd had to pay his dues at the Macy's counter

and going door-to-door selling coffee in the South. In three years, he'd climbed his way from the bottom of the nation's largest advertising agency to the very top. And then, proving that he was still a psychology pioneer, his popular book *Behaviorism* (with a dedication to Stanley Resor—smart move) was published to astonishing reviews. They rolled out over several summer months, and John read each one aloud to me at our quiet, 8 P.M.-or-later dinners. Cora was gone for the day and the boys were asleep, blond heads resting on their pillows, so that John could bask in the order and serenity of our home. (No need to tell him that Jimmy still had fits of colic, or that Billy kept getting those morning stomachaches, making a mockery of our earliest attempts to perfectly train his bowels.)

The Atlantic called John "more revolutionary than Darwin, bolder than Nietzsche." *The New York Times* credited him for launching "a new epoch in the intellectual history of man."

A *new epoch*. Goodness.

"It's to your credit as well," he said once. "I could be as certain and opinionated as I wanted, knowing you'd check me if I went a step too far."

"Oh, that isn't true. When I told you that you were standing too close to the edge, you went a step further."

"Because you were my net. I could risk having a few more enemies with a lover as loyal as you are."

"You always enjoyed having enemies, even before I came along," I said that night, teasing him back, but feeling at the moment warm and safe, confident in his appreciation for our partnership.

More reviews. More congratulations. And surprisingly few objections to John's knocking of William James, of the "older, introspective psychology," and of religion, which perhaps had its prehistoric origins in the "general laziness of mankind," attributing to those individuals too indolent to go out and hunt the discovery that they could make a role for themselves, using fear to control their fellow primitives.

Those primitive days were behind us now. Old psychology and even older religion were behind us now. There was no reason to wallow in useless emotions. Behaviors could be trained into people—and out of them.

On another night, John read aloud to me another review. "It's a little hyperbolic, but listen to just this one line."

"I'm listening."

"'One stands for an instant blinded with a great hope.'"

"Well," I said.

"I always hoped people would listen to reason, but this is more than listening."

"That's marvelous," I said, filling both of our glasses, and then taking a moment to go to the kitchen, to stand there alone, freezer door open, slowly getting more ice.

Blinded with a great hope—was that the right phrase to use in response to John's work? I too had been blinded with *something*—perhaps only my new-wife, new-mother inadequacies. Because I hadn't expected such an effusive public reaction to my very own husband's work. I thought the book was good, the principles and messages—the rationale for studying behaviors instead of mental states, the lack of evidence for human instincts, the basis and conditioning of emotions, a recap of the Albert and other experiments, with several anecdotes from our own boys' childhoods thrown in—all in line with John's previous writings and lectures.

I had done my own part to sand down its rough edges, which weren't many. My main contribution was, perhaps, in talking John into revisiting issues he had oversimplified for many years. He seemed to be groping, at last, for more nuanced explanations—especially about that most difficult subject, the human mind. He had elaborated more carefully this time around, about thought and language, sounding less adamant, less severe. He had always been good at lecturing, and in his best writings, he simply wrote as he talked, like someone you wouldn't mind having to dinner—as long as you didn't mind a few feisty debates—with frequent direct addresses to the reader, and an authoritative and friendly use of *we* to describe the scientists doing the good work of behaviorism.

But I had underestimated the impact of this latest publication. I had perhaps miscalculated the impact of my husband's work, period, even after all these years helping him, defending and promoting him. Now, I felt like a traitor. And I questioned my own contrariness.

John called out from around the corner, "Are you coming, Rar? I have another one to read to you."

"Of course, I'm coming," I said, twisting the trays, holding one cube at a time, feeling the burn on my fingers. The reviews should have made me happy. Why didn't they?

Every one of those reviews should have been a balm for the sting of 1920, our shared *annus horribilis*. I think that even John, accustomed to some notoriety and always ready for a fight, was pushed off-kilter by the gush of praise. It was as if he'd gotten used to leaning hard into a river current that he'd been rowing against most of his life, and then the river had suddenly switched direction.

"So now that you're a JWT VP . . ." I said one night at dinner, having planned my small speech all day: that perhaps after Jimmy's second birthday, or third at the latest, I might like to get another crack at the advertising world, which still seemed both glamorous and intellectually satisfying to me. It wouldn't be all that hard to bring me on board now. I could write copy. I could poll customers on their preferences for testimonial A (older, trustworthy suffragette) versus testimonial B (Eastern European princess). I could run blindfold tests on cola drinkers, cracker eaters, hair-cream users. I could prepare the final graphs and tables to convince clients that our research would benefit their product.

The success of *Behaviorism* had overshadowed the promotion, at least for the moment. At JWT, John couldn't climb much higher. But as a popular author and a scientific spokesperson, there were endless opportunities ahead, beneficial to his reputation as ad man and scientist, both. Too bad he couldn't duplicate himself.

"I need your help here," he said. "Now more than ever."

Here—with the children. Here—with the typewriter and the files and the half-finished articles and the outlines for future books.

He'd said it so clearly, and he'd used that word, *need*. There was little reason for further discussion. The children wouldn't be small indefinitely. The days were long, but the years were short. Part of me fantasized about the time when our sons would be young men, happy and handsome, tall and strong. I could see myself dancing with them, finally able to embrace them without anxiety or censure, because we'd all be adults and their healthy psychological development would no longer be in question. The other part of me knew that day would come all too soon and feared I had missed too much of their precious babyhoods already, so why was I looking for time to pass more quickly? Why had I started having that ridiculous ad-job fantasy again? Why couldn't I appreciate, also, how rare it was for a husband to truly *need* his wife? I was lucky. We were all so very lucky.

"Of course."

"Really?" he asked with that pleading, grateful look I'd once seen in the lab and in the bedroom, and now saw only rarely.

"Really," I said. "We're partners, aren't we?"

In place of answering, he quoted the critic again. "'More revolutionary than Darwin.' Can you believe that?"

It was going to his head. It was going to mine, too, in a different way. I felt so bad about my first contrary reaction to the reviews that I was determined to make up for it now. And never mind my own disloyal reaction. The reviews themselves convinced me of John's greater wisdom. The success of *Behaviorism* worked against my impulse to question, to purge some of the strict behaviorism from our home, delaying my own slowly reemerging independent streak. Yes, I would still be a little softer with the boys when John was not around, but not as soft as I might have been. It was not only John telling me his views were right; it was the whole world now, and if I'd ever questioned him, even a little—about any of the infant tests, about little Albert, about the way we were raising our own children—I only felt grateful that I'd kept most of those doubts to myself. Imagine being the wife or mother of Darwin, telling him not to sail aboard the *Beagle*.

Meanwhile, the ever increasing attention was creating more demands on John's time. Every publication wanted him to write an article.

"These magazines thrive on repetition, and you always know what I'm trying to say, Rosalie. In fact, you say what I want to say, even better. Are you sure you can't get Cora to stay later? Maybe we could hire someone to handle the boys' evening routine, so you can write until I get home. I'll rough out the outline, and if you can start filling it in . . ."

But what touched him most, I think, was the praise from the fellow intellectuals he admired, particularly when they referenced John's views on early childhood.

"Look at all this, Rosalie," he said later that summer, reading me the tenth glowing review, or the twelfth, and bringing out an even bigger stack of requests from magazines, whose continuing publication of John's articles would help the book sell a respectable number of copies, despite its technical nature. "The next book *has* to be a parenting guide. Do you realize how many printings those baby books go through? A self-replenishing market, year after year. Even Mencken ghostwrote one."

Bertrand Russell sent John a particularly touching note. He said that John had convinced him. Russell was going to start raising his own daughter according to the Watson method.

CHAPTER 27

Billy, at the age of three, was a sweetheart, a little lamb. Willing to follow a schedule, to play alone and pick up his toys, independent in his toileting even though constipation and stomach upset plagued him from infancy and all through childhood. (His brother as an older child would suffer even worse, and I later found out that John's first son, Little John, had tummy troubles of his own.)

He was stoic on those mornings when he had to return to his bedroom and lie on his front, stomach pressed into the bed, or on his side, knees curled up to his chest. I took him to a doctor, who found nothing wrong and was only surprised when he asked for specifics on bowel movements that I couldn't provide. After all, Billy used the bathroom unaccompanied. We made sure not to alter routines or give in to coddling when he was sick, because that would be the surest way to make him use illness to gain attention. And we relied on his toileting reports. He seemed a truthful child. Why get in the way of his independence?

The doctor agreed. He was simply surprised. Not too many people were able to trust that a child could take care of himself. But of course, we were special: the family of John Watson—scientist, ad man, popular author.

The only unexpected aspect of Billy's behavior was his firm desire to see his father leave each day for work. Finally, John insisted upon a test.

I was supposed to stand next to John and lightly pummel him. Billy, seeing John being injured, would come to his father's aid, correcting the unhealthy mommy preference.

The charade began just after a normal weekday breakfast, during a lull as John waited for his morning ride to honk at the curb. We stood in the kitchen, between the oven and the breakfast table, Jimmy strapped into his high chair, drinking juice, and Billy on the floor, lining up toy soldiers.

"I'm angry at you, John," I said, with a smirk on my face, feeling a little nervous about this make-believe, afraid I'd be unconvincing to man and boy both.

John lifted his chin and frowned, bettering me with his attempt at a sober expression. "Are you, now?"

He stepped a little closer. I saw the crack of a suppressed smile. He furrowed his eyebrows and folded his arms over his chest.

Little Jimmy had been regarding us, all the while, with a curious, sleepy look, rosy lips parted. But Billy was in his own world, arranging the soldiers in two parallel lines, using the checked pattern of the tiled floor to keep them straight.

John cleared his throat and nodded. I cleared mine, too, feeling positively ridiculous. John and I rarely fought. What could one sensibly fight about in front of children, without raising any sensitive matters?

"You leave a mess wherever you go," I said, grabbing at straws. "Water on the sink. All those—all those—socks on the floor. And sandwich crusts next to your armchair."

I figured that would sound right to Billy. John had chastised him just that morning for leaving a cracker, uneaten, on the breakfast table.

John's expression was sympathetic: *That's the best you can do?*

"And—and," I said, raising my voice, "You never take me anywhere."

He lowered his own to a menacing rumble. "Don't I?"

That made Billy look up, at last: eyebrows raised, one lead soldier closed inside his tiny balled fist.

"I want to see a show," I said.

John nodded, encouraging me to say more and to sound angrier.

Now I was warming up: "I want to see the new Marilyn Miller musical."

"But you hated her in *Sunny*." He said it quickly, carelessly, with a spontaneous and utterly convincing little laugh at the end.

That laugh tripped me up. "No, I didn't."

"Yes," he said. "'That overrated Ziegfield Follies girl.'"

"What?"

"You said she was a good dancer, but a disaster the minute she opened her mouth." He was getting better at improvising, if that's what this was. And he wasn't done. "We went to that chop suey place with Stanley . . ."

"Chop suey?"

". . . and you went on all night about it."

"What are you talking about?" I tried to remember my role. Angry. Threatening. *I* was supposed to be the aggressor. I pushed my balled-up fist against his chest—a little trial tap, like I was knocking at a door. "I haven't seen the Resors since before Jimmy was born."

John's eyes widened, recognizing his gaffe. His mask dropped and my own stomach followed, plummeting. But he thought he could still cover up. "You're wrong about that."

"*I'm* wrong?" I tried a harder tap, mashing my fist into the lapel of his fine jacket.

"Hey."

"Chop suey?" I shouted. "You went to that play without me. You really did. You went on some kind of date." I pounded harder. "No, you really did. I can't believe it. John, you really did!"

"That hurts," he said quietly, obviously unhurt—*always* unhurt, regardless of what was going on around him. I held my breath and punched harder, with both fists now, encouraged by the surprised look on his face.

"All right, Rosalie. That's enough."

"And you didn't even hide it? Out in public?"

"Calm down."

"With the Resors?"

"Just with Stanley and—he brought someone else. Not Helen."

"Oh. *Just* with Stanley and someone else. And another someone else. A double date. That's supposed to make it better? Oh my God, John. Oh my God!"

I had started hyperventilating, and it got worse when John grabbed me by the elbows, trying to push my forearms together, to contain the boxing motions of my fists. I broke free, swung low, and made contact below the belt, which from the sound of John's pained breathing had a pronounced effect. But the satisfaction was short-lived. I felt a pressure against my legs, a tangle of smaller limbs between my knees and John's. I'd forgotten about Billy. Now he was squeezed between us, launching his fists against John's knees with all his might—not at mine, even though I had been the one punching, but at John's. Two against one. Not the Oedipal reversal John had expected. But all of his expectations had gone out the window with his stupid little confession.

"Stop that!" John called out, kicking out once, hard and sharp, with his dress shoe.

And Billy did. He stopped. He fell back to the floor on his rear and scooted back, out of the dangerous tangle of adult legs.

From outside came the honk of a car horn—John's ride to work. He stepped toward the door, jacket askew, breathing hard. I followed.

I grabbed at the sleeve of his jacket, hard enough to hear the rip of stitches. When he spun away, I lunged even harder, grabbing for him, determined not to let him leave without at least answering my question. Not after humiliating me this way.

"Who did you take, John? You're going to tell me. Who was it? How long has this been going on? You always promised me you'd be honest. You claimed you'd always be honest!"

He escaped my grasp. The door slammed. Outside, the car drove away.

In one last fit of frustration I pounded at the closed door with the side of my fist and a moment later saw Billy, no taller than my knee, strut to the door and plant a little kick of his own.

My poor dear. My avenger.

"Oh, sweetheart," I said.

All day I waited for the phone to ring, waited for the sound of a car coming home early to our address, waited for a flower deliveryman, bearing apology roses. I couldn't even bear to take the boys to the park, thinking I'd miss something. I let the boys play on the front porch while I sat inside at the kitchen table, smoking one cigarette after another. I listened at the window, then went back to the bathroom to check my makeup, and then returned to the window. In my own mind, I delivered lectures, heard terrible yet convincing arguments, made threats, accepted or refused excuses. I imagined a woman on John's arm: probably blonde, because I was dark haired, with a girlish giggle or husky, throaty laugh. Or maybe dark haired just like me, but a younger me, the version he favored. I imagined an entire parade of young, fresh, lively women. And when the abstractions of all those dressed-up home wreckers became too hard to sustain, I thought of a single woman. Mary Ickes Watson.

I pictured John's first wife as she was five years ago, hearing the gossip about John and me, haunting the hotel lobby where we'd had lunch, arriving for the first time at my Eutaw Place house, already suspicious and determined to catch John and make him pay. I thought of Mary lying restless in a narrow bed in a low-rent apartment, waiting for John to come home from work, wondering, and in the next room, their daughter, Polly, doing the same, and in another room, Little John, stewing with an adolescent version of the anger that had made our own sweet Billy kick the door. I grew up a little that day. I paid a long-overdue bill.

Cora had asked for the week off, to visit her mother, and the work of watching Billy and Jimmy nearly undid me. It was an Indian summer day, the humid heat rising as the morning wore on, my belted navy-blue dress too hot so I changed to a pale yellow, sleeveless cotton one—worn and not much thicker than a slip. A frumpy housedress, fitting for the day's sour mood. I phoned Viola, a teenage girl who lived down the block, to come watch the boys for the afternoon, and when she came, I closed myself inside the bedroom-that-doubled-as-den, hotter even than the kitchen, and tried to write, filling an entire waste can with balled-up typewriter paper—my first unsuccessful attempt, years ahead of this one, to put my thoughts in order, to try to understand how we'd made this mess. But I wasn't ready then. Jealousy pinned me like a bright, dumb beetle to the present moment, fixated not on the truth but only on my desire to make John pay for his two-timing ways.

Viola gave the boys their lunch and reported to me that Billy's appetite had been off, but that wasn't unusual for Billy. I heated my own bowl of soup and ended up washing it down the sink. When Viola left, it took all my energy just to say goodbye, to smile vaguely, to pretend that everything was fine.

"You're all right, Mrs. Watson?"

"It's just the heat, I think. For Billy, too. Thank you, Viola. Enjoy the rest of your day."

I jumped at the sound of the knock ten minutes later. But it wasn't

John, it wasn't a telegram or flowers. Only the delivery boy who came once a month in a produce truck with his cartons marked FRESH FRUIT, fooling no one.

I pointed to the pantry. "There."

He loped outside again, leaving the door ajar, and came inside with a second carton that he stacked atop the first. Inside there would be bourbon, gin, a few bottles of sherry and wine. Mostly bourbon.

"Goodness, do we go through that much? I guess we do. Thank you . . ."

"Leo," he said.

"Well, thank you, Leo."

Usually the delivery boy came with a stout man, his older brother, but this time, he was alone and chatty.

"That's only half of it," he said, pulling a handkerchief out of his pocket and wiping his brow. "The other half I deliver to your husband's office."

That I had not known. Though it made sense. All those men with their private liquor cabinets in their private offices, and maybe Stanley stocked some of it, but he couldn't keep up with my own husband's pouring schedule.

"I only mention it," he said, "because I need to settle the bill. If you don't mind. We can't carry people any more, is all. Month by month on delivery day, now. Usually, I collect from your husband, but he wasn't in."

"Oh, certainly," I said, wondering if we had enough cash in the house, if I'd have to telephone John at work and make him deal directly with the boy. Man, rather. He was probably nineteen or twenty, wide shouldered, with sun-darkened skin, and a loosened dark lock of hair springing forth from his widow's peak. Trace of an accent. Italian.

Meanwhile, the house was quiet. Viola had given Billy and Jimmy cool baths and put them down for late naps, just prior to leaving.

"You have something on your shirt, there," I said, seeing a bright yellow stain underneath his chest pocket.

He looked down, sheepish. "Mustard. I ate my sandwich in the truck. Usually my brother drives and that's when I eat my lunch."

"You're probably thirsty, then . . . Leo. If you just ate your lunch."

Viola had left a pitcher of lemonade on the counter. I poured Leo a glass and excused myself. There wasn't enough cash in the desk drawer to pay the bill, so I telephoned JWT from the next room. But John wasn't in his office.

"I don't know when my husband will be home," I said, coming out of the den. "Sometimes he doesn't get here until very late." The thought itself, and the question of where John was choosing to be in the middle of a workday, should have made me seethe, but I was too distracted to be angry. Too nervous, and wishing—strange day, strange wish—that I hadn't put on such an ugly dress.

Leo had seated himself at our kitchen table. He had sponged away the mustard, and now his shirt was damp in places, unbuttoned, with a white undershirt showing. Making himself a little too comfortable, I thought. But then again, it was hot in the house. And was I giving the wrong impression? The lemonade, the mention of an absent husband, the absence of children, my own thin dress, unbuttoned at the collar, loose at the waist but a little tight around the hips. Too wide for the flapper look, but John always assured me that real men liked a little more curve, top and bottom. Not every man liked the boyish look of the flapper.

Leo pulled a flask out of his trouser pocket, poured a slug into his lemonade, and noticed me staring. "You don't mind?"

How could I mind? I wasn't Carrie Nation, as he could see from those heavy cartons of clinking bottles.

He asked, "You want any?"

"No," I said, sounding schoolgirlish. "No, thank you."

To make it clear I was only waiting for him to finish his lemonade,

I went to the sink and started washing the few dishes Viola had left behind. I'd thought it the perfect subterfuge, until I realized how I had positioned myself: directly near him, with a front-row view of my backside.

I could picture him sitting behind me: leaning back into the kitchen chair, knees slightly apart, hair around the edges of his face damp with sweat, undershirt tight across his chest. And he could see me: wide hips, feeling his gaze like a warm shaft of sunlight, trying to stand still and not sway even once as I washed the same glass three times and listened to him raise and set down his glass, raise and set down his glass, the ice cubes tinkling. The longer it lasted, with no one saying anything, with him still sitting there even though I could hear his glass was empty, with me keeping the tap running even when I was down to the last triple-washed spoon, the shallower my own breath became and the more obvious our motives seemed. Maybe he was used to this. Maybe other women invited him into their quiet houses all the time. Maybe women invited him and his brother, both. What was supposed to happen next? What was I expecting to happen? Could I do the sort of thing John did? Could I follow it through?

"I suppose I should be leaving," he said, and paused for another awkward moment. "It's a long drive back."

There was a way to do this thing, to have it both ways as married men always seemed to have it in the end—but this wasn't it. I didn't want to get away with anything. I wanted John to care and to come back to me, to want only me.

The delivery man was at my elbow, setting the empty glass on the counter.

"You're very pretty," he said, and the compliment made hot tears spring to my eyes, so that I had to twist away and hide my face over my shoulder. "Thanks anyway. For the lemonade."

He was almost to the door when I said, "Wait."

That was all it took. Nothing clever or seductive, barely any conversation at all. In two minutes we were on the couch, and a moment later, on the living room floor. No time even to pull the drapes. Ten minutes later, he was touching the red rug burn on his knees and pulling up his trousers, while I was tugging my dress down, and trying to decide if I needed to offer him lemonade again. But he understood, as I did, that a quick exit was best for everyone involved. I saw him through the door, bolted it, then went back and poured a strong one, followed by a second and a third, glad that Leo had delivered so many bottles that John would never notice my attempts to equal him in matters of indulgence.

CHAPTER 28

John didn't say anything when he came home late. He left an hour early the next morning—cab at the door, no waiting for a shared ride—with no explanation. But on the breakfast table were two tickets to the comedy musical, *No, No, Nanette.* I looked for a note, even just his name and a line of X's and O's, or a hastily scribbled "Sorry," but he was playing this one close to his vest, maybe because he didn't think he'd truly done anything wrong and didn't want to encourage my hysterics.

The tickets provided a fragile moment of relief, the beginnings of hope and gratitude, but then I felt angry again, and the memories of my own adventure with the deliveryman only made me feel more housebound, more pathetic and alone.

I steeled myself. John would be gone until dinner. That gave me all day to find someone else who wanted the second ticket. I wasn't thinking of other men, honestly. What I wanted most was a night out with a friend—and to make a point, of course.

I left the boys in the house, and I put on a good dress and walked down to the corner, to Janine's house. Four-year-old Tommy answered the door, wiping his nose with the back of his hand. "Mommy's sick."

"Well, can you tell her to stop by my house when she feels better?"

"Grandma's coming to pick me up."

"Well that sounds fun. Make sure to give my message to your mommy, before you go. Can you remember that?"

I heard a door open inside the darkened house, and I saw Janine come forward from the gloom, tightening a belted robe around her waist. "I meant to tell you, Rosalie. I'm going to the hospital."

"Nothing serious, I hope?"

She wrinkled her nose and managed an embarrassed smile. "Female troubles."

"Enough to go to the hospital?"

"They're taking out the parts that don't work."

"Oh Janine, I'm so sorry." She was so young, and she looked so well. I looked down at Tommy, who was glancing up at Janine's face and at mine, trying to decide whether he should be bothered by our conversation. I tried to smile and sound happy for her. "When you come out, you'll feel so much more energetic."

"That's what they say."

I started to go, then turned back. "Tommy can come over any time. If I've never said that before, I should have." Never mind what John thought about Janine's mothering or about Tommy's behavior and his influence on our sons.

She paused a moment before saying, "He'll be at his Grandma's for most of it. But thank you. Really." Then: "I wish I could be more like you, sometimes."

"What do you mean?"

"You seem to handle everything so well, compared to all the other women in this neighborhood—including me." She tried to laugh. "You just—you know—seem to stick it out. Life, the kids. Everything. You don't seem to need anyone."

On the walk back to my house, every step was an effort of will. It was hotter even this day than the day before. It was hard even to breathe.

Back home, I made up a list, and immediately crossed off the first name. Helen Resor and I had never gotten to know each other, after all. She'd be too busy. And though it was possible that she was aware of and unbothered by my husband's extracurriculars, it was equally possible that our family name had become a bitter pill for her, if she knew her husband and my own were running around together.

The next two names on the list were from college: Bee and Vanessa. I gathered up my courage and telephoned them at their apartments in Manhattan. One number was disconnected. At the other, a roommate answered, and told me Vanessa had moved to Seattle, for a job. Two years ago. Hadn't I known?

I swallowed my pride—as well as the drink I'd just poured—and telephoned Mary Cover Jones at her lab. To my surprise, she was at her desk and answered on the second ring.

"A play?" she asked, baffled. "But why?"

"It's been too long. I thought it would be fun."

"But I don't go to many plays."

"That's why I thought of you first."

She puzzled over the details—she and Harold had a baby nurse for the day, but she'd have to find someone for an evening engagement, and this was short notice.

"There's only one extra ticket, unfortunately. I'm sorry. Couldn't Harold watch Barbara?" I knew their daughter would be about two years old now, a year younger than Billy.

"He's great with Barbara. But Lesley's still nursing."

"Lesley?"

"Our other daughter. Didn't John tell you? She's two months old. The truth is, Rosalie, I hate that I spend so much time apart from her, as it is. I bring her to the lab sometimes, but I don't suppose I can bring her to a play."

"No. Probably not."

A second daughter. I made a mental note to pick out a gift the next time I was in a department store, and to chasten John, if we were talking about everyday things anytime soon.

There weren't too many names left on the list. At the bottom was Evelyn. Second from the bottom was my own mother, who immediately asked, "What's wrong? Are the boys ill?"

"The boys are perfectly healthy."

"Are you sure? How is Billy's stomach?"

Why had I ever confessed Billy's stomach troubles to her? Now she'd never let it alone.

"He's fine."

She said, with a little too much eagerness, "Are you and John fighting?"

"Why would you assume that, Mother?"

It was harder to reach Evelyn, and when she finally returned my call, near dinnertime, she sounded exhausted and apprehensive. We had a good chat, long and honest. It was the first time she admitted that she resented my having gone to Vassar, because she hadn't, nor had college even been emphasized much in her time, which was probably true— we were practically of a different generation. She thought Mother and Father had always favored me, and she had gotten tired long ago of hearing about my interests and publications and glamorous life, which made me feel sad, considering I'd never thought our parents were pleased with me and my choices at all. But there was no convincing her. There was no way she could travel several hours to Manhattan for a play. I pressed for a longer visit. She could stay in our house. The night out would be only one part of it. She finally had seen Billy—once—but she'd never seen Jimmy. Why did it take a year or more to schedule every visit?

"Because we're practically strangers, Rosalie," she said.

"I don't want to be."

"It's a little late, don't you think?"

❖   ❖   ❖

When John came home that night, I had nothing to throw back in his face, nor the desire to confide my own vulnerability. The last thing I wanted him to know was that I was friendless. When he came up the drive at 9 P.M., I met him at the door, smartly dressed, neatly coiffed, concealer painted heavily under my eyes to hide the fact that I'd made them sore with rubbing, and with a drink ready in my hand. I wore the new smile I had practiced since the end of my telephone call with Evelyn: impervious.

"So you're taking me out on Friday," I said, handing him the fresh drink. "It's about time."

This next part I can't explain. But it was a tense autumn, and I was losing my husband, or thought I was. John felt our differences had been settled by the evening out and several more like it—restaurant dinners, and a private party at a client's where I watched John flirt with a tall redhead in a green dress (ridiculous how she had to bend down, breasts practically spilling from her dress, to accept a light for her cigarette). Later, he watched me flirt with the same woman's sixty-year-old laundry-soap-magnate husband. We came home from that party and made love twice—once savagely, the second time more tenderly. Far from proving the damaging effects of jealousy, our joint improprieties were only convincing John that jealousy and the occasional argument might have its place, reminding each partner of the other's passion and desirability. He liked to see me flirt or be flirted with, in other words. I can't say the reverse was true.

Yet jealousy still could have its damaging side, he conceded. It was certainly still worth studying, he—never I—insisted.

Twice more he asked me to repeat our little staged fight in front of Billy. The first time had thrown him off, with its unintended eruption of truth. The next two times were more mechanical, and each of these next times John played the aggressor, now that he was convinced that it was pointless playing the victim, because Billy would never come to his defense. I didn't have to do or say much. I just had to stand there and let John shout in my face, loom over me, grab me by the wrists—was this exciting for him, as my sham flirtations with strangers were?—and take note of Billy's reactions, so that John and I could compare notes later.

Each time, Billy reacted instantly, showing clear signs of being greatly disturbed. Eyes wide. Hands over his ears. Mouth open, with tears spilling down his red cheeks. The first time, he ran to my aid, a desperate defense that lasted only a moment before he backed away. The second time, he ran to the next room and from there, shouted for John to stop. The third time, he only stood in the corner, arms up against his ears and hands over his head, twisting back and forth as he wailed for me, "Mama! Mama!" But when I broke away from John's grasp and ran to Billy, finally, he would not let me touch him. His wail had gone quiet, but his mouth was still open. He couldn't seem to get a breath.

John stood at the far end of the room, hands on his own hips, hair sprung loose from its crèmed style, catching his own breath, observing.

"He can't breathe," I said, turning to see John's calm expression, knowing he'd tell me that Billy was fine, that I needed to back away and just observe, to see what came next. But I couldn't take it anymore.

"Go," I shouted, though this was a Sunday morning, not a workday, and there'd be no car horn to break the spell and save us from the simulated conflict, which was no less disturbing for its falseness. "I need to be alone with him. Go!"

"Now, Rosalie . . ." John started to say.

"Never again. Never another damaging experiment on our own boys, or I'm leaving with them, and you'll never see any of us again, no matter how far I need to go."

"It's for a good reason."

"I don't care!"

"You're not being objective . . ."

"Of course I'm not! And if I have to choose between them and you, I'm choosing them, John. My only regret is that I didn't choose sooner."

"All right," he said, and followed my pointing finger, slowly backing toward the door.

That *all right* felt like a tremendous victory. Which felt like the beginning of an entirely new chapter in our lives. Which was tainted only by this afterthought, after he left the house and the boys went off to their naps and I had only my own regrets for company: I could have done it sooner. He wasn't an irredeemable bully. He might even have craved resistance—another opinion, spirited refusal.

Consider the years of evidence: his joy over antagonistic epistolary relationships; his respect for other men who had publicly disagreed with him; his mentorship of Mary Cover Jones, a woman who asked far more questions than I ever had; his pleasure in working with men and women who interrupted, argued, and teased. He'd given me the clues since the first day I met him. He'd come out and said it many times: *Find your spine. Don't just sit there like a scared rabbit.* Our happiest and most passionate moments had come when I'd spoken up, not when I'd submitted. What on earth was wrong with me, that I'd let things go this far?

I could have stood up to him more. I should have. How would I deal with my life now, knowing that?

PART III

NOT SO HIGH A WALL

The past ten years have seen a growing tendency—but one combatted at every point by the old line philosopher—on the part of the "mental sciences" to crawl over the stone wall that separates them from behaviorism.

—John Watson, *Behaviorism*, 1930

CHAPTER 29

To be witty, you can't be worrying who in the crowd gathered around you will laugh or smile, judge or sneer. To flirt, you can't have too much riding on whether your targeted gentleman flirts back. To be a flapper, you have to swing your hips and laugh with your head back, throat bared, and drink like a fish.

It all works best if you don't care too much, and I didn't.

It all works best if you have money, too. We had some—far more than John had ever managed to earn in our Hopkins days—but it was never enough, given that John had an ex-wife and a former family to support and expensive tastes of his own (shirts ordered from a London tailor, only the best suits and shoes, the new boat with its requisite harbor and shore-club fees). So there was always an air of desperation, pushing us to write the next book, the all-important parenting guide, which had to be a smash.

Even though I played some of John's games, and he in turn learned not to violate at least some of my limits where the boys were involved; even though our sex life found its post-baby rhythms again, and he kept his promise of taking me out more than he'd taken me when Billy and Jimmy were very small, it didn't suffice. Not for him. In

1926, John was fired from the last part-time teaching position he would ever hold, at the New School. The day he found the nerve to tell me, he tried spinning an elaborate conspiracy about warring scientific theories and irreconcilable departmental personalities and budget dilemmas. But it had been so sudden. And John's reputation—a boon for that hotbed of progressive ideas—was golden. Dismissals at the New School were unheard of.

"Who did you sleep with?" I finally asked, bored, rising to put away a half-finished casserole.

When he didn't answer, I said, "Must have been a student, not a faculty member."

No answer.

I asked, "Or plural? *Students?*"

Still no answer.

"They're a tolerant bunch," I said, sounding as cool as the banana cream pie I started to slide out of the icebox, and then put back, reconsidering. Gin went better alone. And I had a figure to watch. "I'm guessing they gave you multiple warnings and permission to apologize. But no, that's right. You don't apologize, do you?"

Many months had passed since the firing when Mary Cover Jones invited me to lunch, but still I thought she was inviting me to go over the sordid New School details or to issue some wise, sisterly warning. I wanted none of it. I still remembered her and Harold trying to warn me away from John, all those years ago. I had a hunch, fair or not, that she would also press on the wounds of my continuing absence from an active, public career in psychology.

On the date of our scheduled lunch, Mary nearly had to cancel, which—given the state of my hangover from a Long Island party John and I had attended the night before—didn't seem like the worst thing. She asked if I wanted to come over to her apartment with both children, so that my sons, ages six and three, could play with her daughters, ages five and two. I assured her that Billy was off to summer camp, and Jimmy had his own routines at home with Cora and our new cook, Jeanette. Mary took that comment in stride, agreeing that it was a treat to have a women's date out, worrying neither about work nor children. But then something else came up, and Mary telephoned back to ask, again, if I wouldn't mind tea at her place. I told her I couldn't bear making that much work for her. It was a childless lunch out on the town or nothing.

Lucky me, I thought, when the first step into sunlight made my head throb. But then I took in a few deep breaths and realized I was being silly. It was a beautiful day for driving into the city. Chin up and all that.

We met at a sidewalk bistro just off Central Park. The trees were in sticky full bloom, exhaling green freshness toward us, and the paths were crowded with strolling city dwellers enjoying the summer weather. I knew what I wanted to eat and I handed back the menu within a moment, while Mary continued to puzzle, the menu propped two inches from her face. The waiter came back to take our order, and I went first, but Mary still wasn't ready. The waiter was prepared to leave and come back a third time but I put a firm hand on his soft white sleeve, offering my most charming smile, refusing to let him leave.

"The trout, really?" Mary said. "I'm not sure. With fish you can't be too careful."

"Oh, but you *can* be too careful. You really can be."

I told the confused waiter to bring us two of everything and to get me a soda water before I went into the kitchen and got it myself. Then I lit a cigarette and listened to my old school friend worry aloud, making mountains of molehills.

"I don't know where the time goes," she said. "When Lesley said her first word, that's when it hit me that a year had passed since you'd called, and I'd always meant to find time to see you. We're not living our mothers' lives, are we? They had time for suffragette meetings and rallies and Sunday church suppers, and I have trouble finding a clean blouse to wear in the morning."

"We've achieved the lives they wanted for us," I said, pressing a finger into my temple, still wishing for a stronger drink. "You certainly have, anyway."

I don't think she even heard the second part of my statement, which had cost me some effort to make. She was squinting across the street, toward the park, where an elegant woman was walking, wearing a simple white suit with an unstructured cardigan jacket edged in black, with gold buttons down the front. A small ball of canine fluff, breed unknown, hurried along on a thin leash just behind her, drawing attention to the woman's slim ankles and high heels.

"Chanel," I remarked with appreciation.

"Is that what you call that breed?"

"Not the dog, Mary." I laughed. "The designer of the suit! Really, you're too much."

I expected her to laugh, too, I really did, but instead she looked taken aback. "Of course I've heard of Chanel. I just misheard you." She recovered quickly, pushing her glasses back up her nose. "I can't keep up with that, but maybe I won't have to," she said. "I hear that fashion isn't so up-to-the-minute in California."

"Unfashionable? Los Angeles?"

"Northern California, I meant."

"Is Harold looking at an academic job there?"

She paused, frowning. "We both are. They may have a position for me at Berkeley."

"Mary, that's wonderful. Congratulations."

I had been reluctant to meet with her, and now she was leaving, which was perhaps for the best.

With every passing year there was less chance of running into someone who knew the old me: the Vassar college girl with academic ambitions, or the briefly scandal-plagued young paramour, or even the nervous young mother. It was so easy to remake oneself these days. No one's memory lasted very long, especially if you stopped giving them reminders. Anyway, it was, perhaps, as John had always said: we are simply our present behaviors. My own behaviors lately had not been so virtuous, but my expectations and standards had declined as well. Had we really thought we could make humans happier, healthier, perfect? I was settling, now, for getting through each day. If I seemed brittle, or embittered, perhaps I was.

Carrot soup and green salad. Trout amandine. Black coffee.

Small talk, equal parts domestic and professional, about the difficulty of finding baby nurses and the latest advances in galvanic-response emotion studies. Anything else—fashion, art, real estate, travel, sports, musicals—was a dead end. But perhaps we were each parodying ourselves: Mary only able to engage in laboratory speak and worry about her darling Lesley, and me so very tired of those things, and wishing I could head home in time for a game of tennis.

"Some days it's just a relief to leave the baby at home, and other days I miss her so much I can't bear it," Mary was saying when I tuned back in. "Obviously, I do what I have to do. We all do. But I can't imagine the future John talks about: a future of children raised completely apart from their parents, a future of baby farms. Surely you can't imagine a baby farm, either?"

Chin up or not, my head was refusing to lighten. Everything about Mary that day—her methodical slowness, her gestures, her return to overly familiar subjects—was wearing me down. And the last way to get my sympathy was by questioning John. Perhaps it wasn't a trap, but it felt like one. And maybe I wasn't a great scientist, or even a good mother, but I was a loyal wife at the very least. One leaves or one stays. I had stayed. John had compromised in some if not all ways, and there was no point in my badmouthing his work.

The only way to get through a lunch like this was to half-listen, to nod dreamily, to wait it out and hope the talking would stop.

"Rosalie?" Mary asked. "Hello?"

"Hmmm?"

"My gosh, have you heard a word I've said? Are you all right?" She tried again, "Surely, you can't imagine a baby farm, either? Rosalie? Are you even listening?"

"Of course I'm listening," I said, lighting another cigarette.

"And?"

"And no, I can't imagine it, Mary," I said, finally. "But maybe that's why we need men in this world. Sometimes they're willing to imagine the unimaginable, for the good of us all."

The day was getting hotter. Light glinted off the chrome of cars as they passed. We'd been talking about getting a new car, John and I, even though he still didn't drive. Mary and I didn't finish our coffees.

We turned down the waiter's offer of dessert. When Mary asked, "Did you answer the last Vassar alumnae survey?" I shook my head, busy fishing a lipstick out of my purse.

"I rarely answer those surveys. What would I say: that John is expanding his firm's advertising accounts, or Billy adores his summer camp? Let them all just guess, I suppose."

And I laughed. It was something that required practice, laughing. It was one of the few things children did better than their parents, that you grew out of, rather than into. A woman had to practice or she'd forget how to smile, how to laugh, and then a younger woman would take her place, naturally.

"I'm surprised you don't mind not working in a lab," Mary said. "I remember a time when you read about the field more than I did." She leaned in close and pushed a small vase of flowers to one side, in order to look me in the eye. "You *lived* in the Vassar library, Rosalie."

"I was mousy and shy."

"You weren't."

"Thank goodness that's behind me."

"You were passionate. You once told me you couldn't wait until you had an opportunity to make your own mistakes. Old Washburn said you'd go far, and you'd whisper to me, 'I plan to go *too* far.' Do you remember that?"

"Not really," I said, glancing around for the waiter.

"I was worried about being wrong and you told me, 'If you try new things, if you have any opinions at all, you'll sometimes be wrong. There's nothing wrong in it as long as you keep trying.' You loved risk. You loved the promise of transformation. 'The bubbling over of beakers, the shattering of glass.'"

I looked away from her, out toward the park. "That's a line from one of John's articles."

She stopped short—only incredulous at first, and then honestly disturbed. "It isn't, Rosalie. It's something you said years before either of us had ever met or read anything by John Watson."

We must have sat another few minutes in silence, long enough even for the waiter to finally notice and bring the bill. He was just setting it in the center of the table with a flourish when Mary burst out again, recognizing that the lunch was coming to an end and trying to redeem it, still. "But Rosalie. You're happy? You're well?"

I grabbed the slip of paper before there could be any haggling, and scrutinized the numbers, extending the silence. Then I handed the waiter more than enough cash and smiled until he finally smiled back. "Was that so hard? You're much more handsome when you smile." The waiter blushed.

Just before we got up from the table, Mary said, "So, John's going to Europe?"

"Just for work—J. Walter Thompson accounts."

"Are you going with him?"

"Not this trip," I said, pushing back my chair. "Next time."

How many stifled arguments and sleepless nights compressed into those five words, my only protection from private conflict and public pity. Like a magic trick: making swords and scarves and women disappear. Creating doves from thin air.

CHAPTER 30

John came back from Europe, promising that we'd go together the next year or the one following. It was a long trip with the transatlantic crossing, and then all the required visits with colleagues, city by city by city. For every story he told me about dining regally on the company account with a tire magnate or a testimonial-providing princess, I countered with a story of the Long Island parties I'd attended, or the late-night dinners I'd had with my own friends, gender unspecified, at some cafeteria or Chinese restaurant on Times Square, or the new tennis lessons I'd started taking, to improve my serve.

In place of concealment, there were playful provocations and assertions of independence, his "Maria of Bourbon" in counterpoint to my "doubles" and "sweet-and-sour." He told me I'd never looked more beautiful, but he noticed only when another man was flirting with me. That was the stimulus he needed to recognize me as desirable, and I complied, because I wanted to be desirable. That was the natural state of things. It fit with biology and psychology, and it fit just as well with everything else that decade: the culture of the theater and the street. I winced to remember my awkwardness accepting the tryst with that silly liquor-delivery boy at the house, a year or two earlier. I hadn't known what to say, how to act. But one practices. One learns.

Together, John and I were dining at more restaurants and attending more and more musicals and seeing more movies, at my insistence (John fell asleep during the slow parts), and I couldn't help noticing that our banter—the banter of our entire generation—seemed to be learning its cues from the stage and screen. Flirtation and mild hostility were hard to distinguish, and a couple exchanging witty barbs or angry jealous glances was a couple in love, and the worst thing you could say about anyone was that he was too dull even to know how to make a scene. At parties, I saw beautiful women throw drunken, weak-armed punches, and I saw men sitting on stoops, sobbing, and an hour later, the woman would be kissing someone and the man would be laughing and gay. We were a highly emotional bunch, but we were chic. And best of all: nothing like our parents. On the weekends, I invariably slept late, eye mask and damp washcloth nearby, and both of the boys knew not to wake me. John would kiss me on the cheek before he left (he never stopped kissing me)—off to go boating, in seasonable weather; to do who knows what when the weather was foul—and come back in the early afternoon to work.

Except for the work, we would have been like all the other young, sophisticated, socially active couples we knew—half of them, like the Turners and the Reynoldses and the Bellefield-Wilsons, so praised for their mutual suitability, and having such a good time dashing between Long Island and sometimes the Greek Isles or the Riviera that they'd scarcely notice they were divorcing three or five years later.

It was one of our final purely collaborative and mostly harmonious time periods, those years of 1927 and 1928. John needed me and I needed to be needed, more than ever if that was possible, and we needed the cash because it kept flowing, slick as mercury, through our hands. We wrote up a half-dozen articles for *McCall's*, the foundation for the baby book that John had always wanted to write, and then the baby book itself, which he'd predicted would shore up our finances and change generations to come. From a sample size of two closely observed boys—though John always claimed hundreds, referring to the infant subjects we'd worked with at Hopkins—we told America how to raise its children. On a Sunday afternoon, we'd put our heads together, sitting in the den with a plate of sandwiches and celery or olives and pickles and a bottle of bourbon, and it was almost like old times. Door closed, the sound of Billy and Jimmy and that day's caregiver outside—God forgive them if they even thought to knock at the sacred door between 2 and 5 P.M.—he'd type with me looking over his shoulder, or more often, he'd pace and lecture and I'd type his words, because he thought best on his feet. Last time, the press had called him as wise as Darwin. What could they call him now?

As outrageous as John liked to be, he was walking a well-established path. H. L. Mencken, writing under a pen name, had already lambasted women, grandmothers especially, for germ-infesting and love-smothering their babies, and Dr. Holt, throughout his dozen editions and seventy-five printings, had advocated for years against coddling and in favor of very early potty training. John Watson just said it more memorably and with the added gloss of the latest scientific terminology, plus some twentieth-century frankness about discussing sex openly with young children, for example.

"If it were up to me," John had said one evening, "we'd bring a prostitute directly into the house and let them experience sex with an expert, first, before there's any time for misinformation and humiliation."

"Agreed," I'd said. "But they're still only seven and four. Perhaps it can wait just a few years." My sarcasm was audible, but John didn't mind. Women were supposed to be sharp-tongued.

Psychological Care of Infant and Child was published. To good reviews, mostly, especially from the male scientists and book-column critics; some squeamish comments from various housewives' organizations and so on. The most important thing was the booming sales. Every generation needs its parenting manual, just as John had said, and not since Holt's turn-of-the-century guide had one been as authoritative as this. The publisher was thrilled to have an author who was comfortable with radio, willing to write articles on the side, and man enough to take on the chin a rather snide but ultimately beneficial profile in *The New Yorker*, a rehash of all past scandals: John's U of Chicago days, blinding rats, and his firing from Hopkins and ignominious divorce. They even spelled out how much he was paid per week at his advertising firm, which could only attract the latest round of female admirers. "Dr. Watson says" was on everyone's lips.

In the summer of '28, Father and Mother took a trip to Europe, during which Father felt unwell. A few months later, back home, he passed away. All the thoughts that attend a parent's passing bedeviled me as well: we had done wrong by him, and by the family name. Or he had done wrong by us. He was the world's best father. Or he was too soft and sentimental, the very traits John was arguing against in his and our writing. One night in bed I broke down weeping, and John put his arms around me and said, "Stay busy. That's the cure for everything."

The publicizing of our baby book was a balm to my grief and a way to ensure that my husband spent every Sunday afternoon with me. If Mary Ickes Watson had had the sense to co-author and promote a book with John, maybe I wouldn't have been able to talk him into lunches at Baltimore hotels and weekends in New York City. When newspapers asked if they could interview and photograph Billy and Jimmy, wearing short pants and riding in their wagon—with their healthy bodies and carefree smiles, proof of good parenting—John agreed immediately, but I demurred. The press would stay after them, too. Any story about a Watson boy getting into mischief would make good press, even if it was just about trying to sell used newspapers without a license out on the sidewalk.

But the hardest part of finishing and publishing a book, especially a long-imagined one, is the emptiness that comes afterward. Postpartum depression of a sort—which I had experienced with Billy, though I hadn't known what to call it at the time. Oh sure, John could just keep writing one article after another, pushing the book sales, ten thousand copies at a time, over a hundred thousand copies in just the first years, which made technical or academic writing seem more pointless and esoteric than ever. But our work together was done; our lab work, our making and raising of babies through their most fertile and "interesting" periods, and our writing of the book inspired by those babies.

All this was behind us now: John had taken them canoeing, but mainly to see if they were afraid of water. John had taken them to the Bronx Zoo, but mainly to see if they had any particular fear of certain animals. The rest of the time, the boys were with me and Cora or Jeannette or some other rotating cook or nurse or babysitter. Soon we wouldn't matter, because there'd be school, already for Billy, and soon for Jimmy, too. Camp, and school, and to bed before father came home. *So why don't we go to Europe, then, if we spend so little time with the boys anyway?* John had gone to Europe on business, more than once, and Mother and Father had gone to Europe. When would John and I go together to Europe? Oh yes, and also: I'd turned thirty. "Too old" for John at twenty, I was practically a crone now, and felt it, no matter how fast I drove, no matter how many new dresses or purses or pairs of shoes I bought.

John asked me sometime in 1929, working on one of several articles about marriage, what I thought of this latest statistic he'd read: "Fifteen percent of couples divorce. I think it's higher. I'd say twenty-five."

I replied, "Seems like half of all the couples *we* know."

"And here: look at this. Forty-two percent of married women have affairs. Most of them are so unhappy, I don't understand why more of them aren't cheating."

"Hmmm," I said.

I knew exactly why. If by cheating John meant sex, the answer is that it wasn't usually worth it. Maybe men got immediate pleasure from penetrating women they barely knew, but when it came to the reverse, a meddlesome amount of training was involved. Tennis, swimming, and dancing were all more fun. I'd had a half-dozen consummated affairs after tiring of John's New School shenanigans in 1926. During the last minutes of the final one, in an upstairs room at a friend's party, I had turned to my sexual partner, who had just rolled off me, hand pressed against his lower back, wincing from some spasm caused by our contortions on a narrow couch.

"We aren't finished," I'd said to the forgettable chump.

"What do you mean?"

"I haven't climaxed."

His face, already splotchy from his efforts, went a darker shade of red, and he tucked an already weak chin into his pale chest. "Good God, woman, you have a mouth on you."

"Well, yes, and other parts, too. Including some you seem not to be well acquainted with."

"What do you want from me?"

"Oh, never mind," I'd said, reaching for my discarded dress. "If you have to ask, we don't have a hope. Just get out."

John was too good a biologist, and too much of a perfectionist, to be such a selfish and incompetent lover as that. We'd had our own first few false starts prior to marriage but once we'd learned our way around each other, I'd had no complaints. I was shocked during my stabs at infidelity to realize how many men didn't share his skills—and that's not even counting the men who drank so heavily that they couldn't achieve their own climaxes.

"Forty-two percent?" I said to John as he continued to puzzle over the affair statistics. "That seems about right."

❖   ❖   ❖

At least once a week, a stranger approached me in public, whether in the grocery store, at a hat shop, or at some private party or shore-club affair where someone pointed me out as the wife of John Watson and the co-author of his bestselling psychological baby guide. The ones who had the nerve to approach thanked me.

"I could have ruined little Charlie."

"I finally have a book to show my own mother that everything she did was wrong."

"I finally learned to ignore the crying."

"I'll never let them sit on my lap again."

"My little boy's a gentleman now. He understands a handshake is good enough."

"Every time I start to doubt, I go back and read it again."

"One just can't listen to the older generation. They'd produce a nation of morons if they could."

"Everything my mother did was wrong."

"Everything my father did was wrong."

"He still isn't potty trained, but it must be my fault."

"He still cries, but it must be my fault."

"I stopped talking to my mother after reading your book."

"I ruined the first, but we're trying again."

"I haven't kissed my baby once and now she's two years old and easy as pie."

"Charlie is so quiet now. He never cries. He barely speaks. He's a little adult. We don't see him often but our nurse says he is better behaved than any boy she's ever known."

Only very rarely would a woman, usually older, approach me with a hand on her hip and a smirk on her lips: "What made you an expert, anyway? Fine, your husband then. What made him the expert?"

And then there were people who made comments about the dedication: "To the first mother who brings up a happy child." Which meant there'd never been such a mother, yet.

"Even you. Doesn't that bother you?"

"Of course it doesn't," I said once, a dozen times. "John's absolutely right. I'm not a very good mother. No woman is."

"With an attitude like that, it must be hard to get up in the morning."

"Yes," I'd say, with the most relaxed smile I could muster, "but it's perfectly easy to get up after noon. And that's when fun usually starts."

"I want to go to Europe," I told John. "You promised me."

"Did I?"

"Three years ago."

Another day: "I'm tired of Long Island. I never chose to live here. You chose this cottage for us. I wanted to live in the city."

John was tired, too. Seven years in advertising under his belt. No higher rung to climb. Only more self-promotion, keeping his name on everyone's lips, which benefited JWT and his on-the-side writing and public speaking, both.

"They won't stop talking to me," I told him one day when we were strolling in the park, two women staring as we passed.

"Rar, you're imagining things."

"They recognize you from your picture in the paper. From that silly illustration in *The New Yorker*."

"They recognize me because we're neighbors."

"They love us or they hate us. They thank us or they blame us. I don't know how you can stand it."

"They've bought the book and they'll learn something from it. If I'd worried about every nervous Nellie or angry Maisie telling me I was wrong, I wouldn't have had any kind of career."

"*I* don't have any career."

"You're my wife. That's your career. That's any worthwhile woman's career."

"You didn't used to think that. You used to support women who worked."

"A man learns as he ages, and a woman ages fast, so she'd better get her priorities straight. Anyway, the last printing is allowing us to invest money in our future."

"Well, invest it carefully. Even the ones who thank us seem ready to turn on us any day now. The tides always turn."

"Nonsense."

"And did you have to tell people about the time you made Billy jealous on purpose? Why did you have to tell people how disturbed he was, watching us fight? I could put that out of my mind if it wasn't public knowledge."

"Rar, don't let it bother you. Parents have done far worse, without a good reason. Everything we've ever done was for the best reason there is, which is helping other people avoid mistakes, whether or not they appreciate it."

"And wherever I bring Billy or Jimmy, there are always people watching, to see if they're perfectly behaved or if we've made it all up."

"But that's no problem. They're well behaved enough."

"Not all the time, John. Not everyone can be well behaved all the time!"

"Rar, you're shouting. That's the only reason people are staring."

His articles were always sharp, but it seemed to me that they got sharper in the years that immediately followed the writing of the baby book. "The Weakness of Women" for *The Nation*. "It's Your Own Fault" for *Collier's*. If you read American magazines at all, you couldn't avoid his advice, or his stern and handsome face, which age and silver hair only kept improving: the first popular psychologist, warning, criticizing, and prescribing changes to the entire nation's behavior.

Later, he wrote "Business for Women? Rot!" in the *New York Telegram*. Even the woman reporter noted that this same Dr. Watson had once been a "staunch defender" and "warm admirer" of the working girl but now seemed to think women were good only for being stay-at-home wives. And they needn't bother talking business with their men. Husbands wanted a comfortable home and a pretty and well-maintained wife, not someone to remind them about business. If she didn't have enough to do during the day—and with all the new appliances of the modern age, why would she?—then she could use those empty daytime hours to sleep, "so that she will be fresh and radiant in the evening."

No wonder John hadn't noticed, in the months leading up to my own mental break, how much I was napping, listlessly and melancholically. He'd labeled it "beauty rest" and chalked it up to good sense.

First, the articles seemed aimed at selling books and pleasing editors. Later, perhaps they allowed John to feel the flush of controversy again, or to purge something that was building in him. Three years later, or four, as his ability to maintain an erection became more and more problematic, I could look back and see he'd been trying to make the most of a failing organ, and feeling great anxiety about his own diminishing virility. But it was always hard to distinguish lasting impotence from occasional bourbon-soaked failures.

There was, as always, some truth in what he wrote during this period, but there was venom, too. That old line of his, "Men won't marry fifty years from now," became at last a headline in a June 1929 *Cosmopolitan*. There was good sense in his assertion that divorce should be as easy as marriage, as it was in Sweden. But then there were anecdotes that left me uneasy, even knowing what I knew about John's love of hyperbole, his impish desire to irritate as many readers as he charmed. The average reader didn't know John. They took his statements to heart. His attention-getting prose, accepted and quoted by others, was turning into gospel. I read the first draft carefully, withholding any comment. I looked over the finished, printed copy when it came home from the newsstand, and actually chuckled once or twice at John's outrageous turns of phrase. But late at night, I read it again and felt a sudden sense of panic.

"A woman who exercises and doesn't eat too much is not physiologically old at thirty, yet she has lost that fresh charm of youth . . . Men, on the other hand, are at their prime between thirty and forty-five . . . They are wise; they are sophisticated. They are successful; they know how to do things; they have poise. Their wives look ten years older than they do, ten times tireder, ten times more lifeless, ten times fatter."

It was no wonder, Dr. John Watson told *Cosmopolitan* readers, that the average married man would "take his wife's young friend to the kitchen with him to help crack ice for the evening highball. He, if he is inexperienced, may start a bit of innocent flirting, may even try just a bit of "first-degree" petting . . . He finds himself in pretty deep."

I thought back to parties I'd thrown, and times John had disappeared, with some helpful neighbor woman following close behind, into our kitchen, not to reappear with a tray of highballs for a frightfully long time. I'd never look at our ice trays the same way again. Where had my own recently cultivated attempts at sophistication gone? Out the window and down the drain.

John advised women not to have their first child until the age of thirty, in order to preserve the more beautiful decade for catching and keeping a husband. He truly believed in that advice and made his daughter Polly promise to delay childbearing as long as possible. I wished he would have shown the same wisdom in helping to keep *us* from having children too early. But then again, we needed experimental subjects close at hand, what with John's inability to stay hired in academia. If I hadn't put my foot down, he'd be experimenting on them still.

The poor man who is trying to stay faithful to his wife, Dr. Watson lamented in *Cosmopolitan*, is hunted by the "20,000,000-odd

married women who are not successfully married" and hunted by
the "1,250,000 flappers who reach the age of eighteen every year."

I did not doubt that he had been counting those young flappers as
they stepped across the threshold into adulthood, and welcoming all
women into his objective arms, young huntresses and middle-aged
vixens and sexually frustrated older dames alike.

One weeknight late, I woke to find the bed empty next to me. In the
kitchen, staring at the clock on the wall, I started to pour a drink.
The sound of the shattering glass as it hit the floor woke Billy, who
came into the kitchen, rubbing his eyes.

"Mom. Your foot."

"It's just wet."

"It's red."

"It doesn't matter. Go back to bed. No, wait."

"*Mom.*"

"Pay attention, please. Wake your brother."

Two hours later, I showed up at the Resors' apartment, having left
the car down on the avenue idling, the boys wrapped up in blankets
and sleeping in the backseat.

Stanley opened the door, with Helen standing behind him, hair
piled atop her head and robe tied at her throat.

Breathless, I panted, "Is John here?"

"Of course he isn't here."

"He isn't home. He isn't at the office. I tried telephoning."

"Telephoning? It's three in the morning."

Helen edged her way in front of Stanley. "Rosalie, go home. Go to
bed. John will show up soon. He's probably just out on the town."

"I'm worried about him, Stanley."

"Worried about John?" Stanley put his hand on Helen's shoulder,
and now they stood side by side, both studying me. "He's a night owl,
Rosalie. A tomcat."

"Oh, Stanley," Helen chided.

"But he thinks the world of you, Rosalie," Stanley said. "He can't say enough good things. You're the exception, he always says."

"He's probably home now," I said, starting to laugh. "We might have passed on the bridge. Imagine what he'll think coming home to an empty house!"

"That's right. Go home now," Stanley said.

"Oh, I feel terrible for waking you. I'm sorry."

"Don't be sorry, Rosalie," Helen said. "Where are the boys?"

"Sorry, Helen. Stanley, I'm so embarrassed."

"Don't be embarrassed," Stanley said. "Just drive carefully and go to bed."

Helen said, "Do you need someone to drive you? One of us could get dressed."

"But are you sure?"

"Sure that one of us is willing to drive you? Of course we are."

"No, Helen, *are you sure?*"

"Am I sure what?"

"That John isn't here? That you don't know where he is?"

Helen said, "Rosalie. Darling. Go home."

CHAPTER 31

You might have said I was being fashionable. Ahead of fashion, actually. The crash, about two sleepless weeks after that pathetic visit to the Resors' place. A little one before the big one. I even made the newspapers. The headline in all caps: MRS. ROSALIE WATSON PATIENT AT HOPKINS. Subhead: "Wife of John B. Watson, Former Professor at University, Is Entered There." Under that, caps again: HAS GONE UNDER OBSERVATION. And under that: "Miss Rayner, She Was Once Co-Respondent in Divorce Action Against Present Husband."

Ridiculous that they didn't have more to cover. With all the political scandals and what was to happen soon, with the stocks, perhaps they should have been paying more attention to things other than the mental health of an insignificant woman. There wasn't much more to say, though the reporter tried. "Many persons come to the institution, it was stated, merely for observation after experiencing 'physical upset,' or being in a general rundown condition."

"You scared me, Rar," John said, a week after I'd been checked into Phipps Clinic. He trusted the clinic because he still had colleagues there, including his former boss, Adolf Meyer. Even so, he disliked hospitals in general and wanted me home. He shrugged and tucked his chin into his collar, muttering. "I want to make you better. Just tell me."

John could be unsympathetic about illness—he'd been that way before, with his first wife and with Billy. But he knew this breakdown was serious. He'd had his own nervous breakdown in college, after a long spell of working too hard, and didn't like to talk about it, but the experience had worn a groove of sympathy matched to a precious few situations and symptoms.

"I've got a new apartment picked out," he said. "Park Avenue. We can sell the Malba place. The boys will love the city. You will, too."

I was groggy that day, high on something they'd given me.

"And we'll go to Europe," he said. "Next summer. Would you like that?"

"I don't know," I said, so softly that he had to come closer, leaning over the bed to hear me.

"What do you want?"

"I don't know."

That was the most frightening thing. After years of intense want and frustration capped in the last two weeks by a frantic state in which my own head roared with alarms, I felt dead calm, but also without any desire.

"I love you, Rar. You scared me. Don't do that again. I'll always love you."

I give him credit for not worrying about what the newspapers would say, what his critics would think of a psychologist whose own wife was in the loony bin. But then again, he'd never been afraid of public criticism. And he'd never claimed we were the perfect family. If he had been able to construct a world of his own choosing, then we would be perfect—or his children would be, anyway—but as an environmentalist, he could blame other factors. He wouldn't bother, because he didn't give a damn about explaining. *I* was the one who lived in fear of public criticism. *I* was the one who wanted to shield him from knowing how imperfect we all were.

He put his hand, dry and cool, across my forehead. The touch of him made tears stream out, into my ears, down my earlobes and neck, dampening my pillow.

"What hurts, baby?" he asked.

"Everything."

Psychologist or not, he would have been relieved to blame some specific body part. His way of knowing the world provided little illumination or prescription for a state of general malaise, except to say that I wasn't behaving like myself. *I wasn't behaving.*

Thank goodness I had my break when I did. The treatment involved some hot and cold baths, sedation, and long discussions with the psychologists, who were interested in my everyday activities and reactions. Five years later, I might have ended up in the hands of that decade's eager lobotomists, who thought there was no easier and cheaper fix for melancholia than a quick slice into the old gray matter.

"I love you," he said.

He waited for my response as long as he could. Then he asked, "Do you love me, too?"

What was love? A tickle of certain sensitive erogenous spots? A conditioning to want more of such tickling and stroking? Fear, yes; rage, yes. But maybe we'd all been wrong about love. Maybe it didn't exist in the real world. Maybe it was only a false sentiment, a routine of practiced pretend feelings.

My body was numb. My mind—whatever that meant—was numb, like a foot fallen asleep, and I didn't look forward to the moment it woke up, the return of needling pain. There was nothing and no one, really, who needed me. John would find another wife easily. The boys would do as well with anyone, because we'd labored to ensure their lack of attachment and dependence. My mother was used to loss. She'd lost me once, a decade ago, and we'd never had an honest conversation since. Father was gone, too. What difference did it make?

As for me, I had no work, no real interests. Everything I did was just to pass the time, to make cocktail hour and the weekend arrive more quickly. I had a picture in my mind of pulling a foot out of the stream of life; the water would fill in quickly. There'd be no mark and no empty spot, any more than a hospital bed or a chair in a theater or a restaurant stays empty. *Make way; make room.* The least I could do was make more room. People everywhere, and not enough beds and chairs. And even out in the countryside, the stream keeps running. If I put the boys out of my mind, if I just closed my eyes, I could imagine the relief of falling asleep and never waking up. It wouldn't be a terrible thing.

John said, "Do you really think so?"

I hadn't realized I'd been speaking out loud. I shouldn't have said any of it. I should have kept it to myself.

"You'd rather end it all?

I apologized. I said I was being irrational. I had sent out a tiny spore, spreading an infection on the tail of a thought I hadn't even meant to verbalize, which I couldn't take back.

CHAPTER 32

I had gained some perspective during those dark days. After I was discharged and feeling more like my normal self again, I could sympathize more fully with the way John made everything into an experiment. I'd been his experiment. Billy and Jimmy were his experiments as well. But his life was too, really, and he shied away from very little (only the subject of his own childhood, perhaps), investigating every kind of observed behavior. John had stayed admirably strong during my institutionalization and continued to do so during the swift and multiple life changes that followed—a move to Park Avenue and a trip to Europe without the boys, just as he'd promised. Our family's income proved to be surprisingly Depression-proof compared to many others'. But once I was on the mend, all that strength wore out, and his own moods darkened.

The number of suicides following the stock market crash of fall 1929 was exaggerated in the press, but the general moroseness was real, and talk of suicide became less taboo as the entire nation put its head between its knees. It was like the end of any party, really. We'd all gone overboard during the 1920s and the hangover was bound to be rotten. "Hair of the dog" simply wasn't available for most people who had lost their money, and we started to feel that all of us—everyone in our own social set, especially—had lost our youthful vigor.

"How did an entire nation get so ugly overnight," John said during one of the last times I dragged him to a theater, watching the couples come out into the congested hallway: heavyset women in dark, out-of-fashion clothes, men with trembling jowls and shadows under their eyes. And those were the ones who could afford the tickets. Out on the streets were beggars wearing sandwich-board signs, asking for handouts.

"Why do they even bother?" John asked, outside the theater. "Hoover's not going to help them. They won't last until the turn-around. *If* there's a turnaround."

"There's always a turnaround," I'd said. I'd made some progress from my own darkest days, at least, to be able to make a statement like that.

"What do you know about the stock market?"

"Not a whit," I laughed. It was an authentic laugh, not meant for anyone else, but only because I was beginning to feel better—much better than I'd felt in years—even while my husband, frightened by what he'd seen in my eyes and perhaps what he'd allowed himself to feel in his own tired head and heart, lagged a step behind.

John wrote a letter to a hundred of his friends and colleagues asking them if they'd ever considered suicide. Every one of them took the question seriously. Every single one of them—I felt gratitude for this expression of kindness and respect—wrote back. Some gave reasons for wanting to live. Others admitted they didn't have very good reasons but didn't have the courage to end it, either. John considered suicide a rational choice. He spent a long time writing that article, but the magazine for which it was intended, *Cosmopolitan*, finally rejected it. Too depressing.

❖ ❖ ❖

"Open your eyes," John said after he'd led me inside the Connecticut farmhouse.

The great room was spacious: white walls, exposed dark beams, a fireplace.

"That's where we'll hang a family portrait," he said.

"Yes," I said, and for the first time in a long time, we were in perfect agreement.

"Fifty-five miles from New York City," he said, and then, seeing my concerned frown, "but only eight miles to Westport, and from there, I'd take the train."

"Does it need much work?"

"Not a lot. Some." He had a light in his eyes I hadn't seen for months.

"A few outbuildings to work on. I'd like to put a new roof on the barn. And I'd like to build a stone wall, the old kind, without mortar. The boys can help me with that. They can raise animals, too. There will be room for all kinds of guests. Polly, and your sister and her daughter, if they want to come. They'll all love it here."

It was the thing he'd been missing for years: the chance to work with his hands. And it was true to what he'd said all along: that children should *do* things, have real work and responsibilities, grow things and build things and prove themselves capable. But it wouldn't be just some rustic, utopian farm. It was an estate, and soon enough we'd be playing tennis and swimming laps in the pool, clipping roses tended by our gardener, and eating meals, made by our hired cook, at a long wooden table. Forty acres, and all the comforts. Whip-Poor-Will Farm. Here, it almost seemed that the Depression wasn't happening—that the last few years of the 1920s hadn't happened, either, and that was just as important. Every marriage has its hardest spells, and we'd made our way through ours.

❖ ❖ ❖

Some men just aren't comfortable with babies. Now that Billy and Jimmy were older boys, eager to dig and carry stones for their father, to learn carpentry at his side, to feed the family cow and the family horse, they all got along much better. Jimmy, like Billy, had grown up with some persistent and mysterious tummy troubles, but they lessened at the farm. I found my old spark. Though John still believed in coming home at the end of a long working day to a quiet house, boys already fed and, depending on the hour, sometimes already sleeping, I found ways to do things differently. I'd drive my car to the train station to pick him up, boys in the back seat. "They love the car," I'd remind him, when he stepped out of the station. "And they love watching the train come in. Maybe one of them will take a shine to engineering." As long as the boys' company was in line with some occupational or educational rationale, it was less objectionable to him. He still never hugged or kissed them, but a hair ruffling wasn't entirely out of the question.

In late 1930, I'd published my own article in *Parents* magazine, "I am the Mother of a Behaviorist's Sons," about my own views of John's theories. With his support—and his ad man's confidence that anything I wrote with humor and verve would help sell our 1928 baby book, regardless of the views expressed—I felt free not to agree on every point with the nationally acclaimed Dr. Watson. I admitted I was a bad mother, as John still liked to tease when he gave lectures, to remind people of why they should not judge his theories by his sons' behaviors. But I also said that I couldn't help but resist following scientific parenting in every detail.

Especially now that the most sensitive periods of their young lives were safely behind us, I wanted to be a little more affectionate with my sons. Secretly (or not-so-secretly—I was admitting this in a magazine article, after all) I hoped they'd enjoy just a little bit of coddling. I also hoped they'd grow up with a taste for poetry and the drama of life and the "throb of romance" as I put it in the article, speaking directly to those women readers whom I could count on for softhearted sympathy—no matter that John cared nothing for poetry or drama and was more comfortable talking with the boys about sex than romance. I let American readers know that my sons were mischievous, and I encouraged them to be. We tied up their father's pajamas in knots. We occasionally left hairbrushes under people's blankets. We jumped out from behind doors to scare one another. We liked to giggle. But in the end, John's and my hopes for Billy and Jimmy were the same: to grow up as healthy young men, able to work, love, and be happy. That all seemed within reach.

If I could say all that in a public forum, what else could I say? Perhaps anything. I didn't need the shell I'd been carrying along for the last many years. The bitterness was breaking up slowly and washing away, cleansed by the country rains and the passage of time. It had been so very good to get away from the city, and perhaps even good to hit rock bottom, to let go of so much, to make room for something new.

As before, we rarely dined with our sons, but now John's first set of children were old enough to visit—as long as they made arrangements with John's secretary, Ruth Lieb, back at JWT—and though Little John mostly stayed away, Polly came out on occasion and we all had a swell time. Our ages weren't so very far apart. A young teenager when John and I had first started our relationship, she was in her twenties now, and a good tennis player, and a terrific flirt. When we had large parties with handsome men in attendance, we'd make the rounds together. She was equal parts grown daughter and younger sister, and there seemed to be no residual antagonism between us, though it saddened me to see her still uncomfortable around her father, alternately trying to win his attentions or spurn them. She drank a fair bit, too, and didn't always hold her liquor well. The men she seemed most interested in were often duplicates for John: active, older, domineering types. But time would heal, I felt sure. That's what we had now: space, and time.

❖ ❖ ❖

Jimmy ran into the den, panting. "Dad needs a glass of water."

"Well you know where to get it," I said, smiling. They were out on a sunny spring day working on the stone wall together, a project long in the planning and bound to be long in the doing. It was hot out there, and with the windows all thrown open, I could smell the manure and the green of the fields, and I could hear Gigi barking off in the distance. As quiet as she was sleek, Gigi almost never barked.

"Well, all right," Jimmy said, looking at his dirty hands. He had scrapes on his knees and arms from carrying sharp rocks, and a bruise where his brother had swung a mallet too hard the weekend before, knocking Jimmy in the leg. But they'd had all sorts of adventures: learning to ride our new horse, Moonshine. Chasing after a calf. Falling out of trees. And that was just the previous summer. A few winters earlier, Billy had gotten lost in a Connecticut snowstorm, and our handyman and Jimmy had gone looking for him. They found him hours later, turned around and half frozen—to the joy of local reporters, who never failed to report on any Watson who got into trouble. The town's rescue squad had come out to join the search, but John had stayed at work in the city, insistent that his firstborn son had enough independence and common sense to find his own way home.

"He told me to get you," Jimmy repeated now.

"I'll come in a minute. You bring him the water, first. It must be hot out there. Your father doesn't ask for water very often. You're sure he didn't ask for something stronger?"

I was just starting to work on another article. I'd written one the previous year that had been controversial enough that the editor had printed an overlay commentary, explaining that he didn't endorse the negative things I'd said about the overstated joys of mothering, but only wanted to let varied voices speak and get readers' views in response. Maybe I was finally getting a taste of the thrill John had gotten when he'd written something that made a reader gasp. It was good to make people think, to say the things they felt couldn't be said.

But now that I had been interrupted, I stopped typing and leaned forward to listen. The yap of the dog again. The sound of a cabinet door slamming in the kitchen, and footsteps running back outside. Billy was still out there, and I heard him calling to Jimmy. "Hurry on up, he says!"

That morning, John had received another call from Elsie Bregman, a psychologist—at least the third so far—who had tried replicating the Albert experiment, without success. Various psychologists were evaluating John's parenting advice as well, praising him for some aspects, like his emphasis on establishing routines and his disavowal of corporal punishment, but flogging him for his thwarting of all affection. One highly vocal critic had pointed out that withholding affection would inhibit children from growing and thriving; he pointed to neglected orphans with problems both physical and psychological, owing to the lack of attention they'd received in institutional settings. Just a few weeks ago, John had turned to me in bed and said, "We should have waited a few more years before writing that book. It was premature. We didn't know enough."

I'd frozen in place, waiting to see if he'd say anything more. *John Watson—admit not knowing enough?*

John had once thrived on debate, but things were changing. He was beginning to think about where he'd stand in the annals of psychology and he didn't like to be deemed irrelevant. He'd done his work and he wanted it to stand, uncontested—even when I reminded him gently that science didn't work that way, that it was okay for them to question, and even okay for *him* to question. Science did not remain unchallenged for long. Part of him knew it was true. But when a younger, eager psychologist reached out to him personally, it irritated him, and this particular morning, it had enraged him. I'd heard him call Ruth Lieb even though it was a Saturday and chastise her for giving out his home telephone number too readily.

After the morning calls with Bregman and Ruth Lieb, I'd heard John ask Ray for help bringing down some boxes of files, and an hour later, I saw him pacing the house with an unfamiliar purple folder in hand. I was busy at my typewriter, fighting the forces of distraction, but I could feel him stewing.

When I called out to him and asked which boxes he was digging through, he'd answered only, "Hopkins files."

"What are you looking for?"

In typical John fashion, he refused to answer. "It's a fire hazard up there, you know."

Even all these years later, I still recalled much from our Johns Hopkins days, but this folder rang no bells. Not something from the Phipps side. Maybe something from the Harriet Lane side—the baby-ward files, but ones I'd handled less often. Some other kind of record? Medical? That must be it. I was going to press the point further, but the boys came running into the house, full tilt, voices too loud, colliding in the hallway just outside my bedroom door. John barked at them, and when he turned the corner into the bedroom, to growl at me, I gave him a long, cool look. "Didn't you all have some kind of project planned today, in the healthy outdoors?"

I'd thought the work of building a traditional fieldstone wall at the edge of our property would do him good. It was methodical. It required muscle. He could do it in a silent mood, pointing to the various piles he'd made with the boys' help: stones collected in a way that pleased all three of them, and divided by size and shape, so that you'd have just the stone you needed when the time came.

Or he could do it in a loquacious mood—and I'd come out to watch a few times and knew what an earful any onlooker would get—explaining to the boys how the winter freezes and thaws pushed the rocks up to the soil and Connecticut farmers had to dig them out before plowing, and that's why you'd see piles of rocks here and there in neighbors' fields, and old finished fieldstone walls dating back a century, where the stones had been put to good use marking out boundaries. He could make a math lesson out of it, instructing Billy and Jimmy that even if their wall was only two and a half feet high and only twenty-five feet long, it could take five tons of rock, and how many pounds was that, and how many rocks total if each rock weighed so much?

You didn't start a project like that unless you were prepared to sweat, to know the right way to do certain things, like lifting carefully, and most of all, boys, you had to ignore naysayers. There would always be naysayers, in every good and important and true thing one chose to attempt. Also: change. The nature of the earth was to move and what looked solid would just keep moving, the frozen ground come winter and the thawing ground come spring, but still, they'd better believe it, even without mortar, this wall would stand. The boys didn't know, but I did: John was talking about his entire academic career when he was pretending to talk to them about simple matters of stone.

I sat back in my chair, my own typing and work thoughts interrupted, picturing John instructing Billy and Jimmy on choosing just the right stone, fitting it into place. I'd once imagined my life as a speeding streetcar or roadster which I was all too eager to catch, no matter where it was going. Now I saw life more like this farm, more like John's stone walls: you did what you could to do things good and right, to make things last. You tried to build solid foundations.

Gigi was barking again. More noise in five minutes than she'd made all year, and I didn't like her being outside when it was too hot or cold. When she came in, I'd wipe her with a cloth and make her curl up under my desk, where I could keep a better eye on her.

Jimmy ran in a second time, eyes wide, hair all in a messy shock around his sweaty face. "Mom? He's sitting on the ground."

"Who is?"

"Dad. He can't get up and he can't wait. He keeps calling for you."

John refused to go to the hospital. He let me support his weight, half-dragging him back into the house, and into the bedroom, where he told me to draw the curtains. When I opened the door later that afternoon, he snapped, "How's a man supposed to sleep?" But I didn't want to leave him alone. Why did he have to hate doctors so much? Well—he hated the notion of getting old, of course. Any doctor would tell him to stop hauling rocks, stop working twelve-hour days, maybe lighten up on the cigarettes and cigars and the heavy foods, and above all, stop drinking so damn much. I picked up the telephone from the den and, by God, he had sharp ears when he needed them, and he picked up the extra receiver in the bedroom and said, "You'd better be calling your mother. I don't want Doc Fielding coming around here."

When I tucked the boys into their beds, Jimmy said, "Dad got tired."

"He works hard," I said. "And those rocks were heavy."

Jimmy pulled the sheets up to his chin, a sleepy smile on his face, while from the twin bed opposite, I could feel Billy staring watchfully—old enough to know better, never as easily appeased. He'd be the one to carry grudges, if either of them did. A chip on his shoulder and a wary look in his eye, all these years later, and I knew why.

Jimmy said, "Dad said he built a wall at Stoney Lake once, but the other kids didn't want to help. He said we were better helpers than Aunt Polly."

"She isn't our aunt," Billy said, rolling over to face away from us. Calling her "sister" only confused Jimmy, since Polly looked so old to him.

"Well maybe Polly just didn't like carrying rocks," I said. "That's a woman's prerogative."

"What's a prerogative?"

"Go to sleep now, and we'll look it up in the dictionary tomorrow morning."

I peeked into our bedroom again. A paperback sat on John's chest, the spine broken and the cover torn off. Every weekday, he spent well over two hours on the train, and he read on his commutes, and didn't want anyone to know what he was reading. It was none of their business. He spent his days trying to have an effect on other people's habits—pocketbooks, too—but they had no right to be messing around with his.

I looked hard, to see whether the paperback was rising and falling. I stood by his side and held my own breath, hoping to see a fidget or a twitch. The rubber boots he'd kicked off in a huff were leaning at angles near the foot of the bed. I could see the caked dirt that had fallen from the soles' wavy treads, making a mess on the floor, which he'd complain about even though he'd made it himself. He'd unhooked his work overalls but hadn't allowed me to pull them off, and now the bib hung down, the shoulder straps trailing, and underneath was his broad chest under a clean white sport shirt, motionless. He was ivory haired and handsome, but aged too by his high living, his lack of sleep and his heavy drinking. He'd lived two full lives—he'd certainly had two families, and two careers, and who knows how many lovers. Fifty-five full years.

"John," I whispered. "John."

He stirred, and his arm flopped up and his hand rested on his chest. Stubborn old fool.

"John," I said again.

On his dresser, between a hairbrush and a bottle of cologne, a stack of weathered brown folders threatened to topple. The purple one was somewhere else now, but clearly he'd been actively rummaging.

"No one will write my biography," he'd said more than once since we'd moved to the farm, the last time we'd transported the growing lifelong collection of books and documents, photographs and even a few film reels. He'd resented the burden of all those files. He made it known he didn't expect them to be moved again. "When I'm gone, I want it all burned."

Splayed and snoring, John was still dressed, and anytime I touched him or tried to pull off a half-dangling sock, he grunted and shifted about. The paperback that had slipped from his chest to the bed fell onto the floor, waking him enough to make him grumble.

"Do you want something? An aspirin at least? You'd be more comfortable under the covers—and over on your side."

No answer. No matter. I couldn't sleep anyway.

Plagued by insomnia that night, I did what a woman married to a two-decades-older man does at some point in her middle years, whether she cares to admit it or not: I began to imagine his obituary.

John Broadus Watson, of Travelers Rest, South Carolina, January 9, 1878, to—well, to whenever it would happen to be, and neither of us believed in any kind of providential interference or afterlife. Son of Pickens Butler Watson and Emma Roe Watson, father of four children, and did one mention a former wife? I supposed one did. John's secretary—she'd become "right-hand Ruth" in the last two and a half years, and why didn't that bother me as it would have a few years earlier?—would put the basic details in the right order. I was simply reviewing, and pressing on to what mattered most. Graduate of Furman University and the University of Chicago, founder of Behaviorism, former Johns Hopkins professor, advertising pioneer.

I continued, thinking about which of his studies and views would last. All those early bird and rat studies from well before he thought to study humans, most likely forgotten. The earliest infant studies, published and perhaps still notable. An open attitude to discussing women and marriage and sex, removing taboos. The manipulation of people by advertising via their fears, sexual desires, and loyalties— that might last longer even than the academic contributions. And then there were other things he'd cared so much about and had tried to influence: the fight against eugenics, against racism cloaked in pseudoscientific jargon. Consider what was happening in Germany, with Hitler taking over the Reichstag. John had always warned against leaders like Hitler, though he had also pointed out that America was in just as much danger of being taken over by white supremacists. If it were up to me, my father's daughter and my senator-uncle's niece, I'd wish for John to be remembered for his watchfulness on those forgotten fronts—standing up to superstitious bigots, whether in Europe or at Princeton or Harvard.

Instead, based on that morning's call from Elsie Bregman, he'd be remembered for little Albert. For his experiment with a single infant, which formed his views on conditioning, which informed his views on parenting, which informed his—our—authoritative book on the psychological health of all babies, all children, our own and millions of others. One infant. One "perfectly normal" infant, but only one. How much had rested on those limited sessions, some of them clear in my mind, and others fogged by the competing dramas of those days: kissing and heavy breathing whenever nurses' backs were turned, guilt about Mary and Polly, the thrill of illicit love and the shame of the scandal that followed.

But it was morbid to be eulogizing a man still very much in his prime, to be imagining the headlines in the newspapers, the respectful letters from colleagues, the special conferences to be held in his honor, the posthumous awards that might undo the erosion of respect over the years; wrong to imagine our stoic sons, in their suits and with their forelocks combed into place, at the graveside, and the widow, thirty-five years old, geriatric by the flapper standards of yore, but not so very old, really.

What would I do with my life? How would I live, and where? I had no more idea than my own mother had, only a few years ago. She'd mentioned California, something I'd never imagined coming from the lips of a Jewish second-generation Baltimorean—California! I didn't see how she'd make such a radical transition, and I was half her age. It was wrong to even think about. John wasn't going anywhere. It probably hadn't been his heart, just a spell of heat exhaustion, followed by an even more powerful spell of stubbornness. Yet someone had to think of it, because he would not: how to guarantee that his contributions would be remembered, his mistakes forgotten or at least considered in a fair light.

Late that night, I managed to undress John, and to push him to his side of the bed, though he tossed and turned, and therefore so did I. One never sleeps as easily again, once it's become fully plain that a spouse won't live forever. It is the nature of life that there will nearly always be one person who leaves before the other, and much left undecided, and much left undone.

CHAPTER 33

1935

WHIP-POOR-WILL FARM

"Why are you doing this?" John asks, coming home to the farm from Manhattan, finding me out of bed, at the corner desk, typing.

There is an irony, I am aware, in being the young, ill wife, who not so long ago—only last summer—prematurely eulogized her middle-aged husband. Now, our roles are reversed. I worried and philosophized in response to his brief physical lapse. In response to mine, he has gone about his normal business, racing off to New York on the train, putting in long hours at JWT before coming home, the scent of bourbon evidence that he did not rush home too quickly.

Which is not to say he's been inactive or unsympathetic. If anything, he is upset beyond articulation. He is relying on routine, as men often do, using the familiar as an emotional crutch. My sudden sickness and refusal, despite a period of hospitalization, to get completely better has irritated his logical faculties. There is no reason I should have contracted dysentery in the first place, and no reason why I—thirty-six years old, fond of tennis and swimming—should not be healing at a better-than-average rate. I'd fume too, if I had the physical energy. Instead, I've turned inward.

One day last week when I was feeling sorry for myself, I happened to go to the bookshelf. Lifting a copy of *Behaviorism*, I flipped randomly open to this paragraph:

> No quack can do it for you, no correspondence school can safely guide you. Almost any event or happening might start a change; a flood might do it, a death in the family, an earthquake, a conversion to the church, a breakdown in health, a fist fight—anything that would break up your present habit patterns, throw you out of your routine and put you in such a position that you would have to learn to react to objects and situations different from those to which you have had to react in the past—such happenings might start the process of building a new personality for you.

John's words, not mine: No quack can do it for you. But other things can. A death, a fight, a breakdown in health.

I could see the truth in that—the way, until we have a shock to the system, we hide from ourselves, glued to our routines, unable to change habits. And then we are shoved onto a new set of tracks. The potential benefit of crisis: *a new personality.* Well, that would be nice. I'm not sure I want something that extreme. A little more truth would suit me fine. In my dysenteric state, I am desperately thirsty for something that no amount of water will quench.

"Why are you doing this?" John asked me a long moment ago.

"Doing what?"

"Working so hard when you're supposed to be recuperating. Who's it for?"

When I don't answer, he says, "I heard you asked Ray to bring down some old Johns Hopkins boxes from the attic. I've always said I should get rid of all that stuff up there."

"Not the lab files, surely."

"What's important is already published. I can't see the point in keeping every scrap of paper."

"I suppose that's true."

"And no one's ever going to have a need for my private papers, or yours. Burn it all."

"Burn it *all*."

"When you're dead, you're all dead."

"No proof to the contrary."

"What *were* you looking for, Rar?"

I wait, I think, I bite my tongue, I roam my memories freely. Rebelliously.

I don't trust myself, and I have heard and read enough to be more confused about mind and soul than I ever was, even as an adolescent girl. Still, there is a private "me" inside my physical self, aside from my visible behaviors, that insists on guiding me somewhere.

Hours later, in the middle of the night, I shake John and say, "I've been thinking about the past."

He startles and grunts, as any reasonable person would.

"Why did you let me work for you, at Hopkins?"

Half awake, he says, "Because you could catch."

I wait, but I hear only shifting and finally, his low, rumbling snore.

"John," I say. "John, I need to talk."

"Tomorrow."

It's Tuesday morning, but John hasn't left for work yet. The boys had their own breakfast alone, as usual, and are excited about leaving tomorrow for summer camp. Yesterday, every few hours, they came into my bedroom and asked me about the location of something they needed to pack, and sometimes now, drifting in and out of sleep, I'll once again hear the door opening, the sigh of disappointed Billy or Jimmy, and the door closing as they return to finding the fifth pair of socks or the bandana or the flashlight or whatever is on the camp-provided list. I want to help. I fall back into fragmented sleep and dream about helping them, folding each last thing inside their suit-cases, and closing them tight and turning to give kiss after kiss and a crushing hug.

John has been up for over an hour. When he comes into the bed-room, I prop myself up, a hot water bottle settled onto my stomach, under the covers.

"Fine," he says.

"Fine, what?"

"Tell me where you were a month ago, and I'll tell you something."

This is not what I thought we were on the verge of discussing. "Where I was? In Baltimore."

"And where else?"

"Let's see. I didn't stop in New York City. I didn't care to. Just Baltimore to Connecticut. A long day's drive."

"No snooping around, no stopping in at places you might want to tell me about?"

I'm flustered and confused. All those years when John was the one to disappear suddenly, spending Sundays who knows where, and now I'm the one being questioned. He says, "I got to thinking. About the dysentery. Doc Fielding's weird diagnosis."

"He blames exotic fruit."

"Fruit," John says, shaking his head. He's done his best. He even had our well tested twice, to no avail. "Remember how many times we had to cancel tests because of some small epidemic next door? The home for babies and children next to Johns Hopkins was always raging with diseases."

"I wouldn't say 'raging.' And no, John, I haven't been to Hopkins, not in years."

He says, "Lots of orphanages have the same problem. I wouldn't recommend spending any time in those places."

Well, this is almost funny. We've adopted a horse and a greyhound, but I haven't thought of adopting any new children. It took me long enough to get used to my own.

He says, "You won't find Albert in an orphanage."

Albert?

John has succeeded in surprising me, finally. I wouldn't have expected to find little Albert in an orphanage. He had a mother, last I'd known. I am stunned, most of all, to hear John say the name aloud, since he has avoided saying it whenever possible for the last few years.

Regardless of John's paranoia, I haven't been looking for Albert. Of course, yes, I've been thinking about him. His heavy body and soft limbs in my arms, his tears soaking my blouse, the devastated look in his eyes, the drop of his exhausted head. Even without thinking of him, I can still feel him—smell him. Motherhood has kept fresh in me what I otherwise might gladly have forgotten, that visceral connection to a baby who is fearful and hurting.

John says, "You won't find Albert anywhere. It has nothing to do with our experiment, of course—he left our hands in the same condition as when he started. But you won't find Albert."

"My God, John, what are you saying? If there's something you know, please tell me."

He snaps, "Don't use that surprised tone of voice. Why have you been pestering me unless you thought there was a good story to tell?"

But in truth, I wasn't expecting a new story. Just the old one, told with more honesty, the kind that John always prided himself on, which became more partial and obscure over the years, the less it served him.

"I did want to discuss Albert with you," I say. "But I certainly haven't been looking for him. Isn't he a grown man by now?" And then it occurs to me: "Are you thinking I want you to apologize to him?"

John's face goes blank. I know him too well. There is something he isn't telling me, something beyond my most basic scientific and ethical concerns.

He says, "I don't appreciate the look you're giving me."

"What look?"

"Like you don't trust me. As if you have any right to question me about professional choices I've made, or personal ones either. As if I've ever done anything to let you or the boys down."

At that, I am speechless.

"I've said my piece for now . . ."

"But you haven't explained."

". . . and now I'm going to work."

When I hear the sound of the car that night, the closing of two doors, Ray's gentle "good night" followed by John's footsteps into the house, I can barely wait for him to enter the bedroom. All day, my heartbeat has been fast and irregular. Dehydration. Familiar to me from the last bad spell, three weeks ago now. With a shaky hand, I've actually dialed my mother and asked her to drive up tomorrow, will she, please? But only after the boys have left. Only after, so they don't think her unexpected presence means something troubling. I've called Doc Fielding, too, hoping for a house call, but he wants me to come into town, and I think that's a good idea now. The hospital. With Mother. After the boys have left for camp.

For days, I've been revisiting the past, in more or less orderly fashion. But today, my mind has darted and doubled back and spiraled in and out of the years, looking for whatever was lost or hidden. Forward again to that time when John had heatstroke building the wall; the unfamiliar purple folder in his hand. John's irritation.

I say to John the moment he's in the doorway, his gaze distracted by the empty overnight bag sitting now in the middle of the floor, "You've been thinking about Albert the last few years just as much as I have. It was Elsie Bregman calling you last year. Something made you start thinking about him again."

"Bregman? For Pete's sake, Rosalie. You are feverish."

I won't let him change the subject. "She couldn't replicate the studies, and you were upset. No one has been able to. Something has been bothering you, about our results or our interpretations." I'm only lukewarm, I can tell from his expression. "Or our choice of subject."

"Subject? Why would you say that?"

Oh, John. So transparent.

"Is that it?" I ask. "It's not wrong to question things later. Admit it, John. Please." My heart feels ready to burst out of my chest. I should have relented earlier. An IV drip is the least I need. "And what did you mean this morning—I wouldn't find him now if I looked?"

"I mean," he says, "that Albert died."

"Died?"

A thickening of the tongue. A slowing of the blood. I feel the same drained, hollow ache I felt after giving birth to Billy.

I hear myself asking again: "Died?"

I remember the first infant subject who ever died on our watch, and how we did not mourn him, how John taught me not to mourn him. Subjects die. But this is different. Albert was different.

I still can feel him in my arms. I can smell the top of his head, his breath. It took work to let him grow up in my mind, to imagine him as a boy, and often my mental imaginings regressed, making him an infant all over again, trapping him eternally in that vulnerable state. Of course, he would be more than a boy now. He would be almost a man. I want to feel him, still alive on this earth, outgrowing what we did to him, making his way forward, leaving behind that ridiculous experiment.

"Yes," John says. "I'm sorry. I didn't expect you to take it like this."

"How, John? How did he die?"

"Let me help pack your hospital bag."

John opens a drawer to take out two nightgowns, fresh undergarments. He closes the top drawer, face turned away from me.

"Hydrocephalus."

"When?"

"He would have been six years old."

A decade ago.

"No."

"Why are you acting up?"

"No, John."

"I shouldn't have mentioned it."

I want to hit him. I want to scream. "How did you find out?"

"Makes no difference."

"When?"

"I said, when he was six."

"No, when did you find out?"

"I was at the New School. Right after it happened, I suppose—'25 or '26."

That long ago. And during a difficult time, when we were barely speaking. But it wasn't an excuse for not telling me. "He contracted it suddenly?"

A pause. "Which toiletries do you need packed?"

"In a moment, John. Did Albert contract hydrocephalus when he was older?"

"No."

"Then?"

"He may have had it since birth."

"May have?"

"Probably had."

"But you saw all his medical records. You chose him and we knew everything about him, down to the measles he got right before the first trial."

"Rosalie, this is the least important thing in the world right now."

He has turned back from the dresser now, facing me.

"To you, maybe, John. It's not the least important thing to me."

Outside, wheels crunch on gravel. Car doors open. I hear the voices of Billy and Jimmy, piling out, giddy about camp, naming off the cabins and guessing where they'll be assigned once they arrive.

John says, "I've asked Ray to drive them up early. I called the camp and they say it's fine. That way we can get you to town tomorrow, or if they want to bring you to a bigger hospital. Whatever's best. Your mother called me at work. She's in a fit of worry now and thinks I'm the devil. But you'll be proud of me. I gave her no indication that she's not welcome here. She can stay here all week, if it makes you feel better."

For the first time in his life, he's probably glad to know that my mother will be attached to my side. It will make it impossible for John and me to have any private conversations at all.

"Normal—that's what you called Albert every time. John, you called him perfectly normal. Perfectly healthy. Until we experimented on him, he didn't cry. We couldn't even make him cry. John, that's not a normal baby!"

But now Billy and Jimmy are in the house, and I can hear them rushing into their bedroom, pushing to get in, like a pair of tumbling puppies.

I know they can manage. But it's those last hours when you want to make sure they have what they need and aren't going to forget entirely everything you've taught them, that they'll learn everything you wished you'd taught them. It's those last hours when you wish you could change everything, and do everything all over again, so that you'd make no mistakes, and they'd understand how much you really loved them. But of course, you never can. You can only do your imperfect best.

"You were wrong not to tell me."

"So that what, you would feel bad about it? It doesn't change anything."

Has he lost sight of everything, even the most basic experimental principles? I knew he'd made mistakes, many of them. I had no idea that he'd played with a fixed deck from the very beginning.

"It changes more than one paper. It changes everything, John. You must know better than that."

CHAPTER 34

Three things happened to our family after we moved to Connecticut. First was the farm itself, with its animals and liveliness, its combined gifts of outdoor freedom and work duties, which gave everyone a sense of combined purpose. Second was John's aging—the impotence, and the scare he gave me that day by the fieldstone wall, and the night I first started to imagine life without him, wondering how he'd be remembered and giving myself permission to recall things I hadn't thought clearly about for some time. And third was the woman I've mentioned several times already, who ended up being important to John and me, both.

The first time, I came across her last name only, written at the top of a telephone message: *Lieb*. It was just after my breakdown, actually, and just before we moved to the farm, so I was still tense and suspicious.

Lieb. *Meine Liebe*. I'd heard some of my own German cousins in Baltimore use that phrase: "my love, my sweetheart, my dear." I'd imagined, after my breakdown and John's subsequent depression, that there might be a change in his habits. And then that word scrawled in pencil. I thought: *here we go again*.

But then, a few months later, I heard John talking to a houseguest about his new secretary, Ruth Lieb. He was talking about her in such a no-nonsense way—her typing speed and her way of handling grouchy clients and how much common sense she had compared to the younger girls at JWT—and though any kind of complimentary talk about another woman might have made me jealous in the old days, it didn't make me jealous now. She was Jewish, and I could only hope she was a little matronly. She was certainly nice on the telephone, when I first talked to her, trying to reach John at work.

"You're not sleeping with her, are you?" I asked John later that month, against my better judgment.

"Dames are a dime a dozen," he said, imitating the detective novels that had replaced his Westerns as commuter reading. "But a good secretary is too important to be messed with."

"I'm glad you see it that way."

Billy got to meet her before I did, when he went with John to work one day, to write a school paper about advertising. When Ruth was introduced to him, Billy told me later, she brought out some chocolates from her desk drawer and proceeded to hug him until he couldn't breathe. She pinched his cheek and then planted a lipsticky kiss on the very same spot.

"Good thing your father wasn't there," I said.

"But he was."

"And did he say anything?"

"Oh, you know," Billy said. I was embarrassing him now. John always said *something*.

"And what did Ruth do?"

"She gave me another kiss on the other cheek, even messier than the first."

Good for her, I remember thinking. *Good for Ruth Lieb*.

By the summer after John's little sunstroke episode, she was writing letters to Billy. Not all the time—only when he was at camp. I found a few of them in the back of his dresser drawer, hidden behind his socks. There was nothing inappropriate. She asked him about camp, what he was doing, how he got along with the other boys. She reminded him of his strengths and showered him in endearments.

Once I asked him what he thought about the letters. Anything could embarrass a twelve-year-old boy, but this question didn't seem to bother him in particular.

"Oh, it's just all that mother stuff, like the other boys get."

I might have been offended, but I wasn't.

I could tell he liked the letters, or he wouldn't have saved them. I doubt that he saved the notes *I* wrote to him at camp, which were mostly about what was happening on the farm, which houseguests were coming for the weekend, how the animals were faring. I suppose I'd been so objective for so long that I simply couldn't mimic, even in print, the caring voice in Ruth's letters, even when I threw off caution and tried to be more playful. But playful wasn't the same as tender, I knew. Maybe it wasn't the letters at all, but the letters in combination with how she treated him whenever she saw him in person, with extravagant hugs and kisses. My son was missing something, and he'd stumbled upon a woman outside the family who was willing to provide it, someone who seemed able to work closely with John while disregarding his fiercest convictions, as I should have been able to do. No scientific study was needed to prove there was a hole in my son's life, and one small way to begin filling it.

One of the best things I ever did as a mother—maybe the only truly good thing—was to not get in the way of that.

CHAPTER 35

It is harder than it's ever been to say goodbye to Billy and Jimmy. I insist on coming out to the car and shutting the door for them after they climb into the backseat. Billy is thirteen years old, or almost fourteen, as he'd prefer to say. Jimmy is twelve and sitting with his knees up and his feet resting on his small suitcase, because he doesn't want it out of his sight. No doubt he has packed some contraband about which I am unaware: a slingshot or bar of chocolate. I would not take it away from him even if I knew.

I am thinking about the fact that I'll be in the hospital tomorrow and don't know when I'll get out or whether I'll get to come along at the end of camp to pick them up and get a peek at whittled woodcrafts, teepees built from stripped branches, and other camp treasures on display for the parents who'll arrive to cart home their progeny in a month. They are thinking, of course, about something less serious. Learning the backstroke, or racing frogs.

Even if I were less shaky on my feet, and even if our family was the most typical one in the world, raised to worship instead of condemn sentimentality, I wouldn't manage to hold Jimmy long enough for a proper hug. As it is, I sort of tap their shoulders as they hop into the backseat. I reach out a last time to ruffle the hair on their heads, one after the other, while John remains inside the house, having dispensed his advice and shaken hands with both boys a half hour earlier. He expects our private conversation to continue when all the farewelling is done, and no doubt he's opened a bottle of bourbon and poured himself a few inches, and is numbing himself already to the difficulty of what I might ask or say, now that this illness has freed some witchy impulse in me, turning me into a nag who will not leave him with his secrets. What he doesn't know is that I'm not going to ask him anything more. What he doesn't know is that he has told me enough and there is nothing more for us to do or say.

"More light," Goethe supposedly said on his deathbed, or so our Vassar teachers told us. More light and more truth, indeed. You can keep calling out for it heedlessly, even when it's shining in your face, making you shield your eyes and squint into that fiery horizon.

Sunset, now.

We own two automobiles and a truck, but it's my old canary-yellow Bearcat that the boys wanted to take, with the top down, for their two-hour drive up to the camp. The sky is darkening, the air in a fast-moving car will be too cool, but they won't listen, just as I wouldn't have at their age, or even at my own age. The Bearcat isn't the vehicle that Ray usually drives, and we haven't had it out since last fall, but he is game to try, knowing I've been promising the boys a ride in the old machine for several weeks now and this is their best last chance for a while.

Billy and Jimmy both attempt to direct Ray from the backseat, warning him about the trickiness of the gearshift, but I know they're just trying not to look back at me so they won't have to see that my eyes have become red rimmed, my nose runny. At the last minute, I call to Ray not to back out yet, and as he keeps the car idling, I open the backdoor again and awkwardly lean across and plant a kiss on Jimmy's cheek, then lean over his lap and, with even more effort and much buckling of knees and elbows, plant a kiss on Billy's. They do not ask why. They do not look especially grateful or try to protest, either. Even they seem to realize it is a normal thing, to have to hold still for a mother's kiss. How they could know that after so many years of so few kisses, I have no idea.

Now the car is driving away, and I'm left on the gravel road, my white nightshirt stirred by the light breeze. I am shaking. It occurs to me, when the dust settles and I can't make out even a speck of yellow vanishing around the curve, that I haven't stepped outside in five days and the fresh air smells heavenly, the sweet pepperbush that won't be in full flower for several weeks seems to be blessing the air already with its fragrance, or perhaps my senses, brought alive by the onrush of night, are catching the scent of other trees and flowers, cultivated and wild, things beyond my knowing.

What little energy I have, I use to stand, to stay outside. John's got his bourbon, and much as I will love him always, regardless of everything, still, he doesn't need me as much as he thinks. We are all, in the end, responsible for ourselves.

I won't ever know exactly what John was thinking when he chose an abnormal baby for his most famous experiment, the work upon which he built all of his successive ideas, the sandy foundation on which everything else he ever did unsoundly rests. I do know that he wanted—needed—a baby who was stolid and imperturbable. I had the very same thought, the moment I first held little Albert, with his heavy head, glazed expression, and scarlet cheeks: *Don't bawl. Please, just don't bawl.*

I'll never know for sure whether John understood that his choice of Albert undermined his scientific premise, or if he rationalized it as somehow insignificant. Nor will I ever know if he understood the danger of what he was doing, to one child or later, with the impact of the parenting guide, to a million or more. He wanted proof so badly, and then he invested, and once he had invested a little, it was just too hard not to invest more, and before you knew it, he'd built an entire way of understanding the world on that one little investment, and the world's most avowedly objective person lost his objectivity altogether.

John was wrong about many things but right about at least one: Fear determines so much. Fear of being in the dark. Being alone. Being wrong. Growing old. Losing potency. Losing control. It determined all that happened in response: the booze, the restlessness, the women, the things done to our own dear boys.

Oh John, the worst thing is not only that you created fear in others, but that you lived in so much fear yourself.

There it goes, or rather, it has gone: the sun. Lovely, distant, burning ball.

It's fully dark now. I haven't felt hunger for over two weeks. While my stomach is empty of both food and water, I don't feel the pain that will pinch and stab again the moment anything tries to enter or exit. Better just to be empty for this rare pain-free moment, feeling so blissfully light. Listening to the serenade of insects. Listening to the rush of wind in the tall grasses beyond the barn. There is a glint at my side—I think I'm seeing things, since colors have intermittently flashed at the corners of my eyes over the last few days—but it is a real and welcome sight. Our greyhound, Gigi.

The moon has risen to glow on the grass, which looks oddly black, and on the short hair of Gigi, which in daylight is a grayish-brown but in this light shines like platinum. Silent, loyal, beautiful platinum beast.

I remember the day two years ago when Gigi barked to alert me that something was wrong with John, the day he was working on the fieldstone wall. Weeks later, he and the boys got back to it, but the project lost some of its appeal. Still, John talks about adding more to it each summer, making it longer and maybe a foot or two higher, and maybe he will, and maybe he won't. All that effort: digging a ditch, and moving stone by heavy stone, finding the right pattern, and setting the stones into place in such a way that they won't just topple, even without mortar. Destined to be permanent someday. John declared the first part of it finished, if not his best work, and on this warm, moonlit night before I'm consigned to a hospital ward and while John continues to add bourbon to his foul mood, I decide to go for the shortest of barefoot walks to see it.

Gigi seems to know exactly where I'm going.

I am so light and the air is so warm and fragrant and just a little humid, and I feel I'm hovering or swimming more than walking. We're there in no time. We're there, and it's something less than I remembered. It's surprisingly low to the ground, only a little higher than my knees. An impressive attempt, but no kind of solid barrier. Yet it would seem an insult to ignore its intent and purpose, to treat it as something small or incomplete, an overambitious mistake, a failure of any kind, when John wanted it to be something more, when it was in his nature to try and in all our natures to support with our lives and love and reputations his impassioned projects. Still, it *is* small. I can say that, can't I? There is no harm, now, in just saying it?

There is a flash in the moonlight, as Gigi leaps and clears the stone wall easily, and then looks back at me with her long nose and serene expression, as if to say, *Aren't you coming across? What's stopping you?*

EPILOGUE

Rosalie Alberta Rayner Watson died June 18, 1935, at Norwalk Hospital of bacillary dysentery, with a recorded onset of the illness twenty-nine days prior. Her unexpected death at the age of thirty-six was reported in the press as being due to dysentery or pneumonia. After her death, her sons were called back home from camp. It was one of the only times, recalled James Watson as an adult, that he and his brother were embraced by their father.

Billy Watson fought often with his father in later years and became a Freudian psychiatrist, in opposition to his father's anti-Freudian views. He attempted suicide multiple times, was once discovered and saved by his brother James, and finally took his own life in 1954. James Watson reported that he and his half sister, Polly, also attempted suicide. Polly struggled with alcoholism and depression and was the mother of actress Mariette Harley, who wrote about her mother's mental illness in a celebrity memoir, connecting it with her upbringing and the parenting style of John Watson, Mariette's famous grandfather.

❖ ❖ ❖

After leaving the East Coast with her lifelong husband and research partner, Harold Jones, Mary Cover Jones worked at the Institute for Child Welfare at the University of California–Berkeley, where she became known for her decades-long contribution to the longitudinal Oakland Growth Study, designed to follow the psychological growth of nearly two hundred children through adolescence. Using this data, she published over a hundred studies. Known as the "the mother of behavioral therapy," she received the G. Stanley Hall Award from the American Psychological Association in 1968. She died in Santa Barbara, California, in 1987 at the age of 89.

John B. Watson was deeply affected by Rosalie's death. He switched to another advertising firm, then retired in 1946. Although still assisted by his secretary, Ruth Lieb, he nonetheless became increasingly reclusive over the years, and later sold Whip-Poor-Will Farm to live at a smaller farm, which he rarely left, spending his days drinking heavily. He was honored by the APA for his contributions to psychology in 1957, but embarrassed and emotional, declined at the last moment to attend the ceremony, according to his son James. He burned a large part of his collection of personal papers and letters, and died in 1958 at the age of eighty.

AUTHOR'S NOTE

I wrote this novel to give voice to a woman mostly forgotten by history. While much has been written about John Watson, by himself and others, Rosalie remains an enigma, with only a few publications to her name and surprisingly few sources of evidence for what she thought or others thought about her. Even her own adult children, when interviewed, reflected more about their father's overbearing nature, sparing her the kind of scrutiny that might help us better understand their home and family dynamic. John's penchant for destroying papers may be to blame for the scant record, but even before Rosalie met her future mentor and husband, she had a way of slipping between the cracks, staying out of photos and yearbook notices, for example, though she was clearly a bright woman with a promising future.

For a fiction writer, this lack of documentation can be both vexing and liberating. To write this novel, I had to make decisions about when to follow the historical or scientific record, as it existed, and when to give imagination looser rein. For the purposes of avoiding adding to the misunderstandings that have surrounded the Albert B. story (see excellent work by Ben Harris for an analysis), I tried to remain mostly true to the day-by-day experiment details, as they are known. (Even John

Watson was inconsistent in some details of various descriptions of the experiment.) In one aspect, I had to choose between widely disparate, controversial, and evolving interpretations about Albert B.'s true identity. Two major hypotheses have been advanced: that Albert B. was really a seriously ill baby named Douglas Merritte, who died at age six of hydrocephalus; or, quite to the contrary, that he was a boy named William Barger, who was not ill at the time of experimentation. Neither claim is conclusive, and other possibilities might still be advanced.

There is also the position, of course, that Albert B.'s real identity is not the point. We are fascinated by this experiment, some would say, not just because of the baby who endured morally disturbing, fright-inducing trials, but because it proved to be such a cornerstone of behaviorism—and an astonishingly flawed one at that. Regardless of our much-changed attitudes about experimental ethics (no American psychologists today would ever get away with subjecting infants to the many experiences that were commonplace in Watson's lab), we recognize larger problems with the experiment's design, limited sample size, subjective recording of results, and more.

Historical context should help us understand the limits of Watson's methods and concepts; it would be all too easy to criticize some of his attitudes and experiments, overlooking the areas in which he sincerely attempted to pioneer a new, more objective, experimental approach to psychology. Just as it is tempting to judge him by imposing modern ethical standards, it is too easy to dismiss his scientific contributions now that psychology has enjoyed advances made possible by the cognitive revolution of the 1950s (a counterrevolution to behaviorism). While John Watson is no longer a household name, his influence is undeniable. A 2002 study placed him at number seventeen on the list of the top one hundred eminent psychologists of the twentieth century. (In a limited survey that made up part of the study, Watson earned an even higher ranking—in the fourth position, just behind B. F. Skinner, Jean Piaget, and Sigmund Freud. His lower overall "eminence" ranking is due to several factors, including the fact that his work is not often cited in modern studies, regardless of his broader historical influence.) It is worth noting, furthermore, that B. F. Skinner, number one in the "eminence" and survey rankings, was a behaviorist whose work grew out of Watson's original principles. As readers of this novel will realize, Watson's experimental work was only one aspect of his professional life—and, in terms of time spent and lives affected, perhaps not even the most critical one. In the field of advertising, and as a public figure and popular author with unyielding attitudes against attachment parenting, he had an influence—impressive, and in some ways alarming—that is impossible to quantify.

It will never be possible to know what John Watson and Rosalie Rayner Watson thought, in later life, about the Little Albert experiment, though John began to show signs of doubting some of his work, and Rosalie developed an acerbic, questioning tone in the few articles she published. It's almost impossible to know what Rosalie's final days were like. Only fiction can restore deeply personal, albeit hypothetical, accounts of lives that were deemed not worth recording or not worth protecting from erasure by others.

Beyond the parameters of the Little Albert experiment, Rosalie's mostly undocumented life speaks to the challenges of ambitious young women scientists at that time. In the end, I hope I have been true to the spirit of both people, and I have been grateful for the opportunity to vicariously experience, through them, the social and scientific atmosphere of the late 1910s through early 1930s.

SOURCES AND RECOMMENDED READING:

For those interested in further investigating the mythologizing of the Little Albert experiment and the current debate about Albert's possible identity, I strongly recommend the following scholarly articles:

Beck, Hall P., Sharman Levinson, and Gary Irons. "Finding Little Albert: A Journey to John B. Watson's Infant Laboratory." *American Psychologist* 64, no. 7 (Oct. 2009): 605–14.

Fridlund, Alan J., Hall P. Beck, William D. Goldie, and Gary Irons. "Little Albert: A Neurologically Impaired Child." *History of Psychology* 15, no. 4 (Nov. 2012): 302–27.

Harris, Ben. "Whatever Happened to Little Albert?" *American Psychologist* 34, no. 2 (Feb. 1979): 151–60.
———. "Letting Go of Little Albert: Disciplinary Memory, History, and the Uses of Myth." *Journal of the History of the Behavioral Sciences* 47, no. 1 (Dec. 2011): 1–17.

Powell, Russell A., Nancy Digdon, Ben Harris, and Christopher
    Smithson. "Correcting the Record on Watson, Rayner, and
    Little Albert: Albert Barger as 'Psychology's Lost Boy'."
    American Psychologist 69, no. 6 (Sept. 2014): 600–611.

Most likely, new additions to the debate will follow.

While John Watson was a prolific author, his most important general book, still worth reading today, is *Behaviorism* (London: Kegan Paul, Trench, Trubner, 1930).

In addition to primary documents and works written by John Watson himself, my best source was Kerry W. Buckley's *Mechanical Man: John B. Watson and the Beginnings of Behaviorism* (New York: Guilford Press, 1989). I was also educated and entertained by Ann Hulbert, *Raising America: Experts, Parents, and a Century of Advice About Children* (New York: Knopf, 2003); and Deborah Blum, *Love at Goon Park: Harry Harlow and the Science of Affection* (New York: Perseus, 2002). Both journalistically chronicle the science of behavior and parenting, pre- and post-Watson.

ACKNOWLEDGMENTS

My first thanks go to veteran psychology textbook editor Christine Brune, who may not have known she was inspiring my next novel when she casually told me, at a party in 2012, about John Watson and recent developments in the Little Albert controversy.

Gratitude is due to the scholars who have done considerable detective work and thought deeply about the mythologizing role of textbook classics like the Little Albert experiment. This work is fiction, but it could not have been written without the scientific and historical foundations provided by Ben Harris, as well as Hall P. Beck, Sharman Levinson, Gary Irons, Alan J. Fridlund, and William D. Goldie.

At Soho Press, my editor, Juliet Grames, has played an essential role in the development of my novels and beyond that, kept me sane and hopeful about publishing. Her own love of books, travel, and food is contagious.

I'm also grateful to the support, wisdom and assistance of Bronwen Hruska, Paul Oliver, Meredith Barnes, Amara Hoshijo, Rachel Kowal, Janine Agro, and Gary Stimeling. Thanks to Gail Hochman and Marianne Merola, who kindly helped shepherd this and previous work into print. At Antioch University, in Los Angeles, Steve Heller provided feedback as well as encouragement during this book project's sensitive infancy.

Writing friends and peer readers are invaluable, and mine include Kathleen Tarr, Kate Maruyama, Joan Wilson, Lee Goodman, Karen Ferguson, and family members C. Romano, Honoree Cress, and Eliza Romano, as well as Bill Sherwonit, Eowyn Ivey, the 49 Writers community, my colleagues in the University of Alaska–Anchorage MFA program, and my Antioch buddies: Chrissy, Michelle, Marianne, Wendy, and Jennifer.

This book required several intense rounds of research and writing time, which were facilitated by Trudy Hale at the Porches, a writing retreat in Charlottesville, Virginia, where I spent one of the most enjoyable weeks of my life, by the kind folks at Artscape Gibraltar Point in Toronto, where I enjoyed writing "the end," and by the Alaska Council on the Arts.

Thanks to librarians and the resources made available at Vassar College, Johns Hopkins University, the Library of Congress, and the Archives of the History of American Psychology at the University of Akron, with thanks to director David Baker and special appreciation for the Cedric Larson Collection. Research for this book was made possible in part by a US Artists crowdfunding campaign, and I owe thanks to that organization as well as individuals who generously contributed: Aliza Sherman, Alyse Galvin, Amanda Coyne, Amy Houck, Andy Holleman, Anne Marie Moylan, Anonymous, Barbara Armstrong, Beth Rose and John Levy, Bill Sherwonit, Breawna Power Eaton, Caitlin Shortell, Carol Bryner, Cassandra Stalzer, Cherilynn Romano, Constance Huff, Dale Gardner, Dani Haviland, David Abrams, Don Rearden, Doug Leteux, Ernestine Hayes, Gabriel, Gayle Brandeis, Heather Lende, Jennifer Ettelson, Judith Sara Gelt, Juliet Grames, Karen Benning, Karen Ferguson, Laura Forbes, Linda K., Linda M. Green, Lorena, Lucia Zaczkowski, Mandy Moore, Marianne Cirone, Mike Finkel, Molly McCammon, Monica Devine,

Morgan Grey, Nancy Lord, Olga Livshin, Pamela, Pazit Cahlon, Rosemary Austin, Ruth Glenn, Sherrie Simmonds, Steven Quinn, Susanna Mishler, Thomas Pease, and Wendy Hudson.

I'm also grateful to Stewart Ferguson, Richard Drake, Becky Harrison-Drake (and Mickey and Harrison, too) for friendship and hospitality during our bohemian phase, as well as for all-around family support, to those already named as well as Nikki, Leona, Theo, Evelyn, Sharon, Stewart, and Mildred. A final thanks for serendipitous assistance from D. Craig Elliott and James DiGirolamo of Baltimore.

Last but not least, thanks to my children, Aryeh and Tziporah Lax, and to Brian Lax, who patiently endured countless discussions about behaviorism, blank slates, and classical conditioning while also learning to live beyond all of our comfort zones, and in various time zones, during the writing and editing of this novel.